Memory, Voice, and Identity

Muslim women have been stereotyped by Western academia as oppressed and voiceless. This volume problematizes such Western academic representation. Muslim women writers from the Middle East from Out al-Kouloub al-Dimerdashiyyah (1899–1968) and Latifa al-Zayyat (1923–1996) from Egypt, to current diasporic writers such as Tamara Chalabi from Iraq, Mohja Kahf from Syria, and even trendy writers such as Alexandra Chreiteh, challenge the received notion of Middle Eastern women as subjugated and secluded. The younger largely Muslim women scholars collected in this book present cutting edge theoretical perspectives on these Muslim women writers. This book includes essays from conflict-ridden countries such as Iran, Iraq, Palestine, Syria, and the resultant diaspora. The strengths of Muslim women writers are captured by the scholars included herein. The approach is feminist, postcolonial, and disruptive of Western stereotypical academic tropes.

Feroza Jussawalla, PhD, University of Utah, 1980, has taught at the University of Texas at El Paso and is Full Professor of English and Postcolonial Literatures at the University of New Mexico in Albuquerque, NM. She is the author of *Family Quarrels: Towards a Criticism of Indian Writing in English* (1984), co-editor of *Interviews with Writers of the Postcolonial World* (1992), co-editor of *Emerging South Asian Women Writers* (2017), and the editor of *Conversations with V.S. Naipaul* (1997).

Doaa Omran did her Master's and PhD at the University of New Mexico (2019). She wrote her ground-breaking dissertation titled *Female Hero Mega-Archetypes in the Medieval European Romance* on quranic and biblical female characters as mega-archetypes in Medieval literature. She is currently a visiting lecturer at the University of New Mexico. She received her BA in English language and literature at Alexandria University, Egypt. Her essay "Anachronism and Anatopism in the French Vulgate Cycle and the Forging of English Identity through Othering Muslims/ Saracens" is included in Albrecht Classen's edited volume *Travel, Time, and Space in the Middle Ages and Early Modern Time: Explorations of World Perceptions and Processes of Identity Formation* (2018).

Routledge Studies in Twentieth-Century Literature

For more information about this series, please visit: https://www.routledge.com/Routledge-Studies-in-Twentieth-Century-Literature/book-series/RSTLC

Memory, Voice, and Identity

Muslim Women's Writing from across
the Middle East

Edited by
Feroza Jussawalla and Doaa Omran

Routledge
Taylor & Francis Group

NEW YORK AND LONDON

First published 2021
by Routledge
52 Vanderbilt Avenue, New York, NY 10017

and by Routledge
2 Park Square, Milton Park, Abingdon, Oxon, OX14 4RN

Routledge is an imprint of the Taylor & Francis Group, an informa business

© 2021 Taylor & Francis

The right of Feroza Jussawalla and Doaa Omran to be identified as the authors of the editorial material, and of the authors for their individual chapters, has been asserted in accordance with sections 77 and 78 of the Copyright, Designs and Patents Act 1988.

Library of Congress Cataloging-in-Publication Data
A catalog record for this title has been requested

ISBN: 978-0-367-56976-1 (hbk)
ISBN: 978-0-367-56979-2 (pbk)
ISBN: 978-1-003-10016-4 (ebk)

Typeset in Sabon
by codeMantra

وَلِلَّهِ مُلْكُ السَّمَاوَاتِ وَالْأَرْضِ ۗ وَاللَّهُ عَلَىٰ كُلِّ شَيْءٍ قَدِيرٌ
(آل عمران ‏—۱۸۹)

"God is King of the Heavens and the Earth, and God is
Almighty over everything."
(Quran 3:189)

"The Lord God Omnipotent Reigneth."
(Handel's *Messiah*)

This book is dedicated to peace and safety among all the
peoples written about in this book.

Contents

Contributors

Amel Abbady is a lecturer in the Department of English, South Valley University in Egypt. She was awarded a Fulbright teaching assistantship at St. Edward's University, Texas in 2007. She was also awarded a teaching fellowship in 2016 to teach Middle Eastern literature and culture at Northern Michigan University. She got her PhD in 2017 and her dissertation, "African Cultural Heritage and European Colonialism in Chinua Achebe's Novels: A Study in Narrative and Culture," examined the impact of colonization on Nigerian Igbo culture as depicted in Chinua Achebe's novels. Her current research interests are mostly related to Middle Eastern women writers, as well as contemporary African and Latino women writers. She has previously participated in MLA and ACLA conventions with topics that examined writers such as Alifa Rifaat, Leila Ahmed, and Laila Lalami.

Amel's publications include a paper titled "Women 'The Upholders of Cultural Heritage': A study in Chinua Achebe's *Things Fall Apart* and *Arrow of God*" (Proceedings of the 3rd International Conference on Women and Childhood, Egypt 2015), a paper on "Myths and Folktales in Chinua Achebe's *Things Fall* Apart" (Qena Faculty of Arts Bulletin, Fall 2017), and another on the "Linguistic Features in Chinua Achebe's Novels" (Qena Faculty of Arts Bulletin, Winter 2017) South Valley University, Egypt.

Heba Gaber Abd Elaziz is an English language instructor at Alexandria University, Egypt where she teaches Anglophone and Francophone Civilizations, Critical Thinking, and European Cultural Heritage. She earned her PhD in 2017 which tackled the depiction of London in multicultural British Fiction. In 2011, she got her MA in Comparative Literature entitled, "New Historicism and Postcolonialism in the Autobiographies of Penelope Lively and Radwa Ashour: a Comparative Study." She has presented several research papers in different conferences and universities. Her research interests are postcolonial studies, New Historicism, comparative literature, cultural studies, refugee writings and social media/media influence.

Najlaa Aldeeb is a PhD candidate at Swansea University, Wales, UK. Her dissertation is entitled "Traces of Ideologies in English Translations of the Qur'an: A Comparative Study of Selected Authorized and Unauthorized Versions." She has twenty years of experience in teaching English as a second language (ESL). In 2017, she received a master's degree in Translation Studies—literary translation—from Effat University, Saudi Arabia. She also received an MA in English Language and Literature from Indira Gandhi National Open University in 2008. She is a DELTA holder whose research interests include literary translation, feminist literary criticism, and college writing. On 21 April 2019, her research paper entitled "Ecofeminism in Doris Lessing's *Mara and Dann: An Adventure*" was listed on SSRN's Top Ten download list for WGSRN: Gender & Nature—Feminist Ecology & Sustainability (Sub-Topic). Aldeeb has participated in national and international conferences including The Twenty-first International Conference on Learning, Lander College for Women, New York City, USA.

Lava Asaad is a Postdoctoral Teaching fellow at Auburn University. Her research areas include, but are not limited to: Anglophone literatures, modern British literature, women and gender studies, and Middle Eastern literature. She received her doctoral degree in 2019 from Middle Tennessee State University. She is the author of *Literature with a White Helmet: The Textual-Corporeality of Being, Becoming and Representing Refugees* (2019, Routledge).

Riham Debian is an associate professor of Cultural Studies and Translation at the Institute of Applied Linguistics and Translation, Alexandria University. Her publications and research interest span the fields of translation studies, cultural studies, gender studies, and international politics. She particularly focuses on the politics of knowledge production and its intersection with translation, especially given the latter's reformulation within the field of intercultural communication and international relations. Riham has been awarded Alex-GRI 2014 by Alexandria University, Egypt. She has contributed to a number of national and international conferences at renowned universities in Egypt, Germany, Denmark, and the UK. Her MA thesis tackled the gender politics of modern Arab nation-states in the Levant. Her PhD dealt with the positioning of third-world women between nationalist and fundamentalist discourse in three geographical locations: transnational and multicultural London, modern Nigeria, and modern Iran. Her articles have been published numerous times in various journals, and she has written several books.

Pervine Elrefaei is a Professor of Cultural Studies at the Department of English Language and Literature, Faculty of Arts, Cairo University. Her

PhD was on "The Cultural Conflict of East and West in Selected Novels by Lawrence Durrell, P. H. Newby and D. J. Enright." She has a number of publications on film studies, gender studies, feminism, border studies, and postcolonial literature. Amongst her publications are "Egypt's Borders and the Crisis of Identity in the Literature of Nubia and Sinai," "Egypt and the Prison as a Dual Space of Repression and Resistance: The Dialectics of Power Relations in Literature and Film," "Egyptian Women in the Cartoons and Graffiti of the January 2011 Revolution: A Janus–faced Discourse," "Memory, Identity and Resistance in Susan Abulhawa's *Mornings in Jenin*," "Intellectuals and Activists Writing under the Sign of Hope: Radwa Ashour and Ahdaf Soueif's Manifestos of the 2011 Revolution," "The Cultural Politics of Food in Selected Egyptian Films" (Forthcoming), "The Egyptian Nubian Archival Discourse: Identity Politics in Selected Works by Yehia Mokhtar" (Forthcoming), and "Deconstructing Borders: Arab American Immigrants and Body Politics in Mohja Kahf's *The Girl in the Tangerine Scarf*" (Forthcoming).

Amany El-Sawy is an associate professor of English literature and the chairman of the English Department, Faculty of Education, Alexandria University. She is a playwright and participated with her first play *The Sun* in the 2015 *Women Playwrights International Conference* held in Cape Town, South Africa. Her second play *Eclipse* was performed in Santiago de Chile in 2018. Her other plays are *Eve's Voice, The Apple Tree, Paradise Lost,* and *The Scars.* Her field of specialty in literature has made her interested in human relationships, especially the powerless affairs. She is engrossed in enlightening such powerless groups, thus she participated in *Fortune/State Department Global Women's Mentoring Program* (The Role of NGOs in Promoting Global Women's Issues [A Multi-Regional Project]), which aims at enlightening women by clarifying their roles and rights in their society, highlighting the reasons of their oppression, and suggesting variable solutions to their problems.

Asmaa Gamal Salem Awad did her Master's and her PhD at Ain Shams University in 2012 and 2018, respectively. The Master's thesis was entitled "Globalization and Cultural Disjunction in Selected Novels by Salman Rushdie," and the PhD dissertation titled "Narratives of Power and Subjection: Representations of the Veil in Selected Works by Muslim Women Novelists." She got her BA from The Faculty of Women for Arts, Sciences and Education, Ain Shams University, where she is currently working as an Assistant Professor of English language and literature. Her fields of interest are Cultural Studies, Feminist Studies, Comparative Literature, Gender Studies, Postcolonial Studies, and Poststructural Studies.

Funda Güven received her BA in Turkish language and literature from 19 Mayıs University (Samsun) and her Master's degree in public administration from the Institute of Turkey and the Middle East (Ankara). She completed her PhD degree at the Institute of Social and Political Sciences, Gazi University (Ankara). She has taught at the University of Wisconsin-Madison and is currently an Assistant Professor in the Department of Kazakh Language and Turkic Studies at Nazarbayev University in Nursultan, Kazakhstan. Her doctoral dissertation was entitled "Religious Literature and the Transformation of Religious Identity in Turkey: A Study of Pious Women Writers." She conducts research on Turkish Studies, including Turkish literature, women writers and identity, and other issues.

Magda Mansour Hasabelnaby is a Professor of English Literature at Ain Shams University, Faculty of Women, where she teaches comparative and contemporary US literature. Her publications in both English and Arabic include articles on African and Arabic adaptations of Shakespeare, Arab and Muslim women writers, and postcolonial readings of contemporary poetry and fiction. She has presented her research papers in various conferences held in England, Poland, and the USA, including ACLA 2014 and 2017. In addition, she has visited a number of universities in the USA to give lectures on teaching literature and on Arabic and Arab-American literature. These universities included Miami, Florida; NEIU, Chicago; the University of Oregon, Eugene; and the University of Illinois at Urbana Champaign. Professor Hasabelnaby is a literary translator; she has published a number of translations of American poetry into Arabic, in addition to the translation of a novel, Ray Bradbury's *Fahrenheit 451*, published in 2010 by Dar Alshorouq.

Feroza Jussawalla, PhD, University of Utah, 1980, has taught at the University of Texas at El Paso and is Full Professor of English and Postcolonial Literatures at the University of New Mexico in Albuquerque, NM. She is the author of *Family Quarrels: Towards a Criticism of Indian Writing in English* (Peter Lang, 1984), co-editor of *Interviews with Writers of the Postcolonial World* (University Press of Mississippi, 1992) and *Emerging South Asian Women Writers* (Peter Lang, 2017), and the editor of *Conversations with V.S. Naipaul* (Mississippi, 1997). She has been active in the field of Postcolonial Studies for over forty years, from its inception as Commonwealth Literature and its turn into Postcolonial Literatures. She has published over thirty papers and presented internationally and locally, widely. She also has a collection of poems entitled, *Chiffon Saris*, published by the Kolkata Writer's workshop and the Toronto South Asian Review Press. She helped establish the South Asian Literature Association, a division of the Modern Language Association.

Anna C. Oldfield researches and writes on bardic arts in the Caucasus and Central Asia. Recent publications include a chapter on Azerbaijani women for the *Routledge Handbook of Asian Diaspora and Development* and a collaborative study of Azeri bards in Azerbaijan and Iran for the *Journal of Folklore Research.* Oldfield has worked for several years in Azerbaijan and Kazakhstan as a researcher and Fulbright Scholar. She has been active in cultural exchange with Smithsonian Folkways, the British Library, and the San Francisco World Music Festival, as well as promoting artistic and educational collaboration with the Kazakh Academy of Arts. Oldfield teaches: World Literature, Folklore, and Film as an Associate Professor at Coastal Carolina University.

Doaa Omran did her Master's and PhD at the University of New Mexico (2019). She wrote her ground-breaking dissertation titled *Female Hero Mega-Archetypes in the Medieval European Romance* on quranic and biblical female characters as mega-archetypes in Medieval literature. She is currently a visiting lecturer at the same university where she received her Master's and doctorate. She received her BA in English language and literature at Alexandria University, Egypt. Her awards include a Fulbright Scholarship (2007), the Women of Color award at UNM (2012), Dean of Graduate Studies Dissertation Award (2016), and first place in the Larry Morris Memorial Scholarship (2018). Her essay "Anachronism and Anatopism in the French Vulgate Cycle and the Forging of English Identity through Othering Muslims/Saracens" is included in Albrecht Classen's edited volume *Travel, Time, and Space in the Middle Ages and Early Modern Time: Explorations of World Perceptions and Processes of Identity Formation* (2018).

Rima Sadek is a Visiting Assistant Professor of Arabic in the Department of Modern Languages and Literatures at Kenyon College. She has a PhD in comparative literature from the University of South Carolina (2018). Her areas of specialization include modern Arabic literature, Arab women's literature, literary theory, and women's and gender studies. Her research engages modern literary theory to analyze the elements of deconstruction and resignification in the narratives of contemporary Arab women writers. Her work addresses the broader question, how *Adab* affects and transforms the lived experience of Arab women, exploring how narrative, an imaginative space, is the real space of argumentation and change.

Naila Sahar did her PhD as a Fulbright scholar at State University of New York, Buffalo in the Department of English. The topic of her PhD dissertation is "Reimagining Muslim women: Gendered Religious Life and Resistance in the age of Islamophobia." Her research interests include feminist studies, gender studies, gendered religious nationalism, South Asian studies, and postcolonial studies. Her work has appeared in *South Asian Voices, South Asian Review, Gender Matters*, and *Journal of Commonwealth and Postcolonial Studies*. These days, she is working as Assistant Professor in the English department at Forman Christian College (A chartered University), Lahore.

Arththi Sathananthar is a PhD candidate at the School of English, University of Leeds. Her thesis maps out how the trope of homecoming and the representation of ancestral houses are constructed by Arab Anglophone writers whose narratives are set in conflict zones. She is an Associate Fellow in The Higher Education Academy. She has presented at the MLA International Symposium in Lisbon.

Fatima Sidiya is a senior reporter at *Saudi Gazette* who has ten years of experience in media with specific focus on Saudi Arabia. She has an MTS in translation studies. She has participated in various media conferences, seminars, and workshops and has worked for Arab News, al-Arabiya.net, and Sayidaty. Her research interest is media translation and audiovisual translation. Ms. Sidiya's last paper addressing translating legal terms in newspapers was published in 2018 in the *International Journal of Law, Government and Communication*.

Wafaa H. Sorour is an Assistant Professor & Head of English Department, Faculty of Arts, South Valley University. She worked as a language instructor at Faculty of Arts, University of Assiut until 1992. In 1993, she earned an MA in Irish literature. In 1994, she got a two-month grant in the Integrated English Language Program under the sponsorship of the Fulbright Commission in the USA. In 1997, she got a PhD in American literature from University of South Valley (Egypt) and was appointed as a lecturer of English literature at the same university. She is a member of the Association of Professors of English and Translation at Arab Universities in Jordan. In 2000, she became a member of the Egyptian National Council of Women (in Qena, Egypt). In September 2005, she became the editor of TRANS Arabic web page Redaktion (A cultural journal in seven languages). In July 2007, she had a post-doctor grant at the University of Newcastle.

Brigitte Stepanov is an Andrew W. Mellon Postdoctoral Fellow with the Department of French and Arabic at Grinnell College. Her research interests include Francophone Studies, North and Sub-Saharan African literature and visual culture, and postcolonial studies. She holds a PhD in French Studies from Brown University. Her current book project focuses on representations of atrocities in French, Rwandan, and Maghrebi literature and cinema, arguing that the concept of cruelty is fundamental to any discussion of political instability, war, and crimes against humanity. This work more broadly examines the evolution of warfare over the last eighty years in addition to shifting conceptions of the human in the face of universal manifestations of violence.

Asmaa Ahmed Youssef Moawad is a lecturer of English Literature. She got her PhD in English Literature, Poetry (Alexandria University, Faculty of Arts–2017). She got an Educational Diploma (Alexandria University, 2010) and Tefl Course (Ministry of Defense, 2015). She works at Higher Institute for Languages (Ministry of Higher Education, Mansoura, 2020). She worked at Taibah University (2013–2014), Alexandria (English for Specific Purposes [ESP] Center, 2015–2017), and Matrouh University (2017–2020). She has presented many papers in various conferences, such as Creating Complex Borders within a Borderless World in both Ephraim Sidon's children poetry book *Uzu and Muzu from Kakaruzu* (1987) and Renen Yezerski's film The Invisible Enemy across the Wall: Israeli and Palestinian Children's Perspective of the Other (2015), Cairo University, 2018; Modernization and Nationalism in the 19th Century and 20th in Egypt, Alexandria University, 2019; and *Visual Arts' Manifestation in Poetry: Interdisciplinary Approaches and Techniques in Wallace Stevens's Poetry,* Helwan University, 2019. Her papers have been published in many international magazines such as *The Years of Irish Troubles (1967–1998) in the Poetry of Michael Longley*, Ain Shamas University, 2017, and *Creating Complex Borders within a Borderless World. . .* , 2020; and *The Language of Violence and Reconciliation in the Poetry of Brendan Kennelly*, High-Studies Second Conference, Alexandria University, 2017.

Acknowledgments

We would like to acknowledge our co-editorship to our long association as faculty, student, and co-editors. Doaa Omran and I have been working together since 2014, when Doaa was assigned to be a co-teacher, teaching assistant to my World Literatures surveys. We owe our colleagueship to Dr. Anita Obermeier—Chair of the Department of English, University of New Mexico—for both sending Doaa to work with me and for putting me on Doaa's Medieval Studies committee. She also supported travel to the various seminars and traveled to ACLA in Utrecht to support us. Since then, we have presented at several ACLA seminars beginning in the 2016 ACLA at Harvard, and at the MLA conference. These conference presentations brought together our colleagues who have contributed to this volume. We are grateful to the participants of these seminars for sharing their work with us and for working hard on our submission.

We dedicate this volume to our colleagueship among ourselves, all of us, as faculty, students, and scholars, all who work in the field together.

We are very grateful to Tirzah Reeves, our UNM honors alumni who showed up in the summer to help, took ownership of the project, did all the secretarial work, and helped extensively with her copy editing skills from the Honors undergraduate literary magazine *Scribendi*. Without her, we would not have finished this project.

And finally, we would like to thank our editor Michelle Salyga, for her immense patience and her faith in our project. Feroza Jussawalla would particularly like to thank her for having been her editor previously at Peter Lang also.

Overall, we would like to thank our faith and spirituality in the Omnipotent God of all our traditions for taking us through with help and guidance.

Introduction

Feroza Jussawalla

Women from the Middle East have been telling and writing stories, and recalling memories conveyed orally, since the days of the mythic Scheherazade. Caravans of women moving along the desert lines told each other stories and created tales, didactic, fantastic, perhaps cautionary, thus inspiring the creation of this legend named Scheherazade. Groups of women probably told each other either grandmothers' tales or vividly imagined tales of female strength and heroism. Without getting into the issues of authorship so masterfully dealt with by the exemplary Arab female critic, Ferial Ghazoul, we can envision this mythic figure as the embodiment not only of storytelling, but also of critiquing. Additionally, the Moroccan critic, Fatima Mernissi, in her *Scheherazade Goes West* treats contemporary Western feminism and the treatment of women in the light of Scheherazade. This volume discusses the roles of women as writers and critics, through the eyes of many different critical perspectives.

In a culture rich in oral and written literature that goes back eons, we can envision these forms of telling and critiquing going forward. Hopefully, this book—which is a compilation of readings of contemporary stories, memoirs, novels, poems, and refugee narratives by women scholars largely from the Middle East—facilitates the continuing keeping, reading, and critiquing of these stories. The scholars whose essays are included here—for the most part—live in the cultures of the contexts of the creation of these stories. The stories told here, by women authors, are those of heroism, resistance, immigration, exile, diaspora, and refugeeism. These are records of what Felix and Guattari would call the movements and migrations of peoples over "Mille Plateaux." The authors discussed here are living archives of history and as some of the articles show, their histories are carried forth, either by oral transmission, as in the case of interviews that recall Latifa al-Zayyat, or the singing of Ashiq songs. This book attempts to capture the stories carried forth by women, from one context to the other, through the critiques and analyses of these stories.

Particularly, this volume of essays is a space for showcasing the work of Muslim women writers and scholars, not very well known in the West and whose work is here explicated by younger, mostly Muslim women scholars (with a few exceptions of scholars familiar with the contexts) from the home countries of the writers. This book encompasses writings about exiles, refugees, immigrants, and characters who travel across boundaries and yet retain national, cultural, or religious identity.

While creative writing and literature by Muslim women is burgeoning the world over, the writing has been both neglected by major critics and scholars, with perhaps a few exceptions. There are anthologies of the writings, such as the landmark work by Badran and Cooke, *Opening the Gates: An Anthology of Arab Feminist Writing* (2004), and the foundational encyclopedia *Arab Women Writers* edited by Radwa Ashour, Ferial Ghazoul, and Hasna Reda-Mekdahsi (2008). Our book brings together the older writers with the newer and is more up to date, in terms of considerations of the more recently published writers. Theoretical essays often published in journals, heavy in European theory, bear down on the writings and place the writers out of reach. This is why we deliberately eschewed theoretical approaches that relied on European philosophers and thinkers and chose to simply use the clearest possible theoretical contextualizations to introduce the work of both lesser and better known women writers from the Middle East, some who live(d) at home, some in the Western diaspora, and some who, for compelling political reasons, live in diasporas within the Middle East and beyond. Not only are these women writers often excluded from the canon both of English and of world literature but also they are not included in the canon of postcolonial literatures, though many of the assumptions of postcolonial theory can be seen in their work. Postcolonial literary studies often focus only on those countries liberated from the British empire, such as India, Pakistan, Nigeria, and Kenya, and often exclude even those such as Palestine and relegate them to Middle Eastern Studies. Interestingly, bibliographies of Muslim women writers, such as Marcia Hermansen's "Literature and Muslim women," focus largely on South Asian Muslim women. Robert Young in his influential essay, "Postcolonial Remains," writes "While an intense interest in postcolonial theory has developed in Islamic countries, in 2001 Islam was just as *unreadable*, for most postcolonial theorists in the West, as for everyone else" (emphasis mine, 30). The interest in using postcolonial theory, on the part of the scholars included here, demonstrates this premise of Robert Young's that there is in Middle Eastern countries an interest in espousing "postcolonial theory." Despite this due to what Young calls "the politics of invisibility," and of "unreadability," the literature written about here, and the authors included here have largely not had the *visibility* they deserve. This collection of essays creates this *s/place*. Relevant here also is Leila Ahmed's postulation in *Women and Gender in Islam* that perhaps Western and male travelers and critics in Muslim societies had limited access to women (147). This older formulation is also relevant today. Thus, even recent travelers and critics studying Muslim writing recently have not brought forward writings and explications of writings by Muslim women writers. And therefore, the literature of women had little exposure and, consequently, was neglected.

Indeed, there is not much written on the authors included in this collection, such as Latifa al-Zayyat, Out al-Kouloub al-Dimerdashiyyah, Suad al-Sabah, Sahar Hamouda, or the more contemporary, Ebtissam Shakoush, Tamara Chalabi, and Samar Yazbek. Three authors written about here who are well known in the West are Assia Djebar, Mohja Kahf, and Leila Aboulela. This volume provides more contextualized appraisals of their works.

The purpose of this book then is to let their voices be heard and at the same time to have them interpreted through the voices of critics from their local contexts who provide not just interpretations through European theories, but through critics and theorists local to their contexts. An example of such a working is Doaa Omran's essay on Out al-Kouloub, where she uses the concept of mimicry, together with Ibn Khaldūn and Taha Hussein. These comprise the valid "interpretive community" as formulated by Stanley Fish in his *Is There a Text in this Class?* Indeed, in every way, through our book, as Gayatri Spivak would say, in her seminal essay, "Can the Subaltern Speak?" the subalterns *do* speak.

With such critical interpretations, the authors written about here and the scholars writing about them will have global import. Perhaps it can be considered that they sometimes do inhabit liminal spaces. While they may speak and write from liminal spaces separated by the vast oceans that divide the east and the west, they do bridge the global and the local. Neither the writers written about nor the critics are confined to their contexts, while these essays do attempt to provide more "authentic" perspectives on how writers from the Middle East can be read and their voices carried across cultures into transnational, transcultural humanities.

Essays in this volume encompass a broad range of the Middle East from Turkey to Iran and North Africa, i.e., Mauritania, Algeria, and Morocco. One of the strengths of the book is the inclusion of Mauritanian women writers. Additionally, including the Iranian, Persian women writers extends the notion of Muslim women beyond the Arab world. Hopefully, the essays collected here show how the works written about here should be read in all the canons, across world literatures.

All of the characteristics of what we consider "Postcolonial Literature" apply to Muslim women's writing, not just in South Asia but also in the Middle East, which shares histories of colonialisms of some sort or another, whether in Palestine, Egypt, or Iran. They write against empire; they challenge the assumptions of Western stereotypical representations of them; they are concerned with nationalism, home, and identity, often recalled and reconstructed through memory, often carried trans-generationally, across borders. So that in our volume, we see how a younger writer like Tamara Chalabi and perhaps the better known Mohja Kahf carry the memories of their mothers, grandmothers, "foremothers," and authors across boundaries. In their work, there is always a nationalist longing for home, and if diasporic, whether having moved to the west or whether within the Middle East, as in Sahar Hamouda's *Once Upon a Time in Jerusalem* recollections of home. In these conflicted contexts, how do they construct identity and gender? How are they to be reconciled with their personal religions and faith? And when they fly in the face of the strictures of faith, how does resistance enfold their faith and the expression of it? What are the growing up experiences or *bildungsroman* of these women? What sense of nationality or identity do they grow into, especially in cross-cultural situations, either within their home countries or in cross-cultural conditions? Are they transnational, transcultural, or local? What are the critical criteria to measure them with? And of course, all important, is the question of language: to write in the colonizers' language or not. These essays answer these questions. All of these issues and our current political and societal concerns show the urgency of making the works of the authors and critics compiled here accessible to scholars and readers, whether scholarly, layperson, graduate, or undergraduate. This is why it is important to present accessible theoretical essays grounded in both Western/European theories and local scholarship. To present them through a heavily Europeanized theoretical perspective would have been to "recolonize" rather than decolonize their voices and take away from the "decolonial" import of gathering these essays.

The fact that the literary works written about here are rarely examined is in itself is a major contribution to the field. Additionally, they all represent strong Muslim women, quite contrary to the Western stereotypical representation of Muslim women as oppressed. Edward Said, in his *Covering Islam* (1981), had written extensively about how the Western media misrepresented the Islamic world: "Western and specifically American responses to an Islamic world, perceived since the early seventies, as being immensely, relevant and antipathetically troubled and problematic" (x). Said further writes, "From at least the end of the eighteenth century, until our own day, modern Occidental reactions to Islam have been dominated by a radically simplified type of thinking that may be called Orientalist" (4). This "Orientalist" attitude most affects the depiction of women as subjugated, oppressed, victims of forced female genital mutilation, or restrictions of dresscode and behavior, sometimes ignoring that women may be adopting pious attitudes, or the veil—which has most become the symbol of oppression in the West—out of their own free will, such as the pious Turkish women written about by Funda Güven. Most of all, as Pervine Elrefaei writes in her essay about the Syrian writer Tamara al-Refai who writes about Syrian refugees, the essays here collected show, "women's resilience and pivotal roles as preservers of cultural heritage during traumatic displacement and cultural threat."

Relevant to this discussion is the question that Lila Abu-Lughod asks in a landmark work, *Do Muslim Women Need Saving?* (2013). She emphasizes that since 9/11, 2001, and Laura Bush's championing the cause of oppressed women in Afghanistan, the images of oppressed Muslim women have great currency, even by some well-meaning representatives of the culture like Malala Yousafzai—who despite her speaking out against the Taliban, chooses to cover her head, perhaps as a mark of asserting her identity? This collection shows not only that Muslim women do not need saving, but that they save themselves, and also risk all to save the world. This is especially true of the Iranian women writers under consideration here who show how they literally risk their lives to speak out and attempt to recover their homes as they knew them. Whether women choose to embrace the headscarf or any covering, or whether they choose to reject it, they create an "Islam of their own," and embrace it. A woman like Azar Nafisy chooses not to be veiled and sees it as repressive but retains her Muslim and Persian co-mingled identity.

Major feminist works have been written by Muslim women that embrace both secular and religious Islam and attempt, on the part of women, at making the religion their own, asserting their right to practice it as they would, and yet to keep to it. Asmaa Gamal's essay on the "Burkini," included here, shows how women express their subjectivities through the act of veiling or unveiling. Relevant here is Leila Ahmed's chapter, "The Discourse of the Veil," from her book, *Women and Gender in Islam.* She recounts the severe resistance that had been expressed to Qassim Amin's *Tahir al-mara'a* (*The Liberation of Women* published in 1899). He had argued that "unveiling" was the key to social transformation. Several of the essays in the volume show how and why they embrace or reject this practice today. Amina Wadud's *Qur'an and Woman* defies and challenges male hegemonic *hadith* in favor of women and procreative rights. She quotes from the Quran, verse 4:1 "O humankind. . . have *taqwa* towards Allah in whom you claim your rights of one another and (have *taqwa*) towards the wombs (that bore you)" not only as a statement of respect toward women but also of their "procreative capacity" (Wadud 64).

Sherine Hafez in her *An Islam of her Own* notes that the projects of some women in countries like Egypt lean toward, "modernizing liberal secularism, nationalism, state building agendas, and Islamic discourses in their own understanding of themselves and the world around them" (Hafez 6). Most of the women written about in these articles are attempting to construct their own Islamic worlds, some conservative and some, very young and liberal, like Samar Yazbek and Alexandra Chrieteh. Yet, we are now living in a "post-secular age," where suddenly there is a return to more fundamentalist notions of religion around the world, and there is a return to senses of identity and nationality. The writers discussed in this volume by the contextually informed critics traverse the delicate line of belonging and unbelonging, in what they consider homes, their religion, and their identity. These are stories of women moving across cultures and boundaries, that need interpretive strategies local to their contexts that help illuminate them and their contexts.

The assumptions behind this book have been: (1) to show the strengths of Middle Eastern women as opposed to the Western media's image of them; (2) to contextualize and balance European theoretical approaches and the local critical approaches informed by these perspectives, like even those of Edward Said; and (3) to underscore the importance of local perspectives, in an effort to "decolonize" the interpretive community. A "decolonial" methodology that seeks indigenous forms and ways of thinking is essential to providing validity to these writings, rather than continuing to frame them through Europeanized critical approaches. However, several of the critics have used the theoretical underpinnings basic to postcolonial theory, such as those of Homi Bhabha's notions of hybridity and mimicry, Spivak's speaking subject, the subaltern, and the nostalgia for lost origins, and the basics of postcolonial theory such as Fanon's *Black Skin, White Masks,* intersectionality, and postcolonial feminism. Several of these theories do in fact depend on European theorists and their formulations. This collection is unique in that in most cases we have sought to incorporate and merge local critical perspectives in our effort to show that these are not women who needed "saving," but have always had agency and been speaking subjects.

This volume begins with memories, "recollected in tranquility," often in diaspora homes. What is interesting about the essays in this volume is that diaspora, does not necessarily mean a move to the West. Some writers like Sahar Hamouda, the author of *Once Upon a Time in Jerusalem,* sought diasporic homes in countries like Egypt. Denise Helly writes in Haideh Moghissi's collection, *Muslim Diaspora: Gender, Culture and Identity,* "This new image of the diaspora emphasizes the ties linking local communities originating from a dispersed population rather than underlining exile from a homeland and links with a country of origin" (8). This emphasizes a transnational, transcultural contact. In this collection, there are Palestinian and Syrian refugee women as in Riham Debian's article and Pervine Elrefaei's article that show women building diaspora homes in Egypt, Kuwait, and Saudi Arabia. Among the six essays in the section "Memory and Matriarchy," essays by Arththi Sathananthar, Riham Debian, and Feroza Jussawalla describe rebuilding home in diaspora, through memory. Essays by Magda Hasabelnaby, Anna Oldfield, and Naila Sahar show the building of home, creating of history and archive through memory. These essays survey a vast scope of the Middle Eastern world from Azerbaijan to Algeria. In her essay on Assia Djebar's *Fantasia: An Algerian Cavalcade,* Naila Sahar shows how Djebar reconstructs history and home through memory and documents.

The mobility of Muslim women, refugee or otherwise, show the movements and migrations of women. They attempt to bridge the global and local. Almost all the papers especially those by Wafaa Sorour, Amel Abbady, Arththi Sathananthar, and Fatima Sidiya show how the protagonists move in various contexts from countries such as the Sudan and Mauritania to France, from Morocco to Spain, from Iraq to the UK, from Iran to the USA, and back and forth.

Funda Güven, Doaa Omran, Rima Sadek, and Asmaa Gamal show how religious versus Westernized women traverse the fine line of modernization and sexual politics. Essays like Lava Asaad's on Chreiteh's *Always Coca-Cola* show the precarity of modernization and the need to be recognized as human beings. Intersectionality of race and class color two papers from the Gulf countries: Saudi Arabia and Kuwait. Najla Aldeeb's paper is a critique of class in the Saudi community. Asmaa Youssef's paper explores how a female poet from the ruling family, Suad al-Sabah, addresses her poetry to the male elite, while not touching on topics of class in order not to annoy the ruling class. Suad al-Sabah is a very conservative woman and poet who guards her social status while still speaking out for women's rights.

The last section of the book underscores the importance of Scheherazade in conveying Muslim women's experiences even today. Brigitte Stepanov's chapter along with Amany El-Sawy bring Scheherazade into the present with their discussions of two contemporary writers who rewrite and re-inscribe Scheherazade into contemporary literature: Assia Djebar and Mohja Kahf. Thus, Scheherazade comes alive again.

Scheherazade is the governing trope of this volume. She is the speaking subject, with agency, but also a decolonial myth: the indigenous woman who is the model of women's strength not just for women of her region, but for women everywhere. She is a decolonial myth, not just because as an indigenous myth she "decolonizes" our minds from constantly looking up to European models. She is symbolic of the moment of decoloniality, which is the recognition of the value of the indigenous in illuminating both the colonial and the local. As Walter Mignolo writes, "Decoloniality . . . does not imply the absence of coloniality but rather than ongoing serpentine movement toward possibilities of other modes of being, thinking, knowing, sensing, and living; that is otherwise in plural" (Mignolo 81). In this sense, the project here then is a decolonial project, giving voice to Arab women writers and critics, and yet not restricted to the Arab alone, as we consider the Iranian and some non-Arab Muslim writers and critical perspectives. Myths have always had a "decolonial" purpose, that is to connect a culture with its indigenous or local stories, both at the moment of contact and at the moments of stress. These stories are important as opposed to the overlay of stories and interpretations brought by colonizers and foreigners, *farangi*, as we would say. It distinguishes between "decolonial" and "decolonizing," in highlighting that the "decolonial" moment is the moment of an interaction and awareness that then leads to decolonizing.

So it is in the interest of decoloniality and decolonization of the women's literature from the Middle East, as well as decolonizing the critical approaches to the literature, that the essays here bring together both current Western theoretical approaches combined with local approaches, and interviews, to the work of women writers not very well known in the West, together with some whose names are familiar in the West.

Works Cited

Abu-Lughod, Lila. *Do Muslim Women Need Saving?* Cambridge, Harvard, 2013.

Ahmed, Leila. *Women and Gender in Islam: Historical Roots of a Modern Debate.* New Haven, Yale University Press, 1992.

Delueze, Giles and Felix Guattari. *A Thousand Plateaus.* Minneapolis, University of Minnesota Press, 1987.

Fish, Stanley. *Is There a Text in this Class?* Cambridge, Harvard, 1980.

Hafez, Sherine. *An Islam of Her Own: Reconsidering Religion and Secularism in Women's Islamic Movements.* New York, New York UP, 2011.

Hermansen, Marcia. "Literature and Muslim Women." Oxford Bibliographies, 10 May 2017, doi: 10.1093/OBO/9780195390155-0160.

Mignolo, Walter and Catherine E. Walsh. *On Decoloniality.* Durham, Duke UP, 2018.

Ratti, Manav. *The Postsecular Imagination: Postcolonialism, Religion, and Literature.* New York, Routledge, 2018.

Said, Edward. *Covering Islam.* New York, Pantheon, 1981.

Spivak, Gayatri. "Can the Subaltern Speak?" *Colonial Discourse and Postcolonial Theory*, edited by Patrick Williams and Laura Chrisman, New York, Columbia, 1994, pp. 66–111

Wadud, Amina. *Qur'an and Women.* Oxford, Oxford UP, 1999.

Young, Robert. "Postcolonial Remains," *New Literary History*, vol. 43, 2012, pp. 19–42.

Section 1

Memory and Matriarchy

1 Memory of Latifa al-Zayyat between Influence and Ambivalence

Magda Mansour Hasabelnaby

Latifa al-Zayyat is one of the pioneers of the modern novel in Egypt and the Arab world, and a renowned feminist and political activist. The chapter investigates the assumption that al-Zayyat's influence goes beyond her less famous contemporary, Fawziyya Mahran (1931–2019), to subsequent generations of writers who either saw her as a role model and an inspirational leader (Osman, Personal Interview), or questioned her status as a motivating pioneer altogether (Bakr, Personal Interview). These writers include Etidal Osman (born 1942), Salwa Bakr (born 1949), and the most celebrated Radwa Ashour (1946–2014) whose bond with al-Zayyat was the strongest. al-Zayyat's impact is in fact transgenerational; Rehab Bassam (born 1977) repeatedly speaks in her blog-turned-into-a-collection-of-short-stories of her debt to Latifa al-Zayyat, whom she considered one of her "imaginary friends" (120).[1]

Emphasizing the impact of Latifa al-Zayyat on later Egyptian writers, Ahdaf Soueif says:

> Any summary of the life and work of Latifa al-Zayyat without conveying what she meant for a whole generation of young writers and critics in Egypt would be an injustice to the writer and the woman. Her involvement with young people was lifelong. Her time, advice, support—and at times her praise—were given generously and without stint. (130)

Using interviews along with textual analysis, this chapter will reveal the subtle connection between al-Zayyat, her fellow writers, and later ones. In addition, it will attempt to highlight recurrent tropes in the works of these writers while tracing them in the life and works of al-Zayyat.

The history of acknowledging the value of sisterhood and motherhood in feminist writing in Egypt goes back to the early twentieth century, where the Egypt-based Lebanese writer Mai Ziyada documented her indebtedness to three contemporary and earlier women writers (Malak Hifny Nasif 1886–1918; Aisha Taymur 1840–1902; Warda al-Yazijy 1838–1924).[2] Ziyada documented her appreciation of:

> The efforts of those hardworking women who preceded our generation and opened the road for us. I say "opened the road",

though they have only placed a sign at the beginning of untrod-
den fields. Such sign, however, has a wide usage and a great value,
especially when we take into consideration the time in which it
was placed. (7)

This led Badran and Cooke to consider Ziyada "One of the first women
to evoke a self-conscious sense of literary sisterhood . . . giving public
recognition to foremothers, women with whom she could link herself
in a line that gave weight and substance to what they and other later
women might say" (xviii).

When Mai Ziyada passed away in 1941, she herself turned into a celebrated sister and/or an esteemed foremother for later writers who remembered her successes and cherished her legacy. Huda Shaarawy, the
leader of the feminist movement and the founder of the first female syn-
dicate in Egypt, pointed out the value of the attention Mai Ziyada gave
to women's literary production (al-Rouby 145). The reputation of Ziyada
as a literary critic was posthumously celebrated by Widad al-Sakakini.
al-Rouby suggests that al-Sakakini's book, "*Mai Ziyada: her life and her
legacy* was nothing but a continuation of a tradition which Mai herself
had started when she wrote about her contemporaries motivated by a
passionate feminism and a desire to carve a status for women in the field
of literary achievements" (al-Rouby 145).

This tradition, "achieved a new level of activity in the 1970s and the
1980s, when Arab women increasingly wrote introductions to each other's writings as well critical reviews on essays" (Badran and Cooke xiii).
This level of activity continued to the present and was crystalized in the
bond between Latifa al-Zayyat and her contemporaries.

The renowned male novelist, Bahaa Taher, wrote on this special bond.
In Taher's characteristically novelistic style, he draws a picture of al-
Zayyat's final illness and death as he visited her in the hospital, accom-
panied by their friend, the equally renowned critic Sabry Hafez. In this
scene, Taher pictures, "all her students, friends, and the writers who
learnt from her, standing outside the ICU" (131). He adds, "they have
stayed awake the previous night till 5 a.m.; they would go to their homes
and would come back soon seeking a glimpse of hope from a medical
report on the pulse, or from a passing word from a doctor stepping out
from the ICU" (Taher 131). A conversation between Taher and Hafez,
which took place immediately after that hospital scene, is worth quoting
here in relation to the memory of al-Zayyat:

My friend said as we walked out of the hospital to the road, maybe
in an attempt to expel the blues that befell us: Female writers in
Egypt are more loyal than male ones; I have never witnessed such
attention from writers to a sick male author. I did not answer him. I
did not want to say to him: "And do you know any male writer who

spread all that love, compassion, and support that Latifa al-Zayyat generously extended to her students and companions?" (Taher 131)

The life and the works of Latifa al-Zayyat often underscored the strong ties between women's personal experiences and larger social and political structures, especially in postcolonial Egypt. Her first book, *al-Bab al-maftuh The Open door,* published in 1960 is described by Hoda al-Sadda as:

> A period piece as it typifies the revolutionary fervor and optimism of the 1950s, in the aftermath of the 1952 revolution by the Free Officers, the evacuation of British forces, and the mobilization of resistance to the Tripartite Assault on Egypt in 1956. (*Gender* xi)

The novel does this through its protagonist Layla, whose journey is an inspiring simultaneous discovery of feminist and nationalist identities. According to Amal Amireh, "*The Open Door* was simultaneously a product of its time and ahead of it." Layla's self-liberation, and her final epiphany as she passes through "the open door" and reunites with the nationalist masses, is in many ways reminiscent of Nora's decision to slam the door behind her in Ibsen's *A Doll's House.* Both protagonists mark unique moments of transformational self-awareness and political activism, which stand out in feminist literature, within the two different cultures of Egypt and Norway, respectively.[3] And just as "the door slammed by Nora shook Europe" (Lucas qtd. in Quigley 91), the one opened for Layla impacted gender dynamics throughout the Arab world. Layla's epiphany and her author's free spirit still reverberate in women's lives and writing in Egypt to the present.

Latifa al-Zayyat's final literary work, *Hamlet Taftish: Awraq Shakhsiyya [The Search: Personal Papers]*, likewise blends the personal and the political, and equally balances chronicles of the self and narration of the nation. The journey between *The Open Door* and *The Search* is a journey from innocence to experience, through which the writer never reached *Shaykhukha* [old age], and hardly lost her passion and her revolutionary spirit. This is not to say that al-Zayyat's effervescence was never quenched. Like her protagonist Layla, al-Zayyat went through a phase of withdrawal, which lasted for more than twenty years: *al-Shaykhukha [Old Age]*, her second creative work was published in 1986 and was followed by other works in the 1990s. Publishing after such long "phase of artistic silence" to use al-Sadda's expression (*Gender* xi) was one of many triumphs this writer accomplished.

Yet, it is important to note that al-Zayyat's "artistic silence" during these twenty years never reflected a complete withdrawal, in spite of such "disillusionment." Contrary to hermit-like writers who lived on the fringes of society, al-Zayyat, in the late seventies, co-founded the

Committee for the Defense of National Culture, a group of oppositional intellectuals who worked against Zionism and colonial cultural imposition. She led the committee from 1979 to 1996. Her political activism during this period resulted in her imprisonment by the Anwar al-Sadat administration in 1981.

After earning her PhD from Cairo University in 1957 and twenty-four years before her political activism, al-Zayyat became a lecturer in the English department of the faculty of Women, where I graduated and continued to work there until her death in 1996. During her truce from publishing, al-Zayyat continued to write stories which were published later. She was active and dynamic in alternative arenas; an important one was supporting fellow women writers in academic, literary, and cultural circles—particularly emergent novelists, which is the focus of this chapter.

Of all the writers selected in this study, Fawziyya Mahran was the closest to Latifa al-Zayyat in age; al-Zayyat, who was only eight years older than Mahran, achieved more recognition as a novelist. Nevertheless, their relationship seemed free from competition and was exemplary in its strength and ideal in its quality. Mahran wrote a book about al-Zayyat that was published three years after al-Zayyat's death. The title of the book, *Awraq Latifa al-Zayyat Alsharisa wal Gamila* [*The papers of Latifa Al-Zayyat: The Fierce and the Beautiful*], sums up how Mahran views the life journey of al-Zayyat in a context of both revolutionary struggle and aesthetic production.

An implicit intertextuality can be traced in Mahran's short story "The Talisman" whereby the people's rebellion is similar to the revolution that erupts in al-Zayyat's *The Open Door*. The reader feels the same euphoria and warmth that Layla felt on the day she left school and melted into the masses of demonstrators who marched against the British colonization: "Everything around her was propelling her forward, everything, everyone, surrounding her, embracing her, protecting her. She began all of a sudden to shout again, in that voice that belonged to someone else, a voice that joined her whole self to them all" (al-Zayyat, *The Open Door* 49). In Mahran, the conflict gets bitter between the protagonist of the story and the wolves who chase her, and does not resolve except when she, in search of a talisman, fuses with others and melts with them. Only then, she wins without the need for a talisman:

> I cannot stay still any longer . . . walls split and sounds exploded, rising from alleys and streets . . . These bodies smell of sweat and revolution. Hot bodies are vibrant. . . These are not sleeping people, nor dead people, who carry their shrouds. The sea split and swallowed the magicians with their ropes and sticks. I clung to the warm bodies . . . Shouted with my loudest voice . . . My tongue is a songbird. Until now, I do not know where I lost the talisman . . . It must

have been lost in the crowd. . . . Tread by their feet . . . Or maybe it
melted under the heat of my song. (Mahran 113–4)

Mahran compares revolution to life, and acquiescence to death, a comparison which recalls Mahmoud's letter to Layla in *The Open Door*:

> There is only one solution. The solution is for something amazing
> to happen, something that will shake those people to the core—
> all of those respectable, complacently settled folks. It has to be a
> miracle—only that will compel them to tear their shrouds to bits.
> Otherwise the situation will not change. The shrouds will not be
> torn apart because those folks will be holding so fast to the cloth
> and hiding themselves behind it. (al-Zayyat, *The Open Door* 135)

There is a remarkable difference in style between the two extracts. However, Mahran's surrealism and quranic intertextuality still share with
al-Zayyat the passionate glorification of the masses, which appears in
The Open Door, and reverberates in later works. In *Ḥamlet Taftish,
The Search: Personal Papers*, al-Zayyat speaks of "seeking refuge in the
whole/the masses":

> A sea of young people move in waves over the Abbas bridge in 1956.
> The girl who found refuge in the masses is only a drop of sea water,
> she is fierce joy, and an overflowing active power. The I is the I, but
> the meaning is "we." (al-Zayyat, *Ḥamlet* 61)

In his introduction to Mahran's book, *Awraq Latifa Al-Zayyat Alsharisa
wa Algamila: [The papers of Latifa Al-Zayyat: The Fierce and the Beautiful]*, Hasan Atiyya excludes the idea that Mahran's memory of al-
Zayyat is merely "a proof of creativity in a bygone time." Alternatively,
he invites readers to view that memory as a paradigm for extension in
time, where one generation hands over their fierce and beautiful papers
to the next one. "We hope," Atiyya adds, "that new generations will add
'fiercer papers.'" The present time will not change its course without a
force that realigns its position in favor of the whole (7).

Of the generation of writers that followed al-Zayyat, Salwa Bakr
stands out as one of those fiercer voices, which pushed the revolution
al-Zayyat preached to a whole new level. In an interview with Bakr, she
denies receiving any support from Latifa al-Zayyat or having any special
relationship with her. She even expresses doubt about al-Zayyat's revolutionary and feminist status:

> In fact, we never had a special relationship with each other. She
> wrote about me only when everyone else did. Ali Elraei, Hamed
> Alnassag, and many others celebrated my work before she wrote

anything about it. She even seemed to have a conservative opinion about *The Golden Chariot*. People, however, used to put me with her in one basket, because both of us were affiliated with the left. This is why people assumed we were friends, and that she influenced me. Our writings and our attitudes towards the world and towards women's issues are in fact very different. al-Zayyat's ideas were extremely conservative, and even patriarchal. Her intrinsically patriarchal thoughts, however, put on feminist masks. She was her master's voice. (Bakr, Personal Interview)

The above criticism of Latifa al-Zayyat's attitude, and Bakr's condemnation of her as "conservative" and as a pseudo feminist contradicts with the general attitude of al-Zayyat as a progressive political and feminist activist of her time. However, the perspective Bakr provides here is worth investigating as we attempt to problematize the memory of al-Zayyat.

First of all, it is important to read such criticism in relation to the generational and the class difference between the two writers. al-Zayyat belonged to the upper middle class, had a brother who was appointed a minister, and spent her entire life in the university. She was relatively, or perhaps extremely, progressive in relation to her milieu; yet we cannot expect her to make the subaltern speak in the manner Bakr does in her fiction, neither can we blame her for not feeling enthusiastic about Bakr's project. As Seymour-Jorn rightly points out, "Bakr's lower-middle-class roots, her observation of the hardships and political actions of poor women in her work as an inspector . . . have allowed her access to the worlds of poor urban women and have sparked the anger that drives her critique of Egyptian society" ("A New Language" 173). The language and the narrative techniques Bakr used for representing uneducated Egyptian women may have been shocking for al-Zayyat, who nevertheless felt the talent of Bakr and acknowledged it in her own way. A collection of short stories by women writers, which Latifa al-Zayyat introduced in 1994, bore the title *All that Beautiful Voice Comes from within her*, a title which echoed that Bakr's story in the collection. Critics read al-Zayyat's choice of Bakr's title for the collection, which included established as well as emergent voices in the Arab world at the time, as an honor for Bakr, who was then an emergent writer herself. In his *I'tirāfāt nisā' adībāt. [Confessions of Women Writers]*, Ashraf Mostafa Tawfik points out that al-Zayyat's choice which echoed Bakr's title, with its emphasis on the female voice, reveals her belief that criticism repudiates and marginalizes the achievements of women writers.

In spite of Bakr's feelings that she did not receive her due support from al-Zayyat; the interview conducted with her for this chapter revealed that she still positioned al-Zayyat in a special place. She tells me how when she herself was in prison in 1989 on charges of political conspiracy and pamphleteering, she felt cheered up when she knew that al-Zayyat used to be an inmate in the same cell (Bakr, Personal Interview). Her mixed feelings toward the memory of Latifa al-Zayyat are in fact summed up in the first few words she said to me in this interview: "the issue of Latifa al-Zayyat is a very complex one" (Bakr, Personal Interview).

That Bakr is a fiercer woman than al-Zayyat, with a more inclusive project of representing Egyptian women than both al-Zayyat and her successor Radwa Ashour, should not discourage us from tracing al-Zayyat's legacy in her works. *al-Bab Almaftouh The Open Door* can be read as an implicit intertext in Bakr's "Such a Beautiful Voice" and other stories which underscore female voices.[4]

al-Zayyat uses "voice" as a symbol of activism and as an objective correlative for belonging to a community. She repeatedly underscores the parallelism between oppression and silence on the one hand, and achievement and voice on the other hand. In *The Open Door*, Layla at the age of eleven faces the confiscation of her voice in a short telling scene, in which Latifa al-Zayyat uses suggestive words to express the curtailment of voice:

> . . . Layla rose to her full height quickly and wheeled around to go out, with the measured bounce of the demonstrators, waving her right hand up and down, intoning, "Weapons, weapons, we want weapons. Weapons, wea—" She stopped dead, her arm dropped to her side and the words stalled on her lips. Her father was entering the room. (al-Zayyat, *The Open Door* 12)

The young Layla, however, breaks this silence and goes out in demonstrations against the British occupation, defying the patriarchal authority that stifles women's voices:

> Blood pushed into Layla's head and she felt a surge of energy. She felt alive, at once strong and weightless . . . [she] heard herself calling out with a voice that was not her own . . . Then that new voice was lost, caught up in thousands of others, and she slipped down from her perch . . . She began all of a sudden to shout again, in that voice that belonged to someone else, a voice that joined her whole self to them all. (*The Open Door* 48–9)

This metaphor of the discovered and the discontinuous voice extends throughout the novel; Layla's father responds to her decision to free her voice with physical and emotional violence, which culminates in the beating scene, where she and her mother are instructed to "shut up":

> She heard her father's voice, shouting at her mother—"shut up!"—and again, the crack of the slippers, one blow after another, a momentary silence between each, a pause suppressed breathing, then

the slap ringing out again. Then there was the rustle of her book bag as she dragged it across the tiles, the squeak of teeth on leather as she clenched the bag in her mouth, her father's steps receding, the sharp sound of his door slamming. (al-Zayyat, *The Open Door* 49–50)

The silence imposed in the above scene is made more poignant by the other sounds in the background. Yet, later in the novel, al-Zayyat decides to empower her protagonist and to give her an agency and a voice, which were in perfect accordance with the optimism of the period, the ambitions of the 1952 revolution, and its dreams for a better future for the country and for women. Toward the end of the novel, Layla's brother is startled with the change in her voice: "Her brother looked at her in astonishment, wondering why her voice seemed so strange, someone else's voice. The tone seemed different, too . . . This tone of absolute decision he had never heard from Layla" (al-Zayyat, *The Open Door* 338).

Female voice is an equally recurrent theme with Salwa Bakr. The fluctuation of voice between retention and release that we experience with Layla takes place in Bakr's "Kull dhalika al-sawt al-jamil alladhi ya'ti min dakhiliha'" ["Such a Beautiful Voice that Comes from within Her"]. Sayeda, a low-class woman who is drained by caring for her family tells Abdul Hamid, her husband, that she has just discovered that her once rough, lifeless voice has been transformed into one that is charming and clear. The story however does not end in the optimism of *The Open Door*. Unlike al-Zayyat's generation of the sixties, Bakr's generation, often referred to as the generation of the seventies,

Saw this euphoric national pride shattered in the 1967 defeat at the hands of the Israelis, and furthermore witnessed Egyptians' anger at Nasser's style of rule, which ultimately failed to allow the populace a share in government and used repressive measures to control its detractors. (Seymour-Jorn, "A New Language" 157)

Instead of the supportive male protagonists in *The Open Door*, who recognize and support the change in Layla's voice, Sayeda's husband in Bakr's story convinces her that she has to undergo medical treatment to get rid of the hallucinations she is suffering from.

Whether al-Zayyat and Bakr were aware of such intertextuality in relation to the treatment of the female voice or not, it is interesting to examine such trope and other ones in relation to remembering al-Zayyat. The reiteration of certain images across generations of writers can help us understand the influence and the ambivalence in the relationship between them. The story of al-Zayyat and Bakr is in fact the story of the female voice liberating multiple voices across generations of struggle. It is true, as Hoda al-Sadda claims that: "A voice of her own, both Salwa Bakr and her characters speak a new language that heralds and celebrates the discerning eye of the silenced Egyptian woman, not so silent any more" ("Women's Writing" 142). This voice, however, would never have become free without the earlier efforts exerted by al-Zayyat and her generation.

Unlike Bakr, Etidal Osman was not ambivalent about her relationship with Latifa al-Zayyat. For Osman, al-Zayyat was unquestionably a mentor and a role model. Their relationship started with al-Zayyat comparing Osman to the British author Katherine Mansfield in a short story competition for students of the English Department at Cairo University, where Osman was a student and al-Zayyat was an instructor. According to Osman:

> I still remember the impact of her words and their effect on my psyche. I learnt from her on that day a precious lesson that has stayed with me until today. I learnt that a genuine and honest encouraging word from a great writer to an emergent one can make a dream for a whole life for the young writer, whether a male or a female, and can be a drive for them to continue their writing journey. For me the dream started to come true with the publication of my first short story collection Younis *Elbahr [Jonah of the Sea]* in 1987. (Osman, Personal Interview)

Just as Latifa al-Zayyat spotted the talent of Etidal Osman as a budding writer, hailed the birth of an emergent novelist, and supported her progress, Osman likewise detected the flair of Noha Sobhy (born 1987) after half a century or more. Writing very positive reviews of Sobhy in prestigious journals, Osman was consciously, or perhaps subconsciously, replicating the patronage she received from al-Zayyat, a patronage, which made Osman's own talent visible and her growth possible.[5]

Remembering Latifa al-Zayyat, Osman recalls how al-Zayyat paid a special attention to "al-Sultana" [The Female Sultan], a short story in Osman's collection *Washm Elshams [The Sun Tattoo]*. Osman told me that, she has now come to view the main character in her story as a reflection of al-Zayyat herself. "al-Sultana," as Seymour-Jorn rightly pinpoints, is a story about "a motherly and mysterious village woman who teaches and entertains generations of children through her storytelling" (Seymour-Jorn, "Etidal Osman" 112). In the story, as in the life of Etidal herself, storytelling is an act of survival that one generation hands over to the next.

al-Zayyat's professional and personal patronage to Radwa Ashour is an undoubted common knowledge in the literary circles in Egypt. Ashour was considered by many as al-Zayyat's daughter.[6] On her part, Ashour reveals her indebtedness to and her appreciation of al-Zayyat, both in her autobiographical and in her fictional works. al-Zayyat repeatedly features in Ashour's work as the source of inspiration, support and as a constant healer.

In her *Taqarir alsayida Raa* [*Reports of Ms. R*], published in 2001, Ashour creates the character of Ms. R who represents Radwa herself, and her friend Ms. L, who I read as Latifa (17–21). In a surrealist scene, Ms. R throws herself from the balcony after watching the news on 16 December 1998. The date corresponds with the bombing of Iraq (Operation Desert Fox) by the United States and the United Kingdom, though Ashour does not state that in the text. Latifa al-Zayyat had already passed away on that date; yet, it is Ms. L who saves Ms. R, by rushing down the stairs to rescue her friend/daughter and to fix her body parts together with cellophane tape. The mother-daughter relationship between Latifa and Radwa expressed in such dream-like fashion in 2001 is portrayed in a more factual and confessional one in *al-Ṣarkha a* [*The Scream*], published posthumously in 2015. Radwa pays tribute to Latifa in her final work as she tells of four women: her aunt, her mother-in-law, her biological mother, and Latifa al-Zayyat:

> I met Latifa for the first time in autumn 1967, when I was appointed as a TA in the faculty of Women, Ain Shams University where she used to teach. It should not be a secret for you my dear Ms. reader that just greeting her, or sitting next to her in her car and listening to her talk was impressive for me. I have told you in the first part of this book that seeing a writer from afar was more like the manifestation of a miracle. Let alone if this writer was a female novelist whose mere presence would confirm that taking writing as a profession one day, in the near or far future, was an attainable dream. (Ashour, *al-Ṣarkha* 113)

Not only did Ashour become a renowned writer like her role model, but she also followed al-Zayyat's footsteps in documenting Egyptian modern history through autobiography. Revealing oppression and recording police brutality and people's resistance to it were burdens the mother carried in *Al-Bab Al-Maftouh* [*The Open Door*] and *Ḥamlet Taftish* [*The Search*], and the daughter continued to bear and to share in *Athqal min Radwa* [*Heavier than Radwa*] and *Al-Ṣarkha a* [*The Scream*].

In this chapter, I have attempted to clarify al-Zayyat's impact on, and support for fellow Egyptian women writers, as well as for writers of the later generations on two levels: a personal and a professional one. Through interviews with authors who knew Latifa al-Zayyat, and examination of selections of fiction written during her lifetime and after her death, I have tried to revive her memory and to bear witness to writers' relationships with her across different generations.

I leave the reader now to decide whether the relationship between those writers and Latifa al-Zayyat is purely incidental or that al-Zayyat *is* a literary foremother whose works, and her very existence in the lives of later women writers, affected them. It is also up to the reader to believe, after reading the selections of texts and intertexts in this chapter, whether the reiteration of certain themes and images is not only indicative of broad Arab women's issues but is also? suggestive of some literary heirloom.

Notes

1 In the section for acknowledgements, which follows the book, Bassam indirectly expresses her gratitude again to Latifa al-Zayyat when she thanks a friend of hers, Lobna Abdelmegid Shokry, for introducing her to [the books by] Latifa al-Zayyat (Bassam 122). In addition to these two references to al-Zayyat in the acknowledgements' section, there is an explicit intertextuality in the collection as Bassam refers to *The Open Door*, and to its protagonist's aversion to the corset. Middle-class women in al-Zayyat's time, were required to wear a corset "that would pull in her middle and lift her chest so her price would go up in the market and she could marry" (Bassam 39). Bassam follows this intertextual reference by adding another dress item that she wants to oppose: "I wonder why nobody writes about the transparent *Filet* socks nylon socks," she metafictionally writes, "Maybe I will have to do that in my next story" (25).
2 Ziyada, or Ziade, (1886–1941) was a Christian Lebanese writer who lived in Egypt for most of her life and hosted one of the most famous literary salons in the modern Arab world. She is famous for her long correspondence and platonic love affair with the poet Khalil Gibran (Rappaport 773). It is interesting how such feminist inheritance crosses boundaries of geography and religion within the Arab world.
3 I often teach the two texts simultaneously in courses of comparative literature.
4 Two such stories which show a preoccupation with the female voice are: "Ihda wa Thalathun Shajara Jamila Khadra" ["Thirty-One Beautiful and Green Tree"], and "Umm Shehta Allati Faggarat Elmawdu'" ["The Mother of Shehta Triggers the Whole Affair"].
5 See Etidal Osman's reviews of Noha Sobhi's stories in AlAkhar, and in Alsharqa Althaqafiya.
6 See Hannah Davis Taïeb "The Girl who Found Refuge in the People: The Autobiography of Latifa Zayyat."

Works Cited

al-Rouby, Olfat Kamal. "Mai Ziyada wal Naqd al-Nisawi" ["Mai Ziyada and Feminist Criticism: A Reading of her Book on Aisha Taymur."] *Alif: Journal of Comparative Poetics,* no. 19, 1999, pp. 144–69.

al-Sadda, Hoda. *Gender, Nation, and the Arabic Novel: Egypt 1892–2008.* London, Syracuse, 2012.

———. "Women's Writing in Egypt: Reflections on Salwa Bakr." *Gendering the Middle East: Emerging Perspectives*, edited by Deniz Kandiyoti. I.B. Tauris, 1996, pp. 127–44.

al-Zayyat, Latifa. *Ḥamlet Taftish Awraq Shakhsiyya* [*The Search: Personal Papers*]. Cairo, Dal Elhilal, 1992.

———. *The Open Door*. Translated by M. Booth, Cairo, American U in Cairo P, 2000.

Amireh, Amal. "Remembering Latifa al-Zayyat." *Al Jadid*, vol. 2, no. 12, October 1996. np www.aljadid.com

Ashour, Radwa. *al-Ṣarkha* [*The Scream*]. Cairo, Dar al-Shorouk, 2015.

———, et al., editors. *Arab Women Writers: A Reference Guide 1873–1999.* American U in Cairo P, 2008.

———. *Athqal min Radwa: Maqate' min Sira Thatiyya.* Cairo, Dar al-Shorouk, 2013.

———. *Taqarir alsayida Raa* [*Reports by Ms. R*]. Cairo, Dar al-Shorouk, 2001.

Atiyya, Hasan. Introduction. *Awraq Latifa al-Zayyat Alsharisa wa Algamila: [The Papers of Latifa al-Zayyat: The Fierce and the Beautiful]*, edited by Fawziyya Mahran. Cairo, Matbouat AlHaiaa, 1999.

Badran, Margot, and Miriam Cooke, editors. *Opening the Gates: A Century of Arab Feminist Writing.* Bloomington, Indiana UP, 1990.

Bakr, Salwa. "Ihda wa Thalathoun Shajara Gameela Khadraa" ["Thirty-One Beautiful Green Trees"]. *The Wiles of Men and Other Stories.* Translated by Denys Johnson-Davies, London, Quartet Books, 1992, pp. 12–26.

———. "Kull dhalika al-sawt al-jamil alladhi ya'ti min dakhiliha" ["Such a Beautiful Voice that Comes from within Her"]. *"An al-ruh allati suriqat tadrijiyyan [About the Soul That Gradually Was Spirited Away: Stories]*, Cairo, al-Miṣrīyah lil-nashr wa al-tawzi'"*, 1989, pp. 7–17.

———. Personal Interview. Conducted by Magda Hasabelnaby, 19 May 2020.

———. "Umm Shehta Allati Faggarat Elmawdu'" ["The Mother of Shehta Triggers the Whole Affair"] *Mokhtarat min A'mal Salwa Bakr.* Cairo, Alhy'a al-Misriyah Al'ama lelketab, 2008, pp. 58–67.

Bassam, Rehab. *Orz Bellaban leshakhsein* [*Rice Pudding for Two*]. Cairo, Dar al-Shorouk, 2008.

Ibsen, Henrik. *A Doll's House.* Translated by William Archer, 1879, NY, Eternal Sun Books, 2016.

Mahran, Fawziyya. *Fanar Alakhawein.* Cairo, Markaz Alhadara Alarabiyya, 2003.

Osman, Etidal. "Intabihu Ila hathihi elmawhiba" ["Pay Attention to This Talent"]. *AlAkbar*, October 10.

———. "Noha Sobhi tuḥawel mulamasat alnafs elbashariyya" ["Noha Sobhi Attempts to Touch the Human Soul"]. *Alsharja Althaqafiyya*, January 2020.

———. Personal Interview. Conducted by Magda Hasabelnaby, 10 June 2020.

———. *Washm al-shams* [*Sun Tattoo*]. Cairo, al-hayaa al-Miṣrīya al- 'ama lil-kitāb, 2019.

Quigley, Austin. *The Modern Stage and the Other Worlds.* London, Methuen & Co. Ltd. 2015.

Rappaport, Helen. *Encyclopedia of Women Social Reformers.* Santa Barbara, ABC-CLIO, 2001.

Seymour-Jorn, Caroline. "Etidal Osman: Egyptian Women's Writing and Creativity." *Journal of Middle East Women's Studies*, vol. 2, no. 1, 2006, pp. 95–121.

———. "A New Language: Salwa Bakr on Depicting Egyptian Women's Worlds." *Critique: Critical Middle Eastern Studies*, vol. 11, no. 2, Fall 2002, pp. 151–76, doi: 10.1080/1066992022000007808.

Soueif, Ahdaf. "Latifa al-Zayyat: A Raid: Personal Papers." *Index on Censorship*, vol. 23, no. 1–2, May 1994, pp. 130–34, doi: 10.1080/03064229408535650.

Taher, Bahaa. *Fī Madīh al-riwayah [In Praise of the Novel]*. Dar al-Shorouk, 2018.

Taïeb, Hannah Davis. "The Girl Who Found Refuge in the People: The Autobiography of Latifa Zayyat." *Journal of Arabic Literature*, vol. 29, no. 3/4, 1998, pp. 202–17.

Tawfīq, Ashraf. *I'tirāfāt Nisā' Adībāt. [Confessions of Women Writers]*. Cairo, Dār al-Amīn, 1998.

Ziyada, Mai. *Warda Alyazigi*. Cairo, Hindawi Foundation for Education and Culture, 2012.

2 Rebuilding Baghdad

Placing Memoir in the Archive in Marina Benjamin's *Last Days in Babylon* (2007) and Tamara Chalabi's *Late for Tea at the Deer Palace* (2010)

Arththi Sathananthar

First came the looters, then came the arsonists. It was the final chapter in the sack of Baghdad. The National Library and Archives, a priceless treasure of Ottoman historical documents including the old royal archives of Iraq were turned to ashes in 3,000 degrees of heat. ("Iraq National Library Looted, Destroyed")

Such was the account given by journalist Robert Fisk of the destruction of Iraq's National Library on 14 April 2003. As an old Arabic adage goes, "Cairo writes. Beirut prints. Baghdad reads" (Chalabi 252). However, after the American invasion of Iraq and their destruction of the country's archives, the library's archives which held documents dating back to the Sumerian, Babylonian, and Assyrian civilizations were destroyed (Dimock 1). Nothing was left for Iraqis, whose country was once the zenith of literature and culture. Only the Saddam-era records and archives were safeguarded by the US Department of Defense. Furthermore, with the onslaught of ISIS (Islamic State of Iraq and Syria) a decade later, even more of Iraq's cultural places were destroyed, including archaeological sites and cemeteries (Montgomery 173). As Tamara Chalabi points out in her family memoir on Iraq's lost cultural heritage, "the first system of writing in the world had been devised by the Sumerians in southern Iraq 5,500 years earlier, and the oldest known epic in the world is the Mesopotamian Gilgamesh" (251). As of 2013, only two hundred rare books had been recovered from the three thousand lost (Kingsley). The destruction of Iraq's Archives systematically eradicated, for the most part, accounts of Iraq's rich literary past. The nation which was once the cradle of writing lost a majority of its books which account for the country's history. Art historian Zainab Bahrani, who made it her personal project to recover and restore some of the damaged documents from the archives after the war, claims, "Destruction of archives incites a collective amnesia, an eradication of memory by means of erasing its documentary and historical apparatus, consigning it to the flames." Writing and memory are interconnected, thus reinforcing the importance of writing to preserve a nation's memory. It is the precarious state of the lost records from the National Archives that highlights the need for Iraqis to tell their stories in different mediums in order to escape the clutches of a "collective amnesia."

Archives are not the only holders of a nation's history; it can be found in the writing of memoirs. I focus on two recent memoirs, Marina Benjamin's *Last Days in Babylon: The Story of the Jews of Baghdad* (2007) and Tamara Chalabi's *Late for Tea at the Deer Palace: Lost Dreams of my Iraqi Family* (2010), to elucidate the role that memoir can play in preserving a nation's memory. Chalabi and Benjamin are diasporic Iraqis whose texts reflect on the experience of homecoming as well as the memories and experiences of their foremothers in Baghdad before they had to flee the city and live in political exile. I propose an exploration of women's writing that reflects on the relationship between family and state to curb a "collective amnesia." As Benjamin states in the acknowledgements to her memoir: "This book has tried to capture some of that [Baghdadi Jew] heritage before it slips out of cultural memory and into the obscurity of the forgotten past" (293). Both authors, Muslim and Jewish, give an account of twentieth-century political life in Iraq by focusing on the relationship between the family and the city of Baghdad. I argue that the memoirs are libraries of memory. Chalabi and Benjamin are the custodians of these "libraries" as they work to create an alternative archive. These stories are, of course, not contained in actual libraries but are kept alive within the family and passed down through the generations. This essay seeks to posit an unofficial archive of Iraq. I explore the relationship between these diasporic writers and Baghdad to highlight how space is reimagined and represented in constructing a heterogeneous Iraqi identity tied to Baghdad. I consider these memoirs to be alternative routes to Iraq's archive by foregrounding the voices of its disenfranchised ethnic groups: the Shi'as and the Jews.

I turn to Jacques Derrida's seminal text, *Archive Fever* (1995), to engage with his claim of archive theory and how Chalabi's and Benjamin's memoirs can be understood within this framework. The etymology of the word archive is as Derrida notes, "the meaning of 'archive', its only meaning, comes to it from the Greek *arkheion*: initially a house, a domicile, an address" (9). As I argue, the memoirs are libraries of memory; therefore, the texts are essentially containers or 'domicile(s)' for the archive. Derrida adds:

> There would indeed be no archive desire without the radical finitude, without the possibility of a forgetfulness which does not limit itself to repression. Above all, and this is the most serious, beyond or within this simple limit called finiteness or finitude, there is no

archive fever without the threat of this death drive, this aggression
and destruction drive. (19)

The desire for and destruction of the archive is cyclical; one cannot exist without the other. What is significant about this is that "forgetfulness" or "repression" underscores the need for an archive. I contend that
Chalabi's and Benjamin's texts are alternate archive sources to counteract a "collective amnesia." The collapse of the national archive con-
tradictorily brought forth new possibilities for updating Iraq's history:
"The archivist produces more archive, and that is why the archive is
never closed. It opens out of the future" (Derrida 45). The archive is a
constant and evolving source; it seeks to reinvent and update itself. The
archive does not dwell in the past, but it opens new possibilities for constructing a new identity for the nation.

Derrida's analysis of the archive has paved the way for more recent
critics to purvey the subject. Critics claim that, "'archives' usually de-
notes records which have been recognized as having long term value"
(Thomas et al. iv). However, with the destruction of Iraq's National Archives, different forms such as memoir can be a significant source in
restoring and preserving national memory. It is from this point that I
move to the next aspect of my argument; that archival theory privileges
wholeness (Lowry 3). Memoir, unlike autobiography, does not represent
an entire lifespan or chronological narrative. It focuses on a specific period of time. It is this intense and detailed focus on specific events that
lends memoir its wholeness. However, some critics assert that "Archives
are a form of memory, and record 'a' truth. We must remember that it
is not the whole or only truth" (Thomas et al. 103). As these memoirs
record histories of persons who have been marginalized, minority communities and women, they exhibit the "other" truth that has been obscured in Iraq's history. The role of memoir is significant because it can
be an alternative historical document which bridges the nation's history
to the individual writings of its people. Benjamin's titular reference to
"Last Days" and Chalabi's to "Lost Dreams" evoke impermanence and
transience: their families have to flee Iraq due to political instability.
Although their families no longer reside there, they return to their homeland by documenting a lost time and space.

The function of memoir is no longer relegated to its literary value because "critics' attention has shifted from the 'literary' . . . to the political
and ideological aims of life writing" (Couser 103). This "political" and
"ideological" framework is also reflected in Arab life writing. In her
seminal text, *In The House of Silence* (1998), Fadia Faqir highlights a
"double jeopardy" which Arab female writers are plagued with:

The need which women feel to create their life history is probably
due to their suffering the 'double jeopardy' of being women and

political dissidents in the Arab world. Women face the challenges of the male autobiographer under totalitarian regimes, and also the challenges unique to having a role constructed outside themselves and a 'master narrative' superimposed on them. (9)

Faqir's argument is further repurposed by Geoffrey Nash a decade later: "with respect to Arab women there is a patriarchal complicity behind both the narrative of the colonizer and that of the bourgeois national state" (120–21). With this double bind of oppression at play, Chalabi's and Benjamin's memoirs are important cultural artifacts which are containers to the sites of resistance against an autocratic and patriarchal nation state. By connecting the memoir to the archive, another dimension of Iraqi life is opened up, which is very different from the historiography of Iraq that has been written about the country's male-dominated public life, as the text depicts female experiences and writings. Susan Muaddi Darraj states that Arab women's writings are steeped in the political due to the turmoil in the region as a result of long-standing colonialism in the past century. She notes, "Much Arab literature often focuses on politics, perhaps because the Middle East has been deeply scarred by colonialism, war, and religious strife in the past century" (Darraj 124). Differently to Darraj, what I focus on in these texts are how the family is affected by neo-imperialist powers that privileges the Sunni sect of the country over the other religious minorities. These ethnic tensions result in both Chalabi's and Benjamin's families having to flee the country.

Identity politics plays a major role in the family narratives of Benjamin and Chalabi. Though the Shi'as make up the majority of Iraqis, the Sunni sect are the ruling power in the country. Chalabi, who was born in Lebanon and lived in Jordan and England, is a Shi'a Muslim. The Chalabi family are chiefly involved with the state. Her grandfather and great-uncle occupied public roles in the family's ancestral district Kazimiya in Baghdad. Moreover, her father was directly involved with international efforts (with the USA) to topple the Saddam regime from the 1970s to the early 2000s. He was even chosen as a prime candidate to replace Saddam Hussein. The family's presence in the political landscape can be traced from the late nineteenth century to the twenty-first century. Chalabi also weaves a colorful tapestry of Iraq's past and the nation's position in the wider recent history of the Arab world. Her text includes the influence of Arab nationalism from Egypt in the 1950s, and Iraq's invasion of Kuwait and the Iran-Iraq war in the 1990s.

While Chalabi's text encompasses a vast period of Iraq's twentieth-century history, Benjamin focuses on a single event in this period: the 1941 *farhud*. The word *farhud* refers to the massive riots in Baghdad against the Jewish population. The detonation of Arab-Jewish kinship resulted primarily from the Arab-Israeli conflict in the region, which slowly festered from the Balfour Agreement of 1917 to the creation of Israel in

1948. Hundreds of Jews were killed, public properties were destroyed, and businesses were looted. The Denaturalization Bill was a consequence of this bloody event. It led to a mass departure of the Baghdadi Jews between 1950 and 1951. The government obliged them to renounce their citizenship and surrender property to the state. As Benjamin writes, "the government imposed severe restrictions on what registering emigrants were allowed to take out of Iraq" (200–01). Baghdadi Jews were not only stripped of their nationality, but also of their wealth in an effort by the Iraqi government to render them politically, socially, and economically disadvantaged by living in the diaspora. To study these distinct histories, I focus on the treatment of city and home to explore the socio-cultural aspects of a multi-cultural Iraq identity.

Chalabi's text is illustrative of a lost era of a nation in a time capsule; specifically, Iraq under Ottoman and British rule in the early to mid-twentieth century. She writes to reclaim the significance that this period had in shaping her history of her family and Baghdad. She notes that "Ottoman Baghdad appeared to have retreated into the shadows, leaving few traces of its existence behind other than old buildings and street names. Yet its soul lingered on in the people and the language" (Chalabi 77). Chalabi conveys the Ottoman "soul" through oral tradition that has affected her since childhood:

> My journey to Iraq had really begun in my head many years earlier, in my grandparents' house in Beirut. It was 1981. I was seven years old. A man's voice, sonorous and beautiful, cut across a crowded room, singing about a land I did not know. (xxvii)

Music and song play a major role in her journey to reclaim her Iraqi identity. However, Iraqi space is recollected through a Lebanese locale. The passage highlights Chalabi's diasporic reality; being in Beirut, she is in close proximity to Iraq, but not in it. She imaginatively returns to her homeland through song. It is an anonymous voice, presumably Iraqi, who anchors her to the "land I did not know." The motif of song and voice sets the tone for finding her cultural and familial roots.

Chalabi's first subsection "Fallen Pomegranates" provides an illustrative account of Ottoman control in Baghdad. Bibi sings a popular song about the war (between the British and the Ottomans in 1917):

> The pomegranate tree engulfed me, and the sweet lemon came to my rescue; / I don't want this sweetness, take me home . . . / Oh, mother don't wait for me, there is no point in waiting; I will never abandon my home, there is nothing to be done.
>
> The song was about the Ottomans, referred to as bitter pomegranates, and the British, who were the sweet lemons. The words expressed the longing of a soldier or prisoner for his home, with the

implication being that he wanted neither the sour Ottomans nor the sweet antidote to their bitterness, the British. (Chalabi 62)

Home features prominently in the song lyrics. It being popular during the war, the song highlights the non-native rulers in Iraq: the Ottomans and the British. The resonance of taste is a veiled construct of colonial rule. The "solider or prisoner" does not want neither the "sour Ottomans" nor the "sweet antidote" of the British, as neither offers freedom or liberation for the Iraqi people. It is significant that the Iraqis who ultimately are the victims of this battle of colonial power.

However, Chalabi counteracts this reality of colonialism by creating a romanticized depiction of Baghdad through the melody of the city:

> The streets of Baghdad were filled with music and verse. In the small cafés in the old neighborhood gramophones blared out Egyptian love songs and Iraqi melodies, increasingly performed by female singers. The music of Iraq catered for all tastes: there were popular tunes, Bedouin songs, gypsy songs, songs sung in falsetto by men dressed as women, women's bands for female social occasions, the dirges of official mourners, religious music, the songs of laborers. (166)

Chalabi's relationship to the homeland is conveyed primarily through sensorial motifs which highlight how in absence and separation, the memory of the past can be profoundly felt imaginatively. The passage represents the past through a kaleidoscope of sound. While the previous passages conveyed the gustatory sense, here she emphasizes the olfactory to portray the character of the city. The confined space of the "small cafés" represents Baghdad's rich oral tradition. Although the nation is not independent, its people celebrate life through music. Moreover, the prominent presence of these female singers on the airwaves signals a shift in gendered societal norms which allow women's voices to be publicly heard.

These cafés are also a space where self-expression is heard through poetry:

> Baghdad was in many ways a city dizzy with the glory of the word, with a rich poetic tradition. . . . Besides poetry, there was a long oral tradition which manifested itself in the gossip of the cafés and literary salons, . . . Words were the key means through which people sought to express the complexity and variety of life in Iraq. (Chalabi 251–2)

The city is a hub of poetry and orality, and the cafés and literary salons are the catalyst of these expressions. The oral tradition in the micro-space of the cafés and salons are reflected through the macro-space of the city, which is "dizzy with the glory of the word." Chalabi paints a picture of the cafés and salons as the microcosm of voice for the city. As Lindsey Moore notes, "Arab nationalism and the *nahda* (cultural renaissance or 'awakening') emerged in the latter half of the nineteenth century as much in response to the crumbling Ottoman Empire as to encroachments of European power" (27). Unable to fight back against the Ottomans or the British, Iraqis use words as their "weapons." Their voice is a powerful instrument to record and preserve the reality of living under multiple occupations. Chalabi's documentation of this rich oral tradition functions to memorialize their stories so they may live on in her memoir.

I have established the ways in which the song about a pomegranate tree came to signify the Ottoman rulers of Iraq. The image of the pomegranate is used in both texts, which is not unusual as it is a fruit that is frequently used in Arab cuisine and culture. The motif is common, but the fruit is used in different ways by both authors. Benjamin writes, "'Israel *ghamana*'—Israel is a pomegranate . . . the Baghdadi Jews, like the individual seeds of this unusual fruit, were wrapped within a single skin" (32). She reflects upon the sense of unity that is envisioned through the fruit. In her chapter titled "Jews and Pomegranates" she presents a backdrop of Jewish Baghdad through the Old Quarter of the city which was the epicenter of Jewish Iraqi space and activity. The inside of the pomegranate, with its seeds packed and sealed tightly together by the hard shell of the fruit is likened also to the Jewish Quarter of the city: "It was as if they [the Jewish community] believed that the closer they were bound together the more concentrated their essence would be" (Benjamin 32). The pomegranate is a metaphor for Jewish living space. Benjamin depicts the Jewish Quarter to exert the Jewish presence in Baghdad before their expulsion out of the city in the middle of the twentieth century. Benjamin's narrative seeks to recover obscured Baghdadi Jewish history. Montgomery states:

> The Iraqi Jewish archives was discovered in May 2003 . . . In the Mukhabarat [Saddam Hussein's secret police headquarters], US forces found 2,700 Jewish holy books, Torah scrolls, commentaries and books on Jewish law, and many other water-damaged documents and materials—an invaluable archive of a now dead Jewish community that had been one of the oldest Jewish communities in the world . . . The materials were evidently seized in 1984 from the Bataween synagogue in Baghdad. (170)

After the Allied invasion of Iraq in 2003, the American forces sought to return these Jewish Archives back to Iraq. However, this decision was met with much opposition from Jewish groups and the Iraqi Jewish diaspora because they argued against returning these Jewish cultural materials to the country that eradicated and wiped out the entire community (Montgomery 171).

Due to the Arab-Jewish conflict in Iraq, Jewish spaces and motifs within the city retract and become concealed spaces. Of the Old City, Benjamin notes:

> Elaborately carved twelfth-century gates tucked away in neglected corners, between the noisy souks and bustling coffeehouses. . . . Occasionally, a dark street opens up onto the banks of the River Tigris, where an unexpected burst of sunlight flashes up off the water. But mostly the narrow streets fold in on themselves, hugging their secrets. (xiii)

There is a retracted quality to this space. Each entity from the "gates tucked away" and the streets which "fold in" accentuate the separation of Jewish spaces from the rest of the city. It is as though by shielding their spaces they are shielding their livelihoods from Muslim neighbors to avoid potential frictions. This tightly compact space mirrors the air of privacy. The quality of secrecy is further emphasized: "Its politics are a labyrinthine as its streets. Its crumbling buildings creak under the weight of stories untold" (xiii). Benjamin's memoir unravels the "weight of stories untold." She is asserting the sense of belonging that tethered the Baghdadi Jews to the city. She is rewriting the Baghdadi Jews' history by presenting snapshots of Baghdad's hidden past.

However, it is not the detriments of the *farhud* that make the Baghdadi Jews separate from the city. Benjamin illustrates the intricacies of the Jewish Quarter:

> The typical Jewish house was a personal fortress against the clamor and chaos of daily life in Baghdad. The impregnable facades that faced the street were meant to be uninviting. The hulking wooden doors bolted tightly shut. . . . On the inside, however, home was an oasis of colonnaded walkways and inner courtyards that opened to the sky and rang with the sound of footsteps and laughter. (32–3)

The manner in which the Jewish Quarter was built and inhabited is parallel to the metaphor of the Jews through the prism of the pomegranate. The seeds of the fruit which are individual and separate yet encased within a single shell mirrors how the inner domain of the Jewish home was contained through its "hulking wooden doors." Moreover, the juxtaposition between the community's family life signals a peaceful "oasis" against the city life that was full of "clamor and chaos." These two contrasts highlight the separation between the private and public. Although the community's presence was deeply ingrained within the history of Baghdad, there was still a separation, a distinction that signaled a sense of not wholly belonging to the nation. The distance between the Baghdadi Jew home and the city would be deeply aggravated by the state's many riots. In 1941, during the Iraqi rebels' plot to expel the British out of Iraq, the city shut down and Jews were harassed and targeted because of their longstanding support of British rule (Benjamin 134–5). As a consequence of this, "Many Jews, . . . had lined their front doors with sheets of iron or fitted them with bars" (Benjamin 136). Benjamin continues to assert the significance of doors because they are not only entities to enter the private domain but also barriers against the disastrous forces outside.

The motif of doors is significant in the text. Long after the Baghdadi Jews exodus from Iraq, there are little markers to assert the community's link to Baghdad:

> Small cigarette-shaped indentations in the doorposts of houses where Mezuzahs, long ago pilfered for their silver, had once been nailed, and stars of David ingeniously incorporated into a building's brickwork; empty spaces and silent traces, hinting at prior occupancy. (Benjamin xviii)

Through these "cigarette shaped indentations," Jewish identity is inscribed into the very foundations of these houses. Doors of houses are important elements of the home as they represent the threshold between the public space of the outside world against the intimate space of the home. The religious and cultural aspect of the holy inscriptions, *mezuzahs*, that were pinned to doors highlights that one would be entering a sacred Jewish private space. While the current community has been left disenfranchised from the state, these little vestiges suggest that their presence within the city cannot be so easily forgotten.

To conclude, both Chalabi's and Benjamin's narratives foreground a diverse cultural Iraqi identity that is reflective of a reinvented national archive. Each author projects their diasporic connection to Baghdad in distinct ways. Chalabi illustrates how rich oral traditions are deployed to assuage Iraqis' plight of living under different rulers. On the other hand, Benjamin reinforces the lost Baghdadi Jew identity by detailing the influence of Jewish spaces in Baghdad. Chalabi and Benjamin not only document accounts linked to the creation of the modern state of Iraq, but they delve deep into the past to tell myths of the place and its people. Chalabi notes, "To have an inheritance of exile is a never-ending journey between myth and reality. Part of my coming to terms with Iraq entails accepting a reality that was built on an old dream; the dream of another home" (388). For Benjamin, "This book has tried to capture some of that [Baghdadi Jew] heritage before it slips out of cultural memory and into the obscurity of the forgotten past" (293). Although Iraq's National Archives have been consigned to the flames, these memoirs evidence that the nation's memory lives on in alternate spaces. These texts seek to re-build what was lost and reinvent a new cultural memory for Iraq.

Works Cited

Bahrani, Zainab. "Iraq National Library Destruction: The Incredible Fight to Save Iraq's Collective Memory (PHOTOS)." *Huffington Post*, March 2013.

Benjamin, Marina. *Last Days in Babylon: The Story of the Jews of Baghdad.* London, Bloomsbury Publishing, 2007.

Chalabi, Tamara. *Late for Tea at the Deer Palace: The Lost Dreams of my Iraqi Family.* London, Harper Perennial, 2010.

Couser, Thomas. *Memoir: An Introduction.* Oxford, Oxford UP, 2012.

Darraj, Susan Muaddi. "Writing Relocation: Arab Anglophone Literature of the Last Decade." *Iowa Journal of Cultural Studies*, vol. 2, 2002, pp. 123–30.

Derrida, Jacques. "Archive Fever." *Diacritics*, translated by Eric Prenowitz, vol. 25, no. 2, 1995, pp. 9–63.

Dimock, Wai Chee. "Introduction: Planet as Duration and Extension." *Through Other Continents: American Literature across Deep Time.* Princeton and Oxford, Oxford UP, 2006, pp. 1–6.

Faqir, Fadia, editor. *In The House of Silence: Autobiographical Essays by Arab Women Writers.* Reading, Garnet Publishing, 1998.

"Iraq National Library Looted, Destroyed." *American Libraries Magazine*, 2003.

Kingsley, Suvi. "Interview with Saad Eskander, Director of Iraq National Library and Archives (INLA)." *Ifla*, May 2013.

Lowry, James, editor. *Displaced Archives.* London & New York, Routledge, 2017.

Montgomery, Bruce. "Iraq and Kuwait: The Seizure and Destruction of Historical Patrimony." *Displaced Archives.* Edited by James Lowry, London & New York, Routledge, 2017, pp. 158–79.

Moore, Lindsey. *Arab, Muslim, Woman: Voice and Vision in Postcolonial Literature and Film.* London & New York, Routledge, 2008.

Nash, Geoffrey. *The Anglo-Arab Encounter: Fiction and Autobiography by Arab Writers in English.* Bern, Peter Lang, 2007.

Thomas, David, et al. *The Silence of the Archive.* London, Facet Publishing, 2017.

3 *Once Upon a Time in Jerusalem*

Re-memory and the Storied Geography of Subalterns' Telling of Their S/Place

Riham Debian

> What I remember is a picture floating around out there outside my head . . . the picture of what I did, or knew, or saw is still out there. . . . It's when you bump into a re-memory that belongs to somebody else . . . that place is real. It's never going away. (Morrison, *Beloved* 21)

Crossing the borders of space and place, re-memory, like rewriting, translates past to present/presence, place into discursive space, and identity into placed identities. The latter counters the geographical violence of imperialism (Said 77) and the "carceral geography" or "graduated incarceration" of the metamorphosing geography of colonial occupation through stories of location and relocation (Smith 21, 29). These stories of location and relocation set localized geography as the epicenter of subaltern geographical subjectivity and thus furnish subaltern geopolitics of place and space. This chapter examines the translational re-signification of Sahar Hamouda and her Palestinian mother, Hind al-Fitiany's re-memories in *Once Upon a Time in Jerusalem*. The question of Arab women's meta-narratives on history and theory, their resilient construction of storied geography and their revamping of space into a territorial geographical locale and location through the discursive restoration of the land-based Palestinian geographical identity is important. Maternal legacy of re-memory and its ongoing hold of the Palestinian women's specific resilient strategies help to reconstruct dismembered geography.

Using Morrison's notion of re-memory, Castro's paratextuality, and Littau's Pandora's Tongues, I argue for the semiotic textual construction of subaltern geopolitics of space and place through storied geography— against the de-population and mythical de-peopling of the "land without a people." I pointedly argue for the feminist politics of Palestinian specific women's stories, which is delivered through the feminine re-memories (in distinction from masculine memory) and incarnated in Palestinian specific Pandora's bifurcated tongued narration. The latter becomes the hallmark for the Palestinian woman experience and the imprint for their silenced narrations specifically due to their double marginalization in the mainstream articulation of masculine national narration (delivered in Arabic) and Western feminist theory.

As a minority at the margin of national narration and international relations, Palestinian women face a similar plight to their Afro-American counterparts, yet with a nuance brought about by their non-articulation in established Arab feminist theory. In Black feminist theory against the violence of displacement and "triple marginalization,"[1] re-memory figures as the lead for a subaltern geographical identity enacted through "the subversive retelling of one woman's story during and following the period of slavery" (Purkayastha 3). This subversive retelling in Toni Morrison's remembrance scheme confronts the willful national amnesia through unpacking the subalternity of black slave women's experiences, their invalidating orality, and their incapacitating intersectionality. It becomes the critical to speak what Morrison calls "the unspeakable [things]" of race and gender (Morrison, *Unspeakable Things* 126). According to Morrison, the submerged categories of race and gender in American literature and culture function as the "canon fodder", and the perfect foil for the unspoken-of greatness of American Literature. The latter is hinged on the submersion of Afro-American memory (Morrison, *Unspeakable Things* 126).

Similar yet different from Morrison's fictional remembrance scheme in *Beloved*, Sahar Hamouda's *Once Upon a Time in Jerusalem* enacts this subversive re-memory through auto-biographical recollection of her and her mother's once-upon-a-time memories in their Jerusalemite Dar (house), and the concrete geographical identity that was forever wrought onto their life histories. In this text about women's memories and identities, Hamouda, the writer-critic, fills in the theoretical lacuna in the nonexistence of established Arab feminist theory through writing the Palestinian specific maternal legacy of imparting concrete geographical identities through subversive oral telling in English. Hamouda provides her meta-narrative on history and theory through transposing displacement onto discursive placement and oral accounts into written format that is communicable to international audience.

The text is composed in English with a five-chapter division that is prefaced by a captioned picture of "Abdel Hamid al Fitiani, the last Patriarch of Dar al Fitiani," followed by "Preface," "Acknowledgment," and closes on an epilogue. The epilogue contains a map of "Fitiani Family Tree" linking the now dispersed family members to the last Patriarch of Dar al-Fitiani, Abdel Hamid, the image para-textualizing the text. Hamouda's play with multimodal semiotic resources documents their place-based Jerusalemite identity. Her account builds on Arab women's specific tradition of storytelling, providing for a tactile mold of re-memory that transcribes orally delivered womenfolk's stories into textuality, translating their spaces into mental pictures and models. In doing so,

Hamouda's account figures as the nexus between older women's history-defying tradition of oral storytelling and younger women's spoken word activism delivered to English-speaking audiences. Part of the Palestinian women's specific mode of resistant activism,[2] Hamouda's textually inscribed accounts in English refigures the language policy of nation-narration and the normative geopolitics of political geography to enact the Palestinian-specific subaltern geopolitics of s/place. The latter crosses the statist bounded borders to deliver the "Palestine [Women] know" and populated with mapped stories of placed identities—in defiance of "micro-geographies of occupation" and resilient assertion of the subaltern language politics of s/place (Sharp 21). Moreover, these Palestinian women-specific geopolitics of s/place stands in resilient defiance of postmodern deterritorialization of space, Western feminists' invalidation of nationalism, occupational colonization of place, and their slide into Orientalizing of gender space. Like in Morrison's political poetics, Hamouda's resistant assertion of subaltern orality of s/place is constructed along the unspoken of maternal legacy of remembering and enacted through trans-linguistic and cross-generational narrative mediation—from orality into textuality and onto the performativity of younger Palestinian women's spoken word aesthetic activism.

Living in Egypt with an Egyptian citizenship and identity, Hamouda, a professor of comparative literature in Alexandria University, unpacks the maternal legacy of re-memory through the written word and autobiographical narration of her and her mother's geographical identity placement in Jerusalemite Palestine. Hamouda's maternally centered autobiographical narration figures as the epicenter of Palestinian-specific subaltern geopolitics, which takes different forms in different setting and across different generations. In the performative poetry of Rafeef Ziadah, this maternal legacy of re-memory is articulated through the different medium and mode the spoken art activism.[3] In "The Palestine I Know," Ziadah, a Palestinian women artist of younger generation located in the UK, pinpoints the genealogy in her womenfolk stories in due acknowledgment of their active existence and activist presence across time and s/place:

> This poem is called 'The Palestine I know,' the Palestine I grew up with, the Palestine that taught me everything I know about Palestine. And it mainly came through women, and I think its women who hold the story of their nation. And I think that is why it is very important in the arts to also always acknowledge women, especially as we mark big historical events. Gentlemen, please give us the space to also remember and show solidarity. (Ziadah, "The Palestine I Know" 00:00:03–00:00:32)

Through the "Palestine their women knew," Hamouda recovers the spoken words of her mother's stories to document the key holders to

the stasis of the "nation without a state" (Smith 23) within the localized geographical scheme of her once-upon-a-time spent in her mother's hometown, Jerusalem. Her endeavor unspeaks the unspeakable
right to return through the storied geographies of her and her mother's
re-memories. Her lead is the orality of the subaltern re-memory, which
she bumps into written memory. She recuperates visions and images of
lands, places and spaces peopled by Palestinians, their ordinary ways
of getting by their displacements, and the carceral geography of settler
colonial occupation. Her endeavor bridges the gap between aesthetics
and politics through rewriting history from the position of her and her
mother's intersectional marginality. She simultaneously provides for, "a
richly textured psychological and experiential view of personal and historical events" and enables a take on politics "from below the brilliant
space platform of the powerful" (Haraway 583). More importantly, like
Ziadah, Hamouda's reworking of matrilineal re-memory fashions the
Palestinian-specific feminist translation of subaltern geopolitics through
releasing "local feminist discourses" (Sharoni 117) hinged on "a geopolitical gaze . . . from a marginal position 'within'" (Sharp 3). This
marginal geopolitical gaze defies Western feminist submersion[4] of the
centrality of the question of geography to Palestinian political identity
and feminist cultural subjectivity to speak of the nexus between nation,
intergenerational female oral narration, and the tripartite scheme of
place, land, and identity of Palestinian nationhood.

Deliberately embodying the role of "subversive scribe" (Castro, Introduction 9), Hamouda opens Pandora's Box to transcribe the unspeakable
tirade of place, land, and identity through her mother's re-memories and
retelling of their Jerusalemite identity. As she states in an interview: "My
mother was the most anti-classist and modest person in the world. Yet,
when it came to her being a Jerusalemite, the bells would always ring
in warning" (Debian, Personal Interview). Ringing the warning bells,
Hamouda, the feminist writer and critic, charts space and place of lost
geography and forgotten history in a new historical fashion. Vetting the
orality of her mother's account against written history, Hamouda finds
out that what "the history books say do not really matter," and what
she initially deemed as official history's proof to dynamite her mother's
tales ended up dynamizing the account presenting them as "the truth . . .
though the books did not record it" (Hamouda 10).

Hamouda's incentive is the past: "the Palestinian past" that she found
wanting among her Palestinian students in Beirut. This Palestinian past
"had lived in every corner of [her] house and minds" through her mother's stories (Hamouda viii). Her scheme is the places: "the villages . . .
parents' or grandparents' lives in the country they had been forced to
leave . . . and the small stories of . . . inconsequential lives that make up the
larger mosaic of country and history and monumental past" (Hamouda
viii). To this end, in a discursive combat against the washing away of

family history by "the daily business of living," Hamouda instigates a process of re-memory on herself and her mother's parts (Hamouda viii). The nature of these re-memories falls within the feminist translation theoretical vocabulary and re-politicize its theoretical praxis[5] with respect to the nexus between nation-narration, geographically placed identities and the unspeakable "right to return." Theorizing practice, in her 2018 presentation at Alexandria University, Hamouda recounts the condition of their re-memory of the "once upon a time place in Jerusalem" and their ongoing claim to its storied geography and locale-centric history:

> My mother's tales about her house in Old Jerusalem have always been an integral part of my life . . . stories she told and retold about her family. . . [and the] land which her soul still inhabits . . . her refusal to let go of them, was her own way of holding onto the history of her lost Dar . . . I felt that the core of it rested in the physical location of the Dar itself . . . My first task, therefore, was to record those memories . . . to preserve it from further loss, for if the Dar and its inhabitants were now lost to us, then we should commit them to paper . . . The second task was to collect those memories, and determine the form of narration. . . I didn't know then why I chose to narrate it in two voices . . . I used my voice to fill in the gaps, to comment on her narrative . . . there was an unconscious realization that those memories were mine, and that I was also part of the story. (Hamouda, Presentation)

The centrality of the Dar and the mother-daughter sharing of it hold centerstage the geographical dimension of their re-memories and their enmeshment in the territoriality of the space/place of the Dar in Jerusalem. This foregrounding of the question of geography and physical location undermines the postmodern political organization of space and its consequential de-territorial discourse of peace (Newman 328). It also subverts the Western feminist take on the idea of place as "pure space of total deterritorialization" (Kaplan 42). More importantly, Hamouda's meta-writing account elucidates the process of production and politics of "intercultural ideological mediation" (Castro, "[Re-]examining Horizons" 3) of their re-memories into discursivity, across mediality (orality/textuality), locality, and language borders. Like Ziadah, Hamouda's act of writing comes specifically to respond to the gendered politics of nationalism (its gendering nation-narration) and the engendered carceral geographical occupation of both the mother land and tongue. These gendered politics disallow the "[speaking] in the mother tongue" on account of the ephemerality and incredibility of the orality of women's re-memories. The ascribed discredit to women's orality unwittingly feeds into the occupational politics of the motherland and tongue. It simultaneously territorializes the motherland with andro-centric and politically correct masculine accounts of national telling and fetishizes Arabic as the rightful mother tongue for Palestinian national telling. More specially, this discredit to orality and fetishization of Arabic canonizes the devaluation of what Littau formulates in terms of the forked nature of Pandora's tongue.

In the context of Palestinian diasporic experience and colonial continuing occupation, this forked nature of women's telling becomes the means of resistance passed from mother-to-daughter and upheld by the womenfolk's accounts that telltale the hidden side of history through the mother-forked-tongue. The latter, chiseled to perfection by the momentous enormity of suffering, is "already multilingual" and "the speaker of more than one tongue" (Littau 4). This is specifically due to the weight of Palestinian women's experience, who carry place out of place and hold the keys of the nation without a state. In "Shades of Anger," Ziadah exemplifies this imprint of the mother-forked-tongue employing the interlingual shift between Arabic and English to ideologically mediate the politico-cultural stamp of the Palestinian Pandora's tongue:

اسمحوا لى ان اتكلم بلغتى العربية قبل ان يحتلوا لغتى ايضا

Allow me to speak my mother tongue before
   they occupy my language as well. (Ziadah, "Shades of Anger"
00:00:39–00:00:50)

Speaking in the Palestinian mother tongues of the motherland, Hamouda's *Once Upon a Time in Jerusalem* re-territorializes both the gendered discursive space of national narration and the nationalist gendering occupation of the motherland through unspeaking the storied orality of women space. Her discursive act speaks against both the discursive amnesia of nationalist telling and the colonial myth of "a land without a people to people without a land." Her means is the English language; her tactic is textual form.

A native of Arabic language, Hamouda's language choice does not square neatly with the language politics of *authentic* and *nationalist* cultural claims. However, Hamouda's choice of English as a medium of expression is a political choice and politically correct design. Not only does the choice of English befit what Castro qualifies as the "internationalization of culture and globalization of discourse . . . [where] we all live in a 'translated worlds,'" (Castro, Introduction 6) it also provides for an enabling media that facilities the hearing of Palestinian stories and the reception to a wide international audience. Hamouda states in a 2018 interview: "I chose English because I wanted the story to be heard. I wanted to speak to Western audience. I wanted to tell that there were people in the land . . . that Palestine was not 'a land without people.'" (Hamouda, Personal Interview). The textual form becomes the medium-cum-message or the "medium [as/and] the message" (Littau 56).

Its compositional design simultaneously forks the foreign (colonizing) tongue to bend it to carry (qualifying Achebe) the weight of the Palestinian experience and signifies the forked imprint of its women carriers.

Written in English in the Palestinian Pandora's tongues (through the new-historical/postcolonial leanings of its writer-academic), the text is forked into two voices, two modes of signification and two sign systems. This dualistic compositional formulation instigates an interaction between sound, image, and typographic image (word image and font size), the outcome of which is an audio medial text.[6] The latter, written to be spoken, flaunt the materiality of subaltern feminist textuality through both a tactical capitalization on the tangibility of modes (acoustic/aural and visual) and systems of signification (oral, written and spoken—i.e., written to be spoken), and re-signification of issues of textuality and paratextuality.

Divided into five chapters, the text is prefaced by a captioned picture of "Abdel Hamid al Fitiani, the last Patriarch of Dar al Fitiani." This is followed by "Preface," "Acknowledgment," and closes on an epilogue. The epilogue contains three items: "Sources" (an Arabic Bibliography of the history of Jerusalem), "Glossary" (transliterated Arabic words and their English translation), and "Al Fitiani Genealogy" (commentary on the image of document proving the family lineage). The book closes on "Al Fitiani Family Tree," providing a tree diagram of the family map linking the now dispersed family members to the last Patriarch of Dar al-Fitiani, Abdel Hamid, the image para-textualizing the text. This play with multi-modal semiotic resources in the paratexts is paralleled inside the text. The textual composition adds topographic image to the furnished semiotic ensemble through italicization, which alternately augments the play between image and word and provides for a visual marked signification of the mother-daughter's alternating narrations.

The first chapter, "A Jerusalem Home: Dar al Fitiani," opens with the opening line of *Anna Karenina* on happy and unhappy families where Hamouda humbly *"begs to differ with the [master]"* (1). This marks Hamouda's entry to relate the Jerusalemite-specific happiness of the Dar and her maternal stake in the "Dar . . . an Arabic word which conveys both meanings of 'house': the actual building, and the family" (Hamouda 2). Delivered in the first-person point of view, the brief introduction is followed by the mother's orally inscribed account. The mother's account provides for a pseudo-historical account of the Dar's lineage, architectural structure, inner divisions and geographical and spiritual connection to the Dome of the Rock and the Haram al Sharif: "Saladin chose the family, descendent from the Prophet's family and living within the walls of al Haram al Sharif, as being the family most qualified to hold the *fatwa*," and hence the family name Fitiani (5).

Typographically imaged in roman type (in distinction from Hamouda's italicized narrative voice), the text alternates between mother and daughter's narrations. The latter's italicized accounts feature a scholarly commentary desperately vetting women orality against official history until the narrative begins afresh in the tenth page: "What history books say do not really matter . . . So, let's start afresh. Once upon a time in Jerusalem," (10). This fresh start and linguistic marker of oral storytelling marks a new narrative and voice shift with Hamouda's accounts briefer and personalized functioning as a supplement to fill in the gaps from her childhood memories. Every memory brings a re-memory in a never-ending chain of mother-daughter remembering and in a pictorial formatting of orality.

Pictures start swarming the narrative space with every account embodied in an image. The reader encounters multiple images: images of the Dar (wide shot angles and close-ups), images of historical figures in the Dar, images of high-profile personnel connected to the Dar, images of weddings and outings, images of Hamouda's uncles in different settings, images of toddler Hamouda with her brother in the Dar, etc. The last chapter, "Living in the Diaspora," is solely recounted in Hamouda's voice and is densely populated with images.[7] The last two pictures close the narrative on a scanty note from the mother elucidating the claim of the Dar on its dispersed inmates and their claim to the land on which it resides:

> In 2000, my daughter met Loulou, Taher's youngest daughter. That year Loulou had been to Jerusalem and had wept throughout her stay in the old dar. 'My father is not buried in Cairo', she had sobbed. 'He is buried here. I swear he is buried here, in this dar!' There is nothing strange in what she said. The bones of Taher al Fitiani may still be lying in the cemetery in Cairo, but his spirit has flown home, where we will all surely go. (Hamouda 112)

This profuse instrumentalization of imaging and pictures not only provide for pictorial representation of the Dar and imaged occupation of its locale, it also offers a visual marker for the incarnation of the Palestinian "right to return" home "where we will all surely go." They more specifically flesh out the materiality of subaltern feminist signification as the scheme for mediating the "right to return" through placing people on the land in their habitat in Jerusalem. The outcome is the form, the medial political message that deploys paralinguistic semiotic resources to enact a subaltern feminist geopolitics through a textual space peopled with narratives, narrative space peopled with pictures and pictures populated with imaged stories of lands and its people. These imaged stories relate the tales of men and women's places and spaces in ordinary history and extraordinary geography carrying keys to memories of "ancestral home and leaving it standing as proudly as it has done for the last 400 years" (Hamouda ix).

"The old will die, the young will forget," a quotation attributed to Ben Gurion, places emphasis on forgetfulness and memory elision. In answer to the concerted plan of memory massacre and burial, Palestinian women take re-memory as a foothold and medium to deliver their diasporic Pandora's tongue stories and territorializes the discursive space with the "Palestine women know" and re-member across times, places, and spaces. Hamouda's *Once Upon in Jerusalem* is testament to the power of re-memory and its enactment of subversive telling and formatting through the textual form. The latter's dualistic compositional formulation constructs subaltern geopolitics of s/place through textual enactment of the mother-daughter's agency and the recuperation of the subaltern voices from the traditional submersion and silencing of power politics. A perfect form for the Palestinian specific Pandora Box, Hamouda's dualistic compositional narrative incarnates Littau's formula for Pandora's forked tongue that defies the silencing unanimity of patriarchal discourse through the forked narration of women's stories. The latter become the media for enactment of the materiality of feminist communication specifically on account of its duality and tactile defiance of the unity of national language and telling. It more importantly embodies the validation structure for women's orality and storied geography through the trespassing of the fetishized language politics of national narration to deliver a communicable account of Palestinian women experience. Ultimately, Hamouda's textual signification and embodiment of Pandora's tongue provides a narrative foothold and shape for re-memory as a weapon against history elision and the Israeli long entrenched mythology of a land without valid people. The result is a meta-narrative on history and theory, incarnated through audio-mediality to pump into historical memory an incantation of the cultural key holders of the lost Palestinians' Dars and their continuing "right to return."

In Palestinian cultural politics, Palestinian women, especially elderly women, hold the keys of their confiscated Dars in Palestine, passing it on to younger women in an ongoing chain of re-memories of the land, its maps and s/place. Thus, their actions and ongoing endeavors to keep space out of place becomes the embodiment of Morrison's political scheme for re-memory and re-incarnation of lost territory. Through the forked narration of Pandora's tongue and the triggered off chaos of Pandora's Box, Hamouda articulates Palestinian women ongoing acts of re-memories that incarnates the unspeakable right to return through telling of Palestinian storied geography within the political scheme of Palestinian women's specific re-memories and forked articulation of nation to international readership and globalized culture.

Notes

1 In reading Morrison's remembrance scheme in *Beloved*, Homi Bhabha's words qualifies the language of re-memory as "the indecipherable language of the black and angry dead" (Bhabha 446) that verbalizes what Morrison

describes as the "unspeakable thoughts, unspoken" (Morrison, *Unspeakable Things* 99). In the context of Afro-American triple marginalization, Morrison's employment of re-memory as a means to recuperation of women's tales figures as a feminist strategy to combating the silencing of Afro-American women voices in Western feminism, American canon, and male Afro-American literature.

2 Qualifying the politico-aesthetic function of Black feminist re-memory, Arab women's re-memories enact a process of placement of the selves along both political and matrilineal geography of social relations designed to reformulate identity along the tripartite scheme of land, place, and space in willful designation and embodiment of subaltern national geopolitics.

3 Rafeef Ziadah is a Palestinian spoken word artist and human rights activist based in London, UK. Her performance of poems like "We Teach Life, Sir" and "Shades of Anger" went viral within days of their releases on YouTube.

4 Feminist scholars agree that Western feminist praxis is in the throes of a locational crisis. This locational crisis is evident in what Mojab identifies as methodological fragmentation of "women of the world into religious, national, ethnic, racial and cultural . . . with particularistic agendas" (Mojab 124). The results are twofold: first, the reduction of gender issues to questions of culture and women's place to psychological deterritorialized space; second, an implied encoding of a dichotomy between national and feminist identity and naturalization of the consequential occlusion of the question of place and history in the discursive formation of feminist subjectivity and politics (McClintock 95).

5 The early intervention of the Canadian school of feminist translation, propelled by the cultural turn in Translation Studies, took translation-as-rewriting as a trope and mechanism to simultaneously write into translation history women's eclipsed narrative as writers/translators and rewrite the gendered mythology and metaphoric upon which Translation Studies was theorized. Indeed, due to its origin outside Anglo-American academia, feminist translation scholarly interventions are currently attempting to forge what can be qualified as subaltern feminist geopolitics of translation studies/theories through "woman handling" translation theory along the intersectional paradigm.

6 Mary Snell-Hornby has suggested that we can define four different genres of multimodal texts:

1 *multimedial* texts (in English usually called audiovisual in the form of material for film or television, sub-/surtitling);
2 *multimodal* texts involve different *modes* of verbal and nonverbal expression as in drama and opera;
3 *multisemiotic* texts use different *graphic sign systems*, verbal and nonverbal (e.g., comics or advertising brochures);
4 *audiomedial* texts are those written to be spoken (e.g., political speeches). Multimodal texts are, according to this definition, those written to be performed live on stage (and, of course, for an audience). The distinction between media, modes, and sign systems is of course important, as it is important to acknowledge the possibility of different evaluative frameworks for the same text, e.g., considering its medium, its mode or its sign system.

7 There are images of her mother and father, images at their wedding in Cairo, images of herself and brother in the Dar and in Cairo, and images of her uncle walking next to Abdel Nasser. There is another image of her older aunt "Aisha Fitiani, sitting beside the water well in the Dar." Another image is yet to come of "Hind Fitiani with Sahar Hamouda and Ayman Hamouda" on the Dar's roof overlooking the holy sites.

Works Cited

Castro, Olga. "Introduction: Gender, Language and Translation at the Crossroads of Disciplines." *Gender and Language*, vol. 7, no. 1, 2013, pp. 5–12, doi: 10.1558/genl.v7i1.5.

———. "(Re-)examining Horizons in Feminist Translation Studies: Towards a Third Wave?"*MonTI*, translated by Mark Andrews, vol. 1, 2009, pp. 59–86,

Hamouda, Sahar. *Once Upon a Time in Jerusalem*. Garnet Publishing Limited, 2010.

———. Personal Interview. Conducted by Riham Debian, 9 October 2018.

———. Presentation. Alexandria University, 2018.

Haraway, Donna. "Situated Knowledges: The Science Question in Feminism and the Privilege of Partial Perspective." *Feminist Studies*, vol. 14, no. 3, Feminist Studies, Inc., 1988, pp. 575–99.

Kaplan, Caren. "Deterritorializations: The Rewriting of Home and Exile in Western Feminist Discourse." *Cultural Critique*, no. 6, 1987, pp. 187–198.

Littau, Karen. "Pandora's Tongues." *TTR: Traduction, Terminologie, Rédaction*, vol. 13, no. 1, 2000, pp. 21–35, doi: 10.7202/037391ar.

McClintock, Anne "'No Longer in Future Heavens': Gender, Race, and Nationalism." *Dangerous Liaisons: Gender, Nation, & Postcolonial Perspectives*, edited by Anne McClintock, Aamir Mufti, and Ella Shohat, Minneapolis, U of Minnesota P, 1997, pp. 89–112.

Mojab, Sharazad. "Theorizing the Politics of Islamic Feminism." *Feminist Review*, vol. 69, 2001, pp. 124–46.

Morrison, Toni. *Beloved: A Novel*. New York, Knopf, 1987.

———. *Unspeakable Things Unspoken: The Afro-American Presence in American Literature*. The Tanner Lectures on Human Values. Ann Arbor, University of Michigan, 1989.

Newman, Daniel. "Introduction: Postmodernity and the Territorial Discourse of Peace." *GeoJournal*, vol. 39, no. 4, 1996. pp. 327–330. https://doi.org/10.1007/BF02428495

Purkayastha, Madhamita. "Re-memory as a Strategy for Subversive Representation: A Feminist Reading of Morrison's Beloved." 2013.

Said, Edward. "Yeats and Decolonization." Edited by Terry Eagleton, et al. *Nationalism, Colonialism and Literature*. Minneapolis, U of Minnesota P, 1990, pp. 69–95.

Seymour-Jorn, C. *Cultural Criticism in Egyptian Women Writing (Contemporary Issues in the Middle East)*. Syracuse UP, 2011.

Sharoni, Simona. "Gender and the Israeli-Palestinian Accord: Feminist Approaches to International Politics." *Gendering the Middle East: Emerging Perspectives*, edited by Deniz Kandiyoti, Syracuse, New York, Syracuse UP, 1996, pp. 107–126.

Sharp, J. "Subaltern Geopolitics: Introduction." *Geoforum*, vol. 42, no. 3, 2011, pp. 271–3. ISSN 0016–7185.

Smith, Ron. "Geographies of Dis/Topia in the Nation-State: Israel, Palestine, and the Geographies of Liberation." 2012.

Ziadah, Rafeef. "Palestinian Solidarity Poem. Rafeef Ziadah. 'We Teach Life Sir!' London. 12.11.11." *YouTube*, Uploaded by NoEalamInSL Sri Lanka, 13 Mar. 2012.

————. "Rafeef Ziadah – The Palestine I Know." *YouTube,* Uploaded by Rafeef Ziadah, 20 Oct. 2016.

————. "Rafeef Ziadah – 'Shades of Anger', London, 12.11.11." *YouTube*, Uploaded by Sterchen Productions, 15 Nov. 2011.

————. "Rear Window – RAFEEF ZIADAH POWER OF THE SPOKEN WORD." *YouTube*, Uploaded by The World Today with Tariq Ali, 30 Sep. 2015.

4 "Don't Get in my Face Like Ashiq Peri"

The Legacy of Azerbaijan's Most Famous Woman Bard

Anna C. Oldfield

This study introduces the nineteenth-century poet-minstrel Ashiq Peri and considers the ways in which contemporary Azerbaijani women call on her model to take creative agency in a genre that is embedded within traditional culture. Ashiq Peri wrote and performed poetry in a highly structured Azerbaijani genre that was male-dominated and steeped in gendered tropes. By working from within the genre, she was able to challenge stereotypes and create new roles for herself as a female subject while remaining authentically Azerbaijani. By looking at her legacy as it has been expressed by Azerbaijani minstrel-poets in the Soviet and post-Soviet eras, the chapter looks at how her method of taking agency from within traditional culture has been used creatively by female poet-minstrels to strengthen their creative role in supporting and building an evolving identity of the Azerbaijani woman.

This chapter engages in textual analysis with Ashiq Peri's poetry, as well as my own fieldwork in Azerbaijan with living female poet-minstrels who write and perform in the ashiq genre. My own position as an American precludes me from speaking from inside Azerbaijani culture, but I situate the voices of Azerbaijani women—through poetry, interviews, and scholarship—in the center of my work. I have further put these readings into intersection with the scholarship of Nayereh Tohidi and Farideh Heyat, whose studies of gender and society in Azerbaijan open productive new readings of the figure of Ashiq Peri.

I will begin in Baku in 2005, when I was in the Azerbaijan Republic researching my dissertation. Ashiq is a bardic genre that was originally for epic singing but now includes oral and written poetry as well as improvised verbal dueling. The genre dates back to the sixteenth century and is highly thought of as national folk culture performed by skilled professionals called by the title "Ashiq" (Eldarova 3). Ashiqs sing and accompany themselves on a long-necked lute called the *saz*, and as part of my fieldwork I took saz lessons with Minaya Azafli, who was a member of the women's performance collective, the Ashiq Peri Mejlisi [Aşıq Pəri Məjlisi]. In June 2005, Ashiq Minaya taught me a poem she had written to be sung with a spirited *muxammes* melody I was trying to learn. It was dedicated to Ashiq Peri and began with the following verse:

> Every era has its rule, and she was the ruler of her time, Peri.
> Glances, dimples, and caprice, she was love's physician, Peri.
> Tall in stature, long black hair, she was love's medicine, Peri.
> They say that she was very beautiful, that she was the sultan of
> beauties, Peri. (Xüdiyəv 191)[1]

When I asked Ashiq Minaya to tell me more about Ashiq Peri, her eyes shone: "Oh, she was admirable! Everyone was in love with her, but she was devoted to her art. She's the image of woman, beautiful, and strong. That's why I wrote this song. We would all like our daughters to be like her" (Recorded Saz Lesson). Ashiq Minaya further told me how she had performed the song on television with the Ashiq Peri Mejlisi and it had become quite popular. It was also published in an anthology of women's ashiq poetry called *The Ashiq Peri Mejlisi* (Xüdiyəv). I learned the song and began to think about how the song connected to how the historical Ashiq Peri, who had lived in the nineteenth century. How did a woman who had lived in the nineteenth century become the ideal woman in the twenty-first?

The Azerbaijan Republic in 2005 was one of the Newly Independent Republics that had arisen after the Soviet Union fell. Azerbaijanis speak a Turkic language but have been involved with the Iranian political and cultural sphere for centuries. Most Azerbaijanis are Shi'a Muslims, a religion they are reclaiming after years of religious repression in the USSR. Located in the southern Caucasus, the region has spent millennia at the crossroads of major trade routes and transnational empires, resulting in a lively cultural life and a diverse population (Huseynova 8).

Beginning in the nineteenth century, a major influence on Azerbaijani culture has been its incorporation into the Russophone world, which brought the direct influence of Russian culture and the influence of European culture through Russian translation (Feldman 40). The Russian Empire colonized the southern Caucasus in the nineteenth century, winning the lands and setting a new border with Iran by treaty in 1828. Part of the population of Azerbaijanis ended up in the Russian empire, while a large number remained in northwestern Iran. Families on both sides of the border were separated and lost contact, and the border became hard to cross during the Soviet period. This chapter considers only northern Azerbaijan, which was pulled into the Russian Empire, declared an independent Republic 1918–20, then was incorporated into the Soviet Union 1920–90. The Azerbaijan Republic declared its independence when the USSR dissolved in 1991.

The new Azerbaijan Republic had a traumatic transition to independence, occurring "amid political turmoil, economic collapse, and bloody ethnic and regional conflicts" (Huseynova 236). By 2005, Azerbaijan had stabilized and was in the process of defining itself and its place in the world (Cornell Ch. 5). Having been largely isolated for seventy years from western Europe/America and the Middle East, in the 2000s Azerbaijan was flooded with new influences, from American movies to Turkish pop songs. Another large influence was Iranian Azerbaijanis rejoining their families for the first time in many years (Heyat 2). Individuals were negotiating their way among the attraction of Europe and America offering liberal secular culture, Turkey offering education and a semi-secular brotherly Turkism, and Iran seeking to fold them back into its sphere as a Shi'a authority (Cornell Ch. 4). Women were especially negotiating how these choices intersected with possibly new and evolving gender roles (Tohidi 117). It was in this very fluid situation that individual women were finding their place. The image of Ashiq Peri, so strong and confident in Minaya Azafli's song, could be a resource for Azerbaijani women navigating these confusing times.

The historical Ashiq Peri is well known in Azerbaijan. Anyone who enters the Museum of Musical Culture in Baku will notice a large painting of a woman with flowing hair, saz in hand, and a smile both demure and confident. This is a painting by Tamara Dagistanli of Ashiq Peri (c1811–48?), a native of the village Jebrayil in the region of Marlyan, located in the Karabakh mountain region. Although she is a well-known figure in Azerbaijani culture, little is sure about her life or background, and most of what we know is from the Russian Orientalist, Adolf Berzhe, who traveled the Caucasus on an anthropological study in the early nineteenth century. While in Karabakh, Berzhe noticed a young woman gifted with a very quick wit who competed in verbal dueling contests with men "whom she often defeated." He gave her name as Ashiq Peri and wrote her into his study (Cəfərzadə 28).

Berzhe's brief notes are most of what we know about her biography. Believing her to be eighteen in 1829, Berzhe proposed she was born in 1811 (Kallinikov). Scholar Aziza Jafarzade collected research which stated Peri never married and was said to have gone to Shusha to meet the famous female poet, Natevan (Cəfərzadə 28). Some sources say she was a poet who did not play saz, while some say she apprenticed with Mohammad Bey Ashiq (Kallinikov). Most sources give Peri's death as 1848 without saying how or why she died so young, but when folklorist Sadnik Pashayev inquired in her home village of Marlyan in the 1960s, they told him Peri had married at the age of thirty, had two children, and had lived to a good old age (Pirsultanlı 169). The villagers also told Pashayev that Ashiq Peri was known to have a powerfully quick wit and a formidable talent for debate—there was even a saying in the region, "Don't get in my face like Ashiq Peri!" (Pirsultanlı 168).

Several examples of Ashiq Peri's poetry were published in Azerbaijani in the 1857 anthology *Mecmuə Vagif və muasiri digər [The Author Vagif and his Contemporaries]*. Of her poetry collected from the 1857 edition, most are in the form of poetic duels (Cəfərzadə 47–52). Azerbaijani ashiqs and poets are often part of an artistic collective called a *mejlis* that performs together, often engaging in verbal dueling. A popular mejlis attracted an audience, and sessions were often written down by onlookers, saving a record of the live performances. Ashiq Peri belonged to the Vagif Mejlis, named for the poet Molla Penah Vagif (1717–97) who pioneered using Azerbaijani ashiq verse as a literary medium (Həsənli 184). Creating oral and written poetry in the vernacular Azerbaijani was, at the time, a notable act. In the beginning of the nineteenth century Azerbaijan's literary language was dominated by Farsi, with a parallel vernacular oral tradition kept up by the ashiq minstrels (Eldarova 3). Ashiq poetry, composed orally in the Turkic syllabic metrical system called *heje vezne*, was also used in folksongs, lullabies, and many other oral forms. It was an extremely complex system with highly structured verses with many variations, where the number of syllables and the rhymes were tightly controlled. In verbal dueling, an ashiq would ask a riddle or offer a challenge sung in verse, and the opponent would have to answer in the same verse type, using the same rhyme, making verbal dueling extremely challenging (Eldarova 52). Nineteenth-century ashiqs were often from rural, lower-class communities and many were text illiterate, but they were treasuries of Azerbaijani vernacular poetry and epic passed down by oral tradition over hundreds of years.

In contrast, much of Azerbaijani written poetry in the nineteenth century, associated with urban upper classes, was written in Farsi or in a Farsi-influenced Azerbaijani and used the syllabatonic system of *aruz* verse that was also used in Persian and Arabic. Ashiq Peri's poetry Mejlis distinguished itself by following Vagif's lead in writing and performing poetry in Azerbaijani, using ashiq style verses written in vernacular *heje vezne* meters. It was a sign of rising Azerbaijani national consciousness, when the educated elite were inspired by the folk traditions kept by rural people, and Ashiq Peri was among those who championed her native language and poetic traditions.

The Vagif Mejlis was made up mostly of men, and they were respected poets and local intellectuals including Tufeyli, Mirza Hasan Mirza, and Mirzejan Madatov (Təhmasib et al. 220). Ashiq Peri was the only female in the group, and most of her poems were in some kind of poetic exchange with the other mejlis members. An example is the following verses, which are the beginning of a much longer exchange between Ashiq Peri and Mirza Hasan Mirza:

MIRZA HASAN MIRZA.
I am blanketed in sorrow, in torment,
Your image is ever present in my mind.
There is no remedy for my incurable suffering,
Only with your presence could my pain be eased.

ASHIQ PERI.
Why are you lying there wrapped in a blanket?
Are you sick? What is wrong with you?
It's your love's sickness that makes a doctor out of me.
It's your problem that you let your state depend on me.
(Cəfərzadə 83)

In this poetic dialogue, Mirza Hasan Mirza begins with an excessive dec-
laration of love typical for a male subject in Azerbaijani lyric poetry. Ashiq
Peri answers Mirza's verse point by point but deflates his tone of lofty suffering by answering each hyperbolic claim with an earthy response. Mirza's
poem is filled with concepts that are common in Azerbaijani lyric poetry,
such as the "sorrow" (qəm) and "suffering" (dərd) of love as a sickness,
which needs the "remedy" (dərman) of the beloved's presence to be healed;
accordingly, the beloved is imagined as the "doctor" (tabib), the only one
who can help the suffering victim. Ashiq Peri's response uses Mirza's own
phrases, but makes his claims ridiculous by reframing them in an everyday
context; for example, in response to his metaphor of being "blanketed in
sorrow" (qəm bəstərində) with a "incurable suffering" (dərmansız dərd), she
asks with the tone of a concerned friend, "Why are you lying there wrapped
in a blanket? / Are you sick?" She refutes his claim that only she can heal his
pain by turning the responsibility for the situation back on him: "It is your
love's sickness that makes a doctor out of me." In this way, her verse deflects
his claims by holding up a mirror that recontextualizes his images so they
lose their power. In addition, her answer frees herself, as a female subject,
from the guilt of having caused a man to become sick with love, and simultaneously protects her own honor: "It is your problem that you let your state
depend on me." She clearly prefers the role of a concerned sisterly friend to
that of the "beloved," and rejects all his attempts to force her into that role.

Much of Ashiq Peri's poetry reflects this same playful cleverness, taking a mocking tone toward other Vagif Mejlis members, expressing a
sense of authority and capability much like an older sister (although she
would have been younger than all of them). Many of the Mejlis poems
were devoted to her, the only female in the collective, which reveals the
pivotal role she must have had as the center of attention. The same tone
dominates in her poetic duels with the poet Mirzejan Madatov. Here are
the first and final verses of a much longer exchange:

First Exchange:
MIRZEJAN MADATOV.
I am dying from longing, eh Peri,
Your eyes have intoxicated my soul.
Being near to these glances, flirting, and caprice,
Every time I look in your eyes I am driven to this sweet
    misfortune.

ASHIQ PERI.
As usual, you are talking like out of a fairy tale,
Your eyes will drown in perfidious blood.
You are my rival, I am completely forbidden to you,
Your eyes should not be harassing my dimples.
....
Final Exchange:
MIRZEJAN MADATOV.
Look what I am saying to you, oh bow-browed one,
I will change my religion if you give me the order.
I will sacrifice my life for you,
If only your eyes would look at me, Mirzejan.

ASHIQ PERI.
I am not going to burn up my life in love's fire,
I am not going to carry your charm on my breast.
I am Peri and I am not going to look at you,
Don't let your eyes wander around here.
(Cəfərzadə 46)

In this exchange, while Madatov attempts to draw Ashiq Peri into a poetic relationship using the power of poetic imagery, she refuses the roles
he provides, and instead creates a parallel narrative with an alternative
role for herself, that of the "rival" who is "not going to burn up my life
in love's fire." Ashiq Peri refuses to be drawn into his metaphors, such
as the love story of Layla and Majnun, saying at one point "I am not
inclined to you like Leyla / Even if your eyes are crazy like Majnun's"
(Cəfərzadə 46). As in her exchange with Mirza Hasan, she deflates his
words by using colloquial language to make them seem ridiculous, as in
her warning "your eyes should not be harassing my dimples."
A central image in Madatov's verse is that of the lover suffering from
a flirtatious woman who torments him with her glances. In the original
Azerbaijani his verses repeat "Your eyes" (gözlərin) at the end of every
stanza, and the poetic play with eyes and seeing is at the heart of the struggle. Ashiq Peri refutes his "harassing" eyes, working to escape from his gaze
which objectifies her in a specific system of metaphors. As the exchange goes
on, she continues to deflect his gaze, insisting it is "drunken" and "crazy."
When he attempts to pull her in as the "bow-browed one," begging for the
wounding arrow of her glance, claiming even to change his religion "if your
eyes would only look at me, Mirzejan," she replies firmly, "I am Peri and I
am not going to look at you." She further warns him to keep control over
his eyes, rejecting all responsibility for attracting his glances.
It is clear that the context of being a woman among men influenced
Ashiq Peri's verse, and her poetry reflects her vigorous defense of her

independence. These poetry duels do not reflect on the real-life relationships of Ashiq Peri with either Mirza or Madatov, but rather on her role in the Vagif Mejlis. She was not known to have been romantically involved with any mejlis members; as Ashiq Minaya had told me, "Everyone was in love with her, but she was devoted to her art." In 1903, the literary scholar, Feridun Bey Kocherli, wrote of her importance as a master of verbal dueling, and this type of discursive poetry is the essence of her gift (Təhmasib et al. 221).

All of the above exchanges are in the form of a *qoshma*, which uses eleven-syllable quatrains rhymed ABAB, CCCB, DDDB. The qoshma is a type of *heje vezne* meter and is very popular in written and oral ashiq poetry. It has a quick, singsong rhythm that is good for verbal dueling, while the repetition of the B rhyme throughout gives the verse a strong repeated thematic center. The highly structured verse and constant evocation of familiar tropes creates a strong framework from within the Azerbaijani vernacular tradition. Ashiq Peri is able to fill the traditional structure with her own ideas, rejecting the roles it asks her to play, but while staying within the frame.

In her 1996 article "Soviet in Public, Azeri in Private: Gender, Islam and Nationality in Soviet and Post-Soviet Azerbaijan," Nayereh Tohidi brings out some of the essential contradictions facing women in the 1990s, noting that although women in Azerbaijan "have achieved an impressive level of emancipation, particularly in the realms of education, employment, primary health, and legal rights. . . . their overall emancipation and liberation remain shot through with dilemmas, contradictions, and duality" (111). The contradictions she observed contrasted an emancipated public sphere in a modern Soviet culture that had enabled the liberation of women with the persistence of pre-Soviet gender norms. Tohidi observed that women were embedded in domestic roles that included subservience to the husband, self-sacrificing devotion to family, and expectations of female honor (*namus*) that included modesty, chastity, and loyalty to family, kin, and ethnicity (114). She found this image of the "ideal Azerbaijani women" was held by both women and men and contrasted to the image of the "Russian woman" (Tohidi 117). Reading through a postcolonial lens, Tohidi posits that like in other countries "confronting colonial domination or semi-colonial/imperial intrusion, women's liberation in Azerbaijan has been held hostage to the prescribed responsibility of women as the primary repositories of tradition and national and ethnic identity" (113). She found that educated professional women with considerable social status were continuing to observe patriarchal expectations coded as traditional Azerbaijani values in their family lives.

Tohidi's ideas are echoed and expanded by Ferideh Heyat, who wrote the monograph *Azeri Women in Transition* based on fieldwork in the 1990s combined with extensive historical and archival research.

Heyat also observed the "paradoxical ways" Azerbaijani women who had become "showcases" of the emancipation of Muslim women in the USSR were simultaneously "regarded by their ethnic community as the custodians of ethnic identity and preservers of ethnic custom," noting that "while being highly educated and career-oriented these women were also expected to observe strict sexual standards and carry out oner-ous domestic duties" (3). This, Heyat agreed, was a function of women differentiating themselves from the dominant culture and the "Russian woman" in a postcolonial sense but was further complicated by the Soviet Nationalities policy.

For non-Russian ethnicities, the Soviet Nationalities policy was par-adoxical, both encouraging and discouraging ethnic culture. The USSR encouraged ethnicity in many ways, providing education in native languages, registering each person by ethnicity in their passport, and strongly supporting certain national cultural expressions, such as folk dance and ethnic dress (Hirsch 225). At the same time, national ex-pressions that could challenge Soviet discourses, such as those that con-nected Azerbaijan with its religious past, were repressed (Huseynova 8). Heyat contends that the role of bearing ethnic identity in the Soviet con-text became combined with the anti-colonial role of women in keeping Azerbaijani culture distinct from Russian/Soviet culture (7). Thus, in an-other kind of paradox, by keeping up ethnic identity through observance of traditional Azerbaijani gender roles, women were simultaneously ful-filling and defying the expectations of Soviet culture.

Both Tohidi and Heyat observed that promoting and preserving Azerbaijani ethnicity was a primary expectation of Azerbaijani women in the late twentieth century and was also a role that they enthusias-tically took on themselves (Tohidi 117, Heyat 7). Being "Azerbaijani" encompassed a wide understanding of ethnicity that included customs, traditions, and cultural expressions (Heyat 8). As official practice of re-ligion was repressed in the USSR, in Azerbaijan "Islam was driven un-derground and privatised; informing life-cycle ceremonies and private, family-based rituals, it remained a publicly muted marker of Azeriness" (Heyat 9). However, while much of Azerbaijani culture was driven in the domestic sphere, certain cultural traditions, such as ashiq performance, became rich public spheres where the performance of Azerbaijani cul-ture could thrive.

In 1984, which was 156 years after Berzhe noticed the performance of Ashiq Peri, a collective of ashiqs and poets called the Ashiq Peri Mejlisi had its debut performance. It was not formed by state decree like so many Soviet cultural forms, but by the will and effort of Narinj Avazqizi Jafarova (1930–2006), better known by her pen name Narinj Xatun. Traveling throughout the Azerbaijani Soviet Socialist Republic, Narinj Xatun found female ashiqs and poets in towns and villages and gathered them into Azerbaijan's first all women mejlis (Xatun 2). When asked why she chose the name "Ashiq Peri," she answered, "Ashiq Peri was brave. She was intelligent, intellectual . . . she died very young, at the age of 35. But her spirit lives on in the mejlis" (Abdullazadə 60). The Ashiq Peri Mejlisi' first appearance was held in 1984, at the Writer's Union in Baku. They became very successful and were supported by the government, actively touring and appearing on radio and television (Xatun 4). As Ashiq Minaya, who was with the mejlis from the beginning, told me in 2005, "it was a sensation. Nobody had ever seen anything like it" (Recorded Saz Lesson).

The Ashiq Peri Mejlisi was born in the 1980s, not as a vehicle for Soviet propaganda, but as a voice of growing pride in Azerbaijani ethnicity. Like the original Ashiq Peri's "Vagif Mejlis," the new collective championed traditional Azerbaijani *heje vezne* verse, but in contrast to Russianization rather than Persianization. Linking themselves to their pre-Soviet past, the Ashiq Peri Mejlisi created long, flowing costumes and decorated the stage with traditional Azerbaijani craftwork such as carpets and metalwork bowls. Recordings of the television shows that aired weekly showcased women ashiqs playing saz and singing their poetry. Many shows had themes that showcased ashiqs and poets from earlier centuries, such as Ashiq Peri herself, while others debuted new poetry on themes that were daring in their nationalism, such as Novruz (the ancient spring holiday repressed during much of the Soviet era) or Homeland (Vətən). The Ashiq Peri Mejlisi became part of a larger cultural nationalist movement in the late Soviet era that would lead to overwhelming support for independence in 1991 (Naroditskaya 234, Cornell Ch. 4).

The historical Ashiq Peri had used the traditionally sanctioned framework of the ashiq verbal duel in which to expand her own possibilities of expression as a woman. At the same time, as part of the Vagif majlis, she simultaneously asserted Azerbaijani ethnicity in her vernacular poetry. It was a powerful method for a woman contending with both patriarchy inside the culture and the influence of a dominant outside culture: she challenged gender stereotypes while staying within and affirming ethnic identity through the performance of a traditional genre. She stretched and expanded her role from within Azerbaijani culture.

For the women of the Ashiq Peri Mejlisi, Ashiq Peri could be called on in the shift from domestic to public performance of Azerbaijani ethnicity. Like Ashiq Peri, they worked within a traditional framework and used it to expand women's roles as the "bearers of tradition," bringing that role out of the domestic sphere and into a public venue where they gained a powerful, even televised, voice. Further set within the type of national folklore that was sanctioned by the Soviet Union, they performed a positive Azerbaijani ethnicity in contrast to the Soviet definition of Azerbaijani culture. For women who could not agree with Russian/ Soviet concepts of "women's emancipation" but wanted to expand their opportunities for expression, it offered an alternative pathway from within Azerbaijani culture rather than in defiance of it.

The historical Peri in many ways fits the "ideal Azerbaijani woman" as described by Tohidi: In her poetry exchanges with men she defends her honor, defies their glances, and preserves her modesty. However, there is one "ideal" trait she does not embody, that of subservience. Not only does she keep power over the men she duels with, but also she performed by herself without the infantilizing protection of father, husband, or brother. She is a woman with an assertive public voice, recalling the saying "Don't get in my face like Ashiq Peri." Most importantly, she is a model of a strong, independent woman from within Azerbaijani culture, "the ruler of her time." When Ashiq Minaya said, "We would all like our daughters to be like her," it sounded like the hope of a positive path forward for Azerbaijani women during a time of identity flux. As Tohidi observed,

> In post-Soviet Azerbaijan, people are seeking to reassess, reimagine, and redefine their ethno-cultural and national, as well as individual, identities. In doing so they are looking backward and forward simultaneously; both, digging into their past history, religion, and traditions inwardly and searching among the present and future alternatives in the world community, East and West, outwardly. In this process, women are most acutely engaged in redefining their roles. (118)

With all these issues in mind at this transitional time, it is no wonder that Ashiq Peri would be an appealing figure. As a nineteenth century woman she could be claimed as authentically Azerbaijani, not a Soviet made woman who was influenced by Russian models. As an Ashiq, she was connected to Azerbaijan's most traditional culture. As a woman with a public voice, she gives an Azerbaijani alternative to female subservience and submission.

In the poem Ashiq Minaya taught me, she ends with this stanza, which envisions the Ashiq Peri Mejlisi as a multiplication of many Peris, stepping into "center stage":

> See the power of God!
> "Peri" today is a mejlis!
> Peri is now on center stage,
> A mejlis of Peris.
> She whose name is tied with dastan,
> Narınc Xatun is at the majlis
> The peoples came to see the majlis,
> It was a saz and poetry mejlis,
> Minaya Azafli says,
> Peri should remain on center stage.

By connecting the historical Ashiq Peri with her present, she also expresses a hope for the future: "Peri should remain on center stage." In a choice between competing influences and models from outside and inside, one woman's choice, at least, is clear.

Note

1 This and all poems in this document have been translated from the Azerbaijani by the author. The originals can be found in the sources cited.

Works Cited

Abdullazadə, Fatma, editor. "Aşıq Pəri—15." ["Ashiq Peri at 15 years."] (Azerbaijani Language). *Azərbaycan Qadını*, vol. 6, no. 60, 2000, p. 14.

Azafli, Minayə. Recorded Saz Lesson. Recorded by Anna Oldfield, 5 June 2005.

Cəfərzadə, Əzizə. *Azərbaycanin şair və aşıq qadınları [Azerbaijani Women Ashiqs and Poets]*. Baku, Gənclik, 1974.

Cornell, Svante E. *Azerbaijan Since Independence*. M.E. Sharpe, 2011.

Eldarova, Əminə. *Искусство ашигов Азербайджана [The Art of the Azerbaijani Ashiq]*. Baku, Ishiq, 1984.

Feldman, Leah. *On the Threshold of Eurasia Revolutionary Poetics in the Caucasus*. Cornell UP, 2018.

Heyat, Farideh. *Azeri Women in Transition*. Baku, Chashioglu, 2005.

Hirsch, F. *Empire of Nations: Ethnographic Knowledge and the Making of the Soviet Union*. Ithaca, NY, Cornell UP, 2005.

Huseynova, Aida. *Music of Azerbaijan: From Mugham to Opera*. Bloomington, Indiana UP, 2016.

Həsənli, Bilal, editor. *Ədəbiyyat müntəxəbatı [Literature Collection]*. Baku, Çaşıoğlu, 2002.

Kallinikov, Pavel. "Берже Адольф Петрович" ["Bezhé Adolf Petrovich"]. *Rulex.ru*, Studiya Kolibri, 1997.

Naroditskaya, Inna. "Azerbaijanian Female Musicians: Women's Voices Defying and Defining the Culture." *Ethnomusicology*, vol. 44, no. 2, 2000, pp. 234–56.

Pirsultanlı, Sədnik Paşa. *Ozan-aşıq yaradıcılığna dair araşdırmalar [Research on the Creativity of the Ozan-Ashiq] (Azerbaijani Language)*. vol. 2, Gəncə, Pirsultan, 2002.

Tohidi, Nayereh. "Soviet in Public, Azeri in Private: Gender, Islam, and Nationality in Soviet and Post-Soviet Azerbaijan." *Women's Studies International Forum*, vol. 19, no. 1, 1996, pp. 111–23.

Təhmasib, M., Abbasov, İ., Abdullayev, B., and Ferseliyev, T., editors. *Azərbaycan aşıqıarı və el şairləri [Azerabaijani Ashiqs and Folk Poets]* vol. 1, Baku, Elm, 1983.

Xatun, Narınc. "Aşıq Pəri' məclisi" [The Ashiq Peri Mejlis]. *Aşıq Pəri məclisi – Aşıqlar və əl şairləri*, edited by M. Şükür, Baku, Yazıcı, 1991, pp. 3–4.

Xüdiyəv, Nizami, editor. *Aşıq Peri Məjlisi [The Ashiq Peri Mejlis]*. Baku, Borçalı, 2004.

5 "Exilic Consciousness"

Memoirs of Iranian Women Émigrés

Feroza Jussawalla

> O Mazda, truly it will be like this. Because your path and religion is the best gift for humanity and since this religion is in accord with righteousness, all Persian people will enjoy peace and salvation in two worlds. (*Gathas of Zoroaster*)

As a woman of Zoroastrian, Persian ancestry, an Indian Parsi who immigrated to the US from India carrying her Zoroastrian, Persian religion, and Parsi roots with her, it is interesting for me to contextualize the writings of Muslim Iranian women refugees who escaped or immigrated to the US immediately after the Khomeini revolution. They too carried their religion, Islam—as they saw it—and their ancient Persian ancestry and customs. For these Iranian women, who grew up in a largely Westernized Iran under the Shah, Reza Pahlavi, it was possible to be Muslim, Persian, and Westernized all at once. To be both believing Muslims and Westernized individuals was what comprised their "Secular Islam." In Iran, they were like the vast majority of Muslims in South Asia: secular Muslims. But then, faced with a forced doctrinaire Islam, they recoiled, and chose to follow their paths elsewhere. Several left Iran, finding homes elsewhere, predominantly in the US, where many had studied or traveled earlier. They already embodied the dual consciousness so inherent in the postcolonial condition. After the 1979 Revolution and the consequent exodus, this dual consciousness was further enhanced into what Edward Said has called the *"exilic"* consciousness.

In his Reith lecture for the BBC, entitled "Representations of the Intellectual," Said chose to use the word "exilic," (*The Edward Said Reader* 379)—often used and associated with the period of exile of the Jews in Babylon in the sixth century BCE—not only for the Palestinian condition, but that of all those exiled due to the condition of the world. Edward Said contemplating his own "exiled existence" in several essays—some collected in *Reflections on Exile*—always saw himself as an exile with a dual consciousness and a profound sense of loss. In *Culture and Imperialism*, he writes, ". . . surely it is one of the unhappiest characteristics of the age to have produced more refugees, migrants, displaced persons, and exiles than ever before in history. . . ." (Said 332). Exiles exist in a liminal space of "in-betweenness," the old and the new, the old home and the new one. He proposes that exile is also a *"metaphoric"* condition, the particular consciousness of living in between: belonging and unbelonging at once. In "Intellectual Exile: Expatriates and Marginals," Said writes, "The *exilic* intellectual does not respond to the logic of the conventional but to the audacity of daring" (*The Edward Said Reader* 381). Indeed, we can see this in the writings of so many migrants and refugees that fill our lists of contemporary *New York Times* best sellers or Booker Prizes. We can particularly see the "audacity" of daring in two influential memoirs by Muslim women émigrés from Iran: Azar Nafisi's *Reading Lolita in Tehran* (2004)[1] and Azadeh Moaveni's very powerful *Lipstick Jihad* (2005) in which she chronicles her *bildungsroman* or growing up story, starting in America, going through a journey in Iran, and ending up exiled from both.

Said tell us, "Exiles feel therefore an urgent need to reconstitute their broken lives" (*Reflections in Exile* 422). We see this in both memoirs, as the two characters and their families work urgently to reconstruct the lives they had and the belongings they had owned. We see this in the stories of Iranian Muslim women writers reflecting on their exile as we see in any diasporic community, even mine, that of Parsi Zoroastrians who have been exiles and émigrés from Iran since the eleventh century CE, and now via India, in the US. Another characteristic we see among the writings of the Iranian Muslim women is what Said calls "the most extraordinary of the exile's fates: to have been exiled by exiles: [since there is no solidarity really among exiled communities] to relive the actual process of uprooting at the hands of exiles" (*Reflections in Exile* 424). Both the women writers written about here, Azar Nafisi and Azadeh Moaveni, experience such uprooting several times as they or their families leave due to political constraints, but choose to revisit the homeland and then return to exile due to intolerable conditions and non-acceptance. Political beliefs tear the immigrant community apart further in their new homes. They attempt homecoming, but it always seems out of reach and out of question. The two women written about here express the profound loss, Said notes, as they look back through their exilic consciousness. "Exile is life lived outside habitual order. It is nomadic, decentered, contrapuntal: But no sooner does one get accustomed to it than its unsettling force erupts again" (*Reflections in Exile* 440). Certainly, the two memoirs discussed here illustrate this.

There is a vast body of the Iranian novel of exile and longing for home written in English, post the Iranian Revolution, both by men and women: Hadi Khorsandi's *The Ayatollah and I* (1987), or Hooman Majd's *The Ministry of Guidance Invites You NOT to Stay* (2013). Azar Nafisi's *Reading Lolita in Tehran* (2004) is, of course, the landmark work followed by such works as Azadeh Moaven's *Lipstick Jihad* (2005), and

Davar Ardalan's *My Name Is Iran* (2007). Porochista Khakpour's vast oeuvre and Dina Nayeri's *The Ungrateful Refugee* (2019) are Iranian American novels critical of their host countries that follow in the footsteps of the previously mentioned memoirs of exile, like Azar Nafisi's *Reading Lolita in Tehran* and Azadeh Moaveni's *Liptick Jihad,* which express the gratefulness of being allowed into the US. Both perspectives capture entirely the cross-cultural conflict and the problems of "hybridity" and "mimicry" that so beset the immigrant, diasporic condition, but also cause trouble in the "homeland" that is back in Iran. Hamid Dabashi criticizes some of these women writers, particularly Azar Nafisi as "native informants" and colonial agents. This, however, takes away from the genuine exilic feelings of the profound loss of home conveyed in the writings of Nafisi and Moaveni.

Both Azar Nafisi and Azadeh Moaveni give us a brief history of Iran up to and beyond the 1979 Islamic Revolution. Post the Islamic Revolution of 1979, both talk of their own families' histories. They had previously come to the US in the sixties and seventies like the many students and business people who went back and forth from Iran until the Islamic Revolution: "Until 1979, the year of the great catastrophe that tossed our lives up into the air, scattering us haphazardly like leaves in a storm" (Moaveni 7). Here Moaveni gives us a brief history:

> It came to be known as the Islamic Revolution, though even that term is contested by people like my relatives, who insist it was a populist uprising stolen by fundamentalist clerics. . . . No one agreed on who to blame: Jimmy Carter, the Shah, the CIA, the British, the BBC, the mullahs, the Marxists, or the Mujaheddin. (7, 19)

This history is essential not only to both these memoirs, but also to a consideration of all the stories of the émigrés who left because of the Islamic Revolution.

It is also important to note the role of the US in this revolution, which brought drastic repercussions not only for the US, but for the rest of the world. Seen in the rear-view mirror of the human rights abuses by the Islamic State, the so-called human rights violations of the Shah paled by comparison. President Carter's misguided attempt to bring back the Ayatollah to counter the supposed human rights abuses of the Shah backfired for the world at large.

Since the Islamic Revolution, there have been several attempts by reformists to loosen the grip and chokehold of Islamic "oppression," if it can be called that: the rules and regulations governing behavior, clothing, thought, and language. Since the passing of Khomeini in 1989, moderates like Rafsanjani and Rouhani later attempted softening the regulations, but always came up against conservatives like Ahmadinejan. And the cycle of reform and return to conservativeness goes on. Most of these revolutionary changes and edicts were fought out on the backs and bodies of women with severe punishments for the slightest defiance. But the women were strong and persistent and thus prevailed. It was this oppression in the name of Islam, that the women writers—whose memoirs are here analyzed—were escaping and trying to create a world and "an Islam of their own," by continuing their faith in their religion and yet trying to reconcile it with what they thought were unjust restrictions and practices.

Upon establishing themselves in the US, they revel in a newfound identity and freedom in their new host country. The Muslim women of twentieth-century Iran resisted espousing certain Islamic practices and politics, unpalatable to their democratic and feminist values and perspectives, while retaining their faith in Islam. They also drew strength from the many Persian heroines of their cultural myths: the daughters of Zoroaster—the indigenous prophet of Iran—particularly Chista (1725 BCE, revered as Wisdom), who was also known as Pouruchista, and Havovi. Iran has always had a strong tradition of ancient queens and warriors: Mandana, mother of Cyrus the Great (King of Kings, often invoked by contemporary Persians and Iranians, whose cylinder containing a proclamation for Zoroastrians is still very much revered by all in Iran); Cassandane Shahbanu; Pantea Artheshbod (559–530 BCE) the great military commander, always looked up to by Persian women; Artemisia, a naval admiral, noted by Herodotus as a marvel; and Sura, the daughter of Ardavan the Fifth, who set Zoroastrianism as the official religion of Persia. Most famous of them all is Turandot, immortalized in Puccini's opera and unfortunately, often portrayed as Chinese ("Historical Queens"). But Islam in its ancient form also had strong women leaders, primarily the Prophet Mohammed's first wife Khatija, without whom Mohammed would not have been the businessman and empire builder that he was. Both the Zoroastrian and Muslim women of Iran hail from a lineage of strong women able to reconstruct themselves under all adversity.

Iran, despite several centuries of Arab-Muslim rule, remains what I will here call "Persian," in that it maintained its ancient Mazdayasni roots, i.e., those of the followers of Ahura Mazda, the one monotheistic God, propagated by the still revered prophet Zoroaster, who offered his prayers through the medium of fire. Iranians, or Persians still revere some of these ancient Zoroastrian sites, primarily the fire at a hilltop shrine called "Chak-chak," or "Pir-e-Sabz," where a Zoroastrian princess, Nikbanou, is supposed to have escaped to prevent conversion and rape by the Arab-Muslim invaders. Nikabanou is said to have prayed to Ahura Mazda for protection, whereupon the mountain opened and gave her shelter. It is believed that an ever-flowing stream of water kept her alive, and that the stream originated from her tears. This ancient story gives us a trope for the strength and defiance of Persian-Iranian women and their strength in survival. It also reminds us of the Arab-Muslim colonialism, which pervades and shadows many of the indigenous cultures of the Middle East, even to some extent, Egypt. In *Reading Lolita in Tehran*, Nafisi writes,

> I was reminded of a story I had heard and reheard about the Arab conquest of Persia, a conquest that brought Islam into Iran. By this account when the Arabs attacked Iran they won because the Persians themselves, perhaps tired of the tyranny, had betrayed their King and opened the doors to their enemies. But after the invasion, when their books were burned, their places of worship destroyed and their language overtaken, the Persians took revenge by recreating the burned and plundered history through myth and language. Our great epic poet Ferdowsi had rewritten the confiscated myths of Persian kings and heroes in a pure and sacred language. (Nafisi 172)

Another dominant trope that governs our collection of essays and also the writings of Iranian women is, of course, that of Scheherazade, who is enfolded into Persian culture as their storyteller, as much as the Arabs also embrace her myth. She is the emblem of the Muslim "speaking woman subject," as based on a notion by Gayatri Spivak, developed in her immortalized essay, "Can the Subaltern Speak?" In fact, Azar Nafisi, right at the beginning of *Reading Lolita in Tehran*, invokes Scheherazade as a "Persian" figure: "We read the Persian classical literature, such as the tales of our own lady of fiction, Scheherazade from *A Thousand and One Nights*" (6). Together with Firdousi's *Shahnameh*, this story of Scheherazade originally from Arabia is part of a "hybridized," culture that had existed in Persian Iran, until the resurgence of the newer post-1997 Islamized culture. In fact, *A Thousand and One Nights* governs Nafisi's framework for violence. She writes,

> What had most intrigued me about the frame story of *A Thousand and One Nights* were the three kinds of women it portrayed—all victims of a king's unreasonable rule. Before Scheherazade enters the scene the women are divided into those who are killed before they have a chance to betray and then are killed (the queen) and those who are killed before they have a chance to betray (the virgins), the virgins who unlike Scheherazade have no voice in the story, are mostly ignored by the critics. Their silence however is significant. (Nafisi 19)

Here Nafisi is invoking or calling on those who have accepted that the laws of dress and behavior and readable material, all imposed by the ayatollahs, to resist. She particularly considers these as arbitrary and that she is going to resist. For her, the biggest complaint is against the restrictions on thought and reading. As an intellectual university professor, she objects to the censorship of reading materials and the ways to analyze them. *A Thousand and One Nights* was soon banned, and yet Nafisi assigned them to the students in a private, underground class she had begun to stimulate thinking. Her acts of resistance had begun.

While contemporary Muslims in Iran believe in and follow their religion (even though a new nationalist Zoroastrianism and a turn toward indigeneity is emerging), many of the immigrant and escaped refugees remain wary and skeptical of the overly fundamentalized Islamicism overtaking the world and what they see as their culture and religion, which many would still like to maintain in its secular form. A recent survey reveals a huge change in religious beliefs: only 32% identified as Shi'ite Muslim, 5% as Sunni Muslim, and 8% as Zoroastrian (Maleki and Tamimi Arab 3). And this despite the recent beheading of a Zoroastrian priest for converting Muslims ("Iran-American Zoroastrian Priest Killed"). So, the heavy-handed intolerance continues, contributing to honor killings and suicides among youth, much of which cannot be denied even though we tend to blame the Western media for perpetrating stereotypes. The writings of these women show their bravery and courage to speak out. The subaltern does in fact speak against all odds.

It is the voice of what we could call that of secular Muslim feminism. This then is the major issue for Iranian Muslim women writers: an, "exilic, Muslim consciousness," that asks how to maintain cultural and religious practices while still resisting any form of oppression, freedom of expression and thought, while reconciling them with a religion and belief they love and have faith in, and also in their dual consciousness as Iranian-Americans. Porochista Khakpour wrote of this in an op-ed for CNN in 2017:

> Most of all in my youth [growing up in America] I believed Nowruz might have the power to eclipse the other darknesses of my homeland that played nonstop on television and in the news. I hoped the imagery of beauty and hope and optimism could mean something more. . . . (Khakpour)

She goes on to describe Nowruz as, "the celebration . . . many thousands of years old with roots in ancient Indo-Persian culture, a religion some say the prophet Zoroaster himself created." She talks of her own dual identity embodied in her own name. When people ask her about her name she says, "It is an ancient Zoroastrian name, an unusual one for Iranians" (Khakpour). Indeed, it is the name of one of the daughters of the prophet Zoroaster. Thus, we realize the already inherent hybridity in the culture of Iran.

As Haleh Anvari notes in her lengthy piece on Goli Emami, a translator and bibliophile who was thwarted in her efforts to carry forth the modernization put in motion by Princess Farah Diba by the tsunami of the Islamic Revolution of 1979:

> Then the Islamic Revolution happened. A wave of civil and secular resistance to the Shah's increasingly autocratic rule resulted in widespread and paralyzing strikes and demonstrations in 1978, sending the Shah into exile in January 1979. His reign collapsed in February and Ayatollah Khomeini returned from exile and took power. . . . Almost overnight, Iran was transformed from a relatively secular, Western-looking authoritarian monarchy into an authoritarian, anti-Western theocracy. (Anvari)

It is this transformation and lack of freedoms that many of the exiled, escaped refugees write about and it dominates their sense of loss: the loss of a "Persian," more secular country which, though Muslim, allowed them to be at once, Muslim, Persian, and Western. It is the nostalgia for this way of life that pervades their writings, an almost *recherche du temp perdu*. The sorrow and loss of "homeland," in this unfortunate turn of events pervades the writings of diaspora women from Iran, from the earliest, Mahshid Amirshahi's *Suri and Company* (1995) to Nyeri's *The Ungrateful Refugee* (2019). This spate of writing includes Azar Nafisi's *Reading Lolita in Tehran*, Azadeh Moaveni's *Lipstick Jihad*, Davar Ardlan's *My Name is Iran* (2007), and Goli Taraghi's *The Pomegranate Lady and her Sons* (2013).

The first "refugees" so to speak, Azar Nafisi's *Reading Lolita in Tehran* (2004) and Azadeh Moaveni's *Lipstick Jihad* (2005) look back at the Islamicized Iran never with the recent question of "to be Muslim or not." But they decry the freedoms lost, the inability to teach, think, and dress as they used to. When we look at the strength of the women speaking out against the Mullahs (albeit from overseas), we have to remember the proud heritage of strong Iranian women heroines and see how these women carve their lives out with what Gayatri Spivak would call a "nostalgia for lost origins" (93), and how they reshape identity and their sense of nationalism with an "exilic consciousness." How does diaspora change their view of home, belonging and religion, in their transnational, transcultural context? What is their *representation* of home out of memory? (Re)shaping their religion to make it their own and simultaneously to (re)interpret it for their readers and the West seem to be their primary preoccupations, particularly the concept of jihad. Jihad for them is not what the Westerners decry as a violent holy war, but a self-reflection to reconstruct in their own minds their beliefs and practices: "A jihad, in the classical sense of the word: a struggle" (Moaveni 11).

In *Reading Lolita in Tehran*, Azar Nafisi recoils from the fundamentalist Islam that has overcome her more secular Muslim existence. The book begins with her resignation from the university to start a simple class of her own to a handful of selected students. But even from among them, there is the betrayal.

> Teaching in the Islamic Republic, like any other vocation, was sub-servient to politics and subject to arbitrary rules. Always the joy of teaching was marred by diversions and considerations forced on us by the regime—how well could one teach when the main concern of university officials was not the quality of one's work, but the color of one's lips, the subversive potential of a single strand of hair? (Nafisi 11)

The last sentence of course refers to the prohibition against red lipstick and covering every strand of hair. It is a "lipstick jihad," as in Azadeh Moaveni's book with the same title. Nafisi describes the guards made to walk the streets to "make sure that women . . . wear their veils properly, do not wear makeup, do not walk in public with men who are not their fathers, brothers or husbands" (26). She sees the eroding of women's rights and the freedoms that had been brought to Iran with the modern-ization the Shah had hope for. Nafisi notes, "The Party of God: 'MEN WHO WEAR TIES ARE U.S. LACKEYS. VEILING IS A WOMAN'S PROTECTION.'" The streets had been turned into a "war zone for women who disobeyed the rules" (Nafisi 27). The Republic was waging a war against women. It is then that Nafisi notes wistfully a resentment against her mother's generation. She asks this in the voice of her student Sanaz:

> Is she angry that women of her mother's generation could walk the streets freely, enjoy the company of the opposite sex, join the police force, become pilots, live under laws that were the most progressive in the world regarding women? Does she feel humiliated by the new laws, by the fact that after the revolution, the age of marriage was lowered from eighteen to nine, that stoning became once more the punishment for adultery and prostitution? (Nafisi 27)

Freedom was their matriarchal heritage in Iran before the revolu-tion, the freedom enjoyed by the ancient Persian heroines. It was also Azadeh Moaveni's, but with a twist. Her mother looked at Azadeh's "pro-American" tilt with suspicion, even though her mother found herself materially deprived by the revolution (Moaveni 209). Her matriarchal heritage was unending arguments caused by her mother's "dual consciousness" of nostalgia for a past Iran and yet faithfulness to Iran that meant embracing the Islamicized present (210–11). "If you are a lover of Iran, you love your own remembrance of the past . . . [*recherche du temps perdue*]" (45).

One day, Nafisi told her class that she was going to a protest meeting to oppose the government's attempts to impose the veil and veiling. "A private rebellion" was beginning to manifest for her. Nafisi bemoaned the decrying of literature in the Islamic Republic, except as it spoke to their needs for ideological affirmation. In a poignant scene, she notes a young man denouncing *The Great Gatsby* as capitalistic and immoral (Nafisi 110). Mr. Nyazi tells her, one must be committed to a "higher more sacred love," and that therefore their Imam had decried Western Literature.

> What was more important, to fight against the Satanic influence of Western imperialists, or to obstinately hold onto personal prefer-ences that created division among the rank of revolutionaries? . . . It was not that piece of cloth that I rejected, it was the transformation being imposed upon me that made me look in the mirror and hate the stranger I had become. (Nafisi 165)

Moaveni recollects a similar disgust as she is unpacking upon her return from having gone to Iran in more liberal times to discover "the mother-land" as it were. As she unpacks, she writes,

> As I sort through the clothes, peeling veil from veil, it is like tracing the rings of a tree trunk to trace its evolution. The outer layers are a wash of color, dashing tones of turquoise and frothy pink, in deli-cate chiffons and translucent silks. They are color that are found in life—the colors of pomegranates and pistachio, the sky and bright spring leaves—in fabrics that breathe. Underneath, as I dig down, there are dark, matte veils, long formless robes in funeral tones of slate and black. (Moaveni xi)

It is the move away from the liberal, humanistic, and individual to an ideologic agent of a demagogic state that these women bemoan the most and do not want to be. This was not the Iran of Persian literature, art, and poetry, the Iran of the poet Ferdowsi. It was a new colonialism: the neocolonialism of the Islamic State, though the original colonialization of Iran, by the Arabs remains. This was a further layer, a darker veil, like a palimpsest that darkens with each new veneer.

In the spring of 1981, when Nafisi returns to Iran immediately after the Islamic Revolution, she writes, "I discovered that the same decree that had transformed the single word Iran into the Islamic Republic of Iran had made me and all that I had been irrelevant" (Nafisi 150). *That* is her "exilic consciousness." "It was not until I had reached home that I realized the true meaning of exile. As I walked those dear streets, I felt I was squashing the memories that lay underfoot" (145). She felt exiled in her home, a home she couldn't escape, because of the belonging to it.

And yet not belonging to it. "Until then home had been amorphous and elusive" (145). In her epilogue, she notes that after she left Tehran on 24 June 1997, she felt that, "I left Iran, but Iran did not leave me" (341). Famously, Indian writer Raja Rao had said in his memoir of moving to Paris, "My India I carry with me" (Rao 21).

For me, this is the essence of "exilic consciousness," the deeper connection to one's culture and home, a deeper connection to one's indigenousness, to roots of one's culture, in my case Indian-ness, in the Iranians case, a Persian-ness, a nostalgic return to roots. And yet that deeper connection comes from a forced separation.

This is amply demonstrated in Azadeh Moaven's *Lipstick Jihad* (2005). As a second-generation immigrant, born in the US, she notes her parents' keeping of Iranian culture and the stories of home. Indeed, she tells us that she had grown up thinking she was an Iranian princess, surrounded as she was by stories of home, of objects *d'art*, connected to home and tradition and of course Nowruz . . . the *haftsin* table, the one tradition that brings together all Iranians regardless of religion and belief, just like Christmas does in the West. Humorously, she tells us of her attempts to drown the auspicious fish in the fishbowl placed on the *haftsin* table or a table that has seven items of good luck.

Lipstick Jihad is both a history of one woman's search for her identity and roots and a history of Iran since the 1979 revolution grounded in how an American raised, Americanized product of crossed cultures interacts with the politics of a land she goes to understand. In the midst of it all, she tells us about the hypocrisies of the rich and the Westernized. The palimpsest that overlays both culture and colonialism covers up moral and political corruption. She writes of the fiery radicals of the days of Khomeini who "two decades into the Ayatollah's grand experiment found themselves baffled that their Utopian vision had produced an oppressive, overly sexualized society" (Moaveni 76). She writes openly of her disgust of the Iranian clergy. She writes about being called a CIA agent. She writes about being sexually molested by a *chadori* woman performing a security pat down.

Lipstick Jihad is both a true *bildungsroman* and also a true postcolonial *bildungsroman*[2] because it leads the protagonist into rejecting the colonizer and the colonizer's culture, in this case that of the rigid, fundamentalist Islam that in more recent years had overtaken Iran. For me a "postcolonial *bildungsroman*," is one that leads the protagonist to a knowledge of belonging. The "exilic consciousness," in this *bildungsroman* leads the protagonist to a belonging and yet a non-belonging. The same "exilic consciousness," as that of Nafisi pervades this story of a return to roots, as an awareness of oneself as Persian in a Muslim world, but also one of not belonging in one's "imaginary homeland," as Rushdie would call it.

As in any *bildungsroman*, there is the journey, a journey of self-discovery. I say that Moaveni's is a true *bildungsroman* as it leads us through her childhood, adolescence, experimenting with the young "crowd," and then a return, though not to a country of her citizenship (she currently lives in Beirut, Lebanon), but to an awareness of belonging in unbelonging. In the genre of the "postcolonial *bildungsroman*" there is always a focus on the protagonist's interaction with religion. The protagonist in this work feels "the fatigue with Islam" (Moaveni 88), which always seems like a colonizing religion, particularly to this Americanized, "not-Iranian." More importantly there is a frustration with the language. She speaks, for instance, of not being able to speak Farsi like a native speaker and concludes, "without English, I, as myself, ceased to exist" (Moaveni 89). The "exilic consciousness" is a dual consciousness.

But despite this dual consciousness, both women writers are functioning in a traditional Iranian model of storytelling.[3] Probably the telling had not been easy. But as both women tell us their stories, it is almost as though they are Scheherazades themselves, telling us oral narratives, stories framed with other stories, the oral tale which is the indigenous Persian form of the *dastan*. I had written about it in justifying Rushdie's storytelling method:

> A *dastan* in Persian literature is simply a long-winded stream-of-consciousness tale that incorporates many related and sometimes loosely strung together frame tales and assorted humorous anecdotes—like the Chinese boxes. (Jussawalla, "Rushdie" 66)

Certainly, the works of both these women writers, particularly that of Moaveni, show their fluency and virtuosity in their descriptions and recollections. In several essays in *Reflections on Exile*, Said hearkens to Arab and South Asian writers and forms from Ibn Kaldoun to Naguin Mahfouz, particularly in his interpretations of Adaf Soueif's *In the Eye of the Storm*. What is important to me here is that despite Said's theories being heavily informed by Western theories and thinkers, he does make room to raise our awareness of indigenous forms for otherwise we would be looking at our writers purely through a colonized lens and mentality. In his essay, "Arabic Prose and fiction after 1948" (*Reflections in Exile* 140–81), Said notes the many forms of Middle Eastern literatures: *qissa, sira, hadith, khurafa, nadira*, and *magma*. He talks about *al nakba* as not just play, but as a profound rupture (Said, *Reflections in Exile* 152). It is the profound rupture that gives rise to the sense of profound loss in Middle Eastern memoirs, whether those of Said or the women noted here.

The works of these memoirists, albeit through the perhaps prejudiced or privileged lenses, capture a history that would not be retained through the governmental states. This is why they are important to retain and consider. What does it mean to be Muslim, when one is resisting a state that embodies what it thinks is Muslim? These women resist the despoiling of their religion and beliefs and record the injustices mixing their belief with their diasporic conditions, like fine hands sprinkling spices like *soumak* to flavor Middle Eastern rice. As Moaveni concludes, "Iran like the *Simorgh* was elusive, that it defied being known" (245).

Notes

1 An early version of *Lolita in Tehran* was published as a critical essay entitled "Images of Women in Classical Persian Literature and the Contemporary Iranian Novel." In Afkhami and Friedi, *In the Eye of the Storm: Women in Post-revolutionary Iran,* Syracuse, Syracuse UP, 1994.
2 Postcolonial *bildungsroman*. I developed this paradigm of the *bildungsroman* as defining the postcolonial novel in "Kim, Huck and Naipaul: Using the *Bildungsroman* to (Re)define Postcoloniality."
3 I argued that because Salman Rushdie was using the Persian form of storytelling called the *dastan*, he wasn't really blaspheming.

Works Cited

Anvari, Haleh. "Translating Life in Iran." *Roads and Kingdoms,* 21 Nov. 2018.
Dabashi, Hamid. "Native Informers and the Making of the American Empire." *al-Ahram Weekly,* 1 June 2006.
Fathi, Nazila. "Women Writing Novels Emerge as Stars in Iran." *The New York Times,* 29 June 2005.
Gani, Aisha. "Here's What Muslim Women Authors Have To Say About Finding Their Voice." *Buzzfeed,* 28 Jan. 2017.
"Historical Women: Powerful Women of Persia." *Persepolis,* 23 Sep. 2020.
"Iranian-American Zoroastrian Priest Killed in Kerman." *Iranwire,* 26 July 2020.
Jussawalla, Feroza. "Kim, Huck and Naipaul: Using the *Bildungsroman* to (Re)define Postcoloniality." *Links and Letters,* vol. no. 4, 1997, pp. 25–38.
———. "Rushdie's *Dastan-E-Dilruba The Satanic Verses* as Rushdie's Love Letter to Islam." *Diacritics,* vol. 26, no. 1, Spring 1996, pp. 50–73.
Khakpour, Porochista. "Why This Persian New Year Is Different." *CNN,* 20 Mar. 2017.
Maleki, Ammar and Pooyan Tamimi Arab. "Iranians' Attitudes Toward Religion: A 2020 Survey Report." *Gamaan,* Netherlands, GAMAAN, 2020.
Moaveni, Azadeh. *Lipstick Jihad.* New York, Public Affairs, 2005.
Nafisi, Azar. *Reading Lolita in Tehran: A Memoir in Books.* New York, Random House, 2004.
Rao, Raja. *The Serpent and the Rope.* London, John Murray, 1966, p. 21.
Said, Edward. *Culture and Imperialism.* New York, Knopf, 1993.
———. *The Edward Said Reader.* Edited by Moustafa Bayoumi and Andrew Rubin, Random House, 2000.
———. *Reflections in Exile and Other Essays.* New York, Grantha, 2000.
Spivak, Gayatri. "Can the Subaltern Speak?" *Colonial Discourse and Post-colonial Theory,* edited by Patrick Williams and Laura Chrisman, New York, Columbia UP, 1994, pp. 66–112.

6 Feminist Ethnography, Revisionary Historiography, and the Subaltern in Assia Djebar's *Fantasia*

An Algerian Cavalcade

Naila Sahar

Contemporary fiction writing is an act of breaking silences. It's an act of reinterpreting and reconstructing history. By rewriting history, novelists recover the collective heritage of the nation and thus redefine the role of an author in a society where denial and erasure are primary tools of historiography. Through their novels, writers assert the belief that both history and memory are subject to revision and thus indispensable in shaping a community. Both history and memory engage in imagination and experience to investigate the past and thus are imperative in shaping sound contours of public and personal consciousness and identity. In this respect, ethnographies and fiction writing overlap each other in their objective. In this chapter, I argue that Djebar in *Fantasia: An Algerian Cavalcade* plays several roles in putting together the submerged parts of history; she is an ethnographer, historian, and storyteller simultaneously, and this is what gives most of the appeal to her work. She joins her own voice and life story with the story and voices of Algerian women revolutionaries. Djebar replaces the silence and the colonizer's version of history with a celebration of female experience and expression.

Fantasia is Djebar's combination of autobiographical work with a historical account of French conquest of Algeria in 1830 and Algerian war of mid-twentieth century. While the novel's chapters alternate between the historical and autobiographical, Djebar weaves carefully constructed dialogues that investigate dynamics of both personal and national identity formation through each chapter. Chapters on French colonization of Algeria are based on archives that Djebar, as a historian, has researched, while in an attempt to challenge hegemonic discourses she reimagines, repositions, and rewrites these archives, mingling them with eyewitness accounts written by French officers, artists, and journalists. The archival material that Djebar collects mainly focuses on atrocities committed by French invaders that further challenge French colonial discourse and revise Algerian cultural memory.

Writing the self and social is a part of ethnography. Djebar constantly adapted this strategy of speaking in terms of "I." Just as the French reporters of the Algerian conquest wrote of their personal accounts as well as the reports of the Algerians who could not document their own narratives in the French archives, Djebar documents on behalf of herself, and of Algerian women who cannot write their own histories of exploitation. Indeed, the "I" in her novel has a conspicuously emblematic characteristic. "I" does refer to the narrator herself since there is a clear singular narrative voice at work in the novel, but it also can represent Algerian women collectively. Djebar speaks to the administered silence of Algerian women, elucidating, "How could a woman speak aloud, even in Arabic, unless on the threshold of extreme age? How could she say 'I', since that would be to scorn the blanket-formulae which ensure that each individual journeys through life in a collective resignation?" (Djebar 156). Therefore, in writing the emblematic "I" in *Fantasia*, Djebar acts as the omniscient voice of Algerian women, just as the French archives act as the voice for colonial Algeria. This technique of writing in the memoir genre is shared both by novelists and ethnographers, thus giving them the prospect to simultaneously voice the personal, public, and political.

James Clifford writes, "I treat ethnography itself as a performance emplotted by powerful stories. Embodied in written reports, these stories simultaneously describe real cultural events and make additional, moral, ideological, and even cosmological statements" (Clifford 98). Seen in this perspective, this is the project that Assia Djebar takes up in *Fantasia*. She revises the traditional history in the novel by decentering the official version of history and creating room for women to share the stories of their struggle for national independence. Djebar's project constructs a new model of female subjectivity. Gayatri Chakravorty Spivak writes,

> Between patriarchy and imperialism, subject-constitution and object-formation, the figure of woman disappears, not into a pristine nothingness, but into a violent shuttling which is the displaced figuration of the 'third-world woman' caught between tradition and modernization. (Spivak 102)

Djebar denies this mode of "subject-constitution and object-formation" of women by offering colonial history through letters, diaries, and published accounts of French soldiers and officials. She seeks to destabilize the established Euro-centric and established historical archives for the sake of creating 3D view of Algerian history. She writes, "It is now my turn to tell a tale. To hand on words that were spoken, then written down. Words from more than a century ago . . ." (Djebar 165). Djebar gives voice to third-world women who are perceived as,

> religious (read 'not progressive'), family oriented (read 'traditional'), legal minors (read 'they-still-are-not-conscious-of-their-rights'), illiterate

(read 'ignorant'), domestic (read 'backward'), and sometimes revolutionary (read 'their-country-is-in-a-state-of-war'). (Mohanty 214)

She attempts to prove that although women remained cloistered and confined in their harems, it would be wrong to assume that they remained
immobile and ignorant of their rights during the war of independence
in Algeria.

Paul Stoller argues that the methods of "ethnographic research" include the fabled notion of participant-observation, informally and formally structured interviews, surveys, and archival study. These methods
usually generate data that result in the publication of theoretically informed articles that refine our capacities to understand social and cultural processes. "These same methods sometimes produce results that
are transformed into book-length studies that we call ethnographies"
(Stoller 180). It's this same kind of structure that Assia Djebar follows
while writing her novel. In letters, diaries, and published accounts, she
searches for spaces where the women bubble up to the surface and their
contribution is recorded despite official history's resolve to expunge their
impact and survival. She finds the instants where oppressors are forced
to face the challenging presence of women revolutionaries and offers the
arguments of women freedom fighters themselves, recording their stories
in the sections of a novel titled *Voices*.

While putting the narratives of these women on paper, we can see
Djebar facing the dilemma of being an insider and an outsider at the
same time that Patricia Zavella talks about in her essay "Feminist Insider Dilemmas." Djebar, being an enlightened educated woman and
well-versed in French, is definitely a step above the ladder of social strata
than the women she interviews and writes about, and thus faces the dilemma of continually negotiating her status so to fit in the community
being studied. In *Fantasia*, the autobiographical passages of the novel
emphasize, in particular, Djebar's awareness of her own conflicting role
as a Western-educated, Muslim, female Arab intellectual endeavoring to
recreate the stories of her Arabic ancestors. In *Fantasia*, she writes:

> Can I, twenty years later, claim to revive these stifled voices? And
> speak for them? Shall I not at best find dried up streams? What
> ghosts will be conjured up when in this absence of expressions of
> love (love received, 'love' imposed), I see the reflection of my own
> barrenness, my own aphasia. (Djebar 202)

Thus, to empathize with these women, she focuses on the common de-
nominator between these women and herself, i.e., the shared "aphasia."
Zavella in her essay warns a female ethnographer of her responsibility to construct analysis that are sympathetic to ethnic interests, and
that will somehow share whatever knowledge is generated with them.
While elaborating on the problems that female anthropologists may face

while being an inside outsider, Djebar quotes Maxine Baca Zinn: "These problems should serve to remind us of our political responsibility and compel us to carry out our research with ethical and intellectual integrity" (Zavella 190). According to her, there's a growing acceptance in the field that feminist and other researchers then, must self-consciously reflect upon their status within the field site, on how they are situated within the social and power relations, and place their own work within the changing tides of academic discourse as well. Quoting Jose Limon, Djebar reminds us that however "liberating" a narrative discourse we propose to write, it is always one that is intimate with power, so one must always decenter their own discourse lest it be saturated with domineering power.

In "Can the Subaltern Speak?" Gayatri Chakravorty Spivak elaborates her project of constructing a new model of female subjectivity.

> My readings are, rather, an interested and inexpert examination, by a postcolonial woman, of the fabric of repression, a constructive counter narrative of woman's consciousness, thus woman's being, thus woman's being good, thus the good woman's desire, thus woman's desire. (Spivak 95)

This is the same project as Assia Djebar takes up in *Fantasia* as she decenters the colonizer's version of account and creates space for the participation of women in the struggle for national independence. As Spivak uses the term "subaltern," it signifies someone whose voice cannot be heard, being structurally written out of the capitalist bourgeois narrative. Thus, everything that has a limited or no access to the "cultural imperialism" is subaltern. Spivak's point is not that the subaltern does not cry out in various ways, but that speaking is a transaction between speaker and listener. The subaltern talks, in other words, but does not achieve the dialogic level of utterance.

Using Spivak's theoretical model of the silent subaltern and hegemonic power structure of cultural supremacy, we can investigate how Djebar liberates the silent women's voices that were structurally written out of society's established constructions for political representations. Seen in this way, Djebar attempts at achieving this dialogic level of utterance for the subaltern and brings an Algerian subaltern a transformed model of intellectual discourse. Although Spivak used the term "subaltern" in a different scenario, however, when seen in the perspective and context of historiography, the term closely collaborates to Djebar's project as well. She joins her own voice and life story with the story and voices of Algerian women revolutionaries. They replace the silence and the colonizer's version of history with a celebration of female experience and expression. Djebar neither speaks for, nor to her subaltern sisters, but she speaks with them. She realizes the way in which her own story is intimately linked to the forgotten and silenced testimonies of other women. On the mode of ethnographic writing, she follows in her narrative what Patricia Zavella asks of ethnographers.

> Increasingly, feminist and other fieldworkers realize that we need to be sensitive to differences between our subjects and ourselves as well, and aware of the possible power relations involved in doing research by, about, and for women, and that feminist studies must include a diversity of women's experiences based on race, class, and sexual preferences, among others. (Djebar 186)

Djebar realizes ways in which her story is intimately associated to the overlooked and hushed testimonies of other women.

To write these narratives in *Fantasia*, Djebar goes into the nooks and corners of Algeria finding her subaltern sisters and rendering their utterances at dialogic level. She acknowledges that in Algeria of her times, "The only guilty woman, the only one you could despise with impunity, the one you treated with manifest contempt was 'the woman who raises her voice'" (Djebar 203). Only the "onlooker" one who contented herself with silence was thought to be a perfect jewel. Djebar asks in the novel that if a woman is defined as "Other," can she then speak? Can she express herself and her peculiarly female experiences? And if so, what language or whose voice is she using in doing so? For Djebar as an Algerian woman, the question of Otherness and appropriation becomes doubly acute in the light of colonization, and especially in connection with her French education. Djebar's French education empowers her to escape the fate of her Algerian sisters, providing her with the resources to step out into the public, which is essentially male and the colonizers' space, by enabling her to read, write, and respond in French. However, on the flip side, Djebar's French education also isolates her from the female domain of the harem. This double bind of her education and privileged existence becomes clear at several points in *Fantasia*: "Never did the harem, that is to say, the taboo, whether it be a place of habitation or a symbol, never did the harem act as a better barrier, preventing as it did the cross-breeding of two opposing worlds" (Djebar 128). This barrier that acts as a cloistered cocoon of protection is what Djebar feels is missing from her French-oriented upbringing. She uses this absence to recuperate mutilated voices of her Algerian sisters.

The image of the mutilated hand at the novel's conclusion suggests the connection between body and voice. "Later, I seize this living hand of mutilation and of memory, and I attempt to bring it the qalam" (Djebar 226). According to Danielle Marx-Scouras, the amputated hand symbolizes Algeria, mutilated by a history written by the hands of others (French historians, writers, and artists) but perhaps more importantly for Djebar, it also represents Algerian women severed in their desire to write or express themselves. According to Scouras, the dominant images of the novel—abduction and rape—sexualize the representation of Algeria which becomes female body in final analysis. "If it is on this body that the history of the French conquerors has been written, it is from this body that the desalinization of a people must be written be they men or women" (Marx-Scouras 176).

Djebar's book is a project to resurrect voices that have been long buried under the weight of history, as she attempts at making visible the participants who have struggled for decolonization and have helped in nation building. Djebar states as to how even the silent female prisoners resisted obstinately in the face of brutally imposed power of French, "even when the native seems submissive, he is not vanquished, does not raise his eyes to gaze on his vanquisher. Does not 'recognize' him. Does not name him" (Djebar 56) and does not recognize "victory" of the oppressor. And what is a victory if it is not named, Djebar asks.

Ethnography can sometimes be a bridge that connects two worlds, binding two universes of meaning (Stoller 88). It can be a path that entwines the distant lives of others to our more familiar being, a gift to the world. To counter the distance and bridge this gap with the subaltern Algerian women, Djebar uses words as "torch[es]" which are to be held up to describe the Other's face. "Word seeks all the more to strip us bare" (Djebar 62). It is through writing and analyzing, not in her mother tongue but in "step-mother" tongue, i.e., French, that Djebar has stripped bare the images of monolithic "third-world women" and moved women from border to front position in her recreated history. She takes orality as an essentially female act and fusing these oral accounts of women with written narratives by men, she tries to undo the male/ female binary.

Kamala Visweswaran writes that if we learn to apprehend gender as not the "endpoint of analysis but rather as an entry point" into complex systems of meaning and power, then surely there are other equally valid entry points for feminist work. "Gender is perhaps best understood as a heuristic device and cannot be understood a priori, apart from particular systems of representation" (Visweswaran 616). Telling women's stories through writing, which has hitherto been a male instrument, and using former colonizer's language enables Djebar not only to create a female voice, but also to liberate the surviving heroines of trauma of subjugation. Some passages in *Fantasia* also express the absurdity of using French which was the language of subjugation to convey experiences that were narrated in Arabic. Djebar voices her concerns explicitly: "To attempt an autobiography using French words alone is to lend oneself to the vivisector's scalpel, revealing what lies beneath the skin" (Djebar 156), yet she also emphasizes the playful and imaginative aspect of using French to convey self-experience: "Autobiography practiced in the enemy's language has the texture of fiction" (Djebar 216). Through her written word, Djebar unveils the shrouded and silenced subaltern and her struggles:

> Writing in a foreign language, not in either of the tongues of my native country—the Berber of the Dahra mountains or the Arabic of the town where I was born—writing has brought me to the cries of the women silently rebelling in my youth, to my own true origins. Writing does not silence the voice, but awakens it, above all to resurrect so many vanished sisters. (Djebar 204)

Deborah A. Gordon writes that in Spivak's view, translation offers an opportunity to discover the trace of Other in the self, and since feminist anthropology is always bound up with situations of translation, there are important parallels between literary translation and the translation of ethnography "including its modes of travel, and technologies of listening, recording and writing—and its dissemination" (Gordan 382). Djebar's translation of native Arabic into French gives her an opportunity to discover the trace of Other in the self. Her knowledge of French as well as Arabic enables her replacing history written by the colonizer with the history of gallant women. Knowledge of the French language gives the writer a privileged access to the reports, accounts, and evidence from the past. This "allows me to reach out today to our own dead and weave a pattern of French words around them" (Djebar 78).

Linking language to the female body is another aspect that is crucial for Djebar. Arabic, for example, is described in *Fantasia* as oral. It is open and fluid, flirtatious and sensual. Pronouncing a word such as *hannouni* (my little liver) becomes an experience directly affecting the body: "Sometimes my lips form it silently, awakening it; sometimes it is exhumed by a caress along one of my limbs and the sculpted syllables rise to the surface, I am about to spell it out, just once, whisper it to be free of it, but I refrain" (Djebar 81). Djebar records transcribing her native Arabic into a disruptive language by using French in the novel. Djebar's handling of the veil, her rejection of cloistering, and her access and use of writing proposes that the female body is the milieu of potential power, and her rebellion and knowledge have potential to threaten the status quo of male privilege:

> The fourth language, for all females, young or old, cloistered or half-emancipated, remains that of the body: the body which male neighbors' and cousins' eyes require to be deaf and blind, since they cannot completely incarcerate it, the body which, in trances, dances or vociferations, in fits of hope and despair rebels, and unable to read and write, seeks some unknown shore as destination for its message of love. (Djebar 180)

In this context, Hélène Cixous' "write your body, your body must be heard" becomes relevant (Cixous 250). Djebar explores women's struggle for social emancipation and retrieves the silenced voices of Algerian women back into history. According to Sidonie Smith, speaking the self is linked in important ways to speaking the experience of female embodiment. She speaks of the connection between subjectivity and body that happens in an autobiographical project, a project that Djebar takes up. According to her, when a specific woman approaches the scene of writing and autobiographical "I," she not only engages the discourses of subjectivity through which the universal human subject has been culturally secured; she also engages the complexities of her cultural assignment to an absorbing assignment. "And the autobiographical subject carries a history of the body with her as she negotiates the autobiographical 'I', for autobiographical practice is one of those cultural occasions when the history of the body intersects the development of subjectivity" (Smith 22–3). In telling their stories, Djebar and the women revolutionaries reclaim not only their individual and collective voices, but their bodies as well.

The story of Djebar and women freedom fighters is the story of Algeria's journey from colonization and subjugation to becoming an independent nation. In writing the Arab women's voices and rebelling against childhood taboos, Djebar's novel successfully retrieves those who have been silenced and absent from representation and thus politicizes the everyday experiences of Algerian women in global and historical settings. The way she collects the stories of women underscores the importance of storytelling, because if we will not perform a rewrite of our stories, somebody else might usurp them. Her concept of history is not static and stagnant, but it can be compared to Derrida's concept of "Différance." According to Derrida, the meaning of a word is always in motion and never stays the same. This concept is analogous to Djebar's perception of history, which is constantly subject to slippage and change. The history she talks of does not exist in isolation, severing its ties with the past. Her novel is a palimpsest, where she overwrites the existing history while keeping intact the traces of previous narrations and experiences, opening them up for fresh perspectives and visions.

Judith Stacey addresses the issue of private being made public by a female anthropologist, and thus researching at the risk of intruding and intervening into a system of relationships and values. She thus declares, ". . . the exploitative aspect of ethnographic process seems unavoidable" (Stacey 23). We can see Assia Djebar encountering the somewhat same challenges while researching and interviewing the Algerian women. To counter this challenge of being exploitative on the part of author, Visweswaran writes that working from the genre of feminist testimonial, recent feminist ethnography has elaborated a concern with "giving voice" to its subjects. "Nancy Scheper-Hughes contends that in spite of 'the dissonant voices in the background protesting just this choice of words' that 'there is still a role for the ethnographer-writer in giving voice, as best she can, to those who have been silenced . . ." (Visweswaran 28). Karen McCarthy Brown similarly affirms that "the people who are being studied should be allowed to speak for themselves whenever possible . . ." (Brown 14). In telling their stories, Djebar and the women revolutionaries reclaim their bodies as well.

Silence is not simply proclaimed as protest here; rather silence is enforced onto women and is warranted by "custom" and "tradition." It is also destructive and caustic, as Djebar narrates women's experiences of rape and violence during the French-Algerian war of independence.

> To say the private, Arabic word 'damage', or at the most, 'hurt': 'Sister, did you ever, at any time, suffer "damage"?' The word suggesting rape—the euphemism. . . . One or other of the matriarchs will ask the question, to seize on the silence and build a barrier against mis-fortune. . . . Rape will not be mentioned, will be respected. Swallowed. Until the next alarm. (Djebar 202)

Naming woman's plight or articulating protest, in other words, by unveiling woman's situation and publicizing it, woman is further stigmatized in Arab society: "To refuse to veil one's voice and to start 'shouting,' that was really indecent, real dissidence. For the silence of all the others suddenly lost its charm and revealed itself for what it was: a prison without reprieve" (Djebar 204). Thus, respecting the norms of Arabic language, Djebar avoids using words that were considered curt and blunt in Algerian culture and switching them with words that were ethically and culturally appropriate.

While rewriting the history taken from French archives, Djebar engages with colonial representations so to expose the limits of French accounts and archival sources on colonial Algeria. She writes, "It is now my turn to tell a tale. To hand on words that were spoken, then written down. Words from more than a century ago . . ." (Djebar 165). While colonizer's discourse is systematically accepted as the final verdict (Murdoch 82), Djebar rejects the male-centered version of history and recreates it by moving women from periphery to the center. "In writing of my childhood memories, I am taken back to these bodies bereft of voices" (Djebar 84). She tries to avenge the former silences.

After reading one source by Colonel Pelissier who elaborated how the French crushed a Berber insurrection in the spring of 1845, Djebar writes,

> I, in turn, piece together a picture of that night . . . I imagine the details of this nocturnal tableau . . . I ponder over Pelissier's next order . . . I can't say for sure what the military policy was; this is just

a surmise; I am telling the story in my own way and is it so purpose-
less to imagine what motives these butchers had? (Djebar 70)

Saying this, Djebar elucidates that primary sources are usually stained
by prejudice, and a certain amount of imagination and postulation on
the part of the researcher are required to find inherent meanings. Anne
Donadey states, "History . . . can never be a seamless, linear, grand
narrative. Instead it is presented as a fractured, painfully reconstructed
collage pieced together from a variety of sources" (Donadey xxviii). The
French archival sources that Djebar uses depict the colonizers' version
which was based on French imperial ideologies of the time; however,
Djebar employs her imagination and storytelling embedded in Algerian
cultural memory so as to reenact a new Algerian cultural memory.

Donadey points to the importance for Djebar to emphasize the close
nature of historical writing with fictional narratives, "Foregrounding
the fictional nature of colonial history empowers the writer to seize fiction as a legitimate means of reconstructing her past" (Donadey 46).
Djebar does exactly this in her text, describing from 1830 the records
of chronicler J.T. Merle. Merle is not a military man but rather a 'man
of letters' who prints his account of the capture of Algiers while never
actually being actively involved in the fighting. Djebar remarks on his
writings, stating that "he observes, he notes, he makes discoveries . . . he
is inspired to the heights of eloquence when he portrays . . . [however]
he lags permanently behind any decisive battle; he never witnesses any
actual events" (Djebar 28). History is not static; it lives, breathes, and
transforms by virtue of close retrospection of intellectuals of any society.
Contemporary fiction writers have sensed that the one duty they owe to
history is to rewrite it. Djebar traces the cycle of history in her narratives because she believes that access to information about past mistakes
and their repercussions could guide the decision-makers and citizens in
charting their course in future.

Fantasia has a tone of urgency. Djebar here acquaints her readers to
what is Algeria and what it went through that people hardly know. In
words of Paul Stoller, a memorable ethnography has a sense of locality
through which spaces–places and people of that book become etched in
your memory (Stoller 180). While reading *Fantasia*, one feels like visiting and talking to the women Djebar talks to. In "Tools to Shape Texts,"
Kirin Narayan gives ethnographers tips on improving their ethnographies: "I offer these terms—*story, situation, persona, character, scene,
summary,* and *expository lump*—with the hope that they will prove
helpful to fellow ethnographers" (Narayan 142). Seen this way, these
are the same ingredients that spice up any novella too since, "writing
of ethnography and of fiction may both be enriched by insights carried
across the shifting borders between these genres established by institutional histories and expectations" (Narayan 131). Both literature and

ethnographies are filled with complex insights about the human condition, and the knowledge they impart can enable the humanity to take up challenges of social life.

Djebar's narratives are the collective memoirs of a nation. Both history and memory are subject to revision in her narratives and both are fundamental in the ideological formation of a nation. Memory has the potential to recover the past and alter the present. It urges us to learn from the achievements and mistakes of the past. Djebar keeps on rotating the slide projector of memory to recover the indelible inscription of historical traumas. She knits the fragmented private and public memories which further help her to revise and re-inscribe the dark areas in the history of the Algerian nation. In *Fantasia*, remembering is an act of lending coherence to a history interrupted and subjugated through power.

Works Cited

Brown, K.M. *Mama Lola*. Berkeley, UCP, 1991.

Cixous, Hèléne. "The Laugh of the Medusa." *New French Feminisms: An Anthology*, edited by Isabelle de Courtivron and Elaine Marks, New York, Schocken, 1980, pp. 90–99.

Clifford, James. "On Ethnographic Allegory." *The Postmodern Turn: New Perspectives on Modern Theory*, Cambridge, Cambridge UP, 1994, pp. 205–28.

Derrida, Jacques, Pascale-Anne Brault, and Michael Naas. "To do Justice to Freud:" The History of Madness in the Age of Psycholanalysis." *Critical Inquiry*, vol. 20, no. 2, 1994, pp. 227–266.

Djebar, Assia. *Fantasia: An Algerian Cavalcade*. Translated by Dorothy S. Blair, Portsmouth, N.H. Heinemann, 1993.

Donadey, Anne. *Recasting Postcolonialism: Women Writers between Worlds*. New Hampshire, Heinemann, 2001.

Gordon, Deborah A. "Border Work: Feminist Ethnography and the Dissemination of Literacy." *Women Writing Culture*, edited by Ruth Behar and Deborah A. Gordon, Berkeley, U of California P, 1995, pp. 373–89.

Marx-Scouras, Danielle. "Muffled Screams/stifled Voices." *Yale French Studies*, vol. 82, 1993, pp. 172–82.

Mohanty, Chandra Talpade. "Under Western Eyes: Feminist Scholarship and Colonial Discourses." *Colonial Discourse and Postcolonial Theory*, edited by Patrick Williams and Laura Chrisman, New York, Columbia UP, 1994.

Murdoch, H. Adlai. "Rewriting Writing: Identity, Exile and Renewal in Assia Djebar's L'Amour la Fantasia." *Yale French Studies*, vol. 2, no. 83, 1993, pp. 71–92.

Narayan, Kirin. "Tools to Shape Texts: What Nonfiction Can Offer Ethnography." *Anthropology and Humanism*, vol. 32, 2007, pp. 130–44.

Smith, Sidonie. *Subjectivity, Identity, and the Body: Women's Autobiographical Practices in the Twentieth Century*. Bloomington, Indiana UP, 1993.

Spivak, Gayatri Chakravorty. "Can the Subaltern speak?" *Colonial Discourse and Postcolonial Theory*, edited by Patrick Williams and Laura Chrisman, New York, Columbia UP, 1994, pp. 66–111.

Stacey, Judith. "Can There Be a Feminist Ethnography?" *Women's Studies International Forum*, vol. 11, no. 1, Pergamon, 1988.

Stoller, Paul. "Ethnography/Memoir/Imagination/Story." *Anthropology and Humanism*, vol. 32, 2007, pp. 178–91.

Visweswaran, Kamala. "Histories of Feminist Ethnography." *Annual Review of Anthropology*, vol. 26, 1997, pp. 591–621.

Zavella, Patricia. "Feminist Insider Dilemmas: Constructing Ethnic Identity with Chicana Informants." *Feminist Anthropology: A Reader*, edited by Ellen Lewin NJ, Wiley, 2006, pp. 186–202.

Section 2

Body and Politics

7 Spheres of Piety

Politicization of Muslim Women in Turkish Novels

Funda Güven

> Identity provides one with a sense of well-being—a sense of being at home, in one's body a sense of direction to one's life and a sense of mattering to those who count. (Kroger 63)

Women's participation and appearance in the public sphere from education to work are contested arenas in politics. Women's bodies, dress codes, and the image of Muslim women have become a central topic of Turkish politics, rooted in a West versus East conflict. Although an abundance of work by Muslim women focuses on women's bodies and the state's politics, this article focuses on insightful stories of Muslim women revealing their conflicts through the characters in their novels.

Fatma Barbarosoğlu's biographical novel, *Uzak Ülke* (Distant Country), tells the story of the first pioneering Muslim feminist women and of the author, Fatma Aliye. In the novel *Huzur Sokağı* (Peace Street), Şule Yüksel Şenler narrates a story of a young secular woman who could not find happiness with her secular husband and becomes an observant Muslim herself. In *İkna Odası* (Conviction Room), Yıldız Ramazonoğlu tells the story of a young woman who is trying to obtain a university education while university administration challenges them not to wear a headscarf. Cihan Aktaş tells the story of a young Iranian girl traveling between Turkey and Iran in her novel, *Sınıra Yakın* (Close to the Border). By telling their stories, these female Muslim authors present and project Muslim women as agents in society, creating a space for themselves in the publishing sector so their work becomes visible to others, as well as creating a space in society for those who are otherwise ignored.

Understanding pious Muslim women in the context of socio-political and socio-cultural change in the literary novel is challenged by fluctuations and instabilities in Turkish political life. Turkey experienced two major *coups d'état* in 1960 and 1980 when society split into left and right political camps (Zürcher 6). Starting in the late 1960s, religious authors of novels indulged in political issues more than they had before. Having had modern secular education, authors who were born and raised during the Republican period wrote on new socio-political issues while a grassroots Islamist movement started in the Middle East and Turkey. Turmoil in the streets, oppression from the government, and unstable political and economic situations made pious writers cynical as they shaped the political views of Muslim women who were looking for relief from the social and political burdens in the 1970s. Romanticizing life and offering salvation in the otherworld, Islamist novels became a refuge for younger generations who had access to better education than their parents had experienced. Four major religious political parties were formed between 1970 and 2001, offering Islamic governance as an alternative. While women's organizations took an active role in advocating for women's rights in society, female authors who were a part of this political process wrote "thesis novels" to educate women on the authors' ideology and its place in the political discourse of the day.[1] Female lawyers, architects, and sociologists became activists of right wing political parties and wrote their values and views in the form of novels in order to shape the young female readers' views and teach them how to cover their bodies (Satar 307).

The novel genre in the early period of the Republic of Turkey served the new modern ideology of the state by representing religious functionaries as traitorous or ignorant. It took four decades for religious revivalism to emerge in literature to represent the integration of disengaged Islamists. The Islamist writer, Hekimoğlu İsmail, paved the way for pious Muslim authors with his novel, *Abdullah of Minya,* published in 1967,[2] which became a prototype for the salvation novels in the 1980s (Çayır 10). The book was banned in 1986 under 1982's illiberal constitution, which followed the army coup in 1980. In this period, male authors of salvation novels used nationalist and Islamist discourse to explore the Islamic revolution in Iran and the Russian invasion of Afghanistan. The themes of the male authors were conflicts between individuals and the state, whereas the theme of novels written by Islamist female authors of this period was to find happiness in platonic love with a pious man and Islamic faith. Gündüz argues that female authors of the 1980s were not intellectuals, while well-educated female authors wrote Islamic novels in the next decade (469). Salvation novels of the 1980s called people to unite under the divine message of Islam. Çayır argues that novels of the 1990s undermine the collective identity of Muslims with "the revelation of inner conflicts, non-Islamic thoughts, and non-Islamic experiences." Pious Muslim authors published "more reflexive and self-expressive novels," focusing on "Islamic perceptions of self, ideology and the world" (Çayır 161). Following Çayır's study, I conceptualize the novels of Muslim women published after 2000, when more and more pious Muslim female authors published their stories in Turkey.

The segregated lives of men and women in Muslim societies were criticized heavily by Western and modern secular scholars. Ahmed argues the "segregation of the sexes and use of the veil" is not about Islam per se, but the culture in the Middle East (Ahmed 5). She insists that it is a pre-Islamic practice (Ahmed 17). Following Ahmed's argument, Nikkie Keddie maintains that veiling was an urban class phenomenon in early Mediterranean societies. Many women in Mediterranean societies were subject to live in segregated spaces, isolated from men (Keddie 205). Educated, upper-class Muslim women lived in segregated, private sections of their homes until modernization introduced them to Western-style "saloons" where men and women interacted.[3] One of the first women who interacted with male writers was Fatma Barbarosoğlu, an author and the protagonist of the biographical novel of *Uzak Ülke* (Distant Country). As an activist and founder of a women's association, she not only expanded women's voice in the private sphere, but also led women to be active in the public sphere.

In *Uzak Ülke* (Distant Country), Barbarosoğlu tells the story of the pioneering feminist Muslim woman Fatma Aliye, who spent her life convincing Muslim women to participate social life in the late nineteenth century. The plot is about a university teacher who is also a writer who was locked in a classroom all night, talking about a religious feminist figure who defended both Islamic values and modernization. She emphasizes that the protagonist wore gloves to cover her hands at all times, did not appear in the public sphere, and locked herself in her home late in life. The protagonist advocates for Muslim women's rights without rejecting Islam.

The project of ardent modernization in the Republic of Turkey opened the public sphere to women who adopted Western dress codes, but it did not welcome veiled women. Although there was no law banning the veil, the military-backed governments formed after the coups wrote regulations that aimed to sweep pious Muslim women from the public sphere. Pious Muslims in modern Turkey were only able to be active participants of politics in the 1990s by establishing their own political networks. Rallies and campaigns of Muslim religious parties became meeting points for Muslim women who believed that they were fulfilling their *da^{c}wa*.[4] Despite the government's radical stance of putting pressure on veiled women in the public sphere, pious women did not give up their participation in terms of organizing conferences, panels, auctions, and other public events. The more Muslim women participated in the public sphere, the more they became tolerant of sharing this space with men. Pious Muslim women such as Fatma Barbarosoğlu and Cihan Aktaş participated in panels where gender segregation was not practiced. After the culturally conservative Justice and Development Party took office, the restrictions on veiling were eased. Veiled women showed up on TV screens as anchorwomen, moderators, guest speakers, parliamentary members, and ministers after the decree of 1997[5] decreased the visibility of pious Muslims, especially Muslim women with headscarves. The government lifted the headscarf ban in 2013.[6]

The example of veiling in Turkey illustrates how the modernizing state and its religious citizens are brought into conflict. I aim to provide an understanding of pious fellow citizens who live within the post-secular society and feel a heavy physiological burden when they are forced to follow a profane lifestyle by drawing upon Habermas' suggestion of the "learning process"[7] to explore why pious Muslim women authors narrated their stories during times of social change in Turkey. I argue that the characters in thesis novels show pious Muslim women struggling in public and private spaces, ultimately finding their feet while keeping their Muslim identity.

I firmly believe that Muslim female authors narrate the stories of their own personal identities as a means of developing their Muslim agency in the public sphere. For most Muslims, Islam is not only a religion that belongs to the private sphere; it is a device to help them to feel that they belong to a community where they can reach self-actualization. Francis Fukuyama argues that a person's search for identity starts when a society, standing outside the individual, limits a person's choices. He says that the modern concept of identity consists of recognition of human personality from within and outside the self. In contrast to the utilitarian thinkers of Enlightenment, Fukuyama argues that dignity or esteem is more important for the self than material satisfaction. He describes the "moral self" as an act of choice wherein individuals consider themselves within a moral valuation and evolving concept of dignity when they start asking the question, "Who am I?" (Fukuyama 34–9). In other words, an individual can question their situated identity because of the need for dignity and desire to fulfill self-actualization.

Şule Yuksel Şenler was sentenced for her writings in 1967 and imprisoned in 1971 after the army memorandum in March 1971.[8] Şenler was raised in a relatively secular setting until her brother introduced her to a Naqshbandi sheik, who later formed the Nur movement. She started covering her head in the 1960s and invented a stylish head cover for religious urban women. Her novel, *Huzur Sokağı* (Peace Street), published in 1970, was a precursor of "salvation novels" in Turkey, which allowed female Islamist authors to write about topics that invited readers to genuine Islam (Çaha 124). Şenler took a courageous step in writing an authentic story of two young, pious Muslim sweethearts who find infinite happiness by living an Islamic religious lifestyle in Istanbul. The protagonist of the novel, Feyza, desperately seeks a place in Istanbul's streets where she feels she belongs and can practice Islam without any oppression or harassment by state officials or others around her who are not pursuing an Islamic lifestyle. The title of the book, *Huzur Sokağı* (Peace Street), signals to the reader that Islam guides them to the right path. The metaphor of the word "street" in the novel implies there is no end to the search for happiness. The plot starts with a call to prayer and ends when the protagonist dies with a sound of the call to prayer in her ears, having lived a life of dignity. Through the character of Feyza, pious readers will recognize the fight for their religious lifestyles without losing their dignity, and secular Turks are invited to see how Islam promises "peace" and "brotherhood" for them.

The pious characters in *Huzur Sokağı* (Peace Street) come into conflict with state officials and secular characters when they demand to exercise their religious and educational rights in the public spheres. When one character, Seval, introduces a headscarf to another character named Meral, Meral says, "I will cover my head while I commute to school but not inside of the building. I will keep it on all the time after I graduate" (Şenler, 115, my trans).[9] As an adult, Feyza has a conflict with the school administration when she defends her daughter's right to wear a headscarf and pray secretly in a custodian's closet and criticizes the government, saying, "text books are full of misinformation on Islam" (Şenler 269). Thus, the authoritative voice of the author finds roots in a didactic tone. The protagonist warns side characters by referring to the main sources of Islam that they should confront the non-religious state agents who are considered enemies of the religion, namely Islam (Satar 312).

Feyza continues to challenge secular authority when she transfers her daughter to another school. The principal of the new school asks her not to cover her daughter's head in the school. This time, Feyza asks him to show the regulations. The reader learns that there was no such a regulation. With the help of a pious doctor, Feyza enrolls her daughter in a school with a pious principal. The reader is convinced by the doctor that God tested Feyza in this world and implies that Feyza passed the test with perseverance (Şenler 402).

Huzur Sokağı (Peace Street), became a bestseller in Turkey after the coup in 1980, ultimately selling 1.5 million copies and 101 editions by 2019. Many people in Turkey named their newborn children after the characters of the novel. This is not only an indication of the influence of novels toward the religious sphere, but it also highlights the changing relationship of Muslims with the state.

Jurgen Habermas distinguished the public sphere as a space of transformation and elaborated on the relationship of the actors in this realm, namely state and citizens (*Structural Transformation*). In 1967, a young university student named Hatice Babacan demanded her right to join a class wearing her headscarf and ignited a controversy in Turkey. Pious female university students filled city squares and university malls to demand their constitutional rights of education from the state, which strictly prevented them from entering universities while wearing a headscarf until 2013.[10] In 1998, the Istanbul University administration designed an eight square feet room to interview veiled female students in order to convince them to remove their headscarves to attend the classes. Being state agents, university administrators perceived covered girls as a threat to the secular values of the Republic.

Yıldız Ramazanoğlu's novel, *İkna Odası* (Conviction Room), published in 2003, is about the headscarf ban after the 1980s. The novel
tells the agonizing stories of three female characters who entered the
"conviction room" when they covered their heads and tried to go to
university. Ramazanoğlu utilizes reliable first-person narrators to tell
their own stories as victims of the brutal state. By alternating third
and first-person narrators, the author tries to convince the reader that
these kinds of hurtful stories are abundant in society. She also shows
the reader that conviction rooms were not public spaces since the government agents' hegemonic voice as the body of the state did not give a
chance for the girls to negotiate with them.[11] In conviction rooms, young
women were put in a position to decide who controls their body and
their future. Pious young Muslim women who were trying the participate in university as a public space were reluctantly forced to abandon
those spaces and to become part of university life under the control of
the state by uncovering their heads.

An Islamic presence grew in public life after religious parties took
office, and politicians used religious discourse to frame the political history of Turkey. Elizabeth Özdalga categorizes the tendency of young
girls adopting the headscarf as "religious awakening," "resistance
against the nakedness of modern society," and "proving faith or en-
dorsement." She argues the meaning of the headscarf changed from a
symbol of the protection of female honor and the family or showing
the lower-class status of Muslims in the secular society to a symbol of
faith-based action (Özdalga 162). Jenny White provides an alternative
interpretation of the symbol of the headscarf. White claims the secular
Turkish state has been insecure about the existence of religious symbols
and groups in the public sphere.[12] She presents the headscarf as a meta-
category of threat along with the missionary activities of Christians,
which were highlighted in the discourse of politicians and state officials
as a threat to national integrity (White 182). White points out that with
the rise of Islamist movements in the 1980s, a pious urban youth who
were the offspring of rural migrants came up with a new covering style
that represented them as new, modern, urban Muslims. Young girls from
rural areas attending universities in the cities sought to integrate this
new modern setting with their background. White argues that the headscarf for them is mostly a part of their national political identity, which
allows them to demonstrate their Turkishness, defined as "national"
and "local" in the president's discourse on "new nationalism" in Turkey
after the 2000s (White 88).

The protagonist of *İkna Odası* (Conviction Room), Nermin, does not
accept demands to uncover her head and she quits school, whereas her
close friend Nuray, who invited Nermin to join her in wearing a headscarf, uncovered her head and pursued her goals at the university. Another
character, Seher, does not want to hide beneath a wig, but reluctantly

replaces her headscarf with a wig and attends classes. As a result, she loses her hair and develops allergies. Through these characters, the narrator questions the characters' decisions and judges the state that does not give its citizens the choice to be themselves. The teenage girls seek to finalize the construction of their identity and follow an ideal lifestyle for themselves by seeking respect from others. Demanding dignity (from the secular state officials in this sense) culminates in a political movement that can be seen as a popular Islamic movement in the late 1990s and early 2000s. This interpretation is in keeping with Fukuyama's point that Muslim individuals' appeal to dignity leads them to social-political movements supporting nationalism or Islamism (Fukuyama 59).

Islamic identity is considered as a primordial identity among Muslims; there is not a rite of passage that makes one a Muslim. However, none of the protagonists in Cihan Aktaş' novels adopt their given identity without questioning it. Aktaş' protagonists either challenge any label that modernity forces upon them, or they devoutly adopt religious symbols to express their views. Aktaş mainly focuses on the identity of her veiled protagonists not as a product of the society but a development of the self. This is a motif seen throughout her novels, *Write Me A Long Letter, The One Who Listens to You,* and *Sınıra Yakın* (Close to the Border). Here, I will examine the protagonist of *Sınıra Yakın* (Close to the Border).

Traveling from Istanbul to Tehran on a bus, the protagonist of *Sınıra Yakın* (Close to the Border), Efsane, constructs her identity based on her memories. This two-day long journey to the internal and external world of Efsane reveals that the physically challenged protagonist carries her headscarf as a symbol of her freedom. Having lost the function of her left arm, Efsane symbolizes how leftist ideas lost their popularity among Muslims after Ali Shariati, an Iranian a philosopher and activist, brought Marxist ideas to Iranian society by combining them with Islam in the 1970s. During her journey, Efsane confesses that she engaged in espionage when she reported a fellow passenger and a friend of her mother to the police after the Islamic Revolution in Iran. She still questions her behavior and struggles with the guilt that she feels:

> For the freedom and independence of my people, many people were martyred, I could not remain silent against the insidious spread of counter-revolutionaries. Maybe I got something wrong, and maybe I got it wrong. However, you admit that I would not be expected to act otherwise under those conditions. (Aktaş 541)

The first-person narrator, a young woman taking a trip from Turkey to her home country, Iran, seeks a place where she belongs. The narrator reveals the current state of the identity of Muslim women through non-linear, interwoven flashbacks. The reader learns about her family, marriage, education, job, and the life of Iranian people in the background.

The author herself had moved to Iran from Turkey after getting married to an Iranian and traveled back and forth between two countries until she moved back to Turkey.

The narrator compares Turkey and Iran to how women's bodies and dress codes became symbols of two opposing states' institutions. In Turkey, unveiling women was a symbol of Westernization and modernization, whereas the veiling of Iranian women was the most visible symbol of an institutionalized revolution, and it became a compulsory (Göle 84). In the novel, Efsane runs into the cashier girl whom she saw in the grocery store before in the women's restroom. She was curious and wants confirmation from Efsane of whether authorities beat or imprison women in Iran if they do not wear chadors. The same character asks if Efsane's father forced her to wear a chador. The first-person narrator gives her point of view on covering the body, "Do I look like a person who could be forced?" (Aktaş 327). The same Turkish girl complains that she had to leave university because of her headscarf when she and the protagonist run into each other in the women's restroom:

> She pointed to the headscarf with her hand: 'The reason was the headscarf. I covered my head in the second grade of the university. I was studying dentistry in Sivas and living in an apartment with my friends. How many days can one endure being bullied by the names of birds or bugs, by being refused entrance to the campus gates? Wearing a dirty white wig did not work. Some professors pushed me to the corner, saying that I was fooling them. A teacher was also obsessed with my name. What kind of name is Sümeyra? Where are these fashions coming from? If you love Arabs so much, go and live in Mecca. I'm finally tired. I thought of going to Iran and continue my education there, but my grandfather did not let me go to Iran. I still think that.' (Aktaş 327)

Efsane's mother adopted modernization when it came to Iran in the early 1900s. However, her father, the role model for her perspective, is against modernization that is symbolized by the dress code. The first-person narrator is against the framed perception of Westernization that is limited to physical appearance. Through the character of Efsane, Aktaş gives a message to the reader that covering the body should be above politics. As a vigilant Muslim feminist, she argues that the headscarf should not be a subject of politics. She criticizes the Iranian Islamic Revolution as it yielded an authoritarian regime that persecuted people and resulted in emigration from the country. Mourning her loss, Efsane accuses people of abandoning their country and taking refuge in the West.

Cihan Aktaş and other pious women authors in this article are careful to not to self-identify as feminist authors, even though feminists defend the same idea that women should be able to control their bodies, as that might put them in a position against any new and traditional pious authorities. Following Wollstonecraft's "A Vindication of the rights of Women," Aktaş advocates for this first wave of feminist ideas to demand equality for Muslim women and draws a line between the protagonist and the state, regardless of whether it is secular or religious.

The inner voice of the narrator in *Sınıra Yakın* (Close to the Border) says that covering the body of women should not be the business of the moral police. In the novel, some young girls remove their headscarves as soon as they leave Iran. They carry their scarves with them on the way back to cover themselves at the border control. A character narrates her own story to the protagonist, and the reader sees another point of view on the headscarf. While the cashier girl covers her head as a result of a habit starting at the age of nine, another girl, Mehsa, removes her headscarf in Istanbul and covers her head before getting on the bus to go to Tehran (Aktaş 455). At the end of the journey, when Efsane approaches customs control, the officer warns her against keeping her jacket unbuttoned and tells her a piece of hair is coming out under the headscarf. The first-person narrator mourns that the police take a role to control the women's body after the revolution in Iran. "It should not be like this. It should not be the business of the police" (Aktaş 469). The liberal tone of the narrator's voice tells us that nobody becomes more religious insomuch as they are oppressed.

The fictitious body of Muslim women in these novels written by pious Muslim women authors is depicted in spaces where they questioned their "self." In these novels, the protagonists uncover their feelings under veiled bodies that were oppressed by not only secular, but also religious authoritarian regimes of modernity and people pursuing a modern life. The characters, and by extension their authors, believe they deserve to be treated with dignity for their choices. In the novels' spaces, readers see that they can transform themselves and society to live in peace, advocate for those who are forced to be invisible, fight for their rights for education, and share the identity of women who are connected by primordial ties. The authoritarian role of the narrator transforms their voice from being the voice of "we" to the voice of "I" in time while they question their roles in the society.

Notes

1 Susan Suleiman argues that thesis novels or *"roman a these"* is a genre which is "a work of an 'Other.'" It is "a novel written in the realistic mode (that is based on aesthetic of verisimilitude and representation), which signals itself to the readers primarily didactic in intent, seeking to demonstrate the validity of political, philosophical or religious doctrine" (7).

2 The novel became popular among religious people as soon as it was published in 1967. The novel's plot takes place in a city located in the upper Nile valley in Egypt. Not only did the novel bring Muslims from Ummah into the

consideration of Turks, it also promoted Al Banna and the Muslim Brother-hood in Turkey.

3 See Tuncer for an examination of gendered spaces in Turkey, and Faroqui for a focus on gender in the Ottoman period.

4 *Da^cwa* is an Arabic word for call, appeal, or invitation associated with a missionary activity.

5 The Security Council of Turkey forced the coalition government formed by the Islamist Welfare Party and right-wing True Path Party to resign by sub-mitting a memorandum to the government. After toppling Islamists from the office, army tutelage dominated public life. It has been called the "postmod-ern coup" in the political history of Turkey.

6 The Islamic-oriented conservative Justice and Development party passed a bill to lift the ban on women who wear headscarves. Since 2013 pious Mus-lim women have been able to attend schools with their headscarves and work for the state.

7 Habermas suggests both secular and religious citizens develop a mutual epis-temological understanding through what he calls a "learning process," such that both sides can arrive at egalitarian individualism in the post-secular society ("Religion" 6).

8 In March 1971, the chief of the general staff handed the prime minister a memorandum which demanded for a government who would stop the anarchy on the streets and pursue fulfilling reforms of Kemalist ideology (Zürcher 271).

9 All English translations of Turkish novels are mine.

10 Muslim women became activists in moderate Islamist parties in 1990s and 2000s to gain their rights with their headscarves. The more the secular state put pressure on them, the more women advocated for their rights.

11 Habermas' definition of public space is the place people discuss their views freely without intervention of the hegemony of the state.

12 Although the headscarf issue has been resolved, sensitivity of religious sym-bols is still a question in Turkey.

Works Cited

Ahmed, Leila. *Women and Gender in Islam: Historical Roots of a Modern Debate.* Yale UP, 1992.

Aktaş, Cihan. *Sınıra Yakın* [Close to the Border]. İz Yayıncılık, 2012.

Barbarosoğlu, Fatma. *Fatma Aliye: Uzak Ülke* [Distant Country]. Timaş, 2004.

Çaha, Ömer. *Women and Civil Society in Turkey.* Routledge, 2013.

Çayır, Kenan. *Islamic Literature in Contemporary Turkey.* Palgrave, 2017.

Fukuyama, Francis. *Identity: A Demand for Dignity and the Politics of Resent-ment.* Picador, 2019.

Göle, Nilüfer. *The Forbidden Veiling: Civilization and Veiling.* University of Michigan, 1996.

Gündüz, Osman. "İslâmâ Ve Gelenekçi Söylem." *Yeni Türk Edebiyatı El Kitabı (1839–2000),* edited by Ramazan Korkmaz et al., Grafiker Yayınları, 2007.

Habermas, Jürgen. "Religion in the Public Sphere." *European Journal of Phi-losophy,* vol. 14, no. 1, Apr. 2006, pp. 1–25.

———. *The Structural Transformation of the Public Sphere: An Inquiry into a Category of Bourgeois Society.* Massachusetts Institute of Technology, 1991.

İsmail, Hekimoğlu. *Minyeli Abdullah.* Timaş Yayınları, 1967.

Keddie, Nikki R. *Women in the Middle East*. Princeton UP, 2007.

Özdalga, Elisabeth. *İslâmcılığın Türkiye Seyri Sosyolojik Bir Perspektif*. İletişim, 2006.

Ramazanoğlu, Yıldız. *İkna Odası* [Conviction Room]. Timaş Yayınları, 2003.

Satar, Nesrin Aydın. "Müslüman Kadının Sesi: İslâmcı Romanların Kadın Yazar ve Anlatıcıları." *Muhafazakar Düşünce Dergisi*, Yıl. 13, Sayı. 49, 2016, pp. 295–313.

Şenler, Şule Yüksel. *Peace Street, Huzur Sokağı*. Timaş, 2007.

Suleiman, Susan Rubin. *Authoritarian Fictions: The Ideological Novel as a Literary Genre*. Princeton UP, 1993.

Tuncer, Selda. *Women and Public Space in Turkey: Gender, Modernity and the Urban Experience*. I.B. Tauris, 2018.

White, Jenny B. *Muslim Nationalism and the New Turks*. Princeton UP, 2013.

Wollstonecraft, Mary. *A Vindication of the Rights of Woman: With Strictures on Political and Moral Subjects*. London, Printed for J. Johnson, 1792.

Zürcher, Erik J. *Turkey: A Modern History*. I. B. Tauris, 2004.

8 Muslim Face, White Mask

Out al-Kouloub al-Dimerdashiyyah's *Ramza* as a Mimic (Wo)man

Doaa Omran

Liberation insurgencies against the British and French colonization started in the Middle East during the nineteenth century. These
anti-colonial uprisings were also coupled with worldwide women's liberation movements. This resulted in "the emancipation of women in
Muslim countries." Egypt was no exception; it was in fact one of the
earliest revolutionary countries rising up against the British. Pictures of
the 1919 Revolution against the British mandate of Egypt show women
participating in uprisings while wearing headscarves and partial or no
face covers. In the 1940s, Egyptian women started copying more Westernized norms in their dress code—removing the headcover—ironically
mimicking the "fashion" of the colonizers they had been revolting
against. In the 1980s—and specifically after losing the 1956 and 1967
wars against Israel, England, and France—Egyptian women once more
started restoring the Islamic dress code.

Just as the dress code in Arab countries has been oscillating between the
Islamic and the secular,[1] similarly, the literary contributions of Muslim
women range from the Islamic to the secular/Westernized. Egyptian—
and Arabic—feminism is, thus, manifold and engages a broad spectrum
and is by no means monolithic. It ranges from the obviously Islamic, to
the unambiguously secular that mimics Westernized norms. While the
former depends on models from within that promote pro-women legis-
lations in the Quran and Islamic jurisprudence, the latter is contingent
on Western models in how it combats patriarchy. *Ramza* (1958) by Out
al-Kouloub al-Dimerdashiyyah (1892–1968) is an exemplary secular
Egyptian feminist work that depicts the protagonist as a mimic Muslim
(wo)man who imitates Western ideals during her quest for emancipation.

In his *Muqaddimah* (1377), the Medieval Muslim sociologist Ibn
Khaldūn dedicates a section to imitation in which he states that, "The
vanquished always want to imitate the victor in his distinctive characteristics, his dress, his occupation, and all his other conditions and customs." Ibn Khaldūn attributes this superficial imitation to the fact that
"the superiority of the victor is not the result of his group feeling or great
fortitude, but of his customs and manners" (197). Ibn Khaldūn is the
preferred native scholar whose theoretical formulation I am using here.

In *The Location of Culture* (1994), Homi Bhabha elaborates on the idea of imitating the colonizer, relating it to ambivalence: "Mimicry emerges as one of the most elusive and effective strategies of colonial power and knowledge" (85). Bhabha states that, "colonial mimicry is the desire for a reformed, recognizable Other, *as a subject of difference that is almost the same, but not quite.* Which is to say, that the discourse of mimicry is constructed around an ambivalence" (86, emphasis in original). The reason behind mimicry has also been stated by Franz Fanon in his *Black Faces, White Masks* (1952). Wearing a mask is an act of assuming a superficial identity which is not really one's own. Fanon puts it as:

> every colonized people—in other words, every people in whose soul an inferiority complex has been created by the death and burial of its local cultural originality—finds itself face to face with the language of the civilizing nation; that is, with the culture of the mother country. (9)

Even though Fanon states that the purpose of his book is to "help the *black man* free himself of the arsenal of complexes that has been developed by the colonial environment" (19; my emphasis), his theory similarly applies to the colonized Middle East as both have been resisting superior British-ness/French-ness. "The black man wants to be white" (Fanon 3) and he "becomes whiter as he renounces his blackness, his jungle" (Fanon 3, 9). This imitation trope is not only evident in black men's literature, but also in Muslim women's literature, as will be revealed in Out al-Kouloub al-Dimerdashiyyah's affiliation to the Egyptian Francophone tradition—a convention which the Dean of Arabic Literature, Taha Hussein, critiques in his *Chapters in Literature and Criticism* (1945).

By interweaving theories of post-coloniality and mimicry in reading *Ramza*, I illustrate how it is a Westernized/secular feminist text that conforms to stereotypes about Middle Eastern women as oppressed beings living in cloistered *harems* and forced to wear the veil—headscarf and face cover. Typically, the protagonist renounces her veil together with her indigenous language and traditions. I argue, thus, that Ramza is a mimic (wo)man—to adapt Naipaul's "Mimic Man." Previous research has only read *Ramza* through a feminist lens, hence underscoring Western stereotypes about Muslim women. This paper, on the other hand, attempts a postcolonial reading in order to elucidate aspects that have been neglected in earlier scholarship. According to this reading, the author is mimicking the Other and replicating stereotypes of the salient Western discourse about Muslim women rather than reacting against it. Another aspect that my paper brings to the table is introducing the notion of the liminal Francophone "mimic Muslim (wo)man" to Muslim feminist theory through exposing the hollow mimetic actions that the protagonist implements "as a vanquished" (Ibn Khaldūn 197) colonial subject. Ibn Khaldūn has been studied earlier in conjunction with Homi Bhabha,[2] however their propositions on imitation and mimicry have never been associated with each other. This paper contextualizes Ibn Khaldūn's and Bhabha's theories on imitation of the salient Other within the trope of Islamic feminism. Out al-Kouloub portrays her eponymous protagonist in *Ramza* as a rebellious figure who resists the patriarchy, breaking free from the confines of its cloistered *harem* walls. Ramza has become a feminist celebrity who had "a notorious court case many years earlier . . . in an effort to gain justice for herself but to petition for the rights of women and their emancipation . . . She had fought publicly like a man. But in her heart, she must have suffered like a woman" (al-Dimerdashiyyah 3). Ramza uses her French education to look for liberation in sources from outside her culture. Ramza's days become filled when she is introduced to her father's study that is opulent with French books. However, despite having been educated in France, her father's progressiveness does not extend to giving Ramza the liberty to choose a spouse. Ramza is a stubborn Antigone-like figure who ends up challenging her father and taking him, literally, to court after he annuls her marriage. Eventually, Ramza realizes that she has married a weakling and divorces him. Alas, this happens shortly after she becomes aware of her father's death. Ironically, while combatting misogynist rules, Ramza falls into the trap of emulating colonial norms, forsaking her native "customs [that] contain more wisdom than [she] think[s]" (al-Dimerdashiyyah 155). Ramza "camouflages"[3] into a mimic (wo)man who absorbs the highly esteemed colonial French traditions. This is evident in terms of her ambivalence toward her ethnicity, religion, language, education, dress, and culture.

Fanon's notion that "the black man is a former slave" (44) is reversed in *Ramza*, as her mother is a former Slavic slave and is now married to an Egyptian aristocratic man whose country is politically colonized by the English and culturally monopolized by the French. Being a "transcultural 'hybrid'" of mixed race: half Slavic and half Egyptian, Ramza has what Fanon defines as "two dimensions . . . [and a] divided self" (8). Swinging like a pendulum between two liminal cultures and races, her heart does not fully rest within the confines of either. She is fond of her "blue eyes [which] were said to be one of [her] best features" (al-Dimerdashiyyah 104). She identifies more with the Western side of her mother, Olga, who is ethnically an Eastern European Christian. Her mother recalls how the church in her hometown was:

> ablaze with light, and candles flickering in front of images of people with haloes around their faces. A chandelier hung like a fountain of diamonds from a limitless dome. In front of an altar, a priest with blond hair, a beard, and vestments resplendent with gold embroidery,

gave a benediction, arms raised. In the memory of the child who became my mother, this man was her father. (al-Dimerdashiyyah 8)

These "white" and full-of-light nostalgic church childhood memories
are juxtaposed with the cruelty of the Turkish slave merchants, who
abduct the child from her parents' embrace and change her name to the
Turkish, Indje.

Unlike the warm recollections of her mother's Christian past, Ramza's
rendering of Islamic rituals and practices are described as bland markers
of a lethargic life within the precincts of the harem:

> these women formed a closed circle, a community of females look-
> ing inward. Their days were punctuated with folk and religious rit-
> ual, the rhythm of habitual domestic activity, and the call to prayer
> falling like short showers from the minaret of the neighborhood
> mosque five times daily. (al-Dimerdashiyyah 5)

In his *Covering Islam*, Edward Said argues how "academic experts on
Islam, geopolitical strategists who speak of 'the crescent of crisis,' cultural
thinkers who deplore 'the decline of the West'" (xi) are misleading the
reading public. According to Said, the Western media incessantly distorts
the image of Muslims. Out al-Kouloub's description of the Islamic rituals
is not different from what Said's postulation that "Everyone knows Islam
is a 'place' you must criticize. *Time* did it, *Newsweek* did it, the *Guardian*
and the *New York Times* did it" (Said, *Reflections* 262).

Even though the novel is written in French and, thus, is primarily
directed to a European audience, Out al-Kouloub adopts the strain of
attributing a superstitious side to Islam mimicking Orientalist attitudes.
In *Ramza*, Quranic reciters are deployed in detangling the effect of the
toxic evil eye and magic (al-Dimerdashiyyah 52). Furthermore, reciting
the Quran is coupled with superstitious actions such as: scattering "seven
pinches of course salt in a circle around [one's] head" putting half in the
fire and half in the water, pinching the needle into a paper doll, and invoking the right saint when one gets sick. Ramza who is "not interested
in any of that" (64) disregards mentioning to her French audience that
these practices are pagan—and not Islamic—in essence.

In his *Chapters in Literature and Criticism* (1945), Taha Hussein dedicates a chapter to Out al-Kouloub titled "*Harem*." Even though Taha
Hussein directs his criticism to *Harem*, a novel published before *Ramza*
by twenty-one years, his assessment is valid within *Ramza*'s context:
Taha Hussein states that:

> those who read her book may be sometimes deceived by her, they
> might think that she is a Frenchwoman, writing about the Egyptians.

> She knows a great deal about the Egyptians and does not know what she is expected to be ignorant of [otherwise she will sound like an Egyptian]. (63, my trans.)

Like other post-empire writers who flirt with the West, al-Dimerdashiyyah implies that "the retreat to Islam is 'Stupefaction'" (Said, *Reflections* 257). Like other writers who "are to be castigated for not being Europeans, and this is a political pastime useless to [her]" (Said, *Reflections* 264), al-Dimerdashiyyah sees no harm in "mimicking" the prominent wave of casting some skeptical comments on Islam. Her identification with her white side in terms of ethnicity and religion is best described by Ibn Khaldūn in his depiction of how the colonized/vanquished soul interacts with its oppressor:

> The reason for this [imitation] is that the soul always sees perfection in the person who is superior to it and to whom it is subservient. It considers him perfect, either because it is impressed by the respect it has for him, or because it erroneously assumes that its own subservience to him is not due to the nature of defeat but to the perfection of the victor. If that erroneous assumption fixes itself in the soul, it becomes a firm belief. The soul, then, adopts all the manners of the victor and assimilates itself to him. This, then, is imitation. (Ibn Khaldūn 197).

Being more sympathetic toward the religion of the colonizer as well as to their language, while distancing herself from her ethnic origins gives her the "lactification"—as Fanon puts it (33)—that she aspires to have in order to hybridize herself with the victorious camp.

Homi Bhabha states that "the discourse of post-Enlightenment English colonialism often speaks in a tongue that is forked, not false" (85)—reminiscent of Shakespeare's Caliban's "cloved tongue" (2.2.13). This also applies to the influence of French in English colonized countries whose elite were educated in the French tradition. Coloniality has turned many indigenous objects into bifurcated-tongued Caliban's who "come closer to being a human being—in direct ratio to his mastery of the French [or the English] language" (Fanon 8). Ramza has been so infatuated by the French language that her father hires a French governess, Mademoiselle Hortense, to join their household and teach her French and help her "take on a world, a culture" (Fanon 25). Like the black people of the Antilles who pretend to be French (Fanon 15), Out al-Kouloub, thus, chooses to write the novel in French, not in the national tongue of her country—Arabic—as French was "the preferred language of the upper-class woman of her time" (Atiya xi). Ramza "devour[s] any work of fiction [she] lay[s] [her] hands on, in English or in French, and [her] imagination [takes] flight . . ." (al-Dimerdashiyyah 80).

The dominance of the French language among Egyptian intelligentsia explains the rise of the Francophone tradition that Out al-Kouloub belongs to. She was not alone but was among other prominent Francophone female writers such as Jehan D'ivray and Doria Shafik (*Écrire La "Femme Nouvelle" en Égypte Francophone*). Hussein critiques this Francophone tradition arguing that:

> these works [by women] suffer from a dangerous drawback that hurts and heals, pleases and aggravates, that is: they are not written in our Arabic language. These novels do not reach our Egyptian souls but through indirect ways. These works are written in a foreign language that only a few of us can master. These works are written in French so that the French people can read and praise them. It is this book that I want to talk about today, that Mrs. Out al-Kouloub wrote in French and published in France; it reached Egypt through Paris and did not reach Paris through Egypt. What shall I say! (Hussein 59, my trans.)

This Francophone phenomenon "hurts and heals, pleases and aggravates" Hussein because it promotes Egypt and its writers abroad in foreign literary milieus; in the meantime, it aggravates him because:

> Egyptians should enjoy these works before the French do. It is incumbent that the Arabic language should exclusively claim the production of its offspring. Foreigners should know these works through translating them from Arabic, it should not be that Egyptians know these works and that the Arabic language is enriched by them through translation. (Hussein 60, my trans.)

Hussein's critique of Egyptian elite's replacement of Arabic by French is suggestive of Fanon's position about how the subjects of French colonies imitate their oppressors in their language and manners avoiding local creoles. Out al-Kouloub's adoption of a language different from that of the group into which [s]he was born "is evidence of a dislocation, a separation" (Fanon 14), which gives her "a feeling of equality with the European and his achievements" (D. Westermann qtd. by Fanon 14). Given this predicament of not writing in one's own language, rather than blaming the parents for sending their children to foreign schools sabotaging the latter's mastery of their native tongue, Hussein inculpates the Egyptian state that overlooked updating teaching methodologies of Arabic to the fact that some writers produce their work in French (Hussein 60).

In his *Militant Islam*, Godfrey H. Jansen argues that the local traditional education in most Muslim countries faced "benign neglect" in that it has been outdated "not keeping with the pace of the times" (68).

These native schools had been invested in teaching the Arabic language and the Quran. By the age of nine, the Egyptian child would have memorized the Quran in full, and after that he starts memorizing the colossal thousand-line poem, *Alfiyat Ibn Malek*, which encompasses the rules of Arabic grammar in verse. "Since Arabic and Islamic tendencies were looked upon as dangerous and subversive influences they had to be excluded" (Jansen 68) by colonial regimes.

> For as long as he could, Cromer, the real ruler in Egypt, blocked all attempts to establish a university in Egypt, since it would only 'manufacture demagogues.' Cairo University was finally founded in 1907. When in 1922 the British granted 'independence' to Egypt, conditioned and regulated by a treaty with Britain, the country had its official modern educational sector no more than ten secondary schools with 3,800 pupils (forty-three of whom were girls). (Jansen 70–1)

Cromer—the British Controller-General of Egypt from 1877 to 1907—held that Egyptians should "be persuaded or forced into imbibing the true spirit of Western civilization" (Yahya). This approach is no different from Macaulay's "civilizing" mission in India as stated in the Minute of 1835, in which a "partial reform" of Indians would create a "class of interpreters between us [the English] and the millions whom we govern" (Qtd. in Bhabha 87). In her *Women and Gender in Islam*, Leila Ahmed seconds Jansen's opinion about Cromer, arguing that "the policies Cromer pursued were detrimental to Egyptian women. The restrictions he placed on government schools and his raising of school fees held back girls' education as well as boys'" (153). The result was that the socially and financially less privileged social classes in Egypt could not pursue the exorbitant education fees. Khedive Ismail (1830–95), or Ismael the Magnificent, is also an immanent historical figure in *Ramza*, as he is a friend of Ramza's father. Khedive Ismail ascended the Egyptian throne in 1863 and was a leading figure in the modernization of Egypt. He sent out young people for scholarships to France. It was also during his time that: "the first school for girls opened its doors in 1873, under the patronage of Khedive Ismael's third wife; slavery was abolished in 1877; women began to explore issues surrounding emancipation in tracts and journals as early as the 1890s" (Atiya, xv). Since Egypt was not yet fully afflicted by Cromer, Ramza was basically enjoying the educational privileges of the elite at her time.

The elite sent their sons and daughters to Westernized schools in which they were taught to "scorn the dialect" (Fanon 10), i.e., their native tongue. These children were fonder of speaking the language of the colonizing nations, pretending to be Europeans. European-ness here becomes synonymous with belonging to an elevated social stratum.

Analyzing race as a socioeconomic marker in the US, Herbert Gans in his "Race as Class," posits that,

> race functions as more than a class marker, and the correlation be-
> tween race and the socioeconomic pecking order is far from statis-
> tically perfect: All races can be found at every level of that order.
> Still, the race-class correlation is strong enough to utilize race for the
> general ranking of others. (18)

By analogy, affiliation to European people, languages, and cultures are signifiers of an elevated socioeconomic class in Egypt. By way of expla-nation, speaking the language of a certain race is intersectional with the social class one belongs to. Similarly, Ramza has a French governess and before she joins the elite Sanieh School where she "had a British head-mistress whom [they] feared; Italian teachers for music, art, and sing-ing; a robust young Swede taught [them] gymnastics; and a Swiss lady initiated [them] into the art of home economics. . . . [They] were taught French, Turkish, and English" (al-Dimerdashiyyah 75), and, of course, there is no mention of Arabic. Ramza becomes a product of an alien Western educational system that is not sprouting from native grounds. The result is "flawed colonial mimesis" (Bhabha 87).

Franz Fanon states that, "White civilization and European culture have forced an existential deviation" on their colonial subjects (6) re-sulting in two dimensional characters: "This self-division is a direct result of colonialist subjugation" (8). This "subjugation" extends to student-teacher relationships. A colonized student, like Ramza, prefers to be taught by Europeans; she even esteems her European teachers more than her indigenous ones.

Extending Hegel's Master-Slave dialectic to, what I would name European teacher-indigenous student dialectic, I postulate that Ramza bears low respect for natives who teach her Arabic language, the Quran, and local geography as opposed to the veneration she expresses toward her foreign mentors who teach her about Europe, its geography and its languages. She portrays her two indigenous teachers as idiosyncratically backward. She narrates how Ustez Hefny is a cruel educator who would smack her fingers dryly with a ruler. She enjoyed mocking him by,

> hiding the rags [he used to clean the slate with] and delighted in
> watching Ustez Hefny search for them. If he did not find them, he
> would pull out a huge cotton handkerchief from his *kaftan* to do the
> job. Sometimes he even licked the slate clean, and [she] took pleasure
> in imitating the master. (al-Dimerdashiyyah 55)

Sheikh Nassif, another indigenous teacher, has taught her Arabic gram-mar, composition, and arithmetic so that she can, "to keep household accounts." And he taught her "the Qur'an in order to bring up [her] children in the Islamic faith" (al-Dimerdashiyyah 72). The old-fashioned sheikh was, of course, reticent to teach her geography. Her father had to convince—or rather command—the teacher in a condescending simplistic manner so that the latter's naïve mentality would comprehend that,

> the study of geography is intended us to make us better appreciate God's creation. Even the Qur'an relies on geography when it says Allah is the creator of the Orient and the Occident. I wish for Ramza to understand the meaning of these terms. You will teach her geography.
> The sheikh has to agree, but he did it without grace. (al-Dimerdashiyyah 73)

The depiction of Egyptian teachers as antiquated conforms to Said's ideas of an ancient outdated Orient that needs the "West [to] modernize [it]" (Said, *Orientalism* 43). As a mimic (wo)man, Ramza reiterates Said's theory of "hegemonic" colonialist discourse (Said, *Orientalism* 7).

Europe has been "setting itself off against the Orient as a sort of surrogate and even underground self" (Said, *Orientalism* 3), and European teachers are no exception. Ramza is representative of students belonging to a socioeconomic elite raised in colonial missionary schools who would prefer to have colonial pedagogical "masters" rather than brown-skinned colonized teachers. As far as her French governess is concerned, Ramza declares that she: "feel[s she] owe[s] her a great deal . . . her company and conversation considerably widened [her] horizons. She taught [Ramza] a language, drawing, music, embroidery, manners, and bequeathed to [Ramza] all the trappings of her genteel European upbringing" (al-Dimerdashiyyah 70–1). Mademoiselle Hortense introduces Ramza to European "refinement," and offering her thus what Fanon designates as the cultural "lactification"—as Fanon puts it (33)— one needs to become a European mimic in terms of knowledge, as well as in manners. Hence, Ramza counts on "[Mademoiselle] to raise [her] children" (al-Dimerdashiyyah 134).

In his *Pedagogy of the Oppressed*, Paulo Freire poses the important question of: "How can the oppressed, as divided, unauthentic beings, participate in developing the pedagogy of their liberation?" (48). Freire maintains that the colonially oppressed are possessed "by the fear for freedom" (47) and thus need to acquiesce to the "false generosity" (44) and the "false charity" of the oppressor before they have the faith in themselves to implement "a liberating education" in order to liberate their pedagogy from colonial influences (54). That master, I argue, would rather be a European rather than a native, as colonial students aspire to internalize the colonizer. The teacher has to be a European master who possesses the appropriate up-to-date know-how pedagogical tools.

Unlike the local teacher, who introduce Ramza only to local geography, "it was Mademoiselle who introduced [her] to a greater world picture" (al-Dimerdashiyyah 73).

Not only does the rejection of the native master include teachers, but it also extends to portraying religious authority in a negative light. Just as Ustez Hefny is portrayed as someone who exchanges his teaching assignments for just a *kaftan* (al-Dimerdashiyyah 56), so is the *mazoon* (the man of religion who is permitted to unite couples in marriage). The bribable "*mazoon* had been reluctant at first but had changed his mind when [her husband] put a sum of money in the corner of his desk" (al-Dimerdashiyyah 150). Moreover, Ramza passes the assumption that men dressed in clerical garb are not progressive as she does of Sheikh Mustafa "who although he was dressed in clerical garb, that is he wore a *kaftan*, overcoat, and turban, he had liberal views" (158). Even though Sheikh Mustafa is portrayed in a more positive light than the other three men of religion, the inefficiency of the Sheikh is questioned as he cannot win on the face of her father who also had asked for the help of Lord Cromer who had in turn "intervened on behalf of [her] father in the case" (162) for annulling her marriage. As mentioned above, Cromer had always interceded to impede women's rights in Egypt. The failure of both Sheikh Mustafa—and Khedive Abbas—to help her win her marriage case in the face of Lord Cromer's anti-feminist moves proves, if anything, the failure of her native Egyptians to be reliable masters who can combat patriarchal outdated norms that are supported by the British colonization.

Going beyond incorporating the language of the colonizer and adopting his educational system, mimicry includes various aspects of incorporating the superior's culture into one's life and performing them (Bhabha 142). In his *The Predicament of Culture: Twentieth-Century Ethnography, Literature and Art*, James Clifford puts it: "self-other relations are matters of power and rhetoric rather than of essence" (14). Ramza is representative of leaning toward the heavier side of the scale. Not only, does she disconnect herself from her Arabic and Islamic roots, but also the distant history of her ancestors. She has no interest in the pharaonic "prodigious civilization" (al-Dimerdashiyyah 101) as was "typical of Egyptians of [her] generation. [She] fe[els] indifferent to the civilization of 'our ancestors,' as [her] father called them" (101). She implies that it can even be a subject of mockery if young people go visit the Museum of Antiques (102–3). The Europeanized Ramza fails to comply with Clifford's postulation that "Twentieth-century identities . . . improvise local performances from (re)collected pasts" (14), as she sneaks away also from her Pharaonic heritage and takes refuge in European literature instead. The binding of the Arabic manuscripts may have attracted Ramza's attention (al-Dimerdashiyyah 27), but the contents of the French books feed her soul better. She states that she devoured works of English and French literature such as *Clarissa, The Picture of Dorian*

Gray, and *Les Vieges Fortes*, imagining "like the European and English heroines of stories" (al-Dimerdashiyyah 80).

She admires everything European and wants to live like one. She admires Alexandria as it "was more European, freer, more relaxed than Cairo" (al-Dimerdashiyyah 112). She wants to furnish her matrimonial house with "European furniture [and] a grand piano" (88), she dreams of being courted in French (89). She aspires to be dressed like the French (90–1) verifying Ibn Khaldūn's notion that, "The vanquished always want to imitate the victor in his distinctive characteristics, his dress, his occupation, and all his other conditions and customs" (197). Emulating the victorious is representative of "a system of subject formation—a reform of manners" (Bhabha 87) that requires "colonial appropriation" (Bhabha 86) making the subjected turn into cultural dupes that lean toward the stronger side mimicking the customs of the European colonizer. Going beyond theory, an expression which best describes assimilation of the oppressor exists in the present-day Egyptian dialect; it is عقدة الخواجة "u'qdat al-khawaga" or "the foreigner's complex." "al-Khawaga" specifically refers to the European foreigner. This idiom is widely used to mockingly describe an Egyptian person who imitates the Europeans in order to put an act of equally being superior.

To sum up, I define a mimic Muslim (wo)man as a mottled cultural and linguistic product of the colonialist/post-colonialist establishment. The cultured mimic Muslim (wo)man would sacrifice her local traditions and culture for the sake of European alternatives, considering her Islamic and Arabic values tokens of backwardness, inferiority, and social underprivilege. Thus, lack of knowledge of Arabic and the Quran is no major concern of hers whereas intimate knowledge of English and/or of French are well-sought aspirations. She would rather express herself in French or in English, or would, at least, intersperse her speech using European expressions, superficially mimicking the tongue of her "European mistresses." Despite the fact that Arabic is the language of the Quran—the most revered book in the Muslim world and the only book in history on which a civilization and an empire were founded, the cultured mimic Muslim (wo)man could not care less. Hence, I argue that within the boundaries of Islamic feminism falls the two categories of the mimic Muslim woman and her conservative Islamic counterpart. Out al-Kouloub's Ramza definitely leans more in favor of the cultured mimic Muslim (wo)man extreme.

Notes

1 Secular and Islamic feminisms have been studied in works such as "Between Secular and Islamic Feminism/s: Reflections on the Middle East and Beyond" by Margot Badran and "Dilemmas of Islamic and Secular Feminists and Feminisms" by Huma Ahmed-Ghosh.

2 Ibn Khaldūn *Muqaddimah* and Homi Bhabha's *The Location of Culture* have been studied in conjunction with each other in works such Mohammad R. Salama's *Islam, Orientalism and Intellectual History: Modernity and the Politics of Exclusion since Ibn Khaldūn* and Ahmed Gamal's "Rewriting Strategies in Tariq Ali's Postcolonial Metafiction." However, none of these studies examine their propositions on imitation and mimicry.

3 Bhabha uses the term "camouflage" when he quotes Jacques Lacan's *The Line and the Light of the Gaze.*

Works Cited

Ahmed, Leila. *Women and Gender in Islam: Historical Roots of a Modern Debate.* The American U in Cairo P, 1998.

al-Dimerdashiyyah, Out al-Kouloub. *Harem.* Navila, 2009.

———. *Ramza.* Translated by Nayra Atiya, 1st ed., Syracuse University Press, 1994.

Atiya, Nayra. Introduction. al-Dimerdashiyyah, *Ramza*, pp. xi–xix.

Bhabha, Homi K. *The Location of Culture.* Routledge, 1994.

Clifford, James. *The Predicament of Culture: Twentieth-Century Ethnography, Literature, and Art.* Harvard UP, 1988.

Fanon, Franz. *Black Faces, White Masks.* 1952. Translated by Charles Lam Markmann, Pluto P, 2008.

Freire, Paulo. *Pedagogy of the Oppressed.* 30th anniversary ed., Continuum, 2000.

Gaden, Élodie. *Écrire La "Femme Nouvelle": En Égypte Francophone: 1898–1961.* Classiques Garnier, 2019.

Gans, Herbert J. "Race as Class." *Contexts*, vol. 4, no. 4, Nov. 2005, pp. 17–21.

Hegel, Georg Wilhelm Friedrich, and Terry P. Pinkard. *The Phenomenology of Spirit.* Cambridge UP, 2018.

Hussein, Taha. فصول في الادب و النقد *[Chapters in Literature and Criticism].* Dar al-Maa'rif, 1945.

Ibn Khaldūn, et al. *The Muqaddimah: An Introduction to History.* 1st Princeton classic ed., introduction by Bruce B. Lawrence, Princeton UP, 2005.

Ibn Malik, Mohamed Ibn Abd-Allah. *Alfiyat Ibn Malik wa ma'aha lamiyat al-af'al.* N.p., Dif.

Jansen, Godfrey H. *Militant Islam.* 1st U.S. ed., Harper & Row, 1979.

Naipaul, V. S. *The Mimic Men.* 1st Vintage International ed., Vintage Books, 2001.

Said, Edward W. *Covering Islam: How the Media and the Experts Determine How We See the Rest of the World.* 1st ed., Pantheon Books, 1981.

———. *Orientalism.* Penguin Books, 2003.

———. *Reflections on Exile and Other Essays.* Harvard UP, 2000.

Shakespeare, William and David Lindley. *The Tempest.* Updated edition, Cambridge UP, 2013.

Yahya, Adnan Harun. "British Provocateur: Lord Cromer." *British Deep State*, 22 Nov. 2017.

9 Same-sex Relations in Modern Arabic Fiction between Empowerment and Impossibility

A Case Study of Samar Yazbek's *Cinnamon*

Rima Sadek

Ra'ihat al-qirfah (The Cinnamon's Aroma), by Syrian writer, Samar Yazbek, is first published in 2008 and translated by Emily Dandy as *Cinnamon* in 2012. The in-text references are from Dandy's translation. It is one of several recent works portraying a female same-sex relation between its two protagonists. Representations of same-sex relations in modern Arabic literature spans a wide range of texts. *Innaha London Ya 'Azizi* (Only in London) (2001) by Hanan al-Shaykh, *Hajar al-Dahk* (The Stone of Laughter) (1990) and *Sayyidi wa-Habibi* (My Master and My Beloved) (2004) by Hoda Barakat, *'Imarat Ya'qubyan* (The Yacoubian Building) (2004) by Ala al-Aswani, *Ana Hiya Anty* (I am You) (2000) by Elham Mansour, and Najib Mahfuz's *Zuqaq al-Midaqq* (Midaq Alley) (1947) are but a few examples. Contemporary Arabic novels are increasingly depicting homosexual and homoerotic relationships—an exposure driven by globalization and trans-national connections.

This increased visibility is also drawing mixed and often perplexed responses from literary critics and from the larger Arab society. Often, these responses dismiss similar relations, arguing they are essentially a revolt against socio-political and gender inequalities. Hence, they constitute a temporary, anomalous substitute to the general heteronormative norm. I argue that female same-sex relations exhibit a challenge to the dominant structures of patriarchy, referred to as the norm. This dimension should not be sidelined in the analysis of works like *Cinnamon*. My argument draws mainly on Judith Butler's study on the reciprocity between performativity and agency. Executed through the body, performances that don't conform to the dominant heteropatriarchal norms constitute a subversive political act, a moment of change. Women use their bodies in subversive same-sex relations; a performance that alters and rearticulates the conventional wisdom around oppressive patriarchal "norms."

The Syrian novel *Cinnamon* in its 124 pages chronicles the tumultuous relationship between the older, white, rich, and deranged Hanan al-Hashimi and her young, brown, poor maid, Aliya. The novel, primarily composed of flashbacks, opens with Hanan discovering Aliya in the bed of her husband, Anwar. The "streak of light" left by the open door serves as a motif for Hanan's self-doubt throughout the beginning of the novel. Only as the novel progresses, however, does the reason for her uncertainty and vehemence become clear; she feels not betrayed by her husband, but instead by the true object of her affections, Aliya. Despite these affections, Hanan kicks Aliya out of her mansion. The novel ends with Aliya walking back toward her previous life in the slums of the al-Raml neighborhood outside Damascus, followed by Hanan's mental derangement ensuing the loss of her object of passion.

In *Female Homosexuality in the Middle East, Histories and Representations*, Samar Habib links the dozen negative newspaper reviews on Mansour's novel, *Ana Hiya Anty* (I am You) to the subject-matter of homosexuality: "This onslaught of criticism appeared to be significantly motivated by hidden moral prerogatives" (89). Habib states that *Ana Hiya Anty* is one of the few novels dealing exclusively with the issue of female homosexuality as sexual tendency and identity. On the other hand, Yazbek's *Cinnamon*, for the most part, has received positive newspaper and magazine reviews that praised the novel as well-written and well-structured.

Cinnamon is praised, mainly, on moral grounds, highlighting Yazbek's skillful use of the issue of female same-sex relations to criticize the socioeconomics of the Syrian society. In "The Contemporary Syrian Novel in Translation," Anne Marie McManus mentions that Yazbek's newfound celebrity status as chronicler of the Syrian revolution, may tempt readers to approach *Cinnamon* as a prophetic precursor to the Syrian revolution, triggered in the year 2011: "Yet in this novel about two women's intimate world, readers will be hard pressed to find direct representations of Syrian society on the brink, as it were, of a revolution that has had ambiguous implications for women" (326). This position seems to be echoed by Yazbek's own words in an interview in 2011, quoted here by Martina Censi: "Actually I wanted to talk about the changes in Syrian society, the disappearance of the middle class and the great difference between the world of the upper classes and that of lower classes" (Censi 300). Thus, it appears that *Cinnamon* uses female homoeroticism as a paradigm to criticize the political and socioeconomic injustices of the Syrian society.

In that same article entitled "Rewriting the Body in the Novels of Contemporary Syrian Women Writers," Censi argues that same-sex love affairs between the two protagonists who, at first, appear as an alternative to violent heterosexual relationships, soon exhibit the same violence and oppression of lesbian relationships. She goes on to posit that homosexual relationships are not based on free choice, but on the impossibility of communication between a man and a woman.

In "Out of the Closet: Representations of Homosexuals and Lesbians in Modern Arabic Literature," Hanadi al-Samman states that homosexuality, as portrayed in modern Arabic literature, is predominantly an outlet for feelings of frustration and anger. al-Samman claims that representations of homosexuality, especially lesbianism in this literature is a prelude to, abnormal deviation from, or a temporary replacement of normative heterosexuality. This literature, according to al-Samman, does not give attention to the biological essence of homosexuality or body politics, rather it presents homosexuality as an outlet for feelings of alienation, anger, and outrage experienced by the Arab individual, especially the male individual enduring wars, economic hardships, dictatorships, and colonialism (270). This observation, similar to Samar Habib's, explains the attitudes we find in most reviews, stressing the victimhood of Aliya and the victimhood of women in the novel as a prelude or excuse for having what is considered abnormal sexual relations.

In this paper, I stay away from categorical terms of classification such as "lesbian" or "homosexual" because first, most women engaging in same-sex relations in the novel are married to men and second, they fit Samar Habib's analysis detailing the common reactions to novels portraying homosexual encounters. That is, homosexuality happens for external, most often unfortunate, reasons such as harshness of men, experience of sexual trauma (with men), and a woman's mental derangement. However, central to the exploration in this paper is recentralizing the subversive and progressive effects of female same-sex relations as acts of empowerment despite the constant reminders of the impossibility of such empowerment.

Primarily expressed through her marriage to Anwar, Hanan's heterosexual relationships in the novel are described as passionless. Her parents married her to Anwar at the age of fifteen, and given that he is her cousin, she has felt close familial ties to him. As demonstrated through a flashback, the young Hanan could not expect nor imagine that Anwar, someone like a big brother, would become her husband. At the word husband, "her skin crawled" (Yazbek 117). At the beginning of the novel, later in their marriage, she describes Anwar as "the old crocodile" and is disgusted by his snoring and his "cold body" (Yazbek 11). She seems incredulous that Aliya could even get near his hideous form, feeling inferior by comparison.

Aliya's heterosexual encounters are described not only as passionless, but also as violent and subordinating. In her family home in al-Raml's slum, her father is depicted as a figure of constant abuse: raping her mother, crippling and ultimately killing her older sister, and subjecting his children to unbelievable torment. Aliya's first experiences with heterosexuality are demarcated by rape, be it by watching her parents' abusive relationship, or by discovering her older sister's constant rape by their neighbor, Aboud, while being crippled. Despite these atrocities, her mother insisted to her that: "Any man's better than no man at all" (Yazbek 36). Unfortunately, and unsurprisingly, Aliya's own heterosexual encounters also take the form of sexual violence. As told through flashbacks, Aliya joins a group of children her own age to search through garbage, including a boy named Suzuki. Suzuki eventually gets her on her own and she is brutally raped like her sister before her. Disturbingly, as Yazbek writes, "[t]his had all happened when she was still only ten years old" (83). These heterosexual encounters are entirely sexual and do not prioritize—let alone include—pleasure, something central to the female same-sex relationships in the novel.

The relationship between Hanan and Aliya is revealed to be of a sensual nature about halfway through the novel, again revealed through a flashback. The two women share a bath together while cinnamon tea brews beside them. "I've never felt anything sweeter than the pleasure your fingers give me," Hanan tells Aliya, her words "floating over the foamy bath-water" (Yazbek 50). The dialogue in this scene speaks of burning desire, eternal bliss, and softness, painting a portrait of sensuality and pleasure in stark contrast to the violence and pain witnessed by both women—particularly Aliya—before. In fact, Hanan even makes a direct comparison to heterosexual relationships while they share this moment. "Your fingers are firm—nothing like a limp piece of crocodile flesh," she says to Aliya, comparing the maid's fingers to her husband's genitals. "Do you know what it's like to lie beneath an old crocodile—a foaming, drooling, panting crocodile?" (Yazbek 51) Hanan asks, oblivious to Aliya's own experiences. It is clear that Hanan is expressing a preference for this type of encounter, one with "delicious fingers" as opposed to those that "end in humiliating flaccidity" (Yazbek 51). Though there is a sexual component to this scene, given that the women "made love" with their fingers, it is the overwhelming sensuality that is captured which makes the encounter fundamentally different from the scenes of heterosexual experience in the novel.

Given her youth, Aliya's only same-sex encounter is with Hanan, to whom she is sold at the age of eleven. In many ways, the mansion represents salvation for Aliya from the powerful grip of poverty and violence. Hanan is also a salvation. Aliya describes the scent of the mansion as being profoundly "different to the rotten odor that she had lived with for so many months, that had lingered in her nostrils until Hanan's fingers and the scent of cinnamon tea had washed away all the scents that came before" (Yazbek 77). Furthermore, Aliya gleans self-confidence from these encounters with Hanan: "Aliya had taken her own existence and her own self-confidence from where she had found it: within Hanan's body. Before that, she was nothing. After all, wasn't she now capable of making such a rich, beautiful woman happy!" (Yazbek 94). This indicates an empowerment being gleaned from Aliya's primary same-sex relationship, in stark contrast to the intense disempowerment of her assaults. The sensuality and prioritization of pleasure in her relationship with Hanan subverts the subordination present in the novel's normative heterosexual relationships.

Hanan, due to her age and social mobility, has other same-sex encounters throughout the narrative. In particular, she has a relationship with a woman named Nazek, whom she meets through her husband's social network. These wives of many of Anwar's friends attend functions together in Nazek's home without the company of their husbands, whom Hanan describes as such:

> Most of the girls had married young and each one of them had a female lover. Very few people knew exactly what was going on, since their gatherings were monopolized by women, and the men felt quite secure when their wives were in female company, even if there was something unsettling about their friendship. So long as the relationship remained a secret, there was no problem, but as soon as rumors started, the husband would sever the relationship between his wife and her companion. (Yazbek 71)

These events capture a peculiar dynamic of the female same-sex relationship in *Cinnamon*: companionship. These relationships, though they may very well be sexual in nature, are first and foremost homosocial. They are about female company outside of the male gaze and male expectations. In this same flashback, Nazek describes female same-sex relationships to Hanan in direct comparison to heterosexual relationships. With women, she says, "love is different. When passion takes hold of you and you are completely absorbed in your lover's kiss, she is all of those men in one: a lover, a friend and an everlasting object of desire" (Yazbek 70). In same-sex relationships then, the female lover takes on multiple male roles instead of simply being a lover.

Hanan experiences her first sexual pleasure, which is of homosexual nature, as a child, when she accompanies her mother to a bridal shower in a Damascus *Hammam*. The *Hammam* is a place covered with white marble where women of upper class, mostly naked, have their bodies scrubbed with aromatic soaps and massaged with oils and herbs. The place is associated with white colors, bright sights, appealing fragrances, and soothing, enchanted ambiances. These associations of the bright, beautiful sights and aromatic fragrances, especially the sweet aroma of cinnamon, recur constantly in the novel whenever female sexual encounters happen. The aroma of the cinnamon is the metaphor referring to the nature of these encounters.

Yazbek sets a dichotomy between heterosexual and same-sex relations, among women. The former are, almost exclusively, portrayed as violent, oppressive, objectifying, dull and humiliating. These types of relationships are associated with repulsive scents and unpleasant scenes. On the other hand, female same-sex acts are described as pleasant, appealing, soft, exciting, and gratifying. They are associated with the aroma of cinnamon and with bright, colorful scenes. This dichotomy, I argue, problematizes the notion of natural or moral when it comes to sexuality, portraying female same-sex relations as more natural, compassionate, and moral than their heterosexual counterparts.

The narrative technique of binary oppositions creates an alternative world where both women are sheltered from the hardships and pain they have experienced in their previous lives. Happiness and pleasure prevail in this alternative world where bad odors are replaced with the aroma of cinnamon, where colorful scenes overtake dark ones, alluding to the predominance of female same-sex relations over heterosexual ones. Nevertheless, the binary opposition technique is considered to be incoherent with a feminist writing style and therefore, alludes to the impossibility of the realization of a positive change through same-sex relations. The tragic end of Hanan and Aliya's story, symbolized by the obliteration of the cinnamon's aroma, speaks to this impossibility.

Hanan's adoration and lust for her maid gives Aliya a false impression of equality. The symbolic power structure dynamic is maintained by Aliya leaving Hanan's bed before the break of the dawn, protecting the secrecy of the relationship and the social hierarchy of mistress and maid. When Aliya stays in Hanan's bed until sunrise, Hanan gets mad and kicks her out of her room, primarily to reestablish that social hierarchy. Insulted and hurt, Aliya starts seducing Anwar and would leave his bedroom door half-open to ensure Hanan would see her in Anwar's bed. When this happens, Hanan, in a fit of madness, rage and jealousy, throws Aliya outside her house. Then she drives around hysterically while still in her nightgown looking for Aliya in Damascus' streets.

In "Female Homosexuality in the Contemporary Arabic novel," Jolanda Guardi says:

> *Cinnamon* is a mainstream novel, i.e. it inserts itself in a discourse near to power because it shows us Hanan, the Westernized Bourgeois (presented as) a perverted woman, the "bored woman" and Aliya, who at the end of the novel returns home to her exploited life. There is no real relation between the two characters and no hope for a possibility of empowerment. (Guardi 21)

Guardi contends that Yazbek's novel ends with a sense of despair and does not provide any possibility for hope or empowerment. She bases her argument analyzing the two elements of subject matter and narrative technique being used by Yazbek. On the issue of subject matter, Guardi says that Yazbek's novel does not address homosexuality because the two protagonists do not identify as lesbians. Hence, Hanan and Aliya's relationship is one of exploitation of a poor maid by a rich mistress dissatisfied with her life and marriage. In Guardi's analysis,

Aliya, the victim, finds herself driven to sleep with her master as an act of revenge against Hanan because of the level of inequality between the two. Henceforth, this story is devoid of any real love or affection and is mainly a story about class differences between rich and poor. In such a context, there is no avenue for hope or emancipation, whether futuristic or imaginative: "In *Cinnamon*, the homosexual intercourse is presented as a power relationship between the master and the black slave, thus perpetrating a patriarchal stereotype" (Guardi 20).

The perpetration of patriarchal stereotypes, according to Guardi is also found on the level of the narrative technique based on binary oppositions or juxtapositions. According to Guardi, who uses Sedgwick's analysis, the binary system between homosexual/heterosexual male/female, health/illness, natural/unnatural is a heteronormative epistemological system: "The power discourse, through other related discourses . . . makes our perception of the world possible only through this binary system, and therefore we can perceive sex only as heteronormative (woman/ man) . . ." (Guardi 26). Thus, if a deconstruction through this novel is ongoing, it should break the binary couple. Instead, "the novel's structure does not challenge the heteropatriarchal norm and therefore the presence of a female homosexual character is only functional to reproduce the male structure of society" (Guardi 27).

In "The Lesbian Subjectivity in Contemporary Arabic Literature," Iman al-Ghafari comments on the absence of lesbian literature in modern Arabic fiction, despite the increasing number of novels representing female same-sex relations. al-Ghafari states that lesbian relations are often condemned as a radical feminist tool for liberation, and as such are put under a heterosexist and male-oriented gaze, denying them public visibility and acknowledgment as legitimate self/ identity constructs. Instead, they are confined to the private sphere and to secrecy featuring tragic endings, similar to Aliya and Hana's fate. Commenting on Yazbek's work, al-Ghafari argues: "The author uses the Damascene culture as a means of asserting stereotypes and repeating some pre-conceived ideas about female same-sex relations" (12). Khaled Hadeed uses the term "epistemic closure" to describe a similar position. In his article, "Homosexuality and Epistemic Closure in Modern Arabic Literature," using Eve Sedgwick's notion of "minoritizing view" versus "universalizing view," Hadeed states that most contemporary Arab writers have obeyed an implicit cultural mandate to adopt the "minoritizing view" when dealing with homosexuality. This view sets a clear dichotomy/separation between two groups, gay and straight attributing to each a set of solid boundaries and demarcations instead of a porous one. According to Hadeed: "It's an effort to restrict the meaning of homosexuality to a set of repertoires of genders, desires, and explanatory narrative—what I call 'epistemic closure' . . . reading it as a form of social control" (272).

As mentioned before, this analysis does not assert that Yazbek is advocating for homosexuality, queer, or lesbian sexual identity as elaborated within Western epistemology. As Joseph Massad in *Desiring Arabs* argues, in the Arab world, it is the publicness of sexual identities rather than the sexual acts themselves that elicits oppression: "The campaign of the Gay international misses this important distinction. It is not the same-sex sexual practices that are being repressed . . . but rather the sociopolitical identification of these practices . . ." (Massad 183). In "Thinking Past Pride: Queer Arab Shame in *Bareed Mista3jil*," Dina Georgis materializes this idea in her analysis of *Bareed Mista3jil*, a collection of anonymous true stories of Lebanese queer women and their struggles with their queerness and sexual identity. Georgis argues that these stories reveal a new cultivation and negotiation of sexual identity under a variety of social and geopolitical circumstances very different in nature and form from their Western counterparts. The women telling their stories in *Bareed Mista3jil* are not trying to appropriate Western queer epistemology, but are coming together to imagine ways of reconciliation between their sexual identities and culture. They are trying to organize and find possible ways of living in their specific context. Georgis characterizes this endeavor by replacing the word "pride" and "coming out" with the word "hope" (233).

These voices might help us understand Yazbek's approach concerning the intricacy of Hanan and Aliya's relationship, the element of secrecy in their relationship, the tragic nature of the two characters, and the tragic end of the story altogether. It helps us understand why the text sets a contrast between night and day, where the first symbolizes a utopian, imaginary world represented by the cinnamon's aroma and the second is the world of reality. The only way the former is possible is by respecting the norms of the latter, which are disrupted and twisted in the secrecy of the night, only. This secrecy is featured in all same-sex encounters like Aliya and Hana's relation, in the *Hammam*, as well as in Nazek's house. This element of secrecy and alternation between night and day, between Aliya the servant and Aliya the queen, between Hanan the passionate lover and Hanan the aristocratic hysterical woman represent the fragile nature of the cinnamon's aroma and what it represents. However, the fragility of the alternative world of the cinnamon's aroma does not necessarily eliminate the existence of possible acts of subversion and empowerment found on the level of dissident performative sexual encounters.

Yazbek's novel, like many other novels in contemporary Arabic fiction, lacks attention to the subjectivity of lesbian identity and subordinates same-sex relations to patriarchal-heteronormative structures. However, the lack of subjectivity understood as an essence or a natural trait opens up avenues of female empowerment existing on the level of performance. I refer to Butler to analyze how alternative same-sex relationships provide subversive examples to hetero-patriarchal structures.

In *Bodies that Matter, On the Discursive Limits of Sex*, Judith Butler says, a body that does not confirm her/himself to the heteropatriarchal norm is a subversive political body. According to Butler, sex is material-ized through a highly regulated process of a compulsory power through repetitive reiterations. This compulsory performative power affirms that the subject never exists outside the regulatory norms which constitute him/her as a subject. Hence, if sexed bodies are formed and materialized through compulsory, regulated, and reiterative performances, therefore, agency ex-ists at that same level of performance. Agency is the reactionary behav-ior or the re-articulation of these very norms through which the subject is subjectified at first place. Sexual performance, is one form of reactionary and re-articulatory practice from within the system of regulated norms and practices that have regulated or have constituted the subject as we know it:

> regulatory norms materialize "sex" and achieve this materialization through a forcible reiteration of those norms, that this reiteration is necessary is a sign that materialization is never quite complete . . . Indeed, it is the instabilities, the possibilities for rematerialization, opened up by this process that mark one domain in which the force of the regulatory law can be turned against itself. . . . (Butler, *Bodies That Matter* xii)

Referencing Foucault, Butler contends that power is not only imposed from outside, but is within the regulatory norms that constitute the subjects it comes to control: "regulatory power produces the subjects it controls, that power is not only imposed externally, but works as the regulatory and normative means by which subjects are formed" (Butler, *Bodies That Matter* xxix). Hence, agency, is not necessarily the volun-tary act of a subject existing outside the regulatory norms of power. But agency is performative reiterative acts emanating from within the normative power structures: "it does locate agency as a reiterative or rearticulatory practice, immanent to power, and not a relation of exter-nal opposition to power" (Butler, *Bodies That Matter* xxiii). The queer, the unintelligible, or the deviating from the norm in its definition as compulsory reiterative acts, constitute an opposition to the regulatory power apparatuses. It challenges the symbolic order, constituting a new reworking or re-articulation of that order. It creates, according to Butler, a moment of change. Sex, as a constrained production and highly regu-lated domain, sets the boundaries for what qualifies as body by regulat-ing the terms by which bodies are and are not sustained. Butler studies how what has been banished from the proper domain of sex returns to stir things and rearticulate the symbolic in which bodies come to matter. As such, the performance of sexual acts outside the norm of the restric-tive constraints of sexed bodies, is a reworking and a challenge to those norms, and therefore a potential site of agency.

In addition, performativity, through words and actions, produces gender and sexuality as "constructed" components of one's identity. The act of performance has the potential to displace categories or at least loosen their boundaries opening these categories to new, subversive interpretations. If agency exists at the level of performance, in our case, Aliya and Hanan's agency is figuratively named "cinnamon's aroma" which, in reality, is a sexual performance enacted in opposition to regulated norms. This performance constitutes a re-articulation and reworking of these norms. Performance is a powerful tool of subversion, but also, repetitive performances, in this case sexual performances, produce "essential" gender and sexual identities, or what Butler calls the constituted "I": "the constituted character of the subject is the very precondition of its agency. For what is it that enables a purposive and significant reconfiguration of cultural and political relations, if not a relation that can be turned against itself, reworked, resisted" (Butler et al, *Feminist Contentions* 46). In this sense, rather than establishing a clear demarcation between outside and inside, between identity and performance, Butler presents a more malleable, continuous definition process of exchange between the two entities.

In this regard, *Cinnamon*, can be considered as one of the works cracking what Hadeed calls "epistemic closure"—similar to Barakat's *Sayyidi wa-Habibi*, described by Hadeed as one of the few works that resist the cultural mandate of "epistemic closure" (272). A cracking linked to the very fact of the lack of lesbian subjectivity. *Cinnamon* presents a certain crossing between the two categories of gay/straight through performativity. The novel is mainly about a homoerotic relation between Hanan and Aliya, even though the two women lack a specific lesbian/homosexual self-identity. This crossing—enacted on the level of performance—destabilizes the boundaries between body and culture, between performance and essence, and between gay and straight. In this sense, the novel elaborates the complexities and interconnectedness of homosexual and homosocial boundaries. Hadeed calls this the "universalizing view," that sees homo/heterosexual definition as a continuous and malleable process and that locates the homoerotic within the homosocial, avoiding the epistemic closure that constricts the meaning and boundaries of homosexuality. I would also argue that *Cinnamon* circumvents the binary opposition technique considered a masculine way of writing, as mentioned by Guardi. Instead, it complicates the binary categories by having women perform same-sex relations as acts of dissent and empowerment.

In *This Sex which is Not One*, Luce Irigaray contends that women, sexually speaking, are mainly a use-value, an exchange value, or commodity among men. If women strive to change this reality, they have to set themselves apart from men and discover the love of other women:

For women to undertake tactical strikes, to keep themselves apart from men long enough to learn to defend their desires, especially through speech, to discover the love of other women while sheltered from men's imperious choices that put them in the position of rival commodities . . . these are certainly indispensable stages in the escape from their proletarization on the exchange market. (Irigaray 33)

In *Cinnamon*, women are using their bodies as sites of resistance to an outside social order of objectification and commodification. The figurative world of the aroma of cinnamon alludes to a retreat from the outside, cruel world to an internal world of comfort, companionship, pleasure, and ease. Women, through their bodies and performances are establishing a certain subjectivity and individuality through which they can resist the normative power structures of the outside community. It is a difference established through the body and its sexual performance. This theory of difference, whether implemented successfully or unsuccessfully, constitutes a challenge to the dominant patriarchal narrative and its social structure. In *Cinnamon*, women are using their bodies in subversive same-sex relations to make their bodies matter and challenge the outside communal order.

Female same-sex relations as portrayed in Yazbek's *Cinnamon* oscillate between impossibility and empowerment. They clearly are subversive performances, yet they are confined to secrecy and invisibility. However, the very fact of their existence, in performance and novelistic narrative, constitute a challenge to the dominant patriarchal narrative which establishes itself as the norm. Women, through their bodies, are forming an alternative context in an attempt to redefine dominant narratives resist the power dynamics of their society. As Butler says, agency—which I also call empowerment—exists at the level of performance. Together, they constitute a moment of change. Reading *Cinnamon* between empowerment and impossibility, highlights the resistance posed to patriarchy and its dominant narratives through female same-sex relations.

Works Cited

al-Aswani, 'Ala'. *'Imarat Ya'qubyan [The Yacoubian Building]*. Cairo, Maktabat Madbuli, 2004.

al-Ghafari, Iman. "The Lesbian Subjectivity in Contemporary Arabic Literature: An Absent Presence Disciplined by the Gaze." *al-Raida*, vol. 138, 2012, pp. 6–18.

al-Samman, Hanadi. "Out of the Closet: Representations of Homosexuals and Lesbians in Modern Arabic Literature." *Journal of Arabic Literature*, vol. 39, U. Of South Carolina Libraries, 2008, pp. 270–310.

al-Shaykh, Hanan. *Innaha London ya 'Azizi [Only in London]*. Translated by Catherin Cobham, Beirut, Dar al-Adab / New York, Pantheon Books, 2001.

Barakat, Huda. *Hajar al-Dahk [The Stone of Laughter]*. 1990. Translated by Sophie Bennet, Beirut, Dar al-Nahar / New York, Interlink Books, 1995.

————. *Sayyidi wa-Habibi [My Master and My Beloved]*. Beirut, Dar al-Nahar, 2004.

Bareed Mista3jil: True Stories. Beirut, Meem, 2009.

Butler, Judith. *Bodies That Matter, on the Discursive Limits of Sex*. London, Routledge, 1993.

————, Seyla Benhabib, Durcilla Cornell and Nancy Fraser. *Feminist Contentions: A Philosophical Exchange*. Introduction by Linda Nicholson, New York, Routledge, 1995.

Censi, Martina. "Rewriting the Body in the Novels of Contemporary Syrian Women Writers." *Gender and Sexuality in Muslim Cultures*. Edited by Gul Ozyegin, New York, Routledge, 2015, pp. 297–316.

Foucault, Michel. *The History of Sexuality*. Translated by Robert Hurley, New York, Pantheon Book, 1978.

Georgis, Dina. "Thinking Past Pride: Queer Arab Shame in *Bareed Mista3jil*." *International Journal of Middle East Studies*, vol. 45, U. of South Carolina Libraries, 2013, pp. 233–51.

Guardi, Yolanda. "Female Homosexuality in Contemporary Arabic Literature." *DEP Deportate, Esuli, Profughe*, vol. 25, 2014, pp. 17–30.

Habib, Samar. *Female Sexuality in the Middle East, Histories and Representations*. London, Routledge, 2007.

Hadeed, Khalid. "Homosexuality and Epistemic Closure in Modern Arabic Literature." *International Journal of Middle East Studies*, vol. 45, Kenyon College Library, 2013, pp. 271–91.

Irigaray, Luce. *This Sex Which Is Not One*. Translated by Catherine Porter and Caroline Burke, Ithaca, Cornell UP, 1985.

Mahfuz, Najib. *Zuqaq al-Midaqq [Midaq Alley]*. 1947. Translated by Trevor Le Gassik, Cairo, Dar al-Shuruq / Beirut, Khayat, 1966.

Mansour, Elham. *Ana Hiya Anty*. Beirut, Riyad al-Rayyis, 2000.

————. *I am You (Ana Hiya Anty) a Novel on Lesbian Desire in the Middle East*. Translated and edited by Samar Habib, Cambria P, 2008.

Massad, Joseph. *Desiring Arabs*. Chicago, U of Chicago P, 2007.

Mcmanus, Anne-Marie. "The Contemporary Syrian Novel in Translation." *Arab Studies Journal*, vol. 22, Kenyon College Library, 2014, pp. 322–33.

Sedgwick, Eve. *Epistemology of the Closet*. Berkeley, U of California P, 1990.

Yazbek, Samar. *Ra'ihat al-qirfah [Cinnamon]*. 2008. Translated by Emily Danby, Beirut, Dar al-Adab / London, Arabia Books, 2012.

10 Writing Veiled Bodies Anew

A Study of Maya al-Haj's
Burkini: I ͑tirāfāt Muḥajjaba

Asmaa Gamal Salem Awad

The veil, as a female dress code and as a bodily discourse, is examined in this chapter as a vessel through which women's subjectivity is expressed and linked to freedom/resistance/transcendence, on the one hand, rather than oppression/docility/immanence on the other hand. This work discusses Maya al-Haj's *Burkini: I ͑tirāfāt Muḥajjaba* (2014).[1] The original language of the novel is Arabic, and it does not have a translated edition; therefore, the English quotes taken form *Burkini* are translated by me.[2]

This chapter aims at illustrating the relation of the veiled/unveiled woman to her body, how this relation is evoked, and whether the veil as a bodily extension is empowering or disempowering her on the level of bodily freedom and/or freedom of choice.

Maya al-Haj's *Burkini: I ͑tirāfāt Muḥajjaba* is a very complex, though rich, text. Its richness allows for being open to be read and analyzed from different theoretical perspectives. My argument in this chapter relies on many feminist, phenomenological and post-structural theories of prominent figures like Simone De Beauvoir, Luce Irigaray, Judith Butler, Sandra Lee Bartky, Meyda Yegenoglu, Michel Foucault, and Jean Paul Sartre. Though I frequently use them in the same meaning/direction meant by these theoreticians, I often use the concepts against themselves to be able to examine the main hypothesis underlying my research; i.e., the veil being an instrument of power not only on the corporeal level concerning the body of veiled women but also on the discursive one as it is able to reconcile many binary oppositions between which Western thought failed to find a common ground.

The publication of Simone de Beauvoir's *The Second Sex* highlights the beginning of feminist theorization about the female body. De Beauvoir's concern is not to decipher who a woman is, but rather how she becomes a woman according to gender roles/rules and how her experience as a woman is different from that of a man. Simone de Beauvoir argues that as far as "the body [is] the instrument of our grasp on the world, the world is bound to seem a very different thing when apprehended in one manner or another" (65). This argument evokes the tension she has pointed out between immanence and transcendence. This is further explained in her claims that female costumes are specifically designed to control women's activity in order to protect the male freedom to be the sole social agents. The result is linking the female body to "the inert and passive qualities of an object" (Beauvoir 189–90). This means that the body as an "instrument of our grasp of the world" does not only refer to the materiality/immanence of the female body. Rather, it points out to specific world views which shape our contemporary understanding.

Luce Irigaray holds a different opinion of what constitutes the immanence/transcendence binary opposition. Irigaray believes that for women to achieve pure female subjectivity, their body must develop in the pursuit of achieving transcendence; to reach this end, the sexed nature of the female body has to be reflected in the symbolic order. Thus, she proposes a new way to conceive female bodies as "sensible transcendental" rather than immanent bodies, believing that a "sensible transcendental" body must reconfigure an inter-subjective relation between men and women enabling "a communication or communion which respects the life of the other" (Irigaray 114). This term is Irigaray's attempt to reconcile binaries of man/woman, mind/body, and transcendence/immanence in a way that allows for a more balanced view of each pair.

Whereas de Beauvoir's distinction between immanent/transcendent bodies relies on her critique of the idea of a male "incarnation" of the Divine, Irigaray's method relies on the centrality of respect of others who are "outside" the realm of the sexed self. The former relation could be referred to as a form of "vertical transcendence," where God is re-lated in one way or the other to human beings, while the latter could be described as "horizontal transcendence," a state marked by "the death of God" where the process of becoming relies only on intersubjectivity (Goodenough).

The main difference between these two kinds of transcendence lies in that the former manifests a belief in a special form of hierarchy which should exist in the world in a way that embeds our real temporal world into a higher scheme of eternal reality, i.e., the Divine, to cast a spiritual form of sublimity that elevates human beings, shapes their ethics and behavioral interactions and connects them to their creator at the same time. The latter view of transcendence, however, understands the world as an entity in which human is the center, and only relationships be-tween individuals can shape their future and aspirations; in other words, sublimity here is related to the efforts which humans exert, their mode of understanding their world and the process of human life itself without giving any importance to an abstract world which exists beyond.

The importance of discussing different views of transcendence is two-fold. First, these views determine one's own world view, what de Beauvoir calls "grasp of the world." Second, I believe that following the vertical view of transcendence leads to the emergence of different kinds of religious/spiritual developments in which the body is a major player. Embracing the horizontal view of transcendence, in contrast, results in a purely secular worldview which favors carnal/sensual/corporeal/ material existence over the soul. This tendency, in its turn, strengthens the Western binary oppositions rather than offer different visions of reconciling them, and thus saves the subject position to men and the object status to women, as far as men represent rational/intelligible/forms of existence.

This mechanism of subject/object formation is also found in Judith Butler's claim that the process of subjectification underlies two aspects: Being subordinated to power and being autonomously constituted as a free subject. She says, "there is no formation of the subject without a passionate attachment to subjection" (Butler 67). The process of being subject through subjection is described by Butler to be a kind of ambivalence. She states, "[t]he power imposed upon one is the power that animates one's emergence, and there appears to be no escaping this ambivalence" (Butler 198).

Whereas third-wave feminists like Judith Butler define processes of subjection as an amalgam of subjecthood and subjugation, post feminism marks a postmodern subjection to certain self-technologies which can be described as "fashion beauty complex," to use Sandra Lee Bartky's term (39). Moreover, Bartky cites three ways to discipline the body. One of these is ornamentation which makes the body a pleasant sight (Deleuze 66–71).

In the same vein, Meyda Yegenoglu claims that being unveiled dictates some disciplinary techniques on the unveiled body. Thus, the choice to be unveiled "is no less inscriptive than being veiled" (Yegenoglu 115). Unveiling, according to Yegenoglu, is a culturally conditioned phenomenon. Therefore, it is seen "as one among many practices of corporeal inscriptions" (115).

Regulating the bodily behavior of people could be viewed as a kind of "normalization." The claim that veiled women are emblems of subjection, irrationality, and lack of agency could be interpreted as what Michel Foucault calls "code of normalization" ("Society" 38). At the core of Michel Foucault's understanding of the discursive formation of bodies, however, lies the idea that no subject is formed beyond a specific discourse and that "the individual is carefully fabricated in it, according to a whole technique of forces and bodies" (*Discipline and Punish* 217). As such, disciplinary power has the ability "to subject" individuals in the sense that it subordinates them and makes them subjects at the same time. Viewed as a disciplinary practice, the veil marks women's subjectivity as well as their subjection.

In the same vein, he claims that it is through models offered in collective settings, a person can freely create an ethos perceived in his actions (Foucault, "Genealogy of Ethics" 263). He, thus, proposes a view of what he calls "practices of freedom" as a reference to the idea of agency. He believes that moral agency elements are not solely emerging from the inside of a person. Rather, they are shaped to a great extent by one's culture and society.

Foucault's belief finds ground in Sartrean thought. He states:

> In play, the act is not its own goal for itself; . . . but the function of the act is to make manifest and present to *itself* the absolute freedom which is the very being of the person. (Sartre 732)

Sartre, thus, foregrounds the role of choosing to act/play as opposed to choosing to be. He believes that our actions nurture our uniqueness. In other words, to be authentic is to play/act. Furthermore, Sartre combines the state of being an authentic subject with the freedom and the ability to wear clothes. He claims that, "[t]o put on clothes is to hide one's object state; it is to claim the right of seeing without being seen, that is, to be pure subject" (Sartre 289).

The veil, as a form of cloth, has the power to grant its wearer a sense of subjectivity and agency. By blocking the male gaze, the veil endows women with the power to keep their privacy intact and to break the spell of their objectification in the process of scopophilia. In this sense, veiling could be seen as a practice which urges men to think about the mind beneath the veil, not the body behind it. Thus, women could have be given a chance to be known on the basis of their intellectual worth rather than their sexualized nature.

Seen in this light, the veil could be considered a dual form of power. First: it could be a form of "productive power" in the sense that it is a form of luminosity that produces knowledge. In *Foucault*, Gilles Deleuze argues that Foucault's conception of knowledge is built on those which can be spoken and the visible. He adds that there is a limited number of phenomena that can be both said and seen. The discursive aspect of the phenomenon sets ground for meaning as well as subject formations, while its visible manifestation is a form of "luminosity, created by light itself and allowing things and objects to exist" (Deleuze 60). The process involves the distribution of "the clear and the obscure, the opaque and the transparent, the seen and the not-seen" (Deleuze 64). The veil has a discursive aspect and a visible aspect which allow it to produce some sort of knowledge about veiled women.

Second: the fact that the veil conforms to the criterion of being a "disciplinary power" in the sense that it is "repressive and is exercised directly on the body" (Foucault, *Discipline and Punish* 137–9) induces the veiled woman to put herself under constant surveillance which, though being initially directed toward disciplining the body, takes hold of the mind to induce a psychological state of "conscious and permanent visibility" (Foucault, *Discipline and Punish* 201). In other words, through this quality of self-surveillance,[3] the veil indirectly produces a sense of self-awareness in veiled women which helps them to configure their authenticity.[4] In this sense, the logic of Foucault's disciplinary power as applied to the concept/act of veiling is related to the subjective awareness as well as the truth apprehension activity of the veiled woman. The difference between religious versus secular worldviews is thus constitutive of how the veil is perceived as a source of women's power/subjection.

Chronicling the incidents that happen during one single week in the life of a veiled woman painter who is obsessed with drawing nudity, *Burkini* is narrated by a first-person narrator. At first, being veiled gave the protagonist a predisposition to ignore her body. However, after meeting her fiancé's ex-fiancée, an emblem of femininity and beauty, the protagonist finds herself subject to many attempts to remove her veil in order to show her lover that she is beautiful too. She couldn't remove it: "I won't abandon what I ran into filled with free will and extreme power" (al-Haj 110). She then starts to find out new ways to re-establish her relationship with her body. Through art, love, and veil, the protagonist is able to rewrite her body.

The title of the novel, *Burkini: I'tirāfāt Muḥajjaba,* merges two opposing dress codes; the burqa'[5] and the bikini, to become a *burkini,* meaning a special swimsuit used by veiled women. The two seemingly conflicting dress codes foreshadow the internal conflict of the unnamed protagonist as if the author aims at building a kind of generalization in order to foreground her conflict.

This conflict clarifies that the veil, however, makes her able to hold in herself "the lives of two women" (al-Haj 42), which makes her strong; she says: "I feel that I am more powerful than them [unveiled women] because I am two women, and each one of them is no more than only one" (al-Haj 50). This difference is celebrated by the protagonist to be the "substance of identity formation" (al-Haj 49) which God has put into veiled women's bodies, not to oppress them but to make them distinguished human beings. To illustrate, Saba Mahmoud's seminal work *The Politics of Piety: The Islamic Revival and the Feminist Subject* reveals that veiled women have specific agendas which entail that through submitting to a religious and a social norm, they are aiming at creating models of the self that they wished to achieve. Through veiling, these women have achieved a sense of positive agency that enables them to realize their individual potential as social agents and believers in Allah. To prove her claim that submission can create improvement, Mahmoud gives the example of a pianist who experiences an extended and painful practice hoping to achieve mastery over her piano. Here, the veiled woman as a modern subject "[is treated] not as a private space of self-cultivation, but as an effect of modality of power operationalized through a set of moral codes that summon a subject to constitute herself in accord with its precepts" (Mahmoud 28).

Being a veiled artist and an expert in body painting makes the protagonist communicate better with the world as well as herself. She states:

"I see bodies like languages; each of which has its aesthetics, rules, lines and peculiarities" (al-Haj 16). The veil on her head has sharpened her understanding of the Other. She becomes able to make an analogy between bodies and languages. She can see clearly with her mind's eye that everybody holds some similarities as well as some differences with other bodies.

This ability to see the other's peculiarities means in a sense that choosing willingly to put on the veil makes her a free subject. She is not ready to retreat and occupy the object status when someone suppresses her freedom and claims to know what is better for her. She often says, "the veil which I didn't put on for the sake of somebody is not to be removed for that of anybody" (al-Haj 20). Two outstanding claims lie behind people urging her to drop off her veil. First, it hides her femininity and second, it doesn't suit her social status. She belongs to the elite while the veil is categorized to be "a social code referring to a category of humble, ignorant and backward people" (al-Haj 21).

However, the protagonist is marginalized because of her veil. She ironically explains this situation by saying that "a human being in this world is not worth his value unless he/she imitates others in their style of communication, behavior and dressing" (al-Haj 21), and that it is only through clothes that people become able to discover one's own religion, identity, thoughts, and even social and cultural class (al-Haj 100). People set "normal" codes of dressing and accept only who is similar to them. When she embraces the practice of veiling, she deviates from this "norm." Thus, she is not accepted in her society, and she is stereotyped to be backward and uncivilized (al-Haj 21).

She believes that it is not the fault of her veiled body, it is all people's mistake because most of them "understand the appearance of things and ignore their essence" (al-Haj 36). People believe that she is experiencing an idle lifestyle because she is veiled. The problem, then, is how others look at a veiled woman. They judge her according to their constructed codes, and they do not exert the minimal effort to know the truth behind the veil where a human being lies wanting to be granted due recognition as a result of a continuous pursuit "to impose [her] humanity, rather than [her] femininity" (al-Haj 63). Thus, comes her claim that the veil helps in discovering the human sides of a veiled body as far as being unveiled is a way to reduce women's beauty to be a material: "a woman's beauty is no more than a *lisse* hair and an exposed sexual body" (al-Haj 63). Hence, a veiled woman becomes a fully fledged human being far from being constrained in the confines of a body or a gender (al-Haj 72). Her veil gives her the opportunity to transcend the prewritten patriarchal binary oppositions between mind/body.

This balance between mind and body is the core of the life the protagonist is searching for, recalling Luce Irigaray's concept of the "sensible transcendental" which suggests a sublime unity between the corporeal and the spiritual, the immanent and the transcendental, the secular and the religious. Being close to the Divine by means of her veil as well as her art is what permits the protagonist's body to transcend "a liberal life totally free from its spiritual and religious meanings" (al-Haj 70) because it often steals the real worth of life. She comes to understand that "freedom is not a 'bikini' or a 'mini-skirt'. It is an idea stemming from inside us and takes us far, too far, to be realized without fear or compromises" (al-Haj 60). In other words, she is now convinced that freedom doesn't lie in unveiling the feminine body and exposing it in a seductive way. Freedom, for her, has a spiritual root deeply embedded inside veiled women's souls through the ability to make a choice without being obliged to let go of a dear part for the sake of another.

The protagonist always says that when:

> *al-Iman* (faith) and art (talent) meet in a soul, it is supposed that its bearer (the body) holds a great internal power . . . I was born a child pregnant with her secret and her dream, why do I, then, abandon all my transcendental thoughts for the sake of what is normal and vulgar? (al-Haj 67)

Hybridizing a soul with seeds of both *Iman* and creativity makes it more powerful. Thus, the protagonist's faith in finding the best in her earthly life and in the hereafter due to embracing the practice of veiling could be a clear manifestation of Foucault's "productive power." As a manifestation of her *Iman*, the veil will earn her paradise in the afterlife. As a representation of her peculiarity, it will grant her a strong sense of individuality in a postmodern society which suffers from the excess of images and inauthentic replicas, causing the loss of originality. Being thus a tool of reconciliation between two binary oppositions—secularism and religiosity—the practice of veiling could be seen as a practice of power.

The climax of the protagonist's internal conflict is reached in a café where she and her fiancé meet the man's ex-fiancée who is introduced to be very seductive. The protagonist, however, poses as a sensitive artist while the other woman is a "materialistic" being to whom "nothing is important . . . than trademarks and social appearances" (al-Haj 26). The scene recalls both Lee Bartky's claims that makeup and ornamentation discipline female bodies as far as they control them through imposing special dictates upon them, as well as Yegenoglu's claim that veiling/unveiling are both disciplinary techniques practiced on the female body. In other words, if the protagonist's veiled body is controlled by her veil, the ex-fiancée's unveiled body is controlled by makeup, trademarks, and attractive appearance. However, being extremely beautiful, she seems very naïve as she "acts only on the basis that she is beautiful" (al-Haj 26) though hers is more artificial than natural. Reaching the conclusion that the ex-fiancée is naïve is an indication that the protagonist herself is not. Her veil lifts her body up beyond the level of materialism and objectification to that of sublimity and subjectification which is expressed brilliantly in her alter egos: the heroines of her portraits.

Moreover, for the protagonist, a veiled body is a resistant one, for, "the body which is not in the reach of a man defeats him" (al-Haj 23) states the protagonist. He "satisfies his eyes with the women's naked bodies and inspires his imagination with [the] restricted veiled body" (al-Haj 23). The verb "to satisfy" recalls Sartre's concept of the gaze, denoting that the exposed body is some good to be consumed by lustful hungry eyes. The verb "to inspire" on the contrary means that the veiled body is a subject; an agent that instigates men's fanciful dreams. The veil, thus, is conceived to be a bridge between reality and fancy. The veiled body's domineering presence in reality opens up a gate toward a higher realm of experience. It is powerful in its own ways.

To clarify its strength, the protagonist decides to discover her own veiled body by herself. She stands in front of her mirror in a sexy red dress and she contemplates every single inch of her body, now exposed only to her mirror. She perceives that being veiled, her body does not become flabby. It becomes "blonder and more beautiful" (al-Haj 97). Her charm seduces her to get rid of the veil forever to become able to enjoy the bliss of being a beautiful woman. However, she states, "at the moment, I feel I'm peeling something off me . . . something inside me has collapsed" (al-Haj 108). This confession proves that the veil has become a part of her body and getting rid of it will eventually cause physical as well as spiritual pain. She finally decides not to "take off a veil which has succeeded in bridging the gap inside [her] . . . I won't get rid of something that reminds me that Allah is always with me, . . . I won't abandon what I ran into filled with free will and extreme power" (110).

The protagonist's attempt to rediscover her own body allows her a chance to establish a sense of subjecthood. This is echoed in Irigaray's claim that a woman cannot occupy a place in her society unless she rediscovers her body in all its materiality and brings out her repressed thoughts about it so as to face her fantasies and to counter her sense of corporeal alienation. For Julia Kristeva, the interaction between the semiotic and the symbolic worlds, between identity and language is what constitutes authentic feminine identities. The protagonist's *Iman,* her semiotic realm, as well as her art, her symbolic world, are what constitute her individuality; her subjecthood (Kristeva 40). Her attempt to "di[g] into [her] own flesh to find a meaning," to borrow Frantz Fanon's words (8), helps her to refashion all the kinds of meanings and experiences she is going to confront.

The protagonist's decision of not taking off her veil summarizes the ways in which the veil has empowered her. It causes her to feel inner stability because she felt supported by a divine assistance that endows her with a free will and a total hold onto her body. The novel ends with the protagonist crying because she is now sure that throughout a whole week, she has mistakenly poured her anger on the piece of cloth which preserves her femininity (al-Haj 83).

In the novel, as it seems, the veil is connected to notions of power. al-Haj's protagonist's veiled body is a typical representation of inner and outer conflicts over the female body. Though experiencing marginal existence in the world of postmodern fake beauty, this veiled body attains an outstanding presence on social and private levels due to two main characteristics: fertile imagination and deep faith. In other words, being a typical illustration of Irigaray's sensible transcendental, the veiled body in this novel has the power to reconcile binary oppositions such as secularism/religiosity, immanence/transcendence, and body/mind.

Notes

1 In English, the title could be translated as *Burkini: A Veiled Woman's Confessions*. The original version of this paper appears in Asmaa G. S. Awad's *Narratives of Power and Subjection: Representations of the Veil in Selected Works by Muslim Novelists*.
2 Due to the word limit of this paper, the researcher has decided to include only the English translation of the quotations taken from the novel.
3 Note that Foucault's use of the term self-surveillance is negative. I appropriate the term and assign a positive dimension to it.
4 Foucault's concept of disciplinary power could be related to what Hélène Cixous calls "power over oneself;" a form of power that according to her describes the nature of *"les pouvoir de la Femme"* (483–484).
5 A loose enveloping garment that covers the face and body and is worn in public by certain Muslim women.

Works Cited

al-Haj, Maya. *Burkini: A Veiled Woman's Confessions*. Ḍifāf Publications & al-Ikhtilāf Publications, 2014.
Awad, Asmaa G.S. *Narratives of Power and Subjection: Representations of the Veil in Selected Works by Muslim Novelists*. Cairo, 2018.
Bartky, Sandra-Lee. *Femininity and Domination: Studies in the Phenomenology of Oppression*. Routledge, 1990.
Butler, Judith. *The Psychic Life of Power: Theories in Subjection*. Stanford UP, 1997.
Cixous, Hélène. "Entretien avec Françoise van Rossum-Guyon." *Revue des Sciences Humaines*, 168 (Écriture, féminité, féminisme), 1977, pp. 479–93.
De Beauvoir, Simone. *The Second Sex*. Edited and translated by H. M. Parsheley, Jonathan Cape, 1956.
Deleuze, Gilles. *Foucault*. Translated by Sean Hand, University of Minnesota Press, 1998.
Fanon, Frantz. *Black Skin, White Masks*. Translated by Charles Lam Markmann, Pluto Press, 2008.
Foucault, Michel. *Discipline and Punish: The Birth of the Prison*. Allen Lane, 1977.

———. "On the Genealogy of Ethics: An Overview of Work in Progress in Ethics, Subjectivity and Truth." *The Essential Works of Michel Foucault 1954–1984*, edited by Paul Rabinow, vol. 1, New Press, 1998, pp. 253–80.

———. "Society Must be Defended." *Lectures at the College de France 1975–1976*. Translated by David Macey, Picador, 2003.

Goodenough, Ursula. "Vertical and Horizontal Transcendence." *Biology Faculty Publications & Presentations*, vol. 31, no. 1, 2001, pp. 21–31.

Irigaray, Luce. *The Irigaray Reader*. Edited by Margaret Whitford, Routledge, 1991.

Kristeva, Julia. *Revolution in Poetic Language*. Translated by Margaret Waller, Columbia UP, 1984.

Mahmoud, Saba. *The Politics of Piety: The Islamic Revival and the Feminist Subject*. Princeton UP, 2005.

Sartre, Jean-Paul. *Being and Nothingness: A Phenomenological Essay on Ontology*. 1943. Introduced and translated by Hazel E. Barnes, Washington Square Press, 1992.

Yegenoglu, Meyda. *Colonial Fantasies: Towards a Feminist Reading of Orientalism*. Cambridge UP, 1998.

Section 3

Identity and Crossing Boundaries

11 "A Girl Is Like a Bottle of Coke"

Emptied and Recycled Identities in *Always Coca-Cola*

Lava Asaad

Alexandra Chreiteh is not particularly a familiar name, but her novel *Always Coca-Cola,* written in Arabic in 2009 and translated into English in 2012 by Michelle Hartman, encapsulated from the title to the last page of the novel the idea of the precarity of Arab women. Hartman in the "Translator's Afterword" confesses that she was not fond of the novel when she first read it. Hartman asserts the blatant familiarity of a text with a title that is "the ultimate expression of globalization" may deceive the reader for being about familiar issues tackled by anybody and anywhere in this globalized world (113). Nevertheless, the novel makes it glaringly obvious that the location is the bourgeois west Beirut, where the main events revolve around a student who goes to the Lebanese American University (not to be confused with the American University of Beirut). Hartman explores this deceptive superficial familiarity by acknowledging how Chreiteh is not trying to make the text "'accessible' to a supposed Western audience" instead "it draws on them in order to make poignant comments about the specificities of the local scene and world view of her characters, who are very much part of a Lebanese reality" (114). In other words, the world of the novel saturated with Western products, labels, and cafés doesn't exist to attract a vast worldly readership. It is rather a statement emphasizing that the Arabic novel can no longer ward off Western hegemony that has reshaped the socioeconomical face of the culture. The so-called authenticity and the foreignness that some Western readers expect when approaching a non-euromerican text is increasingly disappearing. The indifference that the reader feels to reading *Always Coca-Cola* might be attributed to the lack of a Muslim female heroine that we are very much accustomed to read about in a World Literature or a Transnational Feminism class. If the readership is looking for some fantastical female Muslim characters to fit into a certain mold, then the novel refuses to lend itself to a stereotypical examination of third-world women where the main character is rebelling against the status quo. For this reason, the novel deserves more attention and acknowledgment than it has received. Chreiteh's strength lies in bringing to the surface a seemingly mundane protagonist only to perhaps be sending a message about the loss of authenticity in an increasingly globalized world where everyone thinks and dreams alike.

On first looking at the cover which has a poster-like female face and on first reading the novel, one can come to the conclusion that this book is a chick-lit novel in which the main character Abeer reconfigures her identity in relation to local and global exigencies. One reviewer on this book also comments on how this seemingly chick-lit novel is more complex in showing "how young women in Beirut today are buffeted by the alternately conflicting and conspiring forces of hegemony, capitalism, and patriarchy—without, vitally, ever using such dry terms" (Garman). Rightly so, the novel pushes the reader to contemplate the intricacies of the superficial and mundane fantasies of a Lebanese woman especially when books about the Middle East mostly cover violent spectacles and unusual events to be read by the West. Another reviewer, Volker Kaminski, praises the novelist for effectively illustrating how the main character's world "on the one hand bombards her with alluring yet delusive images (and songs) of an encitingly glossy world and on the other presents her with traditional values and identity patterns that are hardly a viable alternative for the modern women she is." The protagonist is indeed trying to become a modern woman in her globalized locale, but her attempts come with a heavy price.

Chreiteh's debut novel explores the globalized neocolonial effects on Abeer Ward, whose precarity has been accentuated by industrial trends and Western influences. Oscillating between a conservative and a Westernized society in Beirut, the novel highlights the predicament of maintaining an identity without being tarnished by transnational hierarchies of power that devalue subjects, in this case women in the Middle East. Social, economic, political, and religious aspects make Abeer susceptible to becoming a copy produced by a new global economic vision of erasing identities in the Global South.

The precarization of women like Abeer is multi-stranded; being a woman from a conservative family in the Middle East operating under a failing neo-capitalist paradigms only worsens her indefensible predicament. Judith Butler's seminal contribution on precarity in *Frames of War: When is Life Grievable?* provocatively begs the question of who can be considered worth saving and worth grieving over. In other words, ontologically speaking, how can Abeer's predicaments count as problems when her being is not counted as a life to begin with? Butler opines that there is a direct correlation between someone's precarity and acts of violence enacted upon them: "The apprehension of precariousness leads to a heightening of violence, an insight into the physical vulnerability of some set of others that incites the desire to destroy them" (*Frames* 2). Abeer's life and the final rape incident in the novel come as no surprise to the reader as her vulnerability inevitably leads her to multiple acts of violence against her as a third-world woman. The novel accentuates Abeer's body in the same way that Butler explains how certain bodies are framed within the broader socio-political and economic contexts in which there are "normative conditions for the production of the subject" that would untimely produce "an historically contingent ontology" (*Frames* 4). Abeer builds up and situates her normativity according to her social and religious milieus as dependent, docile, and always preoccupied with how she is perceived by others. This ontological being, Butler argues, can either be "recognized" or "apprehended" by others, where apprehension "is less precise, since it can imply marking, registering, acknowledging without full cognition" (*Frames* 5). Thus, Abeer's life is apprehended without being recognized. She is a subject of the Global South toiling under demanding socio-economic structures that render her invisible. The unshakable reliance on her surroundings enhances her precariousness where her sense of obligation toward the other is irrevocable. Undeniably, her being is disposable and replaceable and "When such lives are lost they are not grievable since, in the twisted logic that rationalizes their death, the loss of such population is deemed necessary to protect the lives of 'the living'" (*Frames* 31). The novel unapologetically focuses on Abeer's situation from a satirical angle wherein the reader is reminded of how common Abeer's situation has become.

The novel, like the title and the story, commercializes and junkifies Abeer's experience as a young Muslim woman. Like the Coca-Cola bottle, a brand name produced in the West but made locally, Abeer's identity aspires to eradicate, or at least to navigate, between her local, traditional self and global expectations of a modern young women. Her precariousness is heightened by her disposability as a commodity whose value, or lack thereof, does not entail her livability and experience as a human. Abeer's life, while still in her mother's womb, was inseparable from the insatiability for Coca-Cola, which was forbidden for her mother to consume because it was part and parcel of American policies—her father insisted. Like the purified water the mother was forced to take, the father presupposed his daughter would have "a natural, a permanent, predisposition for cleanliness" (Chreiteh 2). Abeer's role even before birth was curated to shape her identity. The thirst of the mother for the forbidden beverage leaves a birthmark of a Coke bottle on Abeer's body. Chreiteh cleverly associates Abeer's whole existence, body and soul, to be in a constant thirst for commodity and to commodify herself in her society. One might even recall Žižek's points on how he subtly considers Coke as more than a beverage and where, "Coke has the paradoxical quality that the more you drink it, the more you get thirsty." This statement perfectly fits in what the novel is trying to show. In other words, in a globalized and hyper-capitalized reality, Abeer is the product produced and circulated to satisfy the needs of her conservative society and globalized world at large.

Abeer's identity is further subsumed by the globalized standards of femininity from "fashion models don't ever leave home without using a high-SPF" to the inconclusive debate over whether she should buy tampons from a Starbucks bathroom or continue to use pads like most women in her conservative society do (Chreiteh 29). Western products are readily accessible in the Global South, even if the product is looked upon with suspicion. Chreiteh paints an image of Abeer's misfit-ness as a caricature within an overtly consumptive society. Moreover, upon reading in the magazine that her lips need to always be moisturized like models do, she purchases a lip balm. To her disappointment, Abeer's lips culminate dust after she applies it once she leaves the store. This failed reconciliation with two contrasting lifestyles only leaves Abeer with a sense of confusion and failed emulation of the elusive and perfect standards imported to her culture from the Global North. Relying on Rossi Braidotti's assertion where she aptly describes the paradox of capitalism and politics of inclusion saying that,

> Advanced capitalism is a different engine in that it promotes the marketing of pluralistic differences and the commodification of the existence, the culture, the discourse of "others," for the purpose of consumerism . . . [where] power functions not so much by binary oppositions but in a fragmented and all-pervasive manner. (25)

Abeer on the larger global scheme is no longer an Other with rich and distinctive cultural properties. Her existence is necessary as long as she is a willful partaker in the consumerist society. Regardless where she is from, her existence is consumable and, in fact, disposable.

Abeer has two female friends in the novel. The presence of the two women in Abeer's life sends a conflicting message of how she should behave. Yana, the Romanian model who lives in Beirut is the epitome of beauty for Abeer, whereas Yasmine's butch-like physique makes Abeer reluctant to be seen by other people with Yasmine. Abeer constantly tries to model herself and identity based on Yana's. Abeer's identity within this global economy could only be replicated based off of a product, an image, an idea, or a person imported from centers of Western economy.

As examined in the *Dialectic of Enlightenment,* Horkheimer and Adorno rightly articulated the repeated aspect of creating an identity where, "Being is apprehended in terms of manipulation and administration. Everything—including the individual human being . . . becomes a repeatable, replaceable process, a mere example of the conceptual models of the system" (65). Indeed, Abeer strategically situates her mirror "to reflect the world outside" to her. The outside world was no longer the sea nor the sky as inhabitants of Beirut were accustomed to see, but bigger-than-life Coca-Cola billboards. Yana, who happened to be advertised by Coca-Cola, invades Abeer's consciousness with her sexualized pose and features on the billboard signaling not only a way of being feminine and attractive but also a way of being, of existing for others to emulate; Yana's face is "the face that launches a thousand identifications," as

Baridotti would say. Freezing Yana in time and place reminds us of the countless critics, one of which is Barthes, who linked the fixed image to death and immobility. In this regard, Yana's identity doesn't go beyond her role as an important asset for the advertising agency, and equally so, Abeer's immobility and identity couldn't escape the clutch of the image.

The presence of the billboard functions as a hegemonic power for Abeer and others to enticed by it. In the global economy and in the words of Inderpal Grewal and Caren Kaplan, the product disseminating into other nation-states is part of the multiple "scattered hegemonies" that operate within a system that is decentered but continues to exist in multiple forms of dominance (3). However, following in Yana's footsteps is not that easy for Abeer, a woman who maneuvers her way in and out of a conventional society which, for example, regards buying a pregnancy test for Yana a huge dishonor for Abeer even to be in the same vicinity. Consequently and inevitably, there's nothing redeeming in Abeer's vacillation between the two opposite poles, the pull of the Imam's Friday sermons warning the pious through loudspeakers of "American hegemony" and the power of the overly relied upon globalized and capitalistic city bulldozed by Starbucks and the like. She might be repelling against one tradition only to embrace a new style of being lived by fashion models in magazines who are "one hundred percent cellulite-free!" (Chreiteh 42).

The irony of the clash between two cultures and two ideologies intensify as one day during the night, a person painted over Yana's naked body on the billboard to appear as if she is wearing a black rope, leaving only her face intact. The urge of an Islamic society to "co-exist" with Western influences renders an ad of a socially accepted look of a modest woman holding a Coca-Cola bottle as a successful marriage between the West and the rest. With this new transformation, Abeer could not help but laugh at the image as she says, "the hijab and Yana would never meet—even if the heavens crashed down onto earth or the opposite, if the earth rose up to touch the heavens!" (Chreiteh 65). The paradoxical relationship between what the model and the ad represent in a culture saturated with political and religious repulsions of the West failed to be comprehended by Abeer to realize herself as a mismatched formation of multiple contrasting identities with each edge canceling the other.

The irony continues where a global product seeps into the way local communities define things. Ashraf, Abeer's friend at the university, is a conservative man who has taken upon himself the responsibility of reminding Muslim women like Abeer of the traditional way of living in which women preserve their modesty and virginity. He says to Abeer: "A girl is like a flower, she wilts and her fragrance disappears . . . Actually, she's like a bottle of Coke, it can only be opened once. Who would buy a bottle of Coke that's already been opened?" (Chreiteh 67–8). It is not uncommon from patriarchal discourse to objectify women. The Coke reference is indeed more of an apt description of Abeer's lived reality in which a woman's virginity compared to an uncarbonated Coke is an example that cheaply commodifies her body. Whereas the Coke ad and the concept of consuming the product is characterized by a free and hypersexualized Yana, the receiving society deconstructs the meaning of that product. Chreiteh poignantly and satirically updates the mindset of her society to highlight the clash of two incompatible ideologies.

The clash of the West and the rest is heightened by another example in the text, but this time through how the West continues to define the rest through Oriental fantasies. Chreiteh references Milk and Honey, German duo female singers (one from Germany and one born in Algiers). The group had a couple of hit songs where they would mix Arabic and English and belly dance against the backdrop of a desert and castles. In the text, Yana is supposed to be Milk when she was still in Europe, which led Abeer to remember the lyric of one her songs: "On a dark desert night, in a land far away / you took my heart—that's the price I pay." Yana's idea of Lebanon was intermingled with "tormented love in a dune-filled desert where date palms flourish!" (Chreiteh 92). The exotic East permeates the scene in the clip but Abeer, for the first time, questions the created image about her culture in a conversation with Yana:

> I added that I was born in Lebanon and have lived here my entire life and I've never seen any sand dunes, except those shown on television or depicted on boxes of dates imported from Saudi Arabia and Iran. Moreover, how could she talk like this—after all the time that she's spent here, after all she's seen? At the end of the day, she lives above a Starbucks, of all places! (Chreiteh 93)

The objectification of the culture replays an idea of the place and its people over and over again despite what globalization has promised. The global economies invade localities far away from the center of civilization without admitting that these imported products and ways of thinking would evidently alter the receiving culture. For Yana to accept Beirut as a global city would mean disturbing her fantasies of the Other, she was so desperate to find in this new culture. The scattered hegemony has the ability to recreate through technology a concept, a product like the video clip to be consumed by the viewers. The director, utterly frustrated for not finding desert in Beirut, had to rely on digital effects to turn the house into an Oriental fantasy. Indeed, "Computers can bring the dead back to life" as Abeer exclaims (Chreiteh 95).

So far in the novel, Abeer's precarity has been explained through the gradual objectification of herself and identity. Abeer is only a wishful replica of someone like Yana. Abeer is the image of what her mirror reflects from the outside billboard. Abeer, whose name translates into "fragrance" in Arabic, can only be the epitome of chastity for her family. Despite coming from a bourgeois milieu, her gendered precariousness cannot be saved by her moderate social and economic security. Yana has secured a job opportunity for Abeer at the Coke company so she could spy on Yana's ex-boyfriend, the manager of the company. The text doesn't dwell long on the rape scene when the manager violates Abeer for an unknown reason, beyond the fact that he was exasperated by her work performance. The reader might think that the author did not handle the narration very effectively or that the rape was formed into a clichéd plot. The reader might cringe reading the following: "When he entered me between my legs, I didn't see anything except the edge of his shoulder and the Coca-Cola advertisement, the one Yana appeared in, hanging on the wall behind him" (Chreiteh 81). The indifference of the narration to the rape, however, is only a statement on Abeer's susceptibility in face of the collaboration of symbols of a powerful economy and a lustful patriarchy. Precarity, as Butler defines, includes lives that "Can be expunged at will or by accident; and its persistence is in no sense guaranteed" ("Performativity" ii). Abeer's reaction to the rape does not include grief nor anger at the manager. She was consumed to gratify a momentary satiation, and we might as well remember Ashraf's words, no one would want this Coke once it has been opened. The text trivializes it as another misfortunate accident in Abeer's life which only momentarily forces her to realize her position *vis-à-vis* a dominant patriarchy. Butler pertinently links between performativity and precarity, writing: "The performativity of gender has everything to do with who counts as a life, who can be read or understood as a living being, and who lives, or tries to live, on the far side of established modes of intelligibility" ("Performativity" iv). Everything Abeer learned to aspire to, her modest femininity, her aspiration for a cellulite-free body, and her impeccable reputation crumble instantly as she deliberates on the consequences of the incident:

> If it weren't for the pain, I wouldn't even have noticed that I had been deflowered or that something inside me had completely changed . . . I had always thought that the moment you lose your virginity is a turning point in life . . . [that] in the blink of an eye, I would change from a small, closed-up bud into a blossoming flower, from a tightly cocoon into a brilliant butterfly! But today I realized that flowers and butterflies or any other plants and insects have nothing to do with this, because I'm just exactly who I am. (Chreiteh 82–3)

The momentary rupture of performativity is soon overtaken by the thought that she could be pregnant. Once again Abeer realizes her precarious situation in a conservative society and seeks new ways to perform her gender purity through considering undergoing a hymen restoration procedure, a very popular one in several conservative societies. Abeer's body is disposable once she veers off the righteous path even if she happened to be the victim of the same society. Such procedures, as

Foucault and later on many feminists grasped, are the prime examples of marriage between patriarchy and techno-global capitalism that produce biomedical apparatus seeking to renormalize women. In this case, Abeer internalizes the myth of a "disposable third world woman" which is simultaneously discarded at ease while also needed by global capitalism as a loyal consumer (Wright). This "less developed," "under-developed," or "developing" woman is the embodiment of the tense coexistence of superficial global modernity and local traditions that could only render her confused and insatiate, always pining after the perfect global standards of femininity while also struggling to fit into a more conservative image of womanhood. The disposable third-world woman is trounced by these contrasting ideas alike as she inevitably destined to be an incomplete project, always lacking, and in need of reparation. Chreiteh's so-called protagonist could fit in both worlds but it would be in a similar way to Yana's body on billboard ad, painted in a black robe while sexually pining after the desired beverage. Only this grotesque and incongruous image can surmise Abeer's dilemma and precarity in a globalized and yet still semi-conservative city like Beirut.

Works Cited

Braidotti, Rosi. *Nomadic Theory: The Portable Rosi Braidotti*. Columbia UP, 2011.

Butler, Judith. *Frames of War: When Is Life Grievable?* Verso, 2016.

———. "Performativity, Precarity and Sexual Politics." *Aibr*, vol. 4, no. 3, 2009, pp. i–xiii.

Chreiteh, Alexandra. *Always Coca-Cola*. Translated by Michelle Hartman. Inerlink, 2012.

Garman, Emma. "Alexandra Chreiteh's *Always Coca-Cola*." *Word Without Borders*, Feb., 2012.

Grewal, Inderpal and Caren Kaplan. "Introduction: Transnational Feminist Practices and Questions of Postmodernity." *Scattered Hegemonies: Postmodernity and Transnational Feminist Practices*, edited by Inderpal Grewal and Caren Kaplan, Minneapolis, U of Minnesota P, 1994, pp. 1–36.

Horkheimer, Max, and Theodor W. Adorno. *Dialectic of Enlightenment: Philosophical Fragments*. Edited by Gunzelin Schmid Noerr, translated by Edmund Jephcott, Stanford UP, 2002.

Kaminski, Volker. "The Agony and the Allure." *Qantara.de*, translated by Ron Walker, 17 Aug., 2015.

Wright, Melissa W. *Disposable Women and Other Myths of Global Capitalism*. Routledge, 2006.

Žižek, Slavoj. "The Superego and the Act." *Žižek, UK*, 1 Aug., 1999.

12 Shaping a Female Identity

Feminism & National Identity in Suad al-Sabah's Poetry

Asmaa Ahmed Youssef Moawad

Suad al-Sabah started writing in the 1960s from the perspective of a traditional and conservative writer. She does not introduce shocking topics about the Kuwaiti society, such as rape or class racism. She writes from an aristocratic position, not from an ordinary or a discriminated woman's point of view. This fact is the reason for al-Sabah's powerful voice of nationalism, since her status as a royal family member gives her power to talk about such topics. The poet is a leader in defending her country against the Iraqi occupation of Kuwait in 1990 and has self-confidence in her national identity. Nevertheless, her poetry witnesses an absence of a revolution toward women's economic and political rights within the Kuwaiti society. This is perhaps due to the economic welfare experienced by Kuwaiti people. The Kuwaiti economy is one of the most important economies in the Middle East region, and one of the largest oil-producing countries in the world. The GDP per capita reached its highest level in the 1970s, when it reached 439%, and 91% during the 1990s (*Wayback Machine*). This luxurious life makes women hesitant to take steps toward their rights. In other countries, like the United States, the movement of women's liberation has gone through four waves of feminism. The first wave began in 1849, and emerged out of urban industrialism and liberal, socialist politics. Discussions about suffrage and women's participation in politics opened the gate to an examination of the differences between men and women. Then came the second wave of feminism in 1960s and lasted until 1980s. It started with the movements of civil rights and issues of minority groups around the world. Patriarchy, gender inequality, sexual violence, and reproductive rights were dominant issues. The concepts of sex and gender were introduced. While the former was biological, the later was socially structured. At that period, women sought unity and support, asserting women's social-class struggle. In "The Feminine Mystique" (1963), Betty Friedan criticized the patriarchal, or male-dominated, institutions and cultural practices in the society (31). Besides, the second wave found its way between many movements and theories, such as socialist feminism, Marxism, and psychoanalysis.

With the post-colonial and post-modern thinking, the third wave of feminism began in the mid-90s. The credit for the term "third wave" goes to Rebecca Walker in "Becoming the Third Wave" (1992). She wrote:

> So I write this as a plea to all women, especially women of my generation: . . . Do not vote for them unless they work for us. Do not have sex with them, do not break bread with them, do not nurture them if they don't prioritize our freedom to control our bodies and our lives. I am not a post-feminism feminist. I am the Third Wave. (Walker 40)

Women started to have strong and empowered voices, avoiding victimization, yet they refused to call themselves feminists. They looked at themselves as subjects, not as objects of sex. The third wave saw the emergence of intersectionality, which illustrates how a person's social and political identities may cause forms of discrimination and privilege (Cooper 1). Moreover, by using the web and cyberspace in 1990s and 2000s, women managed to cross gender boundaries and stimulate new, innovative, and creative thoughts.

Fourth wave feminism calls for gender equity and empowerment of marginalized women in politics and business. It is centered on intersectionality, acknowledging women's different experiences and identities, such as being colored, poor, or immigrant women (Crenshaw 04:23–30:46). Fourth-wave feminists use print, news, and social media platforms to engage and rally people. They attack abusers of power and call for justice against violence and harassment.

The feminist movement in Kuwait started slowly in the 1950s and the 1960s at the hands of individual women, and was not supported by the ruling regime or the National Assembly. It was not until 2005 that the government gave women the right to stand for office, or the right to vote in 2009. It is noticeable that much of the progress of Kuwaiti women today is because of individual movements of some women. Nevertheless, some writers, like Khaliel Hiedr and Huda al-Daghfa, claim that "Kuwaiti feminism" became an increasingly classy and bourgeois work during the last decades. In the article, "Is There Any Real Feminism in Kuwait?" (2016), Shiekha al-Bahaweid questions whether Kuwaiti women really struggle for women's rights or for racist and personal interests, since they feel superiority over workers who are not Kuwaiti citizens. She argues that these Kuwaiti women do not support or defend women who are not Kuwaitis (al-Bahaweid 2). Asian women, housekeepers, and workers suffer from persecution, injustice, rape, and sexual persecution. This paper argues that Kuwaiti feminists want to occupy their spare time defending women's rights for the purpose of social prominence or personal concerns. Besides, al-Bahaweid sees that the main essence of feminism is calling for equality, not discrimination, for all women from different nationalities, races, and religions. She is surprised that Kuwaiti women call for giving nationality to Kuwaiti children who have Kuwaiti fathers, but they refuse to give it to the ones from Filipino and Sri Lankan mothers married to Kuwaiti men according to the law (2).

Moreover, al-Sabah is influenced by the second and, in part, by the third waves of feminism; these waves raise many issues, such as gender inequality and domestic violence. The poet introduces these controversial issues smoothly, despite the fact that the Kuwaiti society has not been prepared for such topics. She criticizes patriarchal institutions of marriage—which are not built on love—in which women are marginalized. They are not able to express themselves freely, cannot talk about love, and are forced to have sex. For al-Sabah, the first step toward equality is to have a voice. In "The Abyss" (*In the Beginning* 9), the poet expresses her feelings freely without being ashamed. Expressing love shapes al-Sabah's feminine voice in a conservative society that restricts women in various fields. "Whenever I kiss you insanely / Whenever I have a cliff in front of me / You keep in love professional" (1–3). The speaker explicitly shows her deep love for her man. In another poem, "Democracy" (*In the Beginning* 20), al-Sabah asserts the idea that women must express their feelings freely.

> Democracy is not
> That man says his opinion on politics
> Without objecting to him
> Democracy is when a woman says
> Her opinion about love . . .
> Without being killed by anyone!! (1–7)

She sees that democracy is efficient only when a woman, not a man, is able to talk about love. al-Sabah rejects the Kuwaiti tribal society in which women are not allowed to discuss love.

Alexandra Kollontai, a Russian feminist, has similar views concerning love and marriage. She believes that proletarian family should be replaced by a union of two equal members who are united by love and mutual respect. Kollontai writes,

> Marriage will be a union of two persons who love and trust each other. Such a union promises to the working men and women who understand themselves and the world around them the most complete happiness and the maximum satisfaction. Instead of the conjugal slavery of the past, communist society offers women and men a free union which is strong in the comradeship which inspired it. (qtd in Roelofs 170)

For Kollontai, marriage should be built on love and passion, not on sexual attraction. She insists that egoism, possessing the partner, and patriarchy are the reasons for gender inequality. In her elegy, "The Last Sword" (*Last Swords* 15) al-Sabah laments the death of her husband and sees him as a man of freedom, "It is difficult for the free people to surrender / The destiny of the great, is to remain great" (10–12). She also appreciates his guidance, behavior, and support.

> You were my tribe and my island . . .
> And the bewitched beach, my tent in the middle of wind,
> Who will pass after you my spread tears? (42–4)

The poet recalls the most beautiful moments she lived with her husband, who for her was the tent, the warmth, the tribe, the father, and the unlimited giver. He gave the ultimate freedom and power to his wife on various levels—spiritually, emotionally, and intellectually: "You did not nullify an opinion or suppress a feeling" (60–1).

Moreover, al-Sabah condemns men's patriarchy and gender inequality in her poems, such as "A Subzero Man" (*In the Beginning* 7). In *Sexual Politics* (1970), Kate Millett argues that women's oppression is the result of their femininity. Men and women are not different only because of biological, psychological, and cultural distinctions, but also because of social restrictions (Millet 28–9). According to Millet, patriarchy is a primary cause of women's oppression and is socially constructed. Both Millett and al-Sabah show that women are as capable of choice as men. They can choose to free themselves from men's control. But while Millett believes in women's economic independence and equal education, al-Sabah does not specify what kind of independence. Both writers argue that men put women in the category of the Other to control them and use this point of view as an excuse not to understand women or their problems. This stereotyped relationship is represented in societies dominated by hierarchical power of men. However, al-Sabah cannot fully see that her country itself imposes restrictions and conventions which make women inferior to men. Both writers show that marriage imposes a stiff structure on feelings and passion that should naturally have no strict form.

When women depend completely on their husbands, they are controlled by their husbands and feel inferior to them. A woman's body is humiliated by the hands of abusive men. In "A Subzero Man" (*In the Beginning* 7), she says,

> Oh Hulaguo of this age . . .
> Take away the sword of oppression
> You are a dark man . . .
> Tragic . . .
> Aggressive . . . (1–5)

The speaker, a woman, addresses Hulaguo, a Mongol ruler and a symbol of cruelty who had conquered much of western Asia in the thirteenth century (Robinson 13). The speaker has a savage mind and writes his victories and conquests with his masculinity. The female becomes a paper in Hulaguo's diary. According to the law, a man can discipline a woman if she is really disobedient. But the speaker refuses, "You will not make me enter the House of Obedience" (al-Sabah 18). In the past, the House of Obedience was considered a kind of punishment for oppressed and unvoiced women. The parallels in, "Alienated from the actions of prohibition / And alienated from the actions of order" (20–1) assert the poet's refusal of men's suppressive power. The speaker hates sexual violence, "Your bed is like a grave" (27). She calls first for respect and appreciation, "I am a woman" (20). She has a mind and body; she is not subjugated to a vulgar man.

Suad al-Sabah criticizes sexual and power relationships which are dominated by tyrannical men. This is illustrated by the use of the powerful verb, "woe" in "Woe to women from men if they dominate women" (28). Ruth Rosen posits that women were beaten and raped repeatedly because they were seen as possessions of their husbands in the sixties and seventies (100). Women are similar to inanimate objects, such as fans, warmers, and dolls. This imagery reflects the insignificant position of women, "They want an instrument of entertainment and a matter of desire / And fans in their summer, and warmer in winter" (28–34). The poet condemns the fact that some men abuse women physically without any right. She makes efforts to change gender stereotypes yet does not seek to establish professional opportunities for women which are equal to those for men.

Patriarchy, male supremacy, and capitalism are main factors in determining the oppression of women. Socialist feminists see capitalism as the root of male dominance. The main aspect of socialist feminism is that gender, race, and class participate in shaping gender inequality. al-Sabah does not mention the role of capitalism within the Kuwaiti society, but within the family in which Kuwaiti women mainly depend financially on their husbands. This is a big reason of their suppression. Socialist feminists believe that women's liberation is a necessary quest for social, economic, and political justice. Women cannot be free from subjugation without their financial independence. Their liberation is based on the struggle against patriarchy, race, class, sexual orientation, or economic status (Kennedy 502). While feminists around the whole world were examining the gendered roots of violence, inequality, and poverty, Kuwait feminists accept the norms of the tribe because they are conservative, and the majority has less problems concerning poverty. For example, in "Female 2000" (*In the Beginning* 1), al-Sabah addresses women married to rich husbands and encourages them to leave materialistic properties and seek their freedom, "And I could have / Twinkled with rubies and turquoise" (12–3). The poet believes that jewelry will not grant women any interests or stop persecutions against them.

> I . . . Could have read nothing.
> Written nothing, cared for nothing
> But the limelight, fashions, and travel. (16–9)

The image suggests that reading and writing are ways of defending women's personalities and rights. The poet forsakes materialistic possessions—limelight, fashion, and travel—for the sake of intellectual rewards: reading and writing. The poet announces her war in the last couplet, "But I betrayed the laws of the female / And chose to fight with my words" (30–1). She chooses to face problems, insecurities, and difficulties, "To scream in the face of tragedy" (23).

During the eighties, Islamic groups contributed to a return to traditional values and the rejection of the Western feminist movement. In 1982, these Islamic groups rejected a petition that called for women's right to vote (al-Nagar 328). Under the influence of Islamists and being conservative and religious, Kuwaiti women were very restricted concerning clothing and work. For example, Bedouin women were veiled and not allowed to be educated or work. They accepted the norms of the tribe without any objection. However, because of many factors, including colonial influence, circumstances have changed gradually in the society (Hiedr 2). Many Kuwaiti women travel for scholarships and return back unveiled.

There are other transformations in the Kuwaiti society. In "They Say" (*In the Beginning* 2), al-Sabah frees women from the restrictions of society.

> Why is male singing permissible?
> And the voice of women becomes vice? (1, 10)

For the tribe, virtue is connected with wearing the veil. The speaker breaks the tribe's law with her uncovered hair, "I broke the wall of virtue with my hair" (2). The interrogative question, "How will a poetess be born in the tribe?" (4) demonstrates how she changes the rules of the tribe by writing and singing. The questions express her refusal and sarcasm of this kind of suppression toward women. Changes in dress and physical activity have often been part of feminist movements. Taking off the veil is a sign of rebellion against the norms of the restricted society. al-Sabah does not rebel against the limitations of the society from a Western point of view or an Islamic one, but rather from the perspective of an educated Kuwaiti woman that changes views and beliefs of her people. She does not follow standards of Western feminism and is not influenced by Islamists who have certain agendas. For the veil issue, al-Sabah does not wear it until she turns forty mainly because she becomes more influenced by Islamic modesty. By wearing the common cloth of her tribal women, the poet also accepts the norms of the society without being enforced. In her article "Do Muslim Women Really Need Saving?" (2002), Lila Abu-Lughod tries to discuss why Westerners try to change Muslim women's appearance, and impose their own visions, practices, and conventions on Islamic countries. She believes that Westerners have colonial policies in the Middle East and use women as tools of penetration in formation and transformation of these Arabic countries.

> When you save someone, you imply that you are saving her from something. You are also saving her *to* something. What violences are entailed in this transformation, and what presumptions are being made about the superiority of that to which you are saving her? Projects of saving other women depend on and reinforce a sense of superiority by Westerners, a form of arrogance that deserves to be challenged. (Abu-Lughod 788–9)

Abu-Lughod argues that we need to accept the Other—women, Islamists, or peoples—regardless of their circumstances or appearance. People should accept women in general—cultured and liberated women or indigenous women who lack supremacy—without looking at their histories and circumstances. Instead of saving women, which implies a kind of superiority, Westerners can help women to understand historical changes, achieve goals, and defend global injustice in which women find themselves. Abu-Lughod calls for political and historical investigation concerning oppression, persecution, and equality, instead of a religious and cultural investigation. Dividing the world into East and West, veiled and unveiled women, Muslims and non-Muslims will lead to more divisions and clashes. She sees the intervention to save women in Arabic and Islamic countries as a colonial act. For example, Westerners focus greatly on the issue of Islamic women's veil as a sign of submission but ignore the women's education and health problems (Ahmed 56). She argues that in some Arabic societies, wearing a veil offers modesty, respect, and protection, and believes that women are free to wear what suits them. They are social beings, live in certain social and historical contexts, and belong to communities with distinctive standards and rules. Abu-Lughod sees that it is time not to impose one form of clothing on Muslim women (187). Differences and distinctions are important and required for peoples, groups, movements, and freedoms.

al-Sabah's poetry does not examine women's issues in detail or give any practical solutions to these problems, yet it introduces radical views concerning her nation and nationalism. The concept of nation becomes a cultural heritage, a part of people's identity and life. Nationalism is necessary and has an important role in forming people's thoughts, feelings, and actions. Nationalism is considered an attitude of the individual's positive identification with his nation (Basu 95). Homi Bhabha says, "Nation-ness, indeed, is the most universally legitimate value in the political life of contemporary society" (17). Nationality also becomes a political nation-state relationship. Nation consciousness, shaped by land and culture, gives international dimensions within a bounded space and social boundaries (Holsti 73). Nationalism is the product of political ideology where cultural, physical, and political boundaries influence one's life and society. al-Sabah defends her country in the face of colonizers. She defends her country against Iraq occupation in 1990, and calls for freedom for Arab countries, such as Lebanon and Palestine. Her feminine voice, her royal family, education, and husband shape her personality and sense of national identity.

> Aware of her role as a spokesperson for 'the Arab nation as a whole,' al-Sabah as a woman poet has decided to visit the Arab past in order to show and praise the patriotism of her ancestors and reflect it in her poetry. (Hashim and Alobeid 7)

The poet defends her country in many poems and encourages Arab societies to develop national identity and consciousness whenever they face colonization and wars. In "My Body is a Palm that grows on Bahr al-Arab" (*Fragments* 184), al-Sabah expresses her belonging to her motherland.

> I am the daughter of Kuwait,
> Of the sandy shores that slumber
> By the waters like a gorgeous deer. (1–3)

The imagery in "Then oil came as a cursed devil" (12) reflects the speaker's hate and anger from oil discovery in her land, since it is the main cause of corruption. People become like slaves because of oil, "And men and women slipped at his feet" (13). She demonstrates how Arabs leave their principles and become affected by Western standards. Arabs have illegal relationships with women; they throw money at the women's feet, "And foreign women . . . / perfume our nights / The dinars on the feet are thrown . . . / On the bodies" (30–33). The speaker condemns such behaviors. The metaphor in "Thus my father's enrich sword cries on the wall" (36) reflects the poet's forefathers' struggle and determination. al-Sabah reminds readers with her grandfathers' champions, "They befriended death and tirelessly pursued their dreams" (25). The speaker's anger and feeling of loss express her revolutionary voice, "O land that has slept so long / In bed of gold / Get angry" (52–4).

> Can I ever be anything but an Arab?
> My body is a palm tree fed by the waters of Bahr al-Arab,
> And my soul reflects all the errors, all the sorrows. (99–101)

The image of palm tree expresses her patriotism and love. Although the poet feels bitterness, she ends her poem with hope, "Wait for the roses that / rise from ruin" (119–20). It is her sense of nationalism and patriotism that makes her acute and forceful in resisting colonizers. When Iraq occupied Kuwait in 1990, there were lots of massacres and killings. In her article, "I Bear a Nation File" (1990), al-Sabah wrote:

> What calls for irony is that you see a tank that gives you a lesson in Arab nationalism, the unity of blood, language, religion and destiny, and deals with you on the Nazi or Israeli way of blowing up houses, emptying the land of its residents, and importing new residents instead of them . . . What happened in Kuwait under Iraqi colonialism is a literal and transmitted model of Nazi practices in Eastern European countries . . . and Israeli practices in occupied Palestine. (*Will You Let Me* 9)

al-Sabah makes a comparison between Iraq's invasion of Kuwait and Israel's occupation of Palestine. She sheds light on the Nazi's horrible killings and bombing in Eastern Europe. She also mentions the role of Arabs during the period of Iraq's invasion. Some countries and governments—like Egypt and Saudi Arabia—defended Kuwait; others were silent and betrayed justice. In another article, "Peace upon you. . . . Egypt," al-Sabah thanks Egypt for its role during the Gulf crisis:

> Egypt was great in everything, great in its position, great in its morals, and great in its Arab values and ideals. It did not express any kind of hypocrisy, did not compromise, did not cheat with playing cards, and did not compliment the rich at the expense of the poor, nor the strong at the expense of the weak. Egypt acted as a civilization, as any prestigious and civilized country behaves, and did not resort to Machiavellian, deception, or cheap political tactics, as some did at the summit held in Cairo. (*Will You Let Me* 1)

al-Sabah appreciates Egypt's role in defending Arabic countries and national issues throughout her literary career. The poet fights for freedom against colonization and oppression. In "Three urgent telegrams to my country" (*Urgent Telegrams* 64), al-Sabah faces Arabic tyrants and tyranny, "We Kuwaitis from our manners / reject all kinds of injustice" (20–1). She expresses her pain and sorrow, "O you who planted spears in the ribs of my people / How can a lover take up guns?" (21–2). She believes that colonizers can colonize lands, but they can never "colonize souls" (32). In another poem, "Who Killed Kuwait?" (*Urgent Telegrams* 71), al-Sabah condemns the war on

Kuwait: "How does a rose die without a reason? / How does a palm die without reason?" (3–4). She likens her country to innocent objects, a rose and a palm, and uses interrogative questions to know the identity of the treacherous, "Do you think a foreigner is her killer? / Or an Arab came from the Arab land?" (6–7). She cannot believe that it is an Arab country, Iraq, that has betrayed her homeland, "How can I / Turn a blind eye to the blight of a homeland gripped in the / fangs of terror?" (17–9). The speaker's frustration and helplessness are illustrated by the use of questions, "How can I / Pass over the state of spiritual bankruptcy?" (20–1). The state of national frustration is due to the breakdown of the Arabs' bond. Arabs no longer belong to each other; they attack and cheat themselves. "A skull laments a skull / And shoes are buried near shoes" (44–5). Both the colonized and the colonizer are dead, "Slain crying slain" (43). The poet reflects the futility of killing, and believes that unity, wisdom, and national identity do not develop from massacres.

In conclusion, al-Sabah is a remarkable Kuwaiti voice; she calls for change and freedom of women and Arabs. She supports the liberation principles of women's mind, and resists men's oppression toward women, yet the concept of women's rights is not presented adequately in her poetry. Her analysis and understanding of women's experience are fitted within the requirements and norms of her country. al-Sabah does not have a strong revolutionary feminist voice because of personal and political restrictions. al-Sabah does not call for a rejection of men or a rebellion against oppressive inherited values of her society, but a refusal of men's physical and psychological persecution toward women.

Although al-Sabah writes about women's issues, she does not go deep in exploring various topics of feminism. She talks about women's problems on the level of family only; she focuses on men's patriarchy within the marriage bond. Unlike feminists, who struggle for all women, the poet neglects problems of other women from different races, colors, and religions. She also does not talk about women's rights for divorce, custody of their children, or the minimum age for marriage. She refuses to introduce shocking topics to the Kuwaiti society, and gives general slogans concerning women's suppression to men's passive supremacy. Her poetry does not encourage women for education or taking care of their health.

Nevertheless, the poet has a strong and influential national voice, and defends her country and Arab countries against colonization, injustice, and corruption. Her national and political voice is directed toward colonizers who attack her country, but she does not discuss internal political or economic issues in her poetry, especially those of women inside Kuwait. However, al-Sabah enhances her people's sense of national identity when they face dangers or wars. Her poetry provides a strong struggle against the other's colonial and imperial hegemony.

Works Cited

Abu-Lughod, Lila. "Do Muslim Women Really Need Saving? Anthropological Reflections on Cultural Relativism and Its Others." *American Anthropologist*, vol. 104, no. 3, New York, Columbia UP, 2002, pp. 783–790.

Ahmed, Leila. *A Quiet Revolution: The Veil's Resurgence, from the Middle East to America.* New Haven, CT, Yale UP, 2011.

al-Bahaweid, Shiekha. "Is There Any Real Feminism in Kuwait?" *ElManshour*, 2016.

al-Daghfa, Huda. "Arabic Feminism." *AlFaisl Magazine,* no. 493–4, King Faisl Center for Islamic Search, Saudi Arabia, 2017.

al-Nagar, Baqr Suliman. *Maintaining Modernity in the Arab Gulf: Transformations of Society and the State.* Kuwait, Dar al Saqi, 2018.

al-Sabah, Suad. *In the Beginning Was a Female.* Kuwait, Dr. al-Sabah Publishing House, 1988.

———. "The Last Sword." *Last Sword.* Kuwait, Suad al-Sabah Publishing House, 1991, p. 15.

———. "My Body Is a Palm That Grows on Bahr al-Arab." *Fragments of a Woman,* translated by Nehad Selaiha, Kuwait, Suad al-Sabah Publishing House, 1995, p. 184.

———. *Urgent Telegrams to My Country.* Kuwait, Suad al-Sabah Publishing House, 1992.

———. *Will You Let Me Love My Country?* Kuwait, Suad al-Sabah Publishing House, 1990.

Basu, Aparna. "Feminism and Nationalism in India, 1917–1947." *Journal of Women's History*, vol. 7, no. 4, The Johns Hopkins UP, winter 1995, pp. 95–107.

Bhabha, Homi. *Nation and Narration.* New York, Routledge, 1990.

Cooper, Brittney. "Intersectionality." *The Oxford Handbook of Feminist Theory*, edited by Lisa Disch and Mary Hawkesworth, Oxford Handbooks online 2016, pp. 1–15. Online publication D01:10.1093/oxfordhb/9780199328581/013.20

Crenshaw, Kimberlé. "Kimberlé Crenshaw – On Intersectionality – Keynote – WOW 2016." *YouTube*, uploaded by Southbank Centre, 14 Mar. 2016.

Friedan, Betty. *The Feminine Mystique.* W. W. Norton & Company, 2001.

GDP. "GDP Per Capita, Current US Dollars." *Wayback Machine*, 4 May 2012.

Hashim, Heba M. and Walid Alobeid. "The Arab Girl's Pride of Her National Identity: A Reading of Suad Al-Sabah's Poetry." *European Scientific Journal*, vol. 13, no. 32, Gulf States, 2017, pp 38–48.

Hiedr, Khaliel Ali. "Kuwaiti Feminism and the Religious Trend." 2010, *Eilaf.* London, Eilaf Publishing Limited, 11 July 2020.

Holsti, K.J. *Taming the Sovereigns: Institutional Change in International Politics.* Cambridge, Cambridge UP, 2004.

Kennedy, Elizabeth Lapovsky. "Socialist Feminism: What Difference Did It Make to the History of Women's Studies?" *Feminist Studies*, vol. 34, no. 3, 2008.

Millett, Kate. *Sexual Politics.* New York, Doubleday & Company, 1970.

Robinson, Francis. *The Mughal Emperors and the Islamic Dynasties of India, Iran and Central Asia.* Thames and Hudson Limited, 2007.

Roelofs, Joan. "Alexandra Kollontai: Socialist Feminism in Theory and Practice." *International Critical Thought*, vol. 8, no. 1, 2018, pp. 166–75.
Rosen, Ruth. *The World Split Open: How the Modern Women's Movement Changed America*. New York, The Penguin Group, 2000.
Walker, Rebecca. "Becoming the Third Wave," *Ms Magazine*, 1992.

13 "An Islam of Her Own"
A Critical Reading of Leila Aboulela's *Minaret*

Wafaa H. Sorour

This chapter raises some inquiries on the intricate formation of identity of Muslim women in postcolonial societies. Despite their former acquaintance of Western norms, they confront crucial predicaments far beyond their experience. The paper scrutinizes *Minaret* (2005), Leila Aboulela's second novel which narrates the dilemma of the colonized whose early exposure to Western norms could not save them. For them, appropriateness and modification cannot be easily attained without the least awareness of the positive values of both cultures. Having stumbled into fatal trials and errors, the protagonist of *Minaret* finds it a must to grope for her religious identity. The paper postulates that, eventually, she finds her own faith.

Leila Aboulela is a writer born in Egypt to a Sudanese father and an Egyptian mother. She was raised in Khartoum with a multi-cultural background. Although her novel *Minaret* is not biographical, it is typical of the kind of versatile background in postcolonial Sudan. Aboulela attended the Khartoum American School and a Catholic sisters' girl's school. She grew up reading many Western classics, which was unusual for Arabs at that time. Instead of studying literature, she pursued studying economics at the University of Khartoum. Reflecting on the cultural experience of her childhood in Sudan, Aboulela commented, "Sudan is not Arab enough for Arabs and not African enough for Africans" (Kushkush). Being a Sudanese, an Arab, a Muslim, and a British citizen, she had a difficult time coping with such a multi-cultural background. In an essay titled "And My Fate Was Scotland" (2000), Aboulela recalls the difficult transitions of moving from Sudan to England, and from England to Scotland: "I also moved from a religious Muslim culture to a secular one and that move was the most disturbing of all, the trauma that no amount of time could cure, an eternal culture shock" ("My Fate" 189). Regardless of the different trajectories of life's courses, there are some meeting points; both she and Najwa—her protagonist—raise issues about identity and post-colonialization.

In *An Islam of Her Own*, Sherine Hafez investigates the hidden world of the Egyptian Islamic movement. Gamiyat al-Hilal was a private Islamic organization which flourished during the 1990s in Egypt and succeeded in attracting a huge voluntary participation of women, especially "the educated women of the Egyptian middle class society" (Hafez 3). Hafez was doing research on the controversial relationship between "secular modernity and Islam" (4). Regardless of the principle of collectivity that occurs behind such religious activities, the author finds out that for these women activists, "religion was defined as a personal relationship with God" (Hafez 5). Inspired by the luminous title of *An Islam of Her Own*, I investigate the case of Najwa, the protagonist of *Minaret* whose immanent faith has endowed her with a version of Islam that is her own.

The paper mainly relies upon various postcolonial critiques to understand the protagonist's search for her identity. The British American historian Bernard Lewis made extensive investigation on the diverse components of identities in the Middle East. Lewis considers religion as "the ultimate determinant of identity" (Lewis 13). Lewis' conclusion is summed up in the title Aboulela has chosen for this novel. *Minaret* bears the significance of religious rites of prayers and regular attendance at the mosque. Religion features heavily throughout the novel but is conceived differently according to the context of the narration. The brief introductory part begins with, "Bism Allahi, Ar-rahman, Ar-raheem" (Aboulela, *Minaret* 1). The introductory part ends with a sacred Hadith on mercy. However, in Najwa's case, Lewis' finding requires narrowing since the word "religion" might carry diverse connotations.

Abdulkader Tayob classifies modern Muslim identities in the aftermath of the Iranian Revolution: "These were the reformers (modernist, adaptationists), Islamists (fundamentalists) and traditionalists" (Masud et al. 280). It was then that the Islamic political discourse began to propagate for Fundamentalism anew in Sudan and other Arab countries. The term Fundamentalism may cover "puritan movements perpetuating the Ibn Taymiyya-Wahhabi intellectual tradition. Sufism allegedly combines ill with the basic attitude of such movements" (Bruinessen 157–72). On the whole, these movements are at odds with all aspects of secularism and modernization.

During Najwa's life in Sudan, she is well acquainted with modernity and sheer secularism. Outwardly, Najwa is a privileged classy girl, supposedly a snob. Paradoxically, she says, "I wished I could feel like an emancipated young student driving her own car with confidence" (Aboulela, *Minaret* 16). She is assimilated into the most indulgent part of Euro-oriented practices in dress and lifestyle. Her relationship with religion is remote and vague. She feels emptiness whenever she hears the azan and sees other people go to prayers: "The words and the way the words sounded went inside me . . . A hollow place. A darkness that would suck me in and finish me" (Aboulela, *Minaret* 31). Najwa's mother, with good intentions, tries to inculcate into her some rites on charity taking bags of old clothes, sweets, and lollipops to the handicapped orphans.

Najwa is used to fasting during Ramadan without fully grasping the values associated with this month.

Another key theory is attributed to the Canadian philosopher Charles Taylor who relates the construction of the modern identity exclusively to the age of Enlightenment. Reversely, the French philosopher and psychiatrist, Frantz Fanon stuck to colonization as the most influential factor pertained to the construction of the Muslim identities. According to Taylor, "the notion of identity, cannot be separated from the emergence of a modern, egalitarian state. Identity became important when the state left behind a status-based system for the different classes to which an individual belonged" (Masud et al. 262). Taylor's illumination of his theory attributes to the French Revolution all the evolution "of identity in modernity and the Enlightenment" (Masud et al. 280). This was partly, but negatively, admitted by Fanon who "located it in colonialism and post-colonialism" (Masud et al. 280).

The following analysis will conform with Taylor's and Fanon's theories since they bear witness to the factors molding Najwa's identity. In the first seven episodes of the novel, Najwa recalls in retrospect her university years in Sudan. Through them, Aboulela smoothly hints at the hidden religious turmoil in Khartoum, anticipating the political upheaval which wrecked the city. There are evidences that the political and economic system in Sudan is antiquated and corrupted.

Najwa's family makes an acute paradigm of post-coloniality. The heat of the climate has been customarily incentive for public protest in Khartoum for reasons related to, "resource scarcity and climate change, and their often devastating consequences for vulnerable populations" (Verhoeven 680). The status of Najwa's family is of a privileged minority rated, hierarchically speaking, superior by the power of money to the rest of their Sudanese fellow men. Her father is part of the junta who enlisted "external funds and discourses in their attempts to concentrate wealth and power in Khartoum" (Verhoeven 680). Although the protest was political and economic, it took the form of a religious coup, nominally, fundamentalist. This is the typical masquerading of religion meant by Karl Marx and Friedrich Engels as they condemn "a seemingly religious conflict as a case of class struggle of poor peasants against their oppressors" (Bruinessen 157–72). Najwa's fragility is typical of Taylor's reasons for excluding the status of the family or any "natural inequality" (Masud et al. 263) as antithetical to the formation of a sound modern identity. Najwa's consciousness has been shaped by rather nontraditional parents who spend their money and time on expensive private schooling, Ethiopian servants, parties, Westernized clubs, drinks, and dance. These postcolonial norms were counteracted by the equally vain and extreme form of religiosity. It was as if Najwa had been living up to the standard of the old system, a "status based system" (Masud et al. 262).

The structure of the novel is divided into thirty-six anonymous episodes designed as phases of Najwa's seemingly inconclusive groping for a fixed identity among diverse conflicting ones. The chronological order of its events hovers between the protagonist's present stay in London and recollections from the early years in Sudan. The timing pattern moves from present, to past, and back to the present. At first sight, the scheme of narration seemingly conveys a lack of design, as Aboulela brings twists of perspective between the two discrete cultures. This fits with Najwa's simultaneous lack of fixity. The novel narrates the calamity of Najwa and her family who flee from Sudan and eventually settle in London, England. After a cathartic episode of humiliation, degradation, and impoverishment, Najwa—now a devout Muslim—narrates her life in retrospect. She speaks of her family's tragedy, beginning with her brother's drug addiction and imprisonment, her father's execution, and her mother's fatal disease and death. It is through this radical journey of leaving her home that Najwa grapples to find her true self.

In the opening lines of the novel, the protagonist describes her place of birth humbly in a mode fitting the resilience of a true Muslim: "I've come down in the world. I've slid to a place where the ceiling is low and there isn't much room to move. Most of the time I'm used to it. Most of the time I'm good. I accept my sentence and do not brood or look back" (Aboulela, *Minaret* 1). There are some vague existential alignments between the autumn of London and her being middle-aged: "Now it is at its best, now it is poised like a mature woman whose beauty is no longer fresh but still surprisingly potent" (1). The vastness, commodity, and aura of St. John's Wood High Street reflects a state of modernity characteristic of western civilization. Najwa holds a comparison between the prestigious condition of the building she enters and the luxurious, but devastated condition of her family.

In an interview with Claire Chambers, there is an undertone of suspicion surrounding Aboulela's ignoring 9/11, hinting at Islamophobia, meanwhile overlooking extremism: "There's not really any extremism in your depiction. Is it your experience that extremism isn't terribly prevalent?" (Chambers 99). Aboulela clarifies that she neither glorifies the Islamic values cherished by those movements, nor minimizes the Western norms. "There *is* extremism, but I wanted to explore the lives of Muslims who aren't passionate about politics. I wanted to write about faith itself" (Chambers 99). Najwa's narration articulates the spirit of religiosity in the Sudanese society in the years preceding the 1989 *coup d'état* and among some Arab Muslims in London. At the University of Khartoum, the social prestige of her family alienates her. The utmost antagonism is triggered against Najwa by her communist colleague, Anwar al-Sir. She is stunned by the binary ideological frame of her colleagues and professors. There were the students belonging to the Islamic organization and their counterpart: members of the Democratic Front Party.

She is taught Marxist Economy by a communist professor, reversely, her math professor belongs to the Muslim Brotherhood. Amidst this diverse environment, her father is arrested and later on is to be executed after a political trial. The family moves to London as political refugees. Najwa's eventual leave to London radically transmutes her identity.

Max Weber criticizes the wide chasm between Islam and modernity, and the "polarization between two forms of Islam, . . . dialectic, not complementary" (Masud et al. 39–43). Aboulela points out that most fictional depictions of Muslim characters "are either fundamentalists or completely liberal," she said. "They never write about the people who are in the middle" (Kushkush). The novel presents three categories of Muslim men whose code of religiosity sway between liberalism and commitment. Omar, Anwar, and Tamer represent different attitudes toward religion and modernity. The protagonist's brother—Omar—and her colleague—Anwar—are two negative paradigms of secular Muslim identities. For Omar "anything Western was unmistakably and unquestionably better than anything Sudanese" (Aboulela, Minaret 131). In Sudan, Omar neglected all the aspects related to religion and custom. In London, he is not able to conceive that perseverance and hard work are at the core of Western values. Instead, he spends lavishly on drugs and ends his life in prison.

As for Anwar, he is a hypocrite. He feels at home at the ethnic scene of an Ethiopian restaurant, as "he always became uncomfortable under the gaze of anyone white." Najwa remembers, "for him, more than for me, London was temporarily exotic" (Aboulela, *Minaret* 168). Denying all kinds of values and faith is a basic part of his ideology as a communist. He describes fasting as "a community activity" (231). A good part of his attitude in life is Machiavellian; he squeezes Najwa's money so that he can enroll at university. What is worse, he makes her soul guilt-ridden. Both he and Omar are blind to the fact that they are not good enough for living in the west.

The first time Najwa saw Tamer, she says "I have heard the saying that You can smell Paradise in the young" (Aboulela, *Minaret* 3). In a conversation with Tamer, he expresses the complexity of his identity: "My education is Western and that make me feel that I am western. My English is stronger than my Arabic. So I guess . . . no I don't feel very Sudanese though I would like to be. I guess being a Muslim is my identity" (110). His words reveal that when race, ethnicity, and gender are of minimal worth, religion becomes a crucial aspect of identity. In different degrees, they undergo the negative aspects of post-coloniality. In their cult of everything that is Western, Tamer's family underestimates his desire to study Islamic history. Timidity and lack of self-possession are common traits for Najwa and Tamer. Same as Najwa, Tamer has a keen interest in Sufism. Like many of the young men of his class, he is impressed by Amr Khaled's modernized Islamic TV program. The two of them pay reverence to Ramadan, he spends days in seclusion at the mosque. But the two of them possess what can be described as "sovereignty of soul, between publicness and inwardness" (Masud et al. 13). She cannot completely attain self-fulfillment and self-consciousness unless she is with him. In terms of perseverance to Islamic laws, she is as strict as him; she is pleased by his insistence on halal food, and nearly reminds him of not eating while standing. But she can be more resilient than him. Her self-denial overcomes her love for him. Like a true Muslim, she can never set Tamer into rebellion with his mother. It is her faith which stabilizes her against desire and vulnerability.

Paradoxically, Aboulela brings out a more practical model of religiosity out of the character of Ali, a convert and married to Wafaa, the one who shrouded Najwa's mother. It is the funeral of Najwa's mother which got her acquainted with those women who helped her resolve the conflict between her original identity as a Muslim and her assimilated secular one. Wafaa, Shahinaz, and Um Waleed are part of the fundamentalist community in London who attend religious lessons at the mosque. In dress, they remind Najwa of the other Muslim Fundamentalists who used to gather at university in Khartoum. Yet, their activities and practices materialize the ethical part of the ideology of Islam. In terms of inclusion, they seem alien to the Western mode; Najwa's cousin, Randa, mocks their fertility saying, "You know the type, the wife in hijab having one baby after the other" (Aboulela, *Minaret* 134). However, for Najwa, they act as the perfect guidance for her own mode of religiosity.

Aboulela brings out, beside the protagonist, three other parallel, as well as counterpart female models of secularism: the heroine's mother, her employer Doctora Zeinab, and her self-fulfilled daughter Lamya who is a "a certain type of Arab woman, . . . making the most of the West" (Aboulela, *Minaret* 2). Through them, Aboulela obliquely criticizes the negative aspects of post-coloniality; the unheeded freedom which has been, erratically, conducted by Najwa and her brother in London. Najwa recalls "this empty space was called freedom" (175). Additionally, complacency and self-indulgence ruined her brother's career and life. Vulnerability and lack of self-confidence stuck her into Anwar's abusive grip. "I would hold out and then give in to that side of me that was luxurious and lazy" (172). Paradoxically, her failure of accommodation was never expected, as she remembers, "they often joked about how Westernized I was, detached from Sudanese tradition" (230). With less exposure to such sporadic trials, she could have been like her relative Randa: "An average Sudanese girl, not too religious and not too unconventional" (235). Najwa is impressed by Lamya's success and brags of her integration saying, "I owe myself an absence of envy; I owe myself a heart free of grudges" (73). She says to her brother "If Baba and Mama had prayed, . . . if you and I had prayed, all of this wouldn't have happened" (95).

In another interview with Isma'il Kushkush, Aboulela comments that, "my characters are not role-model Muslims, but they struggle to make choices using 'Muslim logic.'" (Kushkush). Her goal was not to portray a fundamentalist, nor someone who is nominally a Muslim; the goal was rather to portray the vast majority that struggle for identity in between the two extremes. However, *Minaret* cannot be considered as a religious thesis perpetuating any Islamic group. In her investigation into the aftermath of postcolonialism in Sudan, Aboulela is concerned with the dilemma of the individual rather than the state. After the political upheaval of the 1980s, Najwa cannot feel at ease with the fundamentalist atmosphere at campus since it collides with the Western norms of her class. Meanwhile, she has not been sufficiently readied with any cultural maneuvers necessary for adaptation into the proper codes of the Western culture. Hence, she carries the same superficial attitude of post-coloniality with her for a time to London. Perplexingly, she feels the same sense of peripherality that she used to feel in Sudan. Things got worse with her libertine deluding affair with Anwar when the two of them felt, as Najwa says, "conscious that we were free" (Aboulela, *Minaret* 172). As a result, she has an abortion, which was the transformational point in the middle of sporadic and violent transition in Najwa's life. "For the first time, I disliked London and envied the English," but soon after she heated up a tin of soup, Najwa's dislike of London "went away" (174).

After series of catastrophic experiences, Najwa is obliged to come down to earth. Upon failing to enroll at a British university, finding a respectable job, guaranteeing a modest income, she begins to adopt a rigid lifestyle, merging Eastern and Western modes. She becomes conscious of the validity of hard work, self-restraint, and self-discipline. Her practicality is clear as money becomes more meaningful for her than praise or compliments. She is also keen on the utility of the food left over and the strict Islamic orders against throwing it away. In Sudan, she feels dismayed in the presence of the girls who belong to the Muslim Brotherhood. She perceives them according to the standards of her class and its secular upbringing. Paradoxically, it is in London when she embarks on norms that are typically Eastern as well as Islamic. Although she is normally of low profile, she remembers that she was once snobbish and envious of her fellow students in Khartoum who wear traditional dress or hijab, "I gazed at the tobes [hijabs] of the girls, the spread of colors, . . . And when they bowed down there was the fall of polyester on the grass" (Aboulela, *Minaret* 43). She has attained immense humbleness and modesty that she takes the ten-pound note from Doctora Zeinab as a tip. Astonishingly, with all her Western background, she accepts and even welcomes the notion of being a "concubine" (215).

Upon being dispossessed and deprived, Najwa gains moral prosperity. Like a true essentialist, elimination becomes one of her basic trajectories for spiritual evolution (Mckeown). She becomes well-informed of the

Islamic Ordination that she can rightly advise her friend Shahinaz, and the latter agrees saying, "I know it is an Islamic thing for a man to obey his mother" (Aboulela, *Minaret* 104). Najwa's evolution sprang following the climatic episode of her abortion. It is here that cultural clashes occur in their most severe forms: when there is not sufficient recognition of the pros and cons of each culture. Wearing a hijab comes as another crucial moment in Najwa's life. It was in a climactic moment that Najwa realizes the necessity of relating herself to "a collective Muslim identity" (Mustafa 6). Gathering with some Muslim women at the mosque and attending classes of *tajweed* and *tafsir* helps Najwa's self-emulation. Najwa finds refuge in being part of the collective Muslim community of Regent Park mosque. Amidst the Quran *tajweed* and *tafsir* classes, she overcomes timidity and is in her true element. For the first time in her life, she perceives herself with esteem and admiration. "I wrapped the tobe [hijab] around me and covered my hair. In the full-length mirror I was another version of myself, regal like my mother, almost mysterious" (Aboulela, *Minaret* 246). For her, wearing a hijab felt like "the external form of religion paled before the internal quest" (Helminski 89). Though the hijab is commonly mentioned as a symbol of gender oppression and backwardness, it becomes her way of salvation and pride. Aboulela clarifies Najwa's labeling of the hijab as a "uniform" (Aboulela, *Minaret* 186). In her own words, Aboulela thinks that "it does put a distance between you and other people, I think. Something is hidden" (Chambers 92). Quite unexpectedly, it offers Najwa freedom, serenity, and salvation.

Aboulela provides insight into the core of Najwa's identity, which is religious and thoroughly Eastern. The minaret is the symbol of the call to prayer in the Muslim culture; it signifies the place of prayer, the mosque, and the regular attendance of these prayers. It was this spiritual calling that brought Najwa back to the mosque to seek help in bringing forth her religious identity. This identity was suppressed for too long underneath the cultural conflicts of her past. The mosque eventually becomes the safe haven for Najwa, a place of spiritual comfort and eventual identity development for the protagonist. It is because Najwa feels as if she was marginalized in both worlds, the Sudan of her childhood, and her new home in London. It is at the mosque where she sought to reclaim her identity.

It costs Najwa immense loss to approach an eventual identity until she finds religion as a healing element. It is then palpable that the culture of one's childhood cannot be entirely removed. In Sudan and in the early part of her life in London, she dwells on restless speculation, leading an intricate and seemingly inconclusive path, and groping for a fixed identity among diverse conflicting ones. At the closing of the novel, the protagonist yearns for a final repatriation:

> I close my eyes . . . I doze and in my dream I am back in Khartoum,
> ill and fretful, wanting clean, crisp sheets, a quiet room to rest in,

wanting my parents' room. . . . It is a natural decay and I accept it. Carpets threadbare and curtains torn. Valuables squashed and stamped with filth. Things that must not be seen, shameful things are exposed. (Aboulela, *Minaret* 276)

"The past tugs but it is not possession that I miss. . . . Wish that not many doors have closed in my face; the doors of taxis and education, beauty salons, travel agents to take me on Hajj . . ." (Aboulela, *Minaret* 2). This encapsulates the drawbacks of Najwa's upbringing which assimilated her and her brother to the most vulnerable part of the Eastern and Western cultures. It also indicates that her current dreams are no longer mundane, instead, she dreams of the pilgrimage journey to Mecca as her final destination. Aboulela insists that the main protagonist in *Minaret*, "at the end she's relying on her faith" (Chambers 99). She eventually transits toward spirituality, recognizing what Sufi women concluded about "the very substance of life was spirituality" (Helminski 300).

The paper leads into a better awareness of how Muslim women living in Western societies stand perplexed between post-coloniality and modernity on one side, decolonization and religious fundamentalism on the other. Some of them adopt postcolonial Western norms, and others adhere to extreme counterpart. When she discards secularism as a discipline in life, she does not adhere to the rigid laws of Fundamentalism either. The Sufism which fits her nature is void of what is called "The shaykhs of the major Sufi orders (*tariqa, pl. turuq*)" (Masud 59). Her faith is deep and tested enough to understand what the Iranian poet Farid Ud-din Attar says about God's forgiveness: "I've sinned a hundred ways from negligence and found each time Your kind benevolence" (Barmania). To conclude, all the characters in *Minaret* adopt patterns of religiosity swaying between modernity and tradition and they reach a cultural dead end. As for Najwa, she has fashioned her own faith and finally finds "An Islam of her own."

Works Cited

Aboulela, Leila. "And My Fate Was Scotland." *Wish I Was Here: A Scottish Multicultural Anthology*, edited by Kevin Mac Neil and Alec Finlay, Edinburgh, Polygon, 2000, pp. 175–92.

———. *Minaret: A Novel.* New York, Black Cat, 2005.

Barmania, Sima. "Islam and Depression." *The Lancet Psychiatry*, vol. 4, no. 9, Elsevier Ltd, Sep. 2017, pp. 669–70. doi: 10.1016/S2215-0366(17)30322-X.

Bruinessen, Martin van. "Muslim Fundamentalism: Something to Be Understood or to be Explained Away?" *Islam and Muslim Christian Relations*, vol. 6, no. 2, 1995, pp. 157–171.

Chambers, Gail Claire. "An Interview with Leila Aboulela." *Contemporary Women's Writing*, vol. 3, no. 1, June 2009, pp. 86–102.

Fanon, Frantz. *Black Skin, White Masks.* NY: Grove P, 1968.

Hafez, Sherine. *An Islam of Her Own; Reconsidering Religion and Secularism in Women's Islamic Movements.* The American UP, 2011.

Helminski, Camille Adams, editor. *Women of Sufism: A Hidden Treasure.* Shambhala, 2003.

Kushkush, Isma'il. *One Foot in Each of Two Worlds, and a Pen at Home in Both.* Interview with Leila Aboulela, *The New York Times* 21 Mar. 2014.

Lewis, Bernard. *The Multiple Identities of the Middle East.* NY: Pantheon 1998.

Masud, Muhammad Khalid, et al., editors. *Islam and Modernity: Key Issues and Debates.* The American U in Cairo P, 2009.

Mckeown, Greg. "Essentialism: The Disciplined Pursuit of Less." *New York Times,* 2014.

Mustafa, Anisa. Paper for workshop, "Collective Identity, Muslim Identity Politics and the Paradox of Essentialism: Sense of Belonging in a Diverse Britain" 21–22 Nov. 2014.

Verhoeven, Harry. *Climate Change, Conflict and Development in Sudan: Global Neo-Malthusian Narratives and Local Power Struggles.* The Institute of Social Studies, The Hague, 2011.

14 Mobility, Survival, and the Female Body in Laila Lalami's *Hope and Other Dangerous Pursuits*

Amel Abbady

In her essay "So to Speak," Moroccan-American writer Laila Lalami re-examines her own identity as an Arab, Muslim woman who chose to "cast aside the colonial [French] tongue" and write in English so that she can look at her stories "with a fresh perspective" (Lalami, "So to Speak" 20). She recalls that the exact reason she started writing was her deep concern for Arab women who are often portrayed as "silent, oppressed, [and] helpless" (Lalami, "So to Speak" 20). In her debut novella *Hope and Other Dangerous Pursuits* (2005), Laila Lalami addresses the possibilities and limitations imposed on women by presenting two female characters who defy the stereotypical image of Arab women as passive subjectivities. The two characters, Halima and Faten, are not at all related, but their common plight as oppressed women is why they end up on the same boat fleeing from Morocco to Spain hoping to find a better life on the other shore of the Mediterranean. Both Halima and Faten pursue their own migratory projects unaccompanied by a male "guardian," and in the course of their movement they gain an entirely different understanding of their identities as well as of their bodies. The purpose of this article is to examine the complex network of mobility, identity, and the female body in Lalami's novel to emphasize the impact of mobility on the development of the female identity/body.

Because of their poverty, the twenty-nine-year-old Halima and her alcoholic husband always fight, and their fights usually end with her being violently beaten. Halima fears that if she seeks divorce, the judge would never let her keep the children. She tries to bribe the judge but eventually backs down. Instead, Halima decides to use the money to get herself and her three children a place on a boat to Spain. The other female protagonist, Faten Khatibi, is a conservative nineteen-year-old single girl who comes from a poor family. While repeating her final year in college, Faten forges a friendship with Noura, an upper middle-class urban girl with very liberal parents who did not approve of such a friendship. Unfortunately, Faten complains in public about the king and his government, and she is advised by her imam, her religious leader, to immediately migrate to Spain for fear of political persecution.

To emphasize the impact of mobility on the development of the female identity and body, this article adopts a theoretical framework that combines mobility studies with corporeal theory as proposed by Emma Bond in *Writing Migration Through the Body* (2018). In her book, Bond argues that the female body responds to certain acts of mobility in a significant manner that not only reshapes identity, but also allows for the development of a new "bodily identity" (Bond 100). The two central characters in Lalami's novel—Halima, whose body is pigmented and bruised as a result of domestic abuse, and Faten, who obsessively covers up her body from head to toe—undergo a drastic change in their identities and in the way they perceive the capacities of their bodies because of their unconventional acts of mobility.

Mobility as defined by Peter Adey is, "movement imbued with meaning" (*Mobilities* 63); it is not merely an act of moving from one point to another. He further explains that the way mobility is given a particular meaning "is dependent upon the context in which it occurs and who decides upon the significance it is given" (Adey, *Mobilities* 66). In most cultures, men seem to have always enjoyed the freedom of movement, given their physical abilities and, more importantly, the conventional gender roles that entitle them to move in order to fulfill their roles as breadwinners. This freedom of movement bestows even more power on men, compared to women who "are often defined as lacking a 'mobile subjectivity'" (Sheller, "Epilogue" 258). Thus, because women are seen as naturally weaker than men and because of the dangers entailed by the experience of moving, women, "have been routinely associated with stasis, confinement to a 'private sphere,' [and] the containment of bodily capacities" (Adey et al, "Routledge Handbook" 96). However, as evident in the novel, with the escalating political and economic pressures, both men and women have been forced to move in search for better opportunities. In many cases women are obliged to take responsibility for their own survival. Nevertheless, when women move alone, either locally or globally, "even when their physical motion appears to be exactly the same as men's, the meanings ascribed to it are never quite the same—indeed, they are often very different" (Adey et al, "Routledge Handbook" 97). This is particularly true for Middle Eastern women who could be bitterly denunciated if they move unaccompanied by a male "protector."

Women's confinement according to Middle Eastern traditions has a particular purpose; the preservation of the "very fine membrane called a hymen, which is considered one of the most essential, if not *the* most essential, part of her body" (al-Saadawi 51). Thus, on a symbolic level, limiting women's movement could be "linked to the closing of women's boundaries and the protection of their physical openings" (Johansen 81–2). More significantly, as Fataneh Farahani explains, in Muslim cultures "the insistence on the necessity of the virgin female body not only generates a monopoly on women's sexual behaviors, but also has enormous impact on the women's movement" (200). Accordingly, the confinement of women has largely been seen as the best policy to maintain a family's reputation and social standing. Thus, it is not expected to see Arab women depicted as the protagonists of migration narratives in Arabic literature since they, and indeed women in general, are seen as "passive subjectivities who do not follow an independent and personal migratory plan but move in the train of the protagonists" (Marchi 605). However, as depicted in Lalami's novel, the predominant domestic violence in the Middle East sometimes obliges women to risk their reputation by migrating alone.

Although gender-based violence is not associated exclusively with Muslim societies, David Ghanim points out that, "when patriarchal gender relations are supported and sanctioned by culture and religion, societal violence becomes naturalized, tolerated and accessible to everyone" (Ghanim 43). When Halima complains to her mother, the latter ignores the fully visible traces of beatings on her daughter's body and stresses that "The Lord is with those who are patient" (Lalami, *Hope* 53), which is a verse from the holy Quran. This "cultural and religious sanctioning of women's obedience" (Ghanim 44) explains why Halima's mother believes that Halima is the one who has to obey God by not "talking back" to her husband, Maati (Lalami, *Hope* 54). Thus, for Halima's mother, Maati's physical abuse of her daughter is rightfully justified since Halima's "oral ways of expressing [her]self are not mere words; they carry genuine . . . negative values" (Sadiqi 223) that challenge Maati's masculinity and, accordingly, challenge God's dictates.

This conviction is prevalent in almost the entire Arab/Muslim culture where women's obedience to husbands is directly linked to their obedience to God. Thus, unsurprisingly, Muslim women are rarely allowed to report incidents of physical violence, and if some incidents are reported, they "are not taken earnestly by authorities and are perceived as the private business of the family" (Ghanim 44). This "cultural sanctioning" of domestic violence is mostly due to the fact that, even though totally permissible by Islam, divorce in the Middle East is not merely an economic burden on a woman's family, but it could also "expose the family to shame" (Ghanim 52); a woman who fails to be a good wife is certainly not worthy of respect. Therefore, when Halima declares that she intends to seek divorce, her mother "slapped her hand on her thigh, spilling tea on the table" and said "Curse Satan" (Lalami, *Hope* 54), a phrase often used to express rejection of evil or unfavorable deeds. Halima's fear of shame and, more importantly, of losing custody of her children after divorce, force her to put up with her husband's violence, but not for long.

In *Writing Migration Through the Body*, Bond describes the body as "mutable, reactive and expressive archive . . . a mobile site of meaning" (1) that articulates emotions and experiences. Drawing on this argument,

Halima's experience as a submissive, helpless wife is indeed represented in her body, in "the dark patches on her face and the stoop in her shoulder [that] made her look much older" (Lalami, *Hope* 53). These visible markers establish Halima's body as a "site for registering . . . trauma" (Prosser 52) and an essential part of her identity. And although Linda Martin Alcoff refers to ontological, salient features of race and gender when she argues that "[t]he reality of identities often comes from the fact that they are visibly marked on the body itself" (5), Halima's powerless and subjugated identity is actually informed by the temporarily, yet recurrent, visual markers imprinted on her body; the "bubbly welts on her arms and face" (Lalami, *Hope* 52). Thus, aside from her original skin color, the acquired visible patches on her skin stand as signs that entail humiliating interpretations by outsiders.

Unlike the positive notion of ethnic and social visibility, then, these visible markers create a state of *"hyper-*visibility" where misconceptions and judgments are generated by people upon seeing them (Bond 30). Accordingly, Halima's plight is not merely about enduring the physical pain caused by Maati's beatings but, more significantly, in the fact that she is ashamed by her bruised body that would certainly "invite interpretation to discern what is behind it, beyond it, or what it signifies" (Alcoff 7). The shame caused by the visual markers on her body motivates Halima eventually to overturn this negative image by taking certain acts of mobility, since "[a]cquiring mobility is often analogous to a struggle for acquiring new subjectivity" (Cresswell and Uteng 2). Since divorce is never a woman's favorable option as explained earlier, Halima's first act of mobility is a visit to the sorceress whom she believes can help her "'soften' her husband's attitude and thus stop the beatings" (Ricci 49). "It took several weeks and another *three beatings* . . . before Halima managed to save the money to visit the sorceress her mother had recommended" (Lalami, *Hope* 56, emphasis mine). It is truly significant to punctuate Halima's movements with the number of beatings that she can stand, because it illustrates how reactive the body is. And even though Halima does not enjoy full agency, her traumatized body determines her destinations. When the beatings continue Halima takes a second, more daring, act of mobility: to the judge's house to offer him a bribe.

Halima's trip to the judge's house is her first step toward liberating her long-abused body and soul. However, "[t]aking a new route made her anxious, and she stood rigidly at the stop . . . The ride would be nearly an hour long, with many stops along the way, but she sat with her back straight, ready to get up at the slightest sign of trouble" (Lalami, *Hope* 64). Thus, even though Halima is extremely worried for carrying such a large sum of money to a strange place, her body surprisingly displays signs of strength to outsiders, despite her innate fear of being mugged. Being aware of the new place that she is about to experience alone, Halima's body resists her feelings of anxiety and fear and manages to present Halima to outsiders in a different identity frame. Through this act of mobility, Halima slowly recognizes the importance of her body image, particularly to those who do not know her previously and are unable to see the covered debasing markers on her skin, her "identity envelope" (Bond 30). Once she moves away from the familiar traumatic space that is her home, Halima's "bodily identity" shifts and morphs to meet the demands of mobility. The impact of mobility on Halima's identity is further proven through her unsettling encounter with the corrupt judge whom she tries to bribe then changes her mind.

When Halima attempts to take her money back, she "felt her knees tremble" before she speaks (Lalami, *Hope* 68). Despite these signs of weakness, what happens demonstrates that Halima is still experimenting with this new power that her body has gotten ever since she left her house:

> Halima dropped to her knees and clutched [the money] with both hands. The judge grabbed the back of her jellaba and pushed her. She drove her elbow into his gut with all the force she could gather. He bent over in pain, his arms folded over his stomach while Halima stepped outside, a fistful of bills in her hand. (Lalami, *Hope* 68–9)

Halima's encounter with the judge shows a sense of power that develops and grows as she moves to different places seeking her freedom. And now that her home, and the whole country indeed, becomes a traumatic space, Halima decides to "destabilize this pre-established notion by leaving 'home,' 'the country,' 'the inside,' and transcend geographical, historical, and cultural boundaries through the act of migration" (Ricci 43). Because of her earlier acts of mobility and the ensuant sense of agency, Halima recognizes that she can resist the physical and spiritual confinement ingrained in her sociocultural background by migration, which is "almost totally a male experience" (Sarasua 29). This unexpected daring act of Halima challenges the conviction that femininity is "stationery and passive" (Cresswell and Uteng 2) and emphasizes a certain level of development as to Halima's "capacity for agency" (Bond 133).

As explained earlier, Arab women's obligations to traditional gender roles of their culture negatively affect their "mobility potential" (Adey, *Mobilities* 128). In this context, Halima's unconventional acts of mobility, particularly across national borders, are seen as "transgressive actions" (Adey et al 96) that generate shame. Therefore, when her migration fails and she is sent back with her children to Morocco, her husband willingly divorces Halima since she violated the social and religious codes of their society and stigmatized him; hurrying to divorce Halima before she even asks would reinforce her husband's masculinity and recover his honor. As noted before, "Islam rejects the notion of the impurity of women" (Bouhdiba 14). Thus, this religious and cultural insistence on the purity of women's bodies hinders women's free movement because a woman moving alone is rarely expected to be able to protect her body. Although some would suggest that Halima's body disappoints her before and during her migration experience, a close examination of the other female protagonist, Faten, proves the opposite.

As noted earlier, "Arab and Muslim cultures enforce masculine power over women and present stereotypes of women as roaming dangerous creatures that need to be controlled and dominated" (Salhi 34). Clearly, this presumed "dangerous" aspect of a woman lies solely in her body. This has caused the female body in the Middle East to be seen, both by women and their families, as a source of shame, discomfort, and anxiety. Quite expectedly, "[r]eligious practices associated with female modesty (such as veiling, *purdah*, or general separation of the sexes) have prohibited women's travel or made it possible only with the accompaniment of male relatives" (Sheller "Epilogue" 259). Being a Muslim extremist, Faten is depicted as obsessively protective of her body; she even refuses to shake hands with her friend's father because, as part of her strict religious teachings, shaking hands with a man may arouse her or his sexual desires, and so it is strictly forbidden. Despite its lack of practicality on a dangerous illegal sea trip, Faten leaves Morocco wearing her typical Islamic dress; and although she deeply fears the experience ahead of her, she is still preoccupied with covering her body by "pull[ing] her black cardigan tight around her chest" (Lalami, *Hope* 3). Clearly, Faten is still clinging to her religious identity completely unaware of the strikingly different bodily experience that she is about to encounter.

Describing the body as "a malleable and regenerative site that shifts and changes through encounter and movement" (Bond 4) is best illustrated when Faten is obliged to jump into the sea and swim to shore. Faten is entirely helpless as she cannot swim, but now since her life is at stake, Faten's body responds in a manner "entirely alien to the religious and cultural traditions of . . . her identity" (Bond 177). The same person who refuses to shake hands with men, calls out to a stranger, Murad, asking for help. "He turns and holds his hand out to Faten. She grabs it and the next second she is holding both his shoulders. He tries to pull away, but her grip tightens . . . Her body is heavy against his. Each time they hob in the water, she holds on tighter" (Lalami, *Hope* 11). Despite her strict cultural beliefs, Faten's body is instantly changed by her mobility experience. Now that she is more occupied with survival, the anxiety and fear associated with her body disappear. Once she sets foot in Spain, Faten's body continues to shift in the most unexpected manner considering her cultural and religious beliefs.

When she is caught by the coast guards with other illegal migrants, Faten quickly realizes the power of her body when taken out of the context of her Arab/Muslim culture. The female body that on the other shore of the Mediterranean is a burden is here an asset. When Faten sees "one of the guards staring at her . . . [s]he didn't need to speak Spanish to understand that he'd wanted to make her a deal. She remembered what her imam had said . . . extreme times sometimes demanded extreme measure" (Lalami, *Hope* 141). This encounter with the Spanish police officer draws Faten's attention to this innate secret power of her body; she realizes that her "vulnerability and lack of rights" (Castañeda 185) as an illegal immigrant changes her body from a source of shame to a source of empowerment. She is aware that in this society where her true identity as a Muslim is unknown, her body is free; she needs not worry about the "gaze of the other" (Bond 41) anymore because this "Other" does not believe in the same cultural codes, hence would be unable to—or even interested in—judging her.

A foreigner's sense of "cultural invisibility," Bond suggests, could be "damaging." However, for Faten, being invisible comes as a relief to her since now she perceives herself as "shadow" or "ghost" (43). This new "place-based" identity (Sheller and Urry, "New Mobilities" 211) allows Faten to unleash her body potential so much that she even develops a taste for her favorite clients, i.e., "the teenager" (Lalami, *Hope* 127). Although some would sympathize with Faten and justify her behavior, it is completely unjustified that she spends three years in Madrid earning her living as an "odalisque," a prostitute, despite the fact that she is quite aware that prostitution in Islam is a "capital sin" (Bouhdiba 14). Clearly, Faten's body fails to resist, and even seems to enjoy, the temptations of this new agency acquired through the act of migration. However, at some level, Faten struggles "with how to negotiate both external expectations" (Bond 86) as a prostitute, and her inherent cultural and religious beliefs as a Muslim woman.

This internal conflict is articulated mainly through Faten's roommate, Betoul, a Muslim legal migrant who works as a babysitter and sends money to her family. This conflict arises from the fact that, with her roommate, Faten is in direct confrontation with a version of her older self. The image of Betoul as an ideal Arab woman who works hard for her family and, more importantly, still holds on to her cultural identity, is frustrating for Faten who could not live up to the expectations of her culture and her own self-image. Moreover, Betoul every now and then openly looks down upon Faten and accuses her of selling her body; a confrontation that Faten tries to avoid by insisting on getting a roommate "with a day job, someone whom she wouldn't see much" (Lalami, *Hope* 138). Thus, "although the body provides the potential for expressing subjective agency, it also poses a limit to that same agency through the perceptive gaze of the other which can assign meaning and narrative without the knowledge or consent of the subject" (Bond 3). However, Faten remains a prostitute despite that perceptive gaze of Betoul and despite the fact that she now has "the luxury of having faith" (Lalami, *Hope* 138).

Obviously, when cultural boundaries are crossed, the same happens to bodily boundaries as Faten seems to come to terms quite readily with this demeaning yet empowering identity. Thus, in spite of the sense of shame that she resists, Faten realizes that this new bodily agency is essential for her survival as an undocumented migrant. Because of the unsettling journey to a foreign culture and the malleability of her body Faten manages to acquire agency. The freedom of body and mind that she enjoys during her radical acts of mobility allows her to use her body to its fullest capacity, which empowers her.

Unlike Faten, Halima, who does not show much religiosity throughout the story, manages to develop a powerful identity that remains committed to the basic cultural codes. Certainly, her acts of mobility do have an impact on her bodily identity, but not in the same drastic manner as in Faten's case. For example, it is very unlikely for Halima to give in easily to the police officer the way Faten does, should he wish to do the same with Halima, whose body is marked with physical signals of a traumatic life. Throughout the story, Halima's reliance on her body as a protective shield develops as she moves; from her house to her mother's, to the sorcerer's, to the judge's, on the boat trip, and finally when she returns to Morocco and courageously leaves her husband's house, not worrying about his violent attacks anymore.

Thus, although Halima is presented as an oppressed wife, she is by no means a passive victim. Halima is not even financially dependent on her husband as she already feeds herself and her children. Indeed, Halima stands as a countertype to the conventional cultural norms of man as the primary breadwinner, and of Arab families as "agnatic and patriarchal" (Sadiqi 225), which explains all the beatings. Since Halima's vulnerability lies only in her body, Maati uses that body as an outlet for the anger caused by his sense of diminishing masculinity due to his lack of means.

Even though Faten's character also defies the stereotypical image of Arab women as helpless, weak, patient, and obedient (Sadiqi 226), the alternative identity that she develops in the process of migration is not necessarily one to be proud of. The oppressed identity of both Halima and Faten is the production of a "complex map of societal, political and cultural confines that work together" (Bond 82) to subjugate all women. And as the title of the novel suggests, "hope is what drives [Lalami's] characters . . . [but] it's often a perilous leap of faith, exacting a heavy price" (Lodish 30). With every act of mobility that Halima and Faten take, the body pays the price by crossing its boundaries and developing its own unique entity. And despite the unfavorable identity that Faten develops during her journey, she is still empowered by this new bodily agency.

Works Cited

Adey, Peter. *Mobilities*. 2nd ed. New York, Routledge, 2017.

——, et al., editors. *The Routledge Handbook of Mobilities*. London, Routledge, 2014.

al-Saadawi, Nawal. *The Hidden Face of Eve: Women in the Arab World*. Translated by Sherif Hetata, London, Zed Books, 2007.

Alcoff, Linda Martín. *Visible Identities: Race, Gender, and the Self*. Oxford, Oxford UP, 2006.

Bond, Emma. *Writing Migration through the Body*. Palgrave Macmillan, 2018.

Bouhdiba, Abdelwahab. *Sexuality in Islam*. Vol. 20, New York, Routledge, 2008.

Castañeda, Heide. "Illegal Migration, Gender and Health Care: Perspectives from Germany and the United States." *Illegal Migration and Gender in a Global and Historical Perspective*, edited by Marlou Schrover, et al., Amsterdam UP, 2008, pp. 171–88.

Cresswell, Tim and Tanu Priya Uteng. "Introduction." *Gendered Mobilities*, edited by Tim Cresswell and Tanu Priya Uteng, England, Ashgate, 2008, pp. 1–12.

Farahani, Fataneh. "Diasporic Narratives on Virginity." *The Muslim Diaspora: Gender, Culture, and Identity*, edited by Haideh Moghissi, New York, Routledge, 2006, pp. 186–204.

Ghanim, David. "Gender-Based Violence in the Middle East and North Africa: A Ubiquitous Phenomenon." *Gender and Violence in Islamic Societies: Patriarchy, Islamism and Politics in The Middle East and North Africa*, edited by Zahia Smail Salhi, London, I.B. Tauris, 2013, pp. 43–61.

Johansen, R. Elise B. "Resistance to Reconstruction: The Cultural Weight of Virginity, Virility, and Male Sexual Pleasure." *Body, Migration, Re/Constructive Surgeries: Making the Gendered Body in a Globalized World*, edited by Gabriele Griffin and Malin Jordal, New York, Routledge, 2019, pp. 78–91.

Lalami, Laila. *Hope and Other Dangerous Pursuits*. New York, Harcourt, 2005.

——. "So to Speak." *World Literature Today*, vol. 83, no. 5, Sep.–Oct. 2009, pp. 18–20.

Lodish, Emily. "Out of Place." *The Nation*, Jan. 9/16, 2006, p. 30.

Marchi, Lisa. "Ghosts, Guests, Hosts: Rethinking 'Illegal' Migration and Hospitality through Arab Diasporic Literature." *Comparative Literature Studies*, vol. 51, no. 4, 2014, pp. 603–26.

Prosser, Jay. "Skin Memories." *Thinking through the Skin*, edited by Sara Ahmed and Jackie Stacey, New York, Routledge, 2001, pp. 52–68.

Ricci, Christián H. "Laila Lalami: Narrating North African Migration to Europe." *Rocky Mountain Review*, vol. 71, no. 1, Spring 2017, pp. 41–59.

Sadiqi, Fatima. "Women and the Violence of Stereotypes in Morocco." *Gender and Violence in the Middle East*, edited by Moha Ennaji and Fatima Sadiqi, New York, Routledge, 2011, pp. 221–30.

Salhi, Zahia Smail. "Gender and Violence in the Middle East and North Africa: Negotiating with Patriarchal States and Islamism." *Gender and Violence in Islamic Societies: Patriarchy, Islamism and Politics in The Middle East and North Africa*, edited by Zahia Smail Salhi, London, I.B. Tauris, 2013, pp. 12–42.

Sarasua, Carmen. "Leaving Home to Help the Family? Male and Female Temporary Migrants in Eighteenth- and Nineteenth-century Spain." *Women, Gender and Labour Migration: Historical and Global Perspectives*, edited by Pamela Sharpe, London, Routledge, 2001, pp. 29–59.

Sheller, Mimi. "Gendered Mobilities: Epilogue." *Gendered Mobilities*, edited by Tim Cresswell and Tanu Priya Uteng, England, Ashgate, 2008, pp. 1–12.

———, and John Urry. "The New Mobilities Paradigm." *Environment and Planning A*, vol. 38, 2006, pp. 207–26.

Section 4

Moving to Wider Spheres

15 An Intersectional Feminist Reading of *The Dove's Necklace* and *Hend and the Soldiers*

Najlaa R. Aldeeb

Raja Alem's *The Dove's Necklace* (2010) and Badriah al-Beshr's *Hend and the Soldiers* (2006) are two contemporary Saudi novels whose fame resonated for controversial reasons. While the former was awarded the International Prize for Arabic Fiction in 2011, the latter was banned in Saudi Arabia. They were translated by Katharine Halls and Adam Talib (2016), and by Sanna Dhahir (2017), respectively. Alem and al-Beshr, like all authors, are influenced by the ideological tenor of their time, so their works reflect the ideological conflicts of their culture. The two authors disclose challenging issues which are considered taboo in Saudi's conservative society, relating practices—such as female oppression—to the wrong application of the Islamic laws not to Islam (al-Suraihi). The two novels reveal the changes in the Saudi society, highlighting how women are stratified, mainly but not exclusively, based on wealth and ethnicity; the former is pertinent to the wealthy indigenous women while the latter is concerned with the women expatriates from other Arab and Muslim countries.

This chapter examines the ways in which race, ethnicity, and other cultural factors intersect with gender in producing women's experience and class. The underpinning approach of this chapter is intersectional feminism.[1] The term "intersectionality" was coined in 1989 by the civil rights advocate and law professor Kimberlé Crenshaw, "to describe how systems of oppression overlap to create distinct experiences for people with multiple identity categories" (130). Collins and Bilge state, "Intersectionality is a way of understanding and analyzing the complexity in the world . . . and the self can seldom be understood as shaped by one factor" (2). The American activist, Angela Davis, argues that race is one of the intersectional feminist factors (*Women, Race and Class* 10), whereas the Saudi critic Said al-Suraihi states that conformity to social and cultural ideologies are two intersectional elements that affect women's class. Literary works demonstrate that while all women are subject to patriarchal oppression, women's problems in each society are shaped by different elements. For example, in American literature, Toni Morrison's *Beloved* and Alice Walker's *The Color Purple* emphasize race as a factor of a woman's status, whereas in Saudi literature, Alem's

The Dove's Necklace and al-Beshr's *Hend and the Soldiers* deploy the subtler elements of nationality, wealth, and ability among others. This chapter applies the elements of Western intersectional feminism in combination with Arab socio-ideological feminism[2] to cast doubt on the claims of Western critics such as Robert Spencer who attributes the marginalization of women in Saudi Arabia to Islam (Spencer 73–92). Thus, I query how race, ethnicity, ability, divorce, chastity, and sexuality in the two novels intersect with gender and put women in a class stratification.

The Dove's Necklace begins with the discovery of the naked body of a young woman in the Lane of Many Heads, in Mecca.[3] No one claims the corpse because all the people in the lane are ashamed of her nakedness. Detective Nasser suspects the dead woman to be either Aisha or Azza, two of the residents who suddenly disappeared at the time of the gruesome crime. When he investigates Aisha's emails for clues, he discovers a world of crime, religious extremism, exploitation of foreign workers, and above all, exploitation of women. The novel ends without giving any clear-cut answers. It reveals the contradictions in Mecca as the city of Prophet Mohammed's birth and its brutal customs.

On the other hand, al-Beshr's *Hend and the Soldiers* shows how Hend struggles to challenge her conservative society, which is represented by several soldiers. Being a daughter of a military sergeant and failing in her arranged marriage to an army officer, Hend is imprisoned in the community of soldiers, fighting for her independence. The novel gives insight to taboo topics of religion, rape, murder, and sexuality.

While women in Alem's novel struggle to find a place in a patriarchal society, those in al-Beshr's struggle to connect with each other. The two novels, I argue here, showcase that these diverse women in terms of ethnicity and class are, in fact, one woman who seeks equality, a non-fragmented identity, and recognition.

Research done on both novels has focused primarily on writing techniques. For example, Kate Kelsall conducts a thematic study of Alem's *The Dove's Necklace,* arguing that the novel explores themes such as the meaning of exile in a globalized world and highlights the clash between the unique history of Saudi Arabia and its modern identity (11). Kelsall adds that Alem blends traditional and modern themes and styles in an unrivaled way that shows her inspiration by Western literature and philosophy and by the musicality of the Quran and the ancient rhythms of Mecca, the city of her childhood.

Dhahir demonstrates how Alem's *The Dove's Necklace* is a homage to Mecca's heritage. She states that Alem applies techniques in writing that "help overcome heritage erosion with creativity" (Dhahir 127) to enhance young Saudis' sense of history. Dhahir names the techniques as using female symbols like the Great Mother, legends such as that of Hajar—Abraham's second wife—interwoven characterization and symbolism.

Similarly, Marcia Lynx Qualey argues that al-Beshr's techniques in *Hend and the Soldiers* include enriched language (veering between straightforward and lyric), folktales, romances, and dreams. She praises al-Beshr's combination of different styles, which takes contemporary Saudi novels by women from chick lit to stylized literary works. When interviewed by Gregovich, Dhahir, the translator of *Hend and the Soldiers,* states that al-Beshr "combine[s] the clarity and terseness of journalism on the one hand and the craft of a lifelong literary heritage deeply grounded in her readings of Arabic and world texts in translation on the other." She confirms that al-Beshr applies a freer, less formally constrained style than that of men to reflect the experiences of contemporary Saudi women.

Scholars have not focused on how nationality is problematized as social class. Nationality is an intersectional factor in both novels; however, not all nationalities are put in the same class. According to Collins and Bilge, the relationship between systems of oppression constructs the multiple identities that locate women in a social hierarchy of power and privilege (44). In *Hend and the Soldiers*, hierarchies have hardly shifted since King Faisal of Saudi Arabia officially abolished slavery in the 1960s, which means that former slaves are marginalized, denied names, and treated as objects:

> Nweyyir had come from another land . . . [she was] kidnapped from the remote shores of Oman one day when she was seven years old. They carried her and many other children off and made them sleep in burlap bags at night for a whole month. During the day, the men hobbled the children's feet to stop them from running away. They fed them dry bread and water, sometimes adding shriveled dates to their diet . . . She was sold by coastal merchants to my paternal grandfather, Abdul-Rahman, who called her Nweyyir, a diminution of "Noura," erasing all traces of her Omani name. (al-Beshr 6)

Despite the similarities between Oman and Saudi Arabia as both are Gulf countries, Hend's mother and "Black Ammousha," Nweyyir's daughter, are put in different levels because of Ammousha's dark skin. Like black Western women who suffer from the Western glass ceiling[4] — which represents the invisible barrier that keeps women of color from reaching certain positions and puts white women on the top, touching the ceiling—non-Saudi, poor, black women in the novels are put in the lowest social class. According to Collins and Bilge, black women in the globe suffer social inequality (15), and this view is supported by Angela Davis, who adds that racism continues to organize our social and economic lives ("Frameworks" 00:38:20–1:22:58). Similar to black women in the west, Nweyyir and Ammousha are classified at the bottom of the social hierarchy.

In *The Dove's Necklace,* the Lebanese woman is "so unlike the black-cloaked women of the neighborhood . . . no houri, certainly, but enchanting nonetheless with her thick cigars and smoke rings" (Alem 136). The conservative society accepts smoking and overdressing of Lebanese women despite prohibition of this behavior. The diversity in treating women of different ethnicities is also shown when Umm al-Sa'd's brothers evacuate seven families, including their sister and her husband, from a building the brothers inherited. Despite expelling their sister, they "pretended not to notice that the Turkish seamstress was still there" (Alem 306).

The Lebanese and Turkish women are put in a higher class than Jameela, a Yemeni poor, ignorant, fat, fifteen-year-old girl. She is oppressed by both her aged husband and her father. Jameela's husband, Sheikh Muzahim, the father of one of the two missing women, is a local shopkeeper who suffers from dementia. He suddenly proposes to Jameela after she buys a candy bar in his shop. Jameela's father and husband know that Saudis must have approval from the authorities to marry foreign women; however, they violate the system and culture. Her father brings an illegal *mimlik*[5] to write his daughter's marriage contract, gives her to Sheikh Muzahim, receives the bride price—five thousand riyals—and disappears without a word. The old Saudi groom, Sheikh Muzahim, spends the first night of marriage in his shop to store Jameela up and consume her. After he has deflowered her, he leaves to find out about the commotion outside in the lane. He goes home forgetting that he has locked his new bride in the storage room. Like immigrant women in the West, whose position is "closer to their black sisters" than to their white ones (Davis, *Women, Race and Class* 99), non-Saudi women are classified in a lower class than Saudis; nevertheless, Lebanese and Turkish are put in a higher class than Yemenis, Filipinos, Indonesians, and black Africans.

Patriarchy operates differently in various countries as culture affects women's experience and intersects with gender. In Alem's *The Dove's Necklace,* Umm al-Sa'd is entitled by Islamic law, Sharia, to draw income from her late father's property, but she is denied her inheritance by her brothers who do not apply the Islamic laws. They imprison her in a room for years and feed her "just apple peels" during her "years of unconscionable imprisonment" (Alem 80). Out of desperation, she hides her late mother's gold in her vagina, the only place she knows her brother will not touch. Later in the novel, Umm al-Sa'd becomes a stock broker whose success outweighs that of men to the point that, "They entrusted her with what little wealth they had, giving her power of attorney, so she could sell and buy on their behalf" (Alem 79). When interviewed by Ibtisam Azem, Alem expresses her desire to be seen as a human being, not as a woman, nor as an object owned by man (Berner 1). This desire is reflected in Umm al-Sa'd's success: a call for economic equality and freedom for women.

In *Hend and the Soldiers,* non-conformity to social norms intersects with gender and gives women a class. In one of Hend's mother's stories, the mother teaches Hend a moral that the girl's role "must go beyond being the young victim of abduction and rape and murder. Before her death, the girl had to expose her victimizers to prove her innocence and punish the crime" (al-Beshr 75). Hend's dream of a better life after marriage collapses because her husband Mansur never treats her as a dignified person. Hend's self-esteem shatters, and she starts seeing herself as "just an atom in a dark cosmic orbit teeming with women who kept spinning till they rose up in smoke" (al-Beshr 75). Hussein S. Hassan argues that *Hend and the Soldiers* deprives women of their identity (2). He confirms that it is a story of slavery, in which the enslaved person is lost when his flogging frees him. Although gender is one world-wide factor of discrimination, it is exaggerated in Arab countries since women are suppressed by cultural ideologies.

Women are classified as either good girls or bad girls based on sexism. Lois Tyson insists that a feminist reading of a literary work requires examining "the ways in which the novel invites [the reader] to criticize the sexist behaviors and attitudes it portrays" (99). The two novels illustrate women's levels of strength to defy sexual harassment. In *Hend and the Soldiers,* Ammousha—a black, ignorant, poor, and former slave—is submissively abused sexually. In contrast, in *The Dove's Necklace,* Aza—an educated, middle-class Saudi girl—thwarts the attempt. Ammousha fears men, and she stops her daughters from going near them. Her fear is grounded in her low self-esteem, so she becomes a victim of men in her community. Ammousha is sexually exploited by men:

> She told me about a young man, a neighbor of my grandfather, who had followed her to the fields of her "uncle" Jab'an. All the men in the village were her uncles. She wouldn't dare oppose their will. Each had the right to hit her on the head, make a furtive pass at her, or slip his hand between her thighs. She would run away from their advances, being afraid of her mother, who would punish her when she complained about these insolent uncles. (al-Beshr 7)

Complaining about her sexual molestation means more oppression for Ammousha, classifying her as a bad girl. When Obeid sexually abuses her, she "did not scream, afraid of being blamed by others" (al-Beshr 8). Death is the punishment of revealing the incident. Even the religious system does not help her as the imam of the mosque[5] is a symbol of threat in case anyone discovers that she is "the bad-girl," (Tyson 99) who deserves having her throat cut. When Ammousha's mother notices the red smears on the back of her daughter's dress, she gives her a lashing. Ammousha's rape adds another intersectional factor of oppression dragging her down to the bottom of the social hierarchy. Her mother has her marry Fheid, a poor black shepherd and a former slave, and he becomes a burden on her mother's shoulder.

Unlike Ammousha, Hend is strong because she is an educated, Saudi citizen. She plans to use "an electric gadget [to] freeze" (al-Beshr 121) any man who "neither fears God nor is shamed by people's opinion" (al-Beshr 7). Yahya et al. confirm that women reaching higher education are more equipped to face and have an easier time with life's challenges and enjoy gender equality. Consequently, sexism affects the uneducated, poor non-Saudi women more than their educated, middle-class Saudi counterparts.

Rape is an intersectional factor in the Arab world. "Intersectionality as an analytic tool is neither confined to nations of North America and Europe nor is it a new phenomenon" (Collins and Bilge 15). Raped women are considered a source of shame, so they are looked down by the community. It is ideology, not religion, that puts the blame on women, that considers murder "a lesser crime than that of a woman behaving with immodesty" (Fallon). Talking about rape is deemed immoral and categorizes raped women at a low class.

In *Hend and the Soldiers,* the marriage of Heila, Hend's mother, gives an example of rape in marriage. Heila's parents have her get married too young, as is the custom in her community. She falls asleep during her wedding and without saying a word, her husband "pulled her feet beneath him and mounted her, stopping her kicks with his thighs. He stabbed his knife into the tender flesh between her legs and left her bleeding" (al-Beshr 35). Heila's feelings from that night stay with her throughout her life. She could not love her husband and in time, her fear of him turns to disgust, which makes this arranged marriage a symbol of failure.

The same way of treating the bride like a doll is portrayed in Alem's *The Dove's Necklace.* In one of her messages, Aisha, the protagonist and the one suspected to be the killed woman, compares herself and other women in her community to dolls:

> The plastic doll reminded me of me in my *wedding dress*. It reminded me of how Ahmad had carried me as if he were shouldering a bundle of firewood. If you ask me, these mannequins are invading the neighborhood, possessing our bodies, sowing tumors in men's imaginations. (Alem 98, emphasis mine)

The brides in both novels are objectified and endowed roles and positions by their society similar to that position given to Nora in Henrik Ibsen's *A Doll's House,* written in 1879. This analogy shows that contemporary Arab women are struggling because of the imbalance of power among men and women—the same suffering of women in the west in the nineteenth century.

Sexuality as an intersectional factor is inseparably connected to religious ideologies. Heila endures the sexual act until he finishes because she was raised to be obedient, patient, and responsive to her husband in bed; otherwise, as told by her mother, she will be punished by Allah if she refuses her husband's demands. She, similar to many Arab women, consoles herself with being rewarded in paradise (al-Beshr 35). Hassan states that the sexual relationship between husband and wife in Islam is built on mutuality and fairness, which contradicts their relationship in reality. Also, in the Holy Quran in surah[6] Albaqara/The Cow, ayah[7] 228, Allah says, "Women have [rights] similar to their obligations, according to what is fair" (Abdel Haleem 26). Thus, Islam is innocent from these proclamations since the marital relationship in Islam is based on kindness and fairness. These odd marital relationships reflect how much Heila and Aisha's society is dominated by traditional religious ideologies, which can be considered as an intersectional factor that intrudes in shaping their class in the social hierarchy.

Women's chastity determines women's class in the Arab world. Kevin Harrison and Tony Boyd point out that the patriarchy imposes more kinds of social oppression that imprison women within social ideologies (305). *The Dove's Necklace* shows how the Saudi conservative society still punishes women for their biological nature putting them on the bottom of the social hierarchy. For having a "rubber hymen,"[8] Aisha is left by her husband Ahmed. Although her father shows him a medical certificate signed and sealed by a doctor, "Ahmed, who felt duped . . . looked at it blankly" (Alem 157). He gives the father a mysterious glance, that the latter is left unable to decide if it is a mocking or incredulous look. Alem's novel reveals that possessing virginity is an intersectional factor that decides women's position in the ladder of social class. It makes women either embraced in society or neglected and left by their husbands.

Divorce is another intersectional factor that affects women's rank in the social hierarchy. The two novels demonstrate how divorce is deemed a smirch for women but not men. In *The Dove's Necklace,* Aisha is divorced in her second month of her marriage, and she is left neither married nor divorced as her husband does not file for divorce. She does not tell anybody and accepts to be thought of as a neglected and left wife, rather than as a divorced woman (Alem 36). This choice shows how much divorced women struggle because they are rejected from their strict society. In *Hend and the Soldiers,* Hend is divorced because she delivers a baby girl, and she goes back to the domination of her mother who refuses to allow her to work in a hospital, complaining "that the job would entail mixing with men, which would in turn expose me to idle gossip" (al-Beshr 38). Sarah, Hend's employer, is divorced, and she is defied by "male employees under her supervision. They don't listen to her orders simply because she is a woman" (al-Beshr 39). Although the struggle of divorced women in the West is economic (Davis, *Women, Race and Class* 58), it is social for Arab women in closed societies because of the disparity between what is permissible for men versus women. In a society that gives man the right to divorce his wife—who is his cousin—because she gives him a baby girl, divorce intersects with gender to add more pressure on women and gives them a social class lower than the class of married women.

In *The Dove's Necklace,* Alem places the struggle of women with disabilities in the center of the novel by portraying the protagonist as a crippled woman, classified in a class lower than able women. I think this depiction is a way to raise the reader's awareness of the suffering of this category. Crenshaw confirms that those who are concerned with people's plights should focus on the problems of the discriminated, not on "the most privileged group members" to avoid "marginalizing those who are multiply-burdened" (140). In Alem's novel, the suspected victim is called "Aisha the cripple" by people in her community. Whenever Aisha's name is mentioned, the word "cripple" is attached to it. "The accident had put [her] on the shelf, useless and neglected" (Alem 51). Classified in a low social level, Aisha has married Ahmad, the oldest son of the sewage cleaner. "People in the neighborhood say he used to hit her" (Alem 123). Hence, Alem's concern with the torment of the disadvantaged in her community is clear by depicting Aisha, who is humiliated verbally and physically through her label as crippled, to highlight that Aisha's disability intersects with her poverty and divorce.

Another example of intersectional feminist experience is obesity. Janna Fikkan and Esther Rothblum argue that fat is a feminist issue because fat women are subjugated to bias, discrimination, and abuse. They declare, "Women experience multiple deleterious outcomes as a result of weight bias" (Fikkan and Rothblum 575). This view can be seen in *The Dove's Necklace* in the suffering of Jameela, the Yameni, poor, ignorant, plump, underaged, newlywed. Finding herself alone locked in the storeroom on her wedding day, she becomes terrified and ravenously consumes food as days go by. Abigail Saguy postulates that sexism, racism, sexual abuse, and weight-based discrimination in the US contribute to eating problems among minority women (600). This speculation is applied to the non-Saudi poor Jameela since neglect fattened her, turning her to a "threatening creature, gnawing, monstrously fat" (Alem 298). Sheikh Muzahim thinks of Jameela as a rat, skittering around biting constantly. His lust fades, and he starts noticing her flat chin seeing it "like a cushion for her little head. Her waist had filled out, and fat bulged from her chest and hips, weighing down her short frame" (Alem 298). To put an end to his agony, he gives her a sack of sweets and five hundred riyals and pushes her into the street. Alem magnifies obesity as a source of oppression; she sheds light on the impact of neglecting women and on fat as an intersectional factor.

In conclusion, despite the increasing number of novels by Saudi women writers, there is a gap in the study of literary criticism. Muhammad Ghanimi Hilal affirms that Arab literary criticism lacks the founded strategies and relies heavily on Western theories; he emphasizes the need for Arabic literary criticism to raise the readers' awareness of problems in Arab communities (5). This paper aims to fill in the gap in this area, exploring the elements of Western intersectional feminism along with Arab socio-ideological feminism in *The Dove's Necklace* and *Hend and the Soldiers*. The intersectional feminist factors are deemed effective in disclosing the inequality between women in the novels, showing that women, who are located at the intersection of numerous structural inequalities, face additional issues and pressures that classify them on the bottom of the social hierarchy.

Applying these factors show that the source of women suffering is not political, religious, nor purely economic, but ideological. The government gives all women in the community equal rights of employment, health care, and education, and Islam does not differentiate between women of different race, ethnicity, or financial standard. All women characters suffer from people around them, either family members or others in the community. They are not at a disadvantage because of authorities or institutions, but because of social and cultural beliefs, so they boldly defy the patriarchal restrictions imposed on them (al-Samti). The depiction of faceless women in life, in death, and even in dreams in both novels is a call for all women to unite because they are one. The two novels beseech women to connect with each other as shown in Ammousha's attempts to make Hend sympathize with her mother. Thus, my chapter emphasizes the importance of "sisterhood to women's survival" (Tyson 96) as a tool to achieve equality. When oppressed women rise, the whole world will rise with them, even if the oppression is social or ideological.

Notes

1 A reading that describes how different factors of discrimination, such as race, class, language, culture, ethnicity, gender, age, ability, sexuality, and education can meet at an intersection and can affect someone's life.

2 A strand of feminism, coined by the critic, hypothesizing that the abuse and exploitation of women is caused by social and cultural ideologies, resulting in putting women in a social class hierarchy.

3 Also known as Makkah, a city in Saudi Arabia, in which Prophet Muhammad (peace be upon him) was born; only Muslims are allowed in this city, which has Masjid al-Haram (Sacred Mosque) and the Kaaba, built by prophet Ebrahim.

4 A metaphor used to represent an invisible barrier that keeps a given demographic (typically applied to minorities) from rising beyond a certain level in a hierarchy.

5 In Saudi Arabia, a *Mimlik* is a marriage official or registrar, who writes the marriage contract and attests it in a Sharia court if the husband or the wife is non-Saudi.

6 A chapter or set of verses of the Quran.
7 Verses that form chapters of the Quran.
8 A thin membrane that surrounds the opening to the vagina, it does not rip or tear during sexual activity; it needs the help of a doctor.

Works Cited

Abdel Haleem, M.A.S., translator. *The Qur'an*. Oxford, Oxford UP, 2016.

al-Beshr, Badriah. *Hend wa Alaskar [Hend and the Soldiers]*. Translated by Sanna Dhahir, Texas, U of Texas P, 2017.

al-Samti, Abdullah. "Saudi Writers Emerge from Isolation and Turn the Table over the Traditions." *Elaf Morocco Blogs*, 31 July 2010.

al-Suraihi, Said. "Entry into the World of Raja World from the Beginning: The Animal River Flows and Objects Intertwine." *Okaz Newspaper*, 15 Mar. 2011.

Alem, Raja. *Tawq al-hamam [The Dove's Necklace]*. Translated by Katharine Halls and Adam Talib, New York, Overlook Duckworth, 2016.

Berner, Irmgard. "Elegy for a Lost Era." *Qantara.de*. Translated by Michael Lawton, 2011.

Collins, Patricia Hill, and Sirma Bilge. *Intersectionality*. Cambridge, Polity P, 2016.

Crenshaw, Kimberlé. "Demarginalizing the Intersection of Race and Sex: A Black Feminist Critique of Antidiscrimination Doctrine, Feminist Theory and Antiracist Politics." *University of Chicago Legal Forum*, vol no. 1, article 8, 1989, pp. 139–166.

Davis, Angela. "Angela Davis: Frameworks for Radical Feminism." *YouTube*, uploaded by WGBHForum, 27 Jun. 2019.

———. *Women, Race and Class*. New York, Vintage Books, 1981.

Dhahir, Sanna. "Homage to Mecca in Raja Alem's Tawq al-hamam." *Journal of Arabian Studies*, vol. 6, no. 2, 18 Nov. 2016, pp. 127–142. https://doi.org/10.108021534764.2016.1242549

Fallon, Siobhan. "The Dove's Necklace: A Novel." *New York Journal of Books*, 4 Apr. 2016.

Fikkan, Janna L. and Esther D. Rothblum. "Is Fat a Feminist Issue? Exploring the Gendered Nature of Weight Bias." *Sex Roles*, vol. 66, 2012, pp. 575–592.

Gregovich, Andrea. "The Literary Tourist Interviews Sanna Dhahir." *Fiction Advocated*, 24 July 2017.

Harrison, Kevin & Tony Boyd. "Feminism." *Manchester Open Live*, 2018.

Hassan, Hussein Sarmak. "Badriah Al-Beshr in *Hend and the Soldiers*: The Restored Slavery. When the Victim Inherits Her Executioner." *Iraqi Critic*, 26 May 2014.

Hilal, Muhammad Ghanimi. *Alnaqd Aladbi Alhadith / Modern Literary Criticism*. Cairo, Dar Nahdat Misr Liltabaeat Walnashr Waltawzie, 1997.

Kelsall, Kate. "'Lifting the Veil': Three Influential Saudi Novelists." *Culture Trip*, 11 Dec. 2015.

Qualey, Marcia Lynx. "In Fear of Fury." *Qantara.de*, 2017.

Saguy, Abigail. "Why Fat Is a Feminist Issue." *Sex Roles*, vol. 69, no. 9–10, Los Angeles, University of California, May 2012, pp. 600–607.

Spencer, Robert. *Islam Unveiled: Disturbing Questions about the World's Fastest-Growing Faith.* San Francisco, Encounter Books, 2003.

Tyson, Lois. *Critical Theory Today: A User-Friendly Guide.* New York and London, Garland Publishing, Inc., 1999.

Yahya et al. "Review of Women and Society in Saudi Arabia." *American Journal of Education Research*, vol. 3, no. 2, 2015, pp. 121–125.

16 Language and Identity in Postcolonial Mauritanian Muslim Women's Writing

Fatima Sidiya

Samīra Ḥammādī's *Āsmāl al-A'bīd* (Rags of Slaves) written in 2019 and Aïchetou mint Ahmedou's *La Couleur du Vent* (The Color of the Wind) written in 2014[1] are two contemporary Mauritanian novels that highlight the changing lives of women following the settlement of many families in Nouakchott. *Āsmāl* is written in Arabic, while *La Couleur Du Vent* is in French, with both works lacking an official translation. While the languages used are different, the two novels highlight the change in thought and behavior of young women in Nouakchott, Mauritania during the early eighties. Although Mauritanian women are of varying ethnicities,[2] the two novels share their focus on Moors as they follow the lives of French-educated, young, female protagonists whose choices challenge the status quo. The novels reveal the strict traditions applied to young, unmarried women in the Moorish society and how these young women react to them regardless of their social class. *Āsmāl* sheds light on the poor while Ahmedou's novel depicts the life of a middle-class family. The protagonist in *Āsmāl* is less fortunate than the main character in *La Couleur Du Vent* since the former lives in a crowded, poor district of the capital. This chapter looks at Mauritanian women from the lens of intersectionality to see how race and class in addition to sex determines the different types of oppressions single women may face in this conservative Muslim society.

Using the intersectional approach is beneficial to understand the oppression on the two protagonists. The two women face the oppression of their tribal communities as they both belong to Bidān (Moors),[3] and they also face oppression because of their gender. The intersectionality provides a wider scope to understand different oppressions that face women in Mauritania, which can be because of their color and status in the society, or what McCall describes as "multiple subordinate locations" (McCall 1780). Intersectionality has been applied in Western studies and has not been linked to just patriarchy but also race (Patil 853–4).

The novel *Āsmāl al-A'bīd* (Rags of Slaves) by Samīra Ḥammādī and written in Arabic emphasizes the contradictions in the Mauritanian society through its protagonist and other characters. The protagonist of this novel comes from a Moor Bidān family living in a poor and crowded district in Nouakchott. Introduced as Fifi, the protagonist is a teenager who studies in a French school where the majority of the students are Negro-Mauritanian. Through one of her black friends, she gets to know a French man and develops a love story with him, starting a self-exploration experience full of turmoil.

La Couleur du Vent (The Color of the Wind) is a French novel by Aïchetou mint Ahmedou. The novel is centered on the main character Tala, a French teacher who comes from a middle-class family from the Moorish community. Tala develops an amorous relationship with Ahmad; however, the two had to separate because of traditions which forced Ahmad to marry his cousin. Just like Fifi in *Āsmāl*, Tala too challenges traditions but in a less intense manner.

The two writers put Mauritanian women under the spotlight. *Āsmāl* takes a more radical route in depicting extreme feminist actions, including abortion and eloping. The other novel takes a less revolutionary thought by challenging the traditions in a less intense manner. The two novelists addressed issues in their writings like identity, love matters, force-feeding, girls dropping out from school, and marital issues. Other topics include moral issues that emerged in the new capital of Mauritania. The novels describe precisely Moorish lifestyle, costumes, culture, mythology, and folklore.

Ḥammādī, who wrote *Āsmāl*, is from a Moorish community and has been educated in Arabic in Mauritania and Iraq. She lived in Jordon for some time prior to moving to France. Speaking to me, she said, "I have been educated in Arabic, [a language] which I love and believe is rich and deserves admiration" (Ḥammādī, Interview 14 July 2020). Coming from an Islamic society, she says in a previous interview with *Sahafi*, a Jordanian newspaper, "The only sacred matter is religion and everything else can be argued" ("Fāāes"). Ḥammādī is not only cautious in her religious views but also in her views regarding gender. She says in the same interview, "A woman cannot be equal to a man in terms of performing the same duties and thus it would not be fair for her to call for equal rights and status" ("Fāāes"). Probably this statement could be better read in a Moorish context where women enjoy a better status[4] compared to that of women in Arab states. In the words of Ḥammādī, "The Mauritanian woman is strong and enjoys a status that other Arabic women should envy" ("Fāāes"). Her novel, she says, is "pro-diversity" and demonstrated that by posting a photo of herself on her novel's back cover with a veil and not a *Malhafa* (traditional Mauritanian woman clothing).

Speaking about her work, Ḥammādī says that through her novel she wants to demonstrate that Africa has faced Christian missionaries and that "these missionaries use our weak points like those of Fifi" (Ḥammādī, Interview 24 April 2020). Fifi falls in love with Patrick and elopes with him, challenging the conservative community she belongs to. However, after arriving to Paris she finds out that Patrick is a priest who does missionary work and was trapping her to convert her to Christianity. She later decides to leave Patrick and start a new life in Paris, but eventually she goes back to her home country and reunites with her father.

Samīra Ḥammādī, who writes in Arabic, published her novel *Hashaish al-Efyoun* (Opuim Grass) in 2006, in which she addresses the postcolonial period and social change in society following the move from Bedouin life into the city. The writer highlights the contradictions in the society through her depiction of the life of the protagonist Abdulrahman, who leaves Mauritania and his home village. She published *Āsmāl* (Rags) in 2008 and republished it in 2018 under the title *Āsmāl al-Aʿbīd* (Rags of Slaves). Ḥammādī has also published *al-Kanz* in 2015. Ḥammādī is now working on the second section of her novel *al-Kanz* (Ḥammādī, Interview 24 April 2020).

Aïchetou mint Ahmedou's choice of a poetic French language in her novel reveals her background as a Mauritanian educated in a bilingual schooling system. In her words "I have practiced and read French more because French books were more accessible than Arabic ones, and thus I felt comfortable expressing in French being more familiar with it" adding she has been influenced by French classic novelists (Ahmedou, Interview). However, she still believes that Arabic is the language of all Mauritanians, as it is the language of religious teachings and the language of ancestors, unlike the French brought by the colonizer (Ahmedou, Interview). Ahmedou's journey of writing started with publishing articles in newspapers under a penname to avoid being noticed. Things changed as friends convinced her to publish her first novel, but she says, "I don't forget being a woman, I am under family and social pressures that leave me unable to write everything that appeals to me" (Ahmedou, Interview). In another interview, she says about her writings "I don't forget where I come from" in reference to the conservative Moorish tribes (Diallo). Moorish tribes are conservative, and they do not accept criticism to culture or religion, therefore being a female writer from this community, she has to self-censor her writings.

Publishing the first novel was a challenge. From 1993 onward, she tried finding a publishing house in France, Canada, or in her homeland. It was only in 2011 that she managed to publish two hundred copies of her novel at a local publishing house ("al-Kātibah w-al-Mūtarjimah" 00:29:00–00:29:40). In 2014, the novel started to receive better recognition with its second edition. Ahmedou is a writer who tries her hand on short stories, children books, and articles. She is better known for her translation of *Tibraʿ* (local female poetry) into French, many of which she has posted on her personal blog.[5] By using the French language, she opts to expose the contemporary Moorish culture and literature to French speaking readers who are curious to know about Mauritania. As she explains in an interview, "A culture that is not being translated will not be recognized by others" ("al-Kātibah w-al-Mūtarjimah" 00:00:45–00:01:07).

Ahmedou says her novel is about love and social issues that introduce an unknown society with a central focus on women (Ahmedou, 17 July 2020). She wants to put women at the front after being backstage. Speaking about traditions, she says it is not something that can be left behind, because they are deeply rooted through upbringing and education. She believes that some of these traditions should not be left behind but rather they should remain because they are useful (Fall 00:12:14–00:13:34, 00:30:00–00:31:30). Aïchetou mint Ahmedou published her only novel *La Couleur du Vent Il était une fois à Nouakchott* (The Color of the Wind, Once upon a time in Nouakchott) in 2011 and republished it in 2014 with a different cover. Although she is now well-known and appreciated, Ahmedou says she has no intentions to write a new novel: "Nothing has encouraged me to write another one and I no longer think of it" (Ahmedou, Interview).

The choice of language by the two contemporary authors demonstrates a heated topic ever negotiated in Mauritania since its independence. Samīra Ḥammādī, who chooses to write in Arabic, represents the thoughts of the majority of Moors who associate themselves with an Arabic identity. However, Aïchetou Ahmedou, also a Moorish writer, prefers writing in French to better express her message in a language she feels comfortable using (Ahmedou, Interview).

French was the language of the school and institution since the establishment of the first school in the Mauritanian land during the colonization in 1898 in Kaedi (Diagana 62–3). Since independence in 1960, French was the only language taught in schools until 1966 when a few hours of Arabic classes were scheduled. However, this does not mean that Arabic was absent from the scene completely, rather it was present in Mahzara, the traditional religious schooling system of the nomads in Mauritania. The Arabization movement heavily introduced Arabic in education and the judicial system. This resulted in two schooling systems—one in Arabic and another in French—in 1979 (al-Nahawi 437). In 1991, a new constitution made Arabic the official language in the country, but French is still leading in workplace and government administration (al-Šykh). This, al-Šykh says, is attributed to the deeply rooted issue of identity in which language plays a central role. Two opposing social poles have formed in the post-colonial time, which are the Arabs (represented by Moors) and the Africans (represented by the three major African groups). The first believes Mauritania is an Arabic state and should be freed from cultural association with France, thus calling for complete Arabization of the system. On the other hand, the Negro-Mauritanian believe Mauritania is an African state and any effort to move it toward the Arab region is a matter of taking it away from its horizon; in addition, they believe such a move is not supported by history or geography (al-Šykh). While Mauritania is a meeting point for Arabs and Africans thanks to its diverse ethnicities and location, this has created an unstable identity demonstrated in the choice of language following colonization.

Abdallahi Ould Kebd says that Ahmedou's novel uses a simple romantic and catchy style. He elaborates that the use of wind, its changing types and its association with movement and travel, makes the title an inviting one. He notes that the writer has set the scene clearly before making the characters move. He notes that men are marginalized in the novel and they are important only because of their relationship to women. From this he concludes that Ahmedou is feminist even in her imagination. He questioned why she has chosen to use the non-Mauritanian names of Tala among other unfamiliar names like that of individuals and tribes. He says the novel is simple, yet it is a complete depiction of the Mauritanian society, its history, beliefs, religion, traditions, and values. Even more it shows the temptations, hesitations, ambivalences of the society, and the sense of honor (qtd. in Mustapha). Similarly, Mouemel says the novel addresses a complex and difficult to define social movement. He notes that the novelist discusses the change using a careful language without provoking the public. He adds that since Ahmedou is a writer of children stories, she prefers happy endings and thus her novel is completed with a happy scene. However, he still believes that the novel needs a second part to be completed (Mouemel).

Both novels use unusual names for their protagonists, Fifi and Tala are not familiar names in Moorish communities. Kebd pointed this out in his review of *La Couleur Du Vent*: "I did not understand why the author used names of tribes and first names of characters that do not exist or are rare" (qtd. in Mustapha). He adds that it was comfortable to read familiar names like Zahra and Faiza compared to Tala. It can be argued that both novelists try to escape criticism by creating main characters with unusual names.

Aïchetou uses a translation of local female poetry known as *Tibra'* in her novel. It is a very distinctive form of female poetry used in Mauritania. The word *"Tibra'"* is derived from the verb *"Tabara',"* which means to "offer and to give unconditionally" (Esnayd 243). In this context, *Tibra'* means a woman offers short poems to her beloved man in which she describes him, his clothes, his beauty, and she prays to God to connect them without explicitly revealing her affection. She offers all of this in a very short and beautifully structured couplet that is easy to memorize (Esnayd 243). There is no identified starting date for *Tibra'* because it is uttered verbally by women secretly to her female friends, it is not documented, and women who say it remain anonymous (Esnayd 244).

In Ahmedou's novel, Lala—the sister of Tala—starts singing in front of her friends in a typical gathering at home where young ladies exchange

*Tibra*ʿ secretly and away from pubic. Lala says in Hasaniya (Mauritanian Arabic dialect):

*Messab ennebghih ** emle ayniye men aynih*

Translated by Ahmedou into French as:

*Puisse celui que je veux** remplir mes yeux de ses yeux*
May the one I like** [I can] fill my eyes with his eyes. (Ahmedou 54, English translation mine)

With less quality of voice Tala replies:

[Hasaniya] *Ana walah ** elle narjah ou netmenah*
[French] *Sur allah je jurai ** que je le souhaite et l'espérai*
I swear! I hope and wish [to have him]. (Ahmedou 55, English translation mine)

Their friend Toutou explains that love is always associated with less sleep. She sings:

[Hasaniya] *Yan nass ejrouli ** leyatou adou yessrouli*
[French] *Ô! Gens, Courez à mon secours ** la muit me tourmentent les doubeurs de son amour*
O! People, help me out ** the pain of his love approaches me at night. (Ahmedou 96, English translation mine)

Although French colonizers had left Mauritania twenty years prior to the settings of the two novels, these colonizers left behind an influence on language, education, and lifestyle depicted in the life of the two protagonists. Having learned in French schools and introduced to a new lifestyle through the city, Tala and Fifi are considered to be different by their families. In a conservative Muslim community, the reaction of the family members of the two protagonists is a typical behavior of those against all forms of new lifestyle. They associate modernity with the West, this is the distinction between "Those who acquire access to Westernized forms of education, speaking and living and those who remain alien to this cultural setting" (Göle 61). Tala is described by her mother as doing Western hairstyles (Ahmedou 12) and her father thinks that the novels she reads are *dénaturent*, meaning they make her unlike her community (Ahmedou 31).

The two protagonists are aware that they are different. Tala feels uncomfortable after having a dream in which Ahmad tells her that he cannot marry a girl like her who "cuts her hair, paints her nails, and works outside her house, in short, who lives like a Nassraniya [westerner]" (Ahmedou 129). Fifi too has been blamed by her mother for choosing a French school and friends who are not of the same ethnicity (Ḥammādī 25). Fifi, as the narrator explains "the more she grows up and as she gets taller, the more she stays away from the Moorish society" (Ḥammādī 17). In fact, Fifi thinks "her strange spirit has lost its way and fled too far away" and only her body has stayed in Mauritania (Ḥammādī 23–4). Although Tala is more conservative than Fifi, both are described as *Nisraniya*, literally meaning Christian, but in fact meaning inspired by Western culture.

La Couleur Du Vent explains through the main character Tala, who is French-educated and a French teacher, that a person who does not know French is considered illiterate, unclean, closeminded and wears bad outfits, and has a Bedouin spirit. Such a person, in short, a *messauvege*, a local word derived from the French word *sauvage* meaning "barbaric" (Ahmedou 165). By using these labels, the Westernized locals apply Othering as explained by Said, "The Oriental is irrational, depraved (fallen), childlike, 'different'; thus the European is rational, virtuous, mature, 'normal'" (Said 42). Said's views about Orientalism is evident in the relationship between Patrick and Fifi. Patrick was teaching Fifi how to be modernized in the way she dresses, eats, and behaves; this exposes the superiority he thinks his culture has over that of hers. As the relationship between the two ended, Patrick started to abuse Fifi and neglected her in a humiliating manner (Ḥammādī 258).

Tala believes that the Arabization reform in education in the early eighties "had only succeeded in producing an uneducated generation who knew neither Arabic nor French." To her, it also reduced the potentials of those who could have done better (Ahmedou 138). This goes in line with Fanon's views that people who choose the colonizer's language do so because the "mastery of language affords remarkable power" (Fanon 18).

Bidān resisted teaching their children in French schools. For example, Fifi's mother urges her to "leave this futile school" (Ḥammādī 25). By this, the mother is objecting to her daughter being educated in French. In *La Couleur Du Vent* we find similar beliefs from the Moorish community: "We meet whole families who, out of narrow-mindedness, prevent their children from going to school for fear of learning French, considering it the language of the disbelievers and therefore of Satan" (Ahmedou 51). However, the Negro-Mauritanian community "seemed to fear losing their cultural identity and being absorbed by Arab-Berber culture" (Ahmedou 138), thus they were supportive of the French language. In *Āsmāl*, Fifi is a Moor, belonging to an Arabic speaking community, yet "She has chosen to study in French language . . . as if she wants to stay away from Arabic and its speakers, the majority of which are white [Moors]" (Ḥammādī 16–7). It is through the French language that Fifi and those like her can open doors that were barred to them years ago. In fact, the more a colonized person is capable of mastering the language of the colonizer, the more white he/she will be (Fanon 38).

Moors who are against the French language look down on Moors who choose to speak French. Once a stranger addresses Tala after hearing her saying "*pardon!*" he says, "Who are you, devil's wife, to express yourself in French and you are not a disbeliever" (Ahmedou 163). This rejection of French implies an objection to colonization from the Moor community. The creation of the newly formed Mauritania state, just like any previously colonized land, created conflicts between ethnicities exemplified in the choice of language.

Both protagonists belong to Moorish tribal communities. Tala, however, is a working single woman from a middle-class family. Fifi is a teenager who lives in a poor neighborhood. The novels shed light on the different grouping and layers of the Mauritania society. In *Āsmāl*, the novel explains about the two social groups (Moors and Negro-Mauritanian) that "neither of the two groups was able to influence the other, even the mixing and marriage between them remained limited, they were more like two neighboring countries" (Ḥammādī 17). This is exactly what Kennedy explains is a result of decolonization, since countries like Mauritania have a population with different cultural and ethnic groups, there are unsuccessful efforts to incorporate these different groups into one nation (Kennedy 70).

In the same novel, Fifi thinks about a female slave who sits in front of her, that she is "a slave since birth . . . she will remain forever as such" and anyone who comes from her womb will also inherit slavery (Ḥammādī 30). The same classifications are reflected in Ahmedou's novel, where no person is allowed to break the social hierarchy, the person "cannot elevate himself and would never be able to marry a girl from a higher segment" (Ahmedou 197). The Moorish society is explained as "closed clubs" with different layers in each one of them and whose people prefer to marry from the same tribe (Ahmedou 41). The different social classes and groups can be looked at from the intersectionality perspective, where women in these groups are facing simultaneous, complex, irreducible, and inclusive oppressions which result in "constructing institutionalized practices and lived experiences" (Carastathis 307).

Tala styles her hair back like a ponytail and puts in a hairclip (a style known as *Nisraniya*, meaning Western style) unlike the traditional hairstyle in which the hair is styled on the forehead (Ahmedou 12). Although she wears traditional *Malhafa* dress, she says that many women from the Moorish community envy the Negro-Mauritanian women who started to wear Western clothes like dresses and pants (Ahmedou 56). From a young age, Fifi does not like wearing *Malhafa*. She describes it as a "ridiculous cloth that exposes more than what it actually covers" (Ḥammādī 10). In France, she is impressed with the magical cream which helps her straighten her hair. She also tries putting makeup on, wearing perfume, dancing, and listening to loud music (Ḥammādī 225). In Paris, Fifi tries several modern clothes including skinny jeans and colorful shirts (Ḥammādī 222). The two protagonists are interested in the new media; Tala watches TV, likes French comedies, and goes to cinemas in Nouakchott (Ahmedou 51). Fifi borrows magazines to see women who she believes are like her (Ḥammādī 189) and she begs her family to bring a TV to their home (Ḥammādī 94).

The food preferences of the two ladies are not like that of their families. Tala's breakfast consists of French bread, butter, and Coca-Cola, unlike her family who eat *Aish*—a dough made of a mixture of cooked flour, water, and milk (Ahmedou 71). Tala also cooks omelets with a lot of pepper, which is unusual as Moors are not familiar with spices and they do not favor them (Ahmedou 82). Fifi asks her mother to allow her to have a bite of the fresh French bread (Ḥammādī 13). When Fifi moves to France, the meal she likes the most is breakfast with all the different types of pastries, jams, and cheeses (Ḥammādī 225). Another common trait of the two protagonists is they do not favor *Zrig*—a mixture of milk, water, and sugar—a common drink used during the force-feeding process. Fifi describes it as the "torture drink" (Ḥammādī 11). Tala sneaks to the kitchen to drink a glass of water away from her mother's eyes, since the latter believes women should not drink water because it makes the skin pale compared to *Zrig* (Ahmedou 18). In all the styles and choices that the two young women make, they try in one way or the other to imitate the Western modern behavior, which are in the end behaviors brought initially to the country by colonizers. Hence they apply what Bhabha calls mimicry, in which they look like Westerners but not in all aspects. Bhabha defines it as "the desire for a reformed, recognizable Other, as a subject of a difference that is almost the same, but not quite" (Bhabha 86).

The two young female protagonists who live in a patriarchal society know that the only chance for freedom can be achieved through men. In Muslim societies, sexual modesty marks the identity of a woman and it is exemplified in the segregation of sexes, controlling oneself, and veiling (Göle 55). Both girls initially fear meeting men, but soon they develop love stories with them. Tala, for example, would not let herself get in the car of a gentleman before marriage, a person who is not even a family member. To her, this is something "unthinkable and unimaginable" (Ahmedou 34). Fifi has the same concerns initially, "she will not get in a car with a stranger, [he is] not any stranger. A Christian! Her mother has always said they are like dogs and should not be mixed with" (Ḥammādī 35).

Marriage is Tala's primary concern (Ahmedou 25); this is because she knows that, "marriage is the only way to assert oneself and to free oneself from the family slavery . . . It's the only door that opens onto the mysterious universe of men" (Ahmedou 25). Tala just wants to get married to seek her freedom, even if the man does not adhere to family standards. She says: "It doesn't matter to me, rich or not, cousin or not, these are not my criteria of appreciation" (Ahmedou 57). Tala was not successful from the start to marry her love Ahmed because he belongs to another tribe and his family has forced him to marry his cousin. She thus married Hassan, but managed to reunite with Ahmad toward the end of the novel. Fifi chooses to develop a love story with Patrick. To her, everything about this French man "is glowing and clean" (Ḥammādī 100). Patrick, who Fifi will find out later is a priest, has managed in his stay in Mauritania to convince Fifi to start a relationship with him, something that is forbidden in Islam. He is underestimating the importance of Islamic and traditional restrictions. Leila Ahmed explains that "the colonial powers and their agents, and, in particular, the missionaries through the schools they founded did indeed explicitly set out to undermine Islam through the training and remolding of women" (Ahmed 144).

After her relationship with Patrick in Mauritania, Fifi "discovered in herself an immense capability of living with two faces" (Ḥammādī 189): one that fits the traditions and another one that meets her own expectations. Being rebellious, Fifi elopes with Patrick. Her greatest fear has always been that he might leave her (Ḥammādī 119), a reality that happens when she breaks up with him in Paris. She asks herself: "What are you doing in this mega city? A lonely stranger, loitering, shivering just like a bird that drops in water" (Ḥammādī 279). This drives her to go back to Mauritania. She says she "has lost herself after being deceived by the illusion of there" (Ḥammādī 334).

Mauritanian women writers have started to write novels and publish them starting from the early twenty-first century. Although there a number of novels written by women in Mauritania, they still lack recognition locally and internationally. Among challenges faced while writing this chapter was finding the novels or literary criticism about female novels in Mauritania. This chapter examined two novels written by Mauritanian women, namely *Āsmāl al-Aʿbīd* (Rags of Slaves) by Samīra Ḥammādī written in 2019 and *La Couleur du Vent* (The Color of the Wind) by Aïchetou mint Ahmedou. Although the two writers belong to the Arabic speaking community of Moors, their choice of language is different: Ḥammādī has written in Arabic while Ahmedou has written her novel in French. These choices are based on the language they feel comfortable writing in. The two novelists share the concern of young unmarried women and they address the restrictions imposed by society and traditions on women and how young female protagonists seek to break their fear and challenge their communities. The protagonists Fifi, in Ḥammādī's novel, and Tala, in Ahmedou's, belong to the conservative Moorish communities. The two have been raised in the Mauritanian capital and were educated in French schools and they have been regarded by the Moorish community as different and Westernized, which indicates the influence of colonizers on lifestyle and language even after several years of independence. Tala represents a careful move in breaking the norms as she loves a man from a different tribe, while Fifi demonstrates extreme rebellion to the culture as she elopes with a Frenchman. The intersectionality that these two women face in this society is attributed to the social class, race, financial status, and marital status.

Notes

1 Ḥammādī's novel was first published in 2008. It was republished in 2019 by Kitab Publishing. While the first cover is plain, the second has a black woman wearing a black hijab and covering her eyes with her hands while two other hands of different colors block her ears. The word "slave" has also been added to the new edition of the novel. Ahmedou's novel has also been published twice but with different paintings on cover. The first was published in 2011 with a painting of a Mauritanian woman in the traditional dress *Malhafa*, covering her face with only her eyes showing. The second cover depicts the traditional lifestyle of nomads in Mauritania.
2 The Mauritanian population consists of Moors, Pulaar, Soninke, and Wolof with the latter three constituting a segment referred to as Negro-Mauritanian.
3 The Moors consist of both the Sanhājā Berber tribes and Arab immigrants.
4 Although married and divorced women in the Moorish culture enjoy a powerful status, this does not apply to young women who have not been married yet. The freedom of married and divorced women is still under the norms of traditions.
5 http://aichetouma.com/

Works Cited

Ahmed, Leila. *Women and Gender in Islam: Historical Roots of a Modern Debate*. Yale UP, 1992, Z Library, b-ok.asia/book/2563654/31fb11.

Ahmedou, Aïchetou. *Facebook Messenger* interview. Conducted by Khadija Sidiya, 17 July 2020.

———. *La Couleur Du Vent*. Nouakchott, Édition De La Librairie, 2014.

"al-Kātibah w-al-Mūtarjimah Aïchetou Bint Ahmedou Fī Faqarah 'A'yn A'lā' Min Barnāmej Msā' Āḻḫyr." *YouTube*, uploaded by BellewarMedia, 15 May 2014.

al-Nahawi, al-Khalil. *Bilad Shinguit al-Manara Wa al-Ribat*. Arab League Educational· Cultural and Scientific Organization, 1987.

al-Šykh, A'bdy. "A'zmat al-Hawyah Fi al-Mūrītāniyā 'Taš987.Awalī'." *Aghchorguit*, 7 Apr. 2008.

Bhabha, Homi K. *The Location of Culture*. Routledge, 1994.

Blalack, July. "Chapter 18: Mauritania." *The Oxford Handbook of Arab Novelistic Traditions*, by Waïl S. Hassan, Oxford UP, 2017, pp. 325–7.

Carastathis, Anna. "The Concept of Intersectionality in Feminist Theory." *Philosophy Compass*, vol. 9, no. 5, 2014, pp. 304–14.

Diagana, M. *La littérature mauritanienne de langue française: Essai de description et étude du contenu* (Unpublished master's thesis). Thèse de doctorat: Lettres: Paris 12, 2004.

Diallo, Bios. "Mauritanie: Aïchetou Mint Ahmedou Ou La Mécanique Des Mots – Jeune Afrique." *Jeune Afrique*, 8 Dec. 2016.

Esnayd, Esālka. *al-Shir al-Nisāi al-Shingitti al-Qadim*, 1st ed., Ministry of Culture and Traditional Handicraft, 2017.

Fall, Yedaly. "Yedaly Fall, Reçoit Aichetou Ahmedou Lors De Son Émission La Passion Du Livre." *YouTube*, uploaded by Aichetou Ahmedou, 27 May 2018.

"Fāāes: Mā Katebtūho Aʻn al-Jins Taʻdā al-Ḍal-ā A al-Ādabīyah." *Sahafī*, 1 Nov. 2006.

Fanon, Frantz. *Black Skin, White Masks*. Translated by Charles L. Markmann, Pluto Press, 1986.

Göle, Nilüfer. "Islamism, Feminism and Post-modernism: Women's Movements in Islamic Countries." *New Perspectives on Turkey*, vol. 19, 1998, pp. 53–70, doi: 10.1017/S0896634600003022.

Ḥammādī, Samīra. *Āsmāl al-Aʻbīd*. Dār Kitāb for Publishing, 2019.

———. *Facebook Messenger* interview. Conducted by Khadija Sidiya, 14 July 2020.

———. *Facebook Messenger* interview. Conducted by Khadija Sidiya, 24 Apr. 2020.

Kennedy, Dane Keith. *Decolonization: A Very Short Introduction*, vol. 472. Oxford UP, 2016.

Maylūd, Ḥ. *al-Ṣl-l al-Nisāʼī Fi al-Ādab al-Mūrītānī al-MuʻāMuʻ*, 2nd ed., Itid e al-Ūdabāʼ Wa-l-Kūtāb al-Mūrītānīyīn, 2019.

McCall, Leslie. "The Complexity of Intersectionality." *Signs*, vol. 30, no. 3, 1 Mar. 2005, pp. 1771–800.

Mouemel, El Boukhary Mohamed. "La Couleur Du Vent D'Aichetou Mint Ahmedou, Le Récit D'un Profond Mouvement Chaotique Qui Finit En Beauté." *Mauriactu*, 30 March 2018.

Mulāy Ibrāhīm, Muhamed al-Amīn. "Zuhur al-Riwāya al-'Arabiyya al-Mūrītāniyya." *al-Ādāb*, vol. 45, 1997, pp. 51–7.

Mustapha, Ely. "Sortie Du Roman De Aichetou Mint Ahmedou 'La Couleur Du Vent'." *Cridem*, 11 Aug. 2011.

Patil, Vrushali. "From Patriarchy to Intersectionality: A Transnational Feminist Assessment of How Far We've Really Come." *Signs: Journal of Women in Culture and Society*, vol. 38, no. 4, 2013, pp. 847–67.

Said, Edward. *Orientalism: Western Conceptions of the Orient*, Penguin Books Limited, 2003.

17 Documenting Refugee Crisis and Post-migration Living Difficulties in Ebtissam Shakoush's *In the Camps* and Social Media Representations

A Postcolonial Perspective

Heba Gaber Abd Elaziz

In her 2016 short story collection فى االخيام (In the Camps), Ebtissam Ismail Shakoush (1959-) presents a documentation of the living conditions in refugee camps and a depiction of the unspoken challenges that are associated with movement, settlement, and re-settlement. Shakoush's work represents the refugee writer's burden of documentation on several discourses of narration. While the refugee narrative aims at confronting the imperial imposed narrative of refugees' victimization and helplessness, it demonstrates enormous strength and resilience in coping with their re-settlement process. Moreover, the refugee writer's discourse counterparts the marginalization/double marginalization of refugees in camps and host countries by highlighting the impact of refugees on the cultural heritage of displaced subjects. The process of documentation of secret camp lives not only preserves the cultural practices and traditions of displaced subjects, but also introduces changes overshadowed by a dominant Western model. The aim of this chapter is to draw a theoretical framework of refugee/postcolonial theories and apply them on refugee documentation of experiences in Shakoush's work to bridge the gap between the screened refugee world and their victimized representation in literary works and social media photography.[1]

Shakoush is a Syrian writer who has escaped from Hafa, Latakia to Turkey on foot during Ramadan 2012, only to lose her family, job, office, and her comfortable life because of her opposition to the Syrian system. She refused to go to Europe and chose to live in refugee camps with Syrian refugees and write from the camps about the camps. The emotional and psychological stress resulting from the numb, dull, and vacuumed realities in the camps are the main topics of discussion in her writings. Her works are categorized under movement/refugee/revolution and border literature as they echo challenges of resettlement and the strength of refugees to facilitate conditions of loss, change, and poverty. Shakoush declares that she has a mission to educate women and children in camps as part of the social burden of the intellectual, which she considers more imperative than writing to an ignorant audience who cannot even read. She established a cultural center in the camps of Gilan Binar, where she holds seminars and social meetings not only to educate children and women but also to call attention to traditions, norms, language, and stories of parents to preserve a collective identity. Thus, Shakoush embodies the duty of the female figure in exile to document the present and symbolizes the multidirectional role of female generations to construct/reconstruct memory. Shakoush has publications in several periodicals and has written, in Arabic, more than eight novels and ten collections of short stories. She has won many prizes including the Katara Prize for Arabic Novel in 2019. Her famous works include *What a Pity!* (2002), *The Two Orphans* (2009), *In the Camps* (2016), and *Footsteps* (2017).

Several postcolonial views have considered the term "refugee" not only dehumanizing but also demolishing to a person's identity as the term replaces his/her name, face, story, experience, and reality. Building on that postcolonial premise, it would be relevant to link the term "refugee" to key concepts of the theory including nation, nationalism, migration, national identity, violence, community, and citizenship. Because postcolonial theory brings many questions to the table in regards to the structure of society in a postcolonial context and the double consciousness that exists from colonizing forces, an analysis of the current refugee crisis is not complete without considering the implications colonialism has had on the crisis' initial existence. Understanding the effects of colonization on both the colonized and colonizers' worlds allows a better understanding of the term "Othering" as it takes place as the Western world considers the refugee question. Postcolonial critique of the term "refugee" serves as a method of anti-colonial thinking to challenge the international dominant structure and alter the way the world is processed, ideologies are formulated, and terms are coined.

One common ground between refugee and postcolonial issues is the question of nation and landlessness. Shannon Elder stresses that postcolonialism situates landlessness in a historical context and seeks to understand why the term landlessness has come into being. In the Middle East, colonialism divided up the land and drew lines and nations to control the land. In fact, the borders were drawn by the colonizers without consent from the locals living on the land. This resulted in the conflicts taking place today over borders in many places around the world. Hence, violence and conflict in these areas forced people to leave their homes and obliged landowners to become landless refugees. In an article for *The Atlantic*, Nick Danforth discusses how the British and French colonization constructed the idea of the borders for Middle Eastern countries and changed the features of the region:

In Syria, the French cultivated the previously disenfranchised Alawite minority as an ally against the Sunni majority. This involved recruiting and promoting Alawite soldiers in the territory's colonial army, thereby fostering their sense of identity as Alawites and bringing them into conflict with local residents of other ethnicities. The French pursued the same policy with Maronite Christians in Lebanon, just as the Belgians did with Tutsis in Rwanda and the British did with Muslims in India, Turks in Cyprus and innumerable other groups elsewhere. (Danforth 9)

By creating the idea of borders, colonization has found a justification for igniting violence in the region between different groups. "By focusing solely on the colonial borders as the issue, it makes it seem as if violence between differently identified groups is a natural occurrence" (Danforth 4). Against the commonplace notion, accepting tension and violence, neutralizing and justifying them, forces people to leave their homes to create landless refugees who Edward Said, as a refugee himself, declares "have most miserable fates" (*Out of Place* 80).

Robert Young takes this notion one step further to mention that the borders form nations and differentiate them. He writes, "The nation is a kind of corporation. It is the border that allows another nation to recognize it as a nation, to send its representatives there, so that it can participate in the global community of nations. A community without communal values" (Young 60). It thus becomes evident that notions of nation/nationality and borders go hand in hand as tools of imaginary and mythological control, exclusion, inclusion, and separation. Within the same veins, in *Imagined Communities,* Benedict Anderson claims that all the terms related to the nation machine are difficult to define and asserts the necessity of considering their history, connotations and their modern roles. At the same time that Anderson assumes, "nation-ness is the most universally legitimate value in the political life of our time" (3), he hints to the emptiness of the term. He further describes a nation as "an imagined political community—and imagined as both inherently limited and sovereign" (Anderson 6). The imagined facet of the nation comes about because although people of the same nation assume their unity and connectivity, most of them do not know/interact with each other. In fact, the concept of nationalism does not only "invent nations where they do not exist" but also necessitates the presence of nations and borders (6). Furthermore, Anderson relates the two terms community and nation as follows;

[The nation] is imagined as a community, because, regardless of the actual inequality and exploitation that may prevail in each, the nation is always conceived as a deep, horizontal comradeship. Ultimately it is this fraternity that makes it possible, over the past two centuries, for so many millions of people, not so much to kill, as willingly to die for such limited imaginings. (Anderson 7)

In other words, through social categorization, people are united only when they are separated and isolated from "Others" where the landless refugees are not fully recognized, heard, or understood. That is why, postcolonial analysis aims to center on, "linguistic, cultural, and geographical transfer, transformations of positive and negative kinds: changing things into things which they are not. Or showing that they were never that way in the first place" (Young 139). For Young, the coining of the term refugee—which was created by the United Nations after World War II in 1951—resulted in a legal categorizing of individuals into refugees and non-refugees, which is fueled by ideas of nationality and resulted in putting borders on borders.

Franz Fanon, Young, and Anderson consider dehumanization as part and parcel of the refugee marginalization and social alienation. The colonizer ". . . dehumanizes the colonized subject" (Fanon 4) to degrade him/her of his/her rights and justify the process of "Othering." As a result of marginalization, the refugee is deprived of adopting the essentials of the modern colonizer lifestyle, such as capitalism, Christianity, and consumerism. Thus, the landless refugee becomes inferior and less privileged and unable/unqualified to speak for him/herself. Thus, the colonizer makes history/memory/facts and chooses how things are remembered and what things are included/excluded in the dispute over physical land, which is the central struggle of colonialism regardless of any fake ideologies about civilizing missions. Fanon argues that if the dominating colonizer shares with the colonized human characteristics, then the colonized can realize that there is no longer a need to allow colonizers to instill fear in them because their "domination," which is an illusion. For Fanon, and in terms of postcolonial ideologies, the colonized reacts through revolution, decolonization, reawakening, and other tools of violence, language, and a radical lifestyle. Thus, works of art can be considered violent weapons of decolonization for weaponless refugees who face myths created by in/visible borders and divide the human race without adequate justification.

Following the footsteps of postcolonial theorists, Shakoush's writings reflect the psychological traumas, anxiety and mental/emotional burden of refugees starting with the migration process passing by the difficult living conditions in camps to the linguistic, cultural, and ethnic acceptance/rejection of host societies. Her writings about the refugee camp life highlight Abdel Hamid Mohamed's idea about considering the term "refugee" as insulting to the dispersed person who lost his/her spatial/temporal belonging and became a landless citizen (Elsaloom). In a reaction to that, Shakoush "writes" back by highlighting the adjustment techniques of refugees in camps. She presents how refugee citizens change camps into schools and cultural centers in a trial to face the harsh, inhuman conditions and prove to host societies that the refugee can become a part of the wheel of production. In other words, Shakoush does not only pull the marginalized refugee to the center of life, but also stresses the fact that a strong adaptable refugee can add to the host society if accepted and recognized as an important asset.

In fact, Shakoush's collection voices Gayatri Chakravorty Spivak's question "Can the Subaltern Speak?" Most of the protagonists in the short stories are females who narrate the atrocities of the migration and settlement journeys, the losses of their families and homes, and the psychological burden of the trip. The subaltern female subjects are not heard and discussed only; in fact, they have the authority of narration and constituting their own realities and stories. In a trial to assert that notion, Shakoush gives the leading roles to female characters in different age ranges: the grandmother, mother, and child—Khadiga, Aisha, Khansaa, and Fatema. In "A Doll on the Path," for example, the introduction of the female voice takes place through the young girl Khadiga, who during her family's escape trip from Syria finds a doll on the rocky path and asks her mother to take it. Her mother answers back that she cannot hold it because she is carrying Khadiga's younger sister and their few clothes that they managed to take with them. Khadiga decides to hold the doll herself. Extremely happy with the long-dreamt-of-doll, Khadiga hugs the doll and tells it stories and promises to make a swing for it from the berry tree leaves after they go back home. After a while, Khadiga gets tired of holding the doll during the harsh endless walk and decides to place the doll on the path in the hope of coming back one day. Aisha, another girl on the cruel escape trip with her Syrian family, finds the doll on the path and holds it merrily and sings songs for it and when she gets tired, she places the doll in the shadow of a tree and continues her trip toward an unknown fate. Khansaa, another Syrian girl, then finds the doll and repeats the same story. Eventually the writer ends the story as follows:

> The Syrian families are still on their escape trips passing by the difficult rocky thick forest stuffed paths between Syria and Turkey. The doll, bought by a father to his daughter at the beginning of her nursery school, is still on the path exchanging hugs with little refugee girls . . . The doll has not found a safe place yet. It still has this stupid smile and this frizzy blond hair. Her round wide-open blue eyes still watch the events but her plastic brainless head fails to record any of them. (Shakoush, 5, my trans.)[2]

From the above-mentioned quotation, one can deduce that the writer mixes symbols of the adult world (sadness) with the signs of childhood world (joy). The cultural and environmental references to the lost home are also mentioned (berry leaf trees) as terms of loss. The lost cultural emblems document the nostalgic and sudden shift from a prosperous, comfortable life to harsh, poor conditions. The doll symbolizes the trauma of refugees (women in exile) passing from one generation to the other. On a deeper level, the doll might represent Spivak's subaltern who cannot speak because it does not have a voice.

According to Spivak,

> In seeking to learn to speak to (rather than listen to or speak for) the historically muted subject of the subaltern woman, the postcolonial intellectual systematically "unlearns" female privilege. This systematic unlearning involves learning to critique postcolonial discourse with the best tools it can provide and not simply substituting the lost figure of the colonized. (Spivak 91)

In other words, this is very true in the case of Shakoush, because she turns the silenced subjects—subaltern refugees—to speaking ones, not only on the textual level but also schematically. As an intellectual, Shakoush tries to critique the postcolonial view of the refugee by refusing to focus on the trauma story and neglecting the strength and power of the refugees in her stories. This does not only include overshadowing the victimizing Western model that depicts refugees as helpless subjects but also stresses the fact that using the trauma story of refugees alienates them and denies them the right to adapt to unfair living conditions. The refugee subject, especially the female, is depicted as strong and powerful in the face of the tyrannical war. It is interesting to notice that most female figures are either supporters to their husbands, children, grandchildren, neighbors, or daughters. This is extremely clear in "Ritage" where the wife provides great moral support to her husband. This is a subversion of the Western postcolonial model that aims at saving the subaltern from the brown colonized figure by the white colonizer. Instead, the story—among many others—presents a form of solidary regiment in the face of shared trauma. In this story, the husband and wife feel helpless when they cannot find milk for their baby in the camps. The psychological disaster they face drives them toward a moment of collapse where the wife tries to find a solution and thinks of feeding her child crumbs of bread dipped in tea.

> The wife was astonished. She instantly forgot the humiliation and the pain she felt after he hit her. She sat beside him caressing and soothing him, rubbing his head and shoulders. They cried together, they shared torment and helplessness. Only now, she could understand why he insisted on naming their girl, Ritage: maybe he thought her birth would be an end to his misery and the wretched camp life that he never wished for or thought of. In fact, he was plunged into this life after he lost his leg in a battle and came to the camps with these crutches under his arms that stopped him temporarily from Jihad. Now, the child stopped crying and fell to sleep without eating

the crumbs of bread and tea, the only food she will find when she
wakes up . . . and the tears of the hugging couple bear the witness.
(Shakoush 23)

The resilience of the female figure and persistence to live and survive
under the worst living conditions symbolize an answer back to the victimized picture of the refugee who tries to differently reshape history
and provide a new image to the Western ideology.

Among the collection of short stories at hand, two stories strongly
capture the spirit of the work; namely "The Two Tents" and "Burned
Hamza." The multiple techniques used to document the crisis of Syrian
refugees assemble to highlight the immediate effect of the emotional and
psychological trauma on refugees in and outside the camps. First, the
binary opposition technique is used by Shakoush to assert that all funda-
mentals of human culture can only be explicit in relation to one another
and the overall environment. Binary oppositions in cultural studies explore the relationships between different groups of people that cannot
coexist, leading to boundaries between groups of people, prejudice, and
discrimination. The use of binary oppositions in Shakoush underlines
differences between groups of individuals. Examples of binary oppositions include pain and fatigue versus rest and happiness, the world of
grownups and hardships of life versus domains of innocent childhood
life, details of flashbacks of war versus the escape trip, and details of life
in camps versus the absence of everyday routine. The new life in camps
generates new cultural icons that add to, but do not replace the bygone
cultural motifs in Syria. For instance, in "The Two Tents" words like,
"door-less tents, curtains between tents, the rocky land, public baths
and the sponge mattress" are used to describe the difficult living conditions in refugee camps and to oppose to the lost "big house, computers and books, luxurious household and comfortable life in Syria"
(Shakoush 8). Moreover, the opposition between the dispersed families,
spread of diseases, and continuous deaths on the one hand, and the depiction of memories of happy family gatherings back at home on the
other, does not only reflect the new, numb life but also the vacuumed
present and unknown future as part of the helplessness of refugees in
camps. The short story interweaves two narratives, namely, the lives of
Abou Khaled and Om Ahmed to echo the great shift from a rich to a
poor miserable life. In addition to that, it is worth noting how the writer
describes the chaotic life in camps not only on the materialistic level, but
also on the human one. She writes,

The place is packed with waves of tents. All the tents look alike, all
the side ways are similar and the sheets, pillows and covers share the
same color. How can a person memorize the place of his tent? Shame
on whoever was the cause of the misery of all those people. They

have been detached from their villages and cities where the good and the bad people are mixed together: the mujahedeen, the mobs, the vagabonds and the bullies. The respected and well-appreciated men of good reputation can no longer be differentiated from the thieves as they all formed a non-homogenous mixture here in the camps. (Shakoush 8)

The non-homogenous mixture of people in camps is symbolic of the chaotic state of mind of the Syrian refugee, which is swinging between hope and despair. In spite of the miserable life that the refugees lead, the writer always mentions phrases like, "lovely dream," "there will always be a meeting after departure," "he will always find a way to find us," and "Allah is generous" (Shakoush 8). Similarly, in the last story, "Aisha's Teeth," Shakoush sticks to the main axis of the work which swings between moments of hope and despair. The crippled girl Aisha loses her legs in war, and hopes to play with her friends, run and have fun, but she cannot. When she starts losing her teeth, Aisha and her mother exchange the following dialogue,

MOTHER: Don't be sad my little one . . . after few days, you'll grew another tooth . . . prettier and stronger and it will last with you forever.
AISHA: Mum . . . When will I grow new legs to replace my truncated legs? (Shakoush 44)

The continuous fluctuation between hope and despair is another binary opposition technique used frequently by the writer to depict the everyday life misery of refugees.

The second technique used by the writer is related to paying attention to the details of the trauma which are portrayed using themes related to the basic human relationships, as they have become part and parcel of the everyday melancholy and loss of home. Consequently, the depiction of life in the camps is more realistic and felt than that of outside writers/watchers. In "Burned Hamza," for instance, the relationship between the child Hamza and his cancer patient mother signifies the relation between the Syrian refugee and the lost land. When his mother is sick in hospital, Hamza refuses to eat sweets, play with his friends or sit with his grandmother. He instead spends the nights crying and praying for her return in search of security and safety. The detailed description of his beautiful absent mother: her yellow long hair, her lovely face, and her wide eyes are juxtaposed with her ill body, weak figure, and lost hair and eyebrows on her return to the camps. Hamza keeps on searching for a medicine for his mother when he is electrified with a wire and is burnt to death as his mother dies at the same moment. The details of the story symbolize the lost Syria and Syrians. The struggle to survive amidst the conditions of chill, faint light, terror, and diseases is depicted as part of

the resilience and persistence of Syrian refugees. Moreover, the normalization of death scenes, funerals, and tombs, where dead people have
only become numbers to calculate, does not aim at showing the acceptance of refugees, rather it hints at documenting the events and people
with the aim of remembering rather than forgetting the traumas of camp
life. In this prospect, Shakoush ends the story as follows:

> . . . She did not mourn her son, and he did not mourn her too. Their
> souls met in the camp space to continue the trip where thousands
> of souls like them settle peacefully with God All Merciful. The two
> funerals came out from the camps. The administration of the camps
> received the tent with all its components to give it to another refugee
> family. The death shells still bomb the place and still supply the camps
> and tombs with numbers that change every hour. (Shakoush 14)

The writer uses the element of surprise at the end of stories, twisted
endings, and abrupt finales to depict the endings of refugee life stories in
reality. The intertwined stories of a common unknown future emphasize
that refugees with different backgrounds share the same present and
expect the same future.

Third, the reader gets swallowed in events taking place to the defeated heroes/heroines where the events are the real heroes that direct
the story. In accordance with this, the writer mentions the Arabic names
of places and streets to document the absent memories and places. As for
the names of people, Shakoush rarely mentions the names of grownups,
she instead uses titles; Om (the mother of) or Abou (the father of) to
clarify the absent identities of refugees as individuals and assert their
collective identities that are related to their responsibilities and future.
From a different perspective, the usage of the titles Om and Abou is
a reference/assertion to cultural emblems as a way of documenting a
dying culture and heritage. Within the same lines, Shakoush refers to
the absent environment and geography when she mentions the forests,
berry trees, the snow on top of mountains, caves, fruits, and the rivers
as a way of preserving the cultural heritage of the place. However, while
the grownup refugees show a difficulty in adapting to new weather conditions and show a strong relation with the absent environment and geography, younger generations show more adjustment to the weather and
conditions in camps in a reference to the ability of coming generations to
cope and adapt to changing conditions.

By contrast, the critic Mahmoud al-Wahab presents queries concerning whether Shakoush's collection can be considered a literary work in
the first place. He says that it is just a narration of tales that does not pay
attention to the figurative style of the Arabic language as part of focusing on the trauma so that the reader gets involved in the story without
distractions. He claims that literature puts the reader in a space between

reality and fiction, and Shakoush puts the reader nearer to reality where the crimes and atrocities of the story that engage the reader more than anything else. In an answer to that, Shakoush comments that short stories are integral to refugee literature. They spark a flash on part of the scene and leave the reader to imagine the rest. She says short stories are the most convenient form for platform narration, where no preaching takes place but instead only stories of witnesses who record and document the events (al-Abbaso). Moreover, in "'Refugee Literature': What postcolonial theory has to Say," Claire Gallien argues that refugee literature, as examined from a postcolonial stance, experiments with form, genres, and languages. The up-rootedness and geographical alienation of refugees extend them outside national traditional literary forms and force them to experiment with subjective new forms. This is very true in the case of Shakoush who experiments with new forms of narration and tale telling as part of documenting and writing an alternative historical testimony with more concentration on the events rather than the traditional figurative language usage in Arabic literature.

In "Om Hassan," Shakoush illustrates the passive attitude of the media toward the refugee crisis. When a journalist and a photographer visit the camps to report about life in refugee camps, Shakoush comments that their questions are trivial and the answers to the questions are known to the whole world (10). She answers angrily to the meaningless questions of journalists about how they live and get food:

> Why do you record and take photos? Why do you take benefit of our wounds and pain? That's enough . . . For a year and half now, you have been prattling about our stories, twisting facts, forging our words to please your masters. You have neither accomplished any progress nor helped us. Go away for God's sake. (Shakoush 11)

Shakoush's words can direct the attention of the reader to the Syrian refugee photos that spread on social media on the one hand, and the photos of refugees of themselves by themselves on the other hand, as an alternative media platform that challenges the traditional mainstream media representations. Those photos subtly "photograph" back the colonial representations to establish a more real representation of refugees in the new society and hence pave the way for their acceptance rather than rejection.

In *Global Poverty*, Dogra writes, "We come to know the world through its representations. Representations do not re-present facts, but also constitute them" (1). Various social media platforms can thus offer alternative media that counterpart the dominant colonial discourse which contributes to the "Othering" process of refugees (Atton 1). Similarly, in *Covering Islam*, Said highlights the role of the media in directing and manipulating the Western perception of the East/refugees.

Media representations, Said affirms, have distorted the image of Islam as a monolithic entity synonymous with terrorism and religious hysteria which propagated to hostility and Islamophobia. In the Syrian refugee camps, selfies have become ways of recording autobiographies and weapons for these ex-colonials to "photograph" back to the empire.

These photos of co-existence show signs of civilization (schools, wedding parties, clean tents . . . etc.) and represent an assertion of their voices in a context that normally silences them. M. Green and T. Brock state that photos by the refugees from the camps represent narratives that can provoke emotions, modify the approaches of the Other, and act as testimonies (702). The peaceful photos of marriage and birthday parties are forms of revolution, liberation, reawakening, and violence. Cameras in the hands of refugees aim to show that refugees are not an undifferentiated mass. They are rather a miscellaneous group with different experiences and lifestyles. The refugees have the chance to provide their own photo stories instead of having a Western authority represent/misrepresent their experiences distorting the myth of the superiority of the West (Said, *Orientalism* 9). In fact, self-photographs are powerful tools that have the ability to "change a master narrative that seeks to portray the weak or powerless . . . in negative images or social contexts" (Aguirre 147). The photos of the refugees by themselves are considered "the most appropriate voice to tell the story of suffering" as testimonies and not only personal opinions propagated by the West as seemingly true "facts." In fact, replacing a journalist for a citizen on newer media platforms is a bona fide act of witnessing (Chouliaraki 147). Likewise, Clark, Couldry, MacDonald, and Stephansen mention that storytelling using photos on digital platforms provides the opportunity to individuals to exercise agency and show that domination is an illusion (921).

In fact, photography in the hands of the colonized is an act of violence. Clearly, the photographs by the refugees counteract the Western journalist representation of situations and conditions they never lived and thus their representation is not as accurate or real to life like the camera of the refugees. Moreover, the usage of highlighting spatial distance and expressionless faces in press and social media photography encloses immigrants into the margins of the silenced other. Most refugee press photos have been taken from a "safe" social distance and lacked emotional expressiveness that added to the dehumanization of refugees (Batziou 48). However, from a different stance, Batziou assumes that a photo of a suffering face might generate emotional sympathy and could function as a bridge between the subject and viewer and allows the viewer to identify with the subject (45–8). Meanwhile, the photos still do not urge "the Other" to take action but rather to remain negative and remote.

Although postcolonial studies have shed light on refugees as displaced subjects, postcolonial writings have not fully encompassed refugee literature as documents that reflect the violence and unfair living conditions in refugee camps. In fact, postcolonial writings can offer a great opportunity to put refugee literature into effect and create an alternative memory that not only documents the atrocities that refugees face, but also direct the attention toward the silent refugees who continuously and tediously "write" and "photograph" back in the face of the empire. While the refugee writings oscillate between hope and despair, the major themes of the works include highlighting the overshadowed power of refugees by a dominant Western deficit model that defines refugee people as traumatized victims and reestablishing the identity of refugees who are alienated from full inclusion into life by denying their inherent resilience in the face of extraordinary life experiences, language barriers, racism, and discrimination.

Notes

1 The reference to Western and refugee photos circulating on social media does not specify certain photos but targets the widespread photos on social media.
2 All the excerpts from Ebtissam Shakoush's *In the Camps* are translated from Arabic to English by the researcher.

Works Cited

Aguirre, J. Adalberto. "The Personal Narrative as Academic Storytelling: A Chicano's Search for Presence and Voice in Academe." *International Journal of Qualitative Studies in Education*, vol. 18, no. 2, 2005, pp. 147–63.

al-Abbaso, Fayyad. "Interview with Ebtissam Shakoush." The Union of Liberal Writers of Syria, 25 Feb. 2017.

al-Wahab, Mahmoud. "Ebtissam Shakoush: *In the Camps*." *Geroon*, 18 Feb. 2017.

Anderson, Benedict. *Imagined Communities*. Google Books, 1983.

Atton, C. *Alternative Media*. London, Sage, 2001.

Batziou, A. "Framing 'Otherness' in Press Photographs: The Case of Immigrants in Greece and Spain." *Journal of Media Practice*, vol. 12, no. 1, 2011, pp. 41–60.

Chouliaraki, L. *The Ironic Spectator: Solidarity in the Age of Post-humanitarianism*. Cambridge, Polity, 2015.

Clark, W., Couldry, N., MacDonald, R., & Stephansen, H. "Digital Platforms and Narrative Exchange: Hidden Constraints, Emerging Agency." *New Media & Society*, vol. 7, no. 6, 2015, pp. 919–38.

Danforth, Nick. "Stop Blaming Colonial Borders for the Middle East's Problems." *The Atlantic*. Atlantic Media Company, 11 Sep. 2013.

Dogra, N. *Representations of Global Poverty: Aid, Development and International NGOs*. vol. 6, London, IB Tauris, 2015.

Elder, Shannon, "Cameras as Weapons of Resistance: Refugees Disrupting the Colonial Narrative through Photography." *Cultural Studies Capstone Papers*, vol. 14, 2017, pp. 10–11.

Elsaloom, Mohamed. "Syrian Refugee Literature." Harmoon Center for Contemporary Studies, 31 Jan. 2018.

Fanon, Frantz. "On Violence." *The Wretched of the Earth*. London, MacGibbon & Kee, 1963.

Gallien, Claire. "'Refugee Literature': What Postcolonial Theory Has to Say." *Journal of Postcolonial Writing*, vol. 54, no. 6, 2018, pp. 721–6, doi:10.1080/17449855.2018.1555206.

Green, M., & Brock, T. "The Role of Transportation in the Persuasiveness of Public Narratives." *Journal of Personality and Social Psychology*, vol. 79, no. 5, 2000, pp. 701–21.

Rane, H. "Media Content and Inter-Community Relations." *Islam and the Australian News Media*, edited by Rane H., Ewart, J., and Abdalla, M., Carlton, Australia, Melbourne UP, 2013, pp. 104–19.

Said, Edward W. *Covering Islam: How the Media and the Experts Determine How We See the Rest of the World*. New York, Pantheon Books, 1981.

———. *Orientalism*. London, Penguin Books, 1978.

———. *Out of Place: A Memoir*. New York, Vintage Books, 1999.

Shakoush, E. Ismail. فى الخيام *[In the Camps]*. Dar Noun, 2016.

Spivak, Gayatri C. *Can the Subaltern Speak?: Reflections on the History of an Idea*. Edited by Rosalind Morris, NY, Columbia University Press, 2010.

Young, Robert. *Post-colonialism a Very Short Introduction*. Oxford, Oxford UP, 2003.

Section 5

Returning to the Scheherazade Within

18 Djebar and Scheherazade

On Muslim Women, Past and Present

Brigitte Stepanov

I begin by citing the first lines of Hélène Cixous' 1975 essay "Le Rire de la Méduse" ("The Laugh of the Medusa") in order to introduce the body-text link that this chapter explores. Here, calling all women to write, Cixous identifies writing, and namely *what it will do*, as a mode through which to make space for women in law, history, and the world. Through writing, moreover, women must reclaim their bodies:

> I shall speak about women's writing: about *what it will do*. Woman must write her self: must write about women and bring women to writing, from which they have been driven away as violently as from their bodies—for the same reasons, by the same law, with the same fatal goal. Woman must put herself into the text—as into the world and into history—by her own movement. (Cixous, "Laugh of Medusa" 875)

Cixous continues to name the link between body and text throughout her essay, urging women to inscribe their body into their texts as follows:

> We've been turned away from our bodies, shamefully taught to ignore them, to strike them with that stupid sexual modesty. . . . Women must write through their bodies, they must invent the impregnable language that will wreck partitions, classes, and rhetorics, regulations and codes. ("Laugh of Medusa" 885–6)

Women, bodies, texts: these are the key elements present not only in "The Laugh of the Medusa" but also in Assia Djebar's short story "La femme en morceaux" (The Woman in Pieces). Written in June 1996, a moment of acute violence in Algeria's history, and published a year later in a collection titled *Oran, langue morte* (*The Tongue's Blood Does Not Run Dry: Algerian Stories*),[1] "The Woman in Pieces" is a rewriting of "The Story of the Three Apples," a tale from the *Thousand and One Nights*, or the *Arabian Nights* as they are also known. But the text does more than simply recount the events of "The Story of the Three Apples." Djebar's short story juxtaposes the past—the era of

Scheherazade[2]—with the text's present—the Algerian Civil War known as the "Black Decade" (1992–2002)—while also forging a link between a fragmented narrative and a fragmented, or cut-up, body.

The project of this chapter is to wrestle with the complex legacy that Scheherazade poses for Muslim women by examining the particular case of Djebar's "The Woman in Pieces" and, notably, the inscription of body into her short story. I will show that the body as described in "The Woman in Pieces" is a device that parallels—specifically through its fragmentation—the construction of Djebar's text, which is dislocated and fractured in similar ways. By thus analyzing the short story's narrative structure, I argue that it is through what I call the flattening out of the narrative stacking at the end of "The Woman in Pieces" that the figure of Scheherazade is expulsed from the text and that Djebar's protagonist Atyka can demand, even reclaim a voice of her own. Placing Atyka within a larger conversation about the rejection of Scheherazade epitomized by Tunisian writer Fawzia Zouari's 1996 work *Pour en finir avec Shahrazade* (To Put an End to Shahrazad), I will demonstrate how "The Woman in Pieces" ultimately reconceptualizes contemporary Muslim women beyond the storyteller of the *Thousand and One Nights*. In the final analysis, this chapter engages with a historical and literary archive of women's narratives and addresses how Djebar's tale gives voice to those who have found themselves in the shadow of a storied narrator.

Women, bodies, and texts, or rather, Muslim women, severed bodies, and framing and fragmented texts motivate this analysis. I would like to explore these thematic paths and expound on how my chapter fits into the parameters of this collected volume before delving deeper into a close reading of "The Woman in Pieces." The *Thousand and One Nights* is a crucial intertext for Djebar, and the figure of Scheherazade has played a critical role in the reception of Muslim women writers and narrators. Muhsin J. al-Musawi has persuasively shown the deep Islamic roots of the stories in question. As he explains,

> The *Thousand and One Nights* . . . has always been considered one of the world's most entertaining books, but its title and concerns are Arab-Islamic, and thus it has drawn and should draw more attention as a repository of popular memory, collective consciousness, and cultural dynamics. (al-Musawi 1)

Additonally, he asks us to consider how this backdrop imbues the descriptions of the spaces that characters occupy or the objects that they carry, noting: "The nonverbal narrative properties in the *Thousand and One Nights* have more Islamic character than we might assume. They permeate medieval narratology, history, and hagiography" (250). Clarisse Zimra, who has written extensively on Djebar, further underscores the Islamic context of the *Thousand and One Nights* while simultaneously emphasizing the multiple frames of the short story that interests us here: "In its intertextual uses, *Arabian Nights* inflecting 'La femme en morceaux,' as the Q'ran could be said to inflect *Arabian Nights*, Djebar revisits the primal scene of ruthless politics in her native land" (Zimra 116).

Djebar provided illuminating reflections on Muslim women throughout her life. Born Fatima-Zohra Imalayen in Cherchell, Algeria in 1936, she became the first female Muslim student at the École normale supérieure. She published her first novel, *La Soif* (The Mischief), in 1957, taught French at the universities of Rabat and Algiers, and later in life held distinguished professoriates at Louisiana State University and New York University. In the midst of a prolific career of textual and cinematographic works in French, Djebar was awarded the Neustadt International Prize for Literature in 1996 and elected to the Académie française in 2005. Evelyne Accad notes that the Algerian writer and filmmaker "was able to synthesize her traditional Muslim background and her European education" (802),[3] but while her background provides important context, it is not her upbringing alone that made her one of the preeminent voices on Muslim women. Every aspect of her corpus contemplates women, oppression, brutality, the politics of gender, and (post)colonialism. Furthermore, all of Djebar's works examine, if indirectly, Islam in various temporal spaces (past and present) and physical spaces (private or public), systematically providing a poignantly introspective account of the people who constitute them.

Djebar's most apparent reflections on Islam are found in *Loin de Médine (Far from Medina)* (1991). The historical novel tells the story of the prophet Muhammad from the perspective of a group of women, including his daughter Fatima, whose voices, Djebar contends, have been silenced in the archive. Hanan al-Sayed offers a compelling critique of the Algerian writer's stance, identifying it as an anachronistic reading of early Islamic sources that does not fully acknowledge women's voices already present within them. Nevertheless, Djebar's project in *Far from Medina* undeniably shows us, to echo Cixous' words, what writing can *do* with respect to inscribing women into history—at the very least reminding us that women do, in fact, constitute it.[4]

Djebar's most obvious connection to the *Thousand and One Nights* specifically appears in her novel *Ombre sultane* (1995), strikingly translated into English as *A Sister to Scheherazade*. This text has garnered much scholarly attention that draws parallels between the protagonists of Djebar's book, Isma and Hajila, who are married to the same man, and the figures of Scheherazade and her sister Dinarzade. Djebar's collected stories *Femmes d'Alger dans leur appartement* (Women of Algiers in Their Apartment) (1980) and novel *L'amour, la fantasia* (Fantasia: An Algerian Cavalcade) (1985) have also prompted analysis vis-à-vis Scheherazade's storytelling. Suzanne Gaucho's *Liberating*

Shahrazad: Feminism, Postcolonialism, and Islam (2006) focuses on the figure of Scheherazade in these texts, as well as in the works of Fatima Mernissi, Tahar Ben Jelloun, Leïla Sebbar, and Moufida Tlatli. Her study, one of many analyses of contemporary versions of Scheherazade and the intertextual appearances of the *Thousand and One Nights* in modern works, makes it clear that Djebar inscribes herself into a long genealogy of permutations of the renowned storyteller and her tales. Dominique Jullien, known for her ground-breaking study of Proust in relation to the *Thousand and One Nights*, has more recently published *Les amoureux de Schéhérazade: variations modernes sur les Mille et une nuits* (2009), in which she identifies a similar tradition and provides a feminist reading of *A Sister to Scheherazade.*[5]

In addition to examinations of Muslim women in Djebar's literary universe and interpretations of Scheherazade in her texts, readings of her corpus that focus on the body are manifold. Indeed, the volume of scholarly work on Djebar and women's corporeal identities, and specifically on Djebar, Cixous, and body politics, is enormous. Brigitte Weltman-Aron's *Algerian Imprints: Ethical Space in the Work of Assia Djebar and Hélène Cixous* (2015), for instance, reflects on the limits of the body and argues for its de-limitation as a way of rethinking the contours of Algeria (5), a country of profound significance to both Djebar's and Cixous' lives and writing. As Cixous recalls in *La Jeune Née* (*The Newly Born Woman*) (1975), accentuating increasingly somatic experiences: "I learned to read, to write, to scream, to vomit in Algeria" (70). Notably, Djebar features this very line as the epigraph to the first short story of *The Tongue's Blood Does Not Run Dry*, thus herself acknowledging Cixous' (bodily) presence within her work. In *Polygraphies: Francophone Women Writing Algeria* (2012), Alison Rice also discusses the links between Djebar and Cixous, clearly delineating why the body is so present in Djebar's corpus by reminding us that the Algerian writer called autobiography, a genre that has informed much of her work, as a *mise à nu* or stripping naked (46).[6]

Far less scholarly work, however, has been conducted on the intersections between Djebar and Fawzia Zouari. Zouari, who has written both fiction and theory and has fondly reflected in *Jeune Afrique* on Djebar's relationship to Algeria, France, and the French language, has also extensively examined women, oppression, and the body in her own work. Josefina Bueno-Alonso discusses these themes alongside language and, in particular, body language through a feminist lens in Zouari and Djebar, while Claudia Mansueto draws parallels between Djebar's *Les nuits de Strasbourg* (Strasbourg Nights) (1997) and Zouari's *La retournée* (The Traitor) (2002). Mansueto highlights both authors' ability to acutely describe details of the private lives of Maghrebi women, the relationship between their private and public spheres, and, more broadly, identity politics (15). The link between Djebar and Zouari is natural and, I argue, necessary. Indeed, "The Woman in Pieces" and Zouari's *To Put an*

End to Shahrazad, which were notably written in the same year, both offer distortions, or rather, complete rejections of Scheherazade. This study offers an investigation of these parallels and demonstrates how Djebar's short story enacts, literally *embodies* the call espoused in the title of Zouari's work.

Before putting an end to Scheherazade, however, let us begin with her. "The Story of the Three Apples" tells the tale of the murder of a woman cut up into pieces, then hidden in a trunk at the bottom of the Tigris. In disguise one night in Baghdad, the caliph and his vizier, Djaffar, find this chest with the help of a fisherman. The caliph is infuriated and shocked that such crimes could take place under his rule. He orders Djaffar to find the murderer—if not the vizier himself and forty members of his extended family will be hung. Fortunately, the murderer presents himself at court three days later and explains that his crime was one of jealousy. His wife was sick and longed for an apple, he states. Wanting to satisfy her wishes, he traveled for days to find three. But when he returned, she no longer desired the apples. A few days later, the jealous husband sees the coveted fruit in the possession of a slave who tells him that his lover had given it to him. In rage, he kills his wife only to discover that the slave had lied: he had stolen the apple from the man's son, who had been playing with the fruit. The story concludes with the discovery that the slave belongs to Djaffar. The vizier, eager to save his slave, decides to recount a story to the caliph in hopes that the narrative will postpone any deaths. Three dimensions thus structure the *Thousand and One Nights* at this moment: first, the frame, the story of king Shahrayar and Scheherazade, who each night puts off her death thanks to narration; second, the framed text, Scheherazade's stories; and, third, another layer of framed text encased within the framed text, Djaffar's story within that of Scheherazade. We see from this example alone why the *Thousand and One Nights* has elicited reflections on temporality, women's storytelling, and the power of Scheherazade's voice to expose the stakes of narration. In "The Woman in Pieces," Atyka's voice does the same.

Though also constructed through nested stories, Djebar's text is not solely a rewriting of "The Story of the Three Apples," but also a restaging of the narrative against the backdrop of Algeria's Black Decade. Djebar's short story gives voice to Scheherazade, but gives center stage to Atyka, a professor of French reading the *Thousand and One Nights* with her students. "The Woman in Pieces"—oscillating between the past and 1990s Algeria, coming and going between the Atyka and Scheherazade frames—is consequently interrupted and broken up much like "The Story of the Three Apples." Even the font of the tale—italics chosen for Atyka's story and standard type used for the rewriting of the *Thousand and One Nights*—demonstrates a material fracture within the text. The fragmented body of the woman from "The Story of the Three Apples" can be seen to articulate the textual fragmentation in

Djebar's short story. Here, body becomes text; text becomes body. As Djebar writes:

> The pieces are wrapped carefully in a veil. . . . The veil is folded inside a carpet. . . . The carpet, rolled halfway, is kept in a coffin, a large coffin made of palm leaves. . . . The coffin made of palm leaves has been sewn carefully with yarn, good red yarn. Sewn tightly. The coffin itself is preserved in an olivewood trunk, a sealed trunk. . . . The chest lies at the bottom of the Tigris. (97)

Describing the nesting-doll-like organization of the limbs found at the bottom of the river, Djebar underlines the encased structure of her own text, thus marrying body to narrative form. She accentuates the place of flesh in "The Story of the Three Apples," or rather, *adds* corporeality to the story. This incorporation is even more palpable in the description of the wife while she is still alive. In the original tale from the *Thousand and One Nights*, the woman who will later be killed is described in a single five-sentence paragraph spoken by her husband. As he states, eluding the details of her illness or interiority more generally, "On the first day of this month she fell gravely ill and kept getting worse, but I took great care of her until by the end of the month she slowly began to recover" (Haddawy 185). In the Djebar/Atyka version, however, the description is eleven pages long. It speaks of the wife's weariness, solitude, and servitude. This portion of the story addresses her fatigue and boredom, her feelings of abandonment in the absence of confidants or other women. The account also focuses heavily on her body. As the excerpt below underscores, her distress stems from her fear of another pregnancy:

> A fourth! . . . Ah, if it were only possible for her to avoid being weighed down with another burden, to avoid the arrival of a fourth baby. Sapped anew of her powers, she wonders who she can confide in. Who can she tell that she is weary of life, especially of the charge of giving life? . . . Is it wrong not to want to be weighed down so? Alas, whether they are males or not, they are milking, demanding, flesh that devours. (Djebar 101)

This passage describes a woman tired of sharing her body with others, be it her children to feed them or her husband to please him. Indeed, in Djebar's rewriting, the apples much more directly equate to sex, and the husband is compelled to find the fruit in order to taste carnal pleasures: "the husband has become obsessed with the fruit. He can almost taste the juice, can already feel the skin snapping under his teeth. And the night of reciprocated desires that lies ahead" (Djebar 105). And yet, the young wife gains control over her sexualized body by not giving it to him: "At night, between the sheets, by her favourite citronella candle, she silently moves away from the husband. A first time. A second time. It makes his heart freeze" (101). Here is a woman reclaiming her own body for herself, craving apples or sex on her terms, rhythms, and conditions. This reframing of the narrative through an accented corporeality puts into obvious practice Cixous' conceptualization of women's writing as:

> an act which will not only 'realize' the decensored relation of woman to her sexuality, to her womanly being, giving her access to her native strength; it will give her back her goods, her pleasures, her organs, her immense bodily territories which have been kept under seal. ("The Laugh of the Medusa" 880)

Bodies permeate "The Woman in Pieces." They infuse every part of the story and, when dismembered, mirror its form. Atyka's body plays an even more crucial role in bringing corporeality to both the content and structure of the short story. Toward the end of "The Woman in Pieces," Atyka is murdered by a group of violent radical Islamists who find her teachings intolerable. Her body, like the wife's in Scheherazade's story, is cut into pieces—her head is detached from her body—and at this horrific moment, the text undergoes a change of form. The fonts are standardized and Atyka's murder, like that of the woman from "The Story of the Three Apples," is recounted in roman typeface as follows:

> Five imposing men have entered [the classroom], four of them in gendarmes', or soldiers', uniforms, bearded, armed and impassive. . . . [Atyka] stares at them and in Arabic she asks forcefully, 'Who are you and what do you want?' . . . The man with the gun is still facing Atyka, who is standing stiffly. In good French, he says, 'You are Atyka F., a self-proclaimed teacher who, it appears, nonetheless tells these young children obscene stories?' . . . Standing, Atyka gets a bullet in the heart. . . . Then, with a long and sure gesture of his other hand, he slits Atyka's throat. (Djebar 121–3)

Atyka's murder, not set in italics like the rest of her narrative, enacts a flattening out of the framing and framed texts, of Atyka's story and the tale from the *Thousand and One Nights*. The fonts become uniform and the narrative distance between the professor and what she is teaching collapses: "Atyka is at once there, in Baghdad—where the vizier and his strange master are struggling—and here, now, in this city" (Djebar 121), the narrator notes. Moreover, Atyka's body is described in much the same way as the woman's from "The Story of the Three Apples." It is now *her* body that is enveloped in veils; *she* who is identified as the woman cut into pieces: "Atyka's body and head, wrapped in white linen, rest within the chest inside the two coffins. The body of the woman cut into pieces" (125).

But her gruesome death also calls into question what happens to her voice. There is a brief moment, immediately following her murder, in which the font reverts back to italics. This passage begins with the words *"Atyka, her head severed, the new storyteller"* (Djebar 123), but ends with her voice breaking off: *"Atyka's voice is beginning to sound stifled, as if the words were drowning, stewing in the blood that drips and flows over the wood of the table"* (124). The narrator explains how one of Atyka's students, Omar, *"will say later that her last words were not Scheherazade's, no, but her own, Atyka's, the professor they had liked so much"* (124). This grisly description of mutilation puts a clear end to Atyka—both to her body, dripping in blood, and to her voice, drowning in it. But not before she owns her last words; she is the *new storyteller.* And yet, her story ends here. Stifled until silent, Atyka's voice does not go on narrating. Indeed, while there are similarities between Atyka and the woman from "The Story of the Three Apples," Djebar draws a stark contrast between Atyka and Scheherazade. Although both are storytellers, Djebar distances Atyka from the famous teller of tales through her voice that, like her body, is no more. As the end of Djebar's text shows, the rupture of body, that which holds the larynx, leads to a rupture of voice. Through her death, Atyka's voice has been killed off and is thereby unable to be endlessly recuperated in narrative, a fate that could not be further from the destiny that entraps Scheherazade.

Drawing on her analyses of *Far from Medina*, Monia Kallel also underscores Djebar's desire of distance from the mythical storyteller. Citing the title of Zouari's 1996 work, Kallel writes,

> one thing is clear: like many Maghrebian women writers, Djebar thinks that 'it is necessary to put an end to Scheherazade' by updating the space, purpose, and mode of her speech, while preserving the essence of this voice that oscillates between silence and eruption, absence and flow. (140, my trans.)

This observation is persuasive and recalls Christiane Chaulet Achour's cogent analyses identifying the very ways in which Scheherazade's space, purpose, and mode of speech have changed in fourteen literary examples ranging from 1981 to 2007. These include Zouari's 1999 novel *Ce pays dont je meurs* (I Die by This Country), which puts into practice her urge to do away with Scheherazade's storytelling through the story of sisters Nacéra and Amira, and Leïla Sebbar's *Sherazade* trilogy, whose protagonist's name offers a certain rejection of Scheherazade with its missing syllable.

But does a simple update or change *put an end to Scheherazade?* Kallel, after all, reminds us that in *Ces voix qui m'assiègent* (These Voices that Besiege Me) (1999), Djebar presents herself as Scheherazade's inheritor (Kallel 131) and concludes her study of *Far from Medina* (alongside George Sand's *Consuelo*) with the following observation: "these voice-bodies and corpora combine with other voices and participate in the interminable speech-scene so that Scheherazade no longer falls silent at dawn" (Kallel 143). Unending narration that equates to survival has always been Scheherazade's power, however. As Tzvetan Todorov cogently explains, "narrating equals living. The most obvious example is that of Scheherazade herself, who lives exclusively to the degree that she can continue to tell stories; but this situation is ceaselessly repeated within the tale" (233). If the story continues infinitely, never dying off, Scheherazade never dies either, and as a result eclipses many—if not all—other voices.

Indeed, undying cultural specters and avatars of Scheherazade abound. For centuries she has been the literary prototype—even for Djebar—for how women are to be heard when oppressed or threatened with other forms of violence. In a chapter on feminist revolt, colonialism, and Islam, Jane Hiddleston concludes her analyses of a breadth of Djebar's works, though not *The Tongue's Blood Does Not Run Dry*, by summarizing that,

> through Fatima and Scheherazade, she shows how eloquence and storytelling can be deployed to achieve the practical liberation of women from oppression, and literature itself emerges as a site of questioning, an invitation to the reader or listener to think differently. (242)

Hiddleston is careful to note Djebar's complex feminist stance, explaining that "her contribution to feminism is at once this multifaceted exploration of Islamic feminist rebellion through literature, and an anxious revelation of the tensions that feminist self-affirmation might bring in its wake" (242). And yet, in "The Woman in Pieces," something different takes place. Self-affirmation does not occur through the figure of Scheherazade and certainly not through her voice. Although the storyteller has systematically been the figure of resistance and liberation, in this case to resist her is to liberate oneself.

In "The Woman in Pieces," Atyka is able to reclaim her voice. Although she ultimately dies and her italicized narrative, ending with an ellipsis, is killed off just as she is, in the process she also puts an end to the enduring universe of Scheherazade. The flattening out of the embedded narratives and the standardization of the fonts carried out by Atyka's death reduce the distance between herself and "The Story of the Three Apples" to zero, replacing Scheherazade's eternal, mythical voice with her own ephemeral voice. Scheherazade, with her stories that never end, is like a woman without a body. In other words, if she can continue to narrate to eternity, she is immortal, not corporeal. Djebar's body-inscribing rewriting of "The Story of the Three Apples," however, brings mortality, *corpo-reality*, to the narrative. By espousing flesh—and brutally rupturing it along with the voice it holds— "The Woman in Pieces" silences Scheherazade as Atyka is silenced. The professor has brought the storyteller's narrative, which was alive through her voice as she taught it to her class, to an end. She has, as a result, enacted a reconceptualization of voice, a coming to storytelling for women and certainly Muslim women that no longer occurs in the shadow of myth or adopted teller of tales.

This is not to suggest that refusing Scheherazade implies a "liberation" of Muslim women nor that the homogenizing figure of Scheherazade should be replaced by an equally homogenizing antithesis that would obfuscate individual voices. Instead, putting an end to Scheherazade constitutes a form of personal revolt—for Djebar, for those who could not speak during the Algerian War, for Muslim women in general. As Zouari writes:

> For centuries, you have narrated in my place, Shahrazad! Your voice has covered mine. You aroused admiration and astonishment. You fixed for eternity the contours of the woman, both cunning and frail, victim and persecutor, that I must be. And I, I no longer feel a sense of community with you, Shahrazad. . . . Every time that I was tempted to speak, there was a new tale of Shahrazad's that silenced me. Her stories never end: there my torment lies! (11, my trans.)

Zouari's emphatic passage justifiably reveals rage and pain as it underscores Scheherazade's relentless narration and its suppression of other voices. Closely paralleling Cixous' words, Zouari further remarks that "when Shahrazad narrates, she does not *do*" (13). I disagree with this position to an extent, as Scheherazade's narrative does actively push back her death. However, it is precisely through death that Atyka's narrative does indeed *do*. Although her voice is silenced through murder, Atyka's story reveals this censorship and exposes the injustices committed against teachers, journalists, and artists—especially those operating in French—during Algeria's Civil War. "The Woman in Pieces" stresses what Zimra and many others identify as the "necessary distinction between Islam and Islamism" (118n15), as well as specifically foregrounds the gender-based violence of the war. As Anissa Daoudi highlights, "Women were also targeted by Islamists. In *Oran, langue morte*, Djebar draws on the language tension and the violence associated with it in Algeria to discuss the killing of women language teachers" (53). Djebar contemporizes the death described in "The Story of the Three Apples," rejects the storied figure of Scheherazade, and as a result gives way to new perspectives. In the process, she confirms Gayatri Chakravorty Spivak's belief that "rethinking woman in Islam is crucial in the context not only of Algeria but that internationality, called 'Islamic,' which does not have the convenient name of a continent" (78–9). Rethinking and inscribing women in Islam into history, does Djebar not also provide a contextualized response to Cixous' urgent calling women to writing?

In the final analysis, Djebar's short story, by inserting body into text, moves away from the immortality of the *Thousand and One Nights*. When "The Woman in Pieces" becomes formally uniform, that is, when the framing/framed structure of the text collapses and flattens, Scheherazade is ultimately silenced. The result is significant. As Zouari asserts, "It is when Shahrazad keeps quiet that I begin to speak. My speaking comes at the cost of her definitive silence" (11). The closing of Djebar's text is thus also an opening up, a rallying cry urging women to find their own voice, an invitation for women writers to embody their own bodies and texts. Writing, according to Cixous, "is precisely *the very possibility of change*, the space that can serve as a springboard for subversive thought, the precursory movement of a transformation of social and cultural structures" ("The Laugh of the Medusa" 879). "Write!" she says, "Writing is for you, you are for you; your body is yours, take it" (876). To put an end to Scheherazade—and Atyka—paves the way for other women to tell the stories that expose the conditions of their existence.

Notes

1 The title of the English translation refers to the book's afterword and its epigraph from Djebar's *Vaste est la prison* (*So Vast the Prison*) (1995): "*Blood does not run dry, it simply dies out*" (209).
2 Spelling variants of the storyteller's name are many. I have used the common "Scheherazade," while "Shahrazad" is a more direct transliteration of her name.
3 See Accad's article for a thorough bio-bibliography of Djebar's life and production prior to 1996.
4 As Elsayed explains, "To a large extent, previous scholarship on *Loin de Médine* seems to accommodate the claim made by Djebar in the 'Avant-propos' about the 'silence' of early Muslim male historians [with respect to women]. In fact, this claim has been largely repeated like a refrain and never problematized. In this article, I begin by questioning the 'silence' of the official history: I examine women's presence in the historians' texts by returning to the original sources themselves" (92).
5 Jullien in fact puts forth four readings of modern versions of Scheherazade: political, aesthetic, feminist, and introspective (12).
6 For more on autobiography, see Natalie Edwards's *Shifting Subjects: Plural Subjectivity in Contemporary Francophone Women's Autobiography* (2011), in which she explores this genre in the works of Julia Kristeva, Cixous, and Djebar.

Works Cited

Accad, Evelyne. "Assia Djebar's Contribution to Arab Women's Literature: Rebellion, Maturity, Vision." *World Literature Today*, vol. 70, no. 4, 1996, pp. 801–12.

al-Musawi, Muhsin J. *The Islamic Context of the Thousand and One Nights*. Columbia UP, 2009.

Bueno-Alonso, Josefina. "Representations of Motherhood: Between Absence and Rebelliousness." *Narrating Motherhood(s), Breaking the Silence: Other Mothers, Other Voices*, edited by Silvia Caporale-Bizzini, Peter Lang, 2006, pp. 123–140.

Chaulet Achour, Christiane. "Des écrivaines contemporaines et *Les Mille et Une Nuits*." *À l'aube des Mille et Une Nuits: Lectures comparatistes*, edited by Christiane Chaulet Achour, Saint-Denis: Presses universitaires de Vincennes, 2012, pp. 113–160.

Cixous, Hélène. "The Laugh of the Medusa." *Signs*, translated by Keith Cohen and Paula Cohen, vol. 1, no. 4, 1976, pp. 875–93.

——, and Catherine Clément. *The Newly Born Woman*. Translated by Betsy Wing, U of Minnesota P, 1986.

Daoudi, Anissa. "Algerian Women and the Traumatic Decade: Literary Interventions." *Journal of Literature and Trauma Studies*, vol. 5, no. 1, 2016, pp. 41–63.

Djebar, Assia. "La femme en morceaux" ("The Woman in Pieces"). *The Tongue's Blood Does Not Run Dry: Algerian Stories*, translated by Tegan Raleigh, Seven Stories Press, 2009.

Elsayed, Hanan. "'Silence' and Historical Tradition in Assia Djebar's *Loin de Médine*." *Research in African Literatures*, vol. 44, no. 1, 2013, pp. 91–105.

Gaucho, Suzanne. *Liberating Shahrazad: Feminism, Postcolonialism, and Islam*. U of Minnesota P, 2006.

Haddawy, Husain, translator, and Muhsin Mahdi, editor. "The Story of the Three Apples." *The Arabian Nights*. Norton, 2008.

Hiddleston, Jane. "The Woman Who Said 'No': Colonialism, Islam, and Feminist Resistance in the Works of Assia Djebar." *Literature and the Development of Feminist Theory*, edited by Robin Truth Goodman, Cambridge UP, 2015, pp. 230–242.

Jullien, Dominique. *Les amoureux de Schéhérazade: variations modernes sur les Mille et une nuits*. Geneva, Droz, 2009.

Kallel, Monia. "Sand et Djebar: sur la voie (voix) de Shéhérazade." *Études littéraires*, vol. 42, no. 1, 2011, pp. 129–44.

Mansueto, Claudia. "Franchir les frontières territoriales et identitaires à travers l'expérience sexuelle: *La Retournée* (2002) de Fawzia Zouari et *Les Nuits de Strasbourg* (1997) d'Assia Djebar." *Planeta Literatur. Journal of Global Literary Studies*, vol. 1, no. 2, 2014, pp. 1–15.

Rice, Alison. *Polygraphies: Francophone Women Writing Algeria*. U of Virginia P, 2012.

Spivak, Gayatri Chakravorty. "Ghostwriting." *Diacritics*, vol. 25, no. 2, 1995, pp. 65–84.

Todorov, Tzvetan. "Narrative-Men." *The Arabian Nights Reader*, edited by Ulrich Marzolph, translated by Richard Howard, Wayne State UP, 2006, pp. 226–238.

Weltman-Aron, Brigitte. *Algerian Imprints: Ethical Space in the Work of Assia Djebar and Hélène Cixous*. Columbia UP, 2015.

Zimra, Clarisse. "Sounding Off the Absent Body: Intertextual Resonances in 'La femme qui pleure' and 'La femme en morceaux.'" *Research in African Literatures*, vol. 30, no. 3, 1999, pp. 108–24.

Zouari, Fawzia. *Pour en finir avec Shahrazade*. Tunis, Cérès, 1996.

19 Cultural Trauma and Scheherazade's Gastro-national/ Transnational Discourse in Tamara al-Refai's Writings

Pervine Elrefaei

The ongoing fragmentation of Syria by sectarianism is the culmination of a civil war in which extremists like The Free Syrian Army, al-Nusra Front, Jaysh al-Islam, al-Qaʿeda, and ISIS have played major roles.[1] Consequently, national identity crisis has become a focal theme for many Syrian writers. This chapter examines selected Arabic literary articles by the Syrian writer Tamara al-Refai published in the Egyptian newspaper *Elshorouk* and translated here by the present researcher. Also, this chapter draws on memory studies, food studies, gender studies and the field of feminist geopolitics that "demonstrates how the 'apolitical,' 'feminine' private realm is a key component in the operation of global power" (Massaro and Williams 470). The study argues that the articles are basically centered on identity, cultural trauma, and memory, interlaced with Syrian women's resilience and pivotal roles as "cultural transmitters" and "cultural signifiers of the national collectivity" (Yuval-Davis 621) during traumatic displacement and cultural threat. al-Refai utilizes female storytelling that is anchored in the *Arabian Nights* and the Scheherazade motif as an empowering tactic of survival and resistance to threatening Islamism, authoritarianism, and Western imperialism.

As a secular Sunni Muslim, al-Refai foregrounds the history of a multilayered secular Syrian identity through the sovereignty of the nation as "an imagined political community" (Anderson 6). The term "gastro-nationalism" highlights the political role of food as a discourse that "buttresses national identity against perceived threats from outsiders who wish to eliminate certain objects or practices" (Desoucey). As a Scheherazade figure, al-Refai transforms the kitchen from a private domestic space that is associated with the stereotypical discourse of the invisible harem world conjured up by the ongoing threats to a political public space where food becomes a metaphor of memory, and cooking becomes a performative act of identity reconstruction, agency, solidarity, and nation building. Food is delineated as "commemorative," representing "the accumulated wisdom" of Syrian "ancestors," granting them "to partake each day of the national past" (Barthes 27). However, al-Refai's deliberate remembering of a gastro-national discourse leads to a transnational discourse and a new meaning of home in the diaspora that transcends the borders of religion, race, gender, ethnicity, and class.

Previously working for the International Committee of the Red Cross, and later for the Human Rights Watch Organization, al-Refai is an activist and supporter of Syrian women refugees worldwide. She is the founder of "Zeit Zeitoun," or "Olive Oil," a food project in Cairo, Egypt, that sells Syrian food cooked by Syrian women refugees for economic empowerment. al-Refai weaves polyphonic stories within stories about her nation and culture in an attempt to struggle against cultural trauma and draw a "meaningful connection of this past to the current situation in which the memory is retrieved" (Neumann 336).

In her article "On the memory of scent and food," Tamara al-Refai utilizes memory and food discourse to highlight identity formation as opposed to the ongoing cultural trauma. She writes,

> How can we, Syrians, explain that . . . there are various scents, voices and tastes that visit us . . . from that country that is enveloped today by the smell of death and gunpowder? Memory has the power to bring back feelings and means of communication with the surroundings in a way that keeps us there in spite of being here! . . . I think a lot about the horrendous condition that the Syrians have come to in the diaspora; their estrangement and loss of everything, particularly the dwindling of memory; our memory; specifically the memory of scents exuding from the stoves and kitchens and emanating from the arranged plates on the tables . . . There is a memory that Syrians need to start documenting today to block extinction, starting with the dialect and the use of some expressions and proverbs, to the kitchen and the daily customs and practices related to food (al-Refai, "On Memory").

As J. C. Alexander puts it, "Cultural trauma occurs when members of a collectivity feel they have been subjected to a horrendous event that leaves indelible marks upon their group consciousness, marking their memories forever and changing their future identity in fundamental and irrevocable ways" (1). Deliberate remembrance is thus an indispensable therapeutic strategy of resistance and identity reconstruction that al-Refai implements in all her articles.

al-Refai embarks on a tempo-spatial journey through the different devastated Syrian cities which are torn apart between Islamists, the oppressive Alawite regime, and the competing imperial powers. In "Aleppo, the City of the 1001 Stories," she documents the traumatic impact of war on individual/collective identity. The present reality of a devastated Aleppo that has turned into "the city of the 1001 deaths" is set in contrast to its glorious cross-cultural past as "the largest Syrian city and one of the oldest, if not the oldest, inhabited cities of the world." The city that witnessed successive civilizations, from the Aramaic to the Islamic, and later the Western, during colonization, is cast in the light of a beautiful woman that has been violated by oppressive powers. The historical transformation is delineated through the multigenerational narrative of the father, grandfather, and great grandfather. Recollecting the secular hybrid identity of her family/nation/land, Tamara al-Refai narrates,

> I imagine the old city . . . that in 1986 the UNESCO counted as a World Heritage site . . . I listen to the call to prayer from the Umayyad Mosque . . . I sit in Cairo with my father and a family friend, both from Aleppo . . . Both men conjure up names of bygone places and persons . . . My father was brought up in a home run by a father/ intellectual/poet who was secularly inclined, and a grandfather who preached the Friday sermon, led the prayers in Aleppo's big mosque, and taught his disciples in the other . . . big Ottoman Mosque . . . My father was educated in the Marist Fathers School, . . . so he studied all the subjects in French. He and his siblings were taken care of by a Jewish nanny from Aleppo. This was in the forties and fifties in the last century. All lived in one house and learnt that each individual had his specificity, religion, and beliefs. The Prophets' stories that the great grandfather daily narrated interconnected with the stories of Christmas and Resurrection my father came back with from school. ("Aleppo, the City")

The ambivalent role of missionary schools in shaping Syrian identities was highlighted by many scholars. While Albert Hourani amongst others emphasized its positive impact on modernizing Arab identity, it was seen by others as part of the hegemonic colonial enterprise (al-Sadda 214). The above quote highlights al-Refai as a secular writer who supports Hourani's perspective through the tolerant and inclusive transcultural discourse of coexistence she deliberately remembers. However, I argue that the above quote depicts knowledge production and "geopolitics as a masculinist enterprise" that is anchored in "hierarchies of race and gender" (Massaro and Williams 569).

In "From there, this is Damascus," al-Refai delineates the cultural trauma of the Syrian diaspora through a dramatic scene that takes place at a restaurant in Berlin. The article is a story within a story anchored in multilayered memory as al-Refai encompasses her husband's memory of his experience abroad. A male Syrian waiter is represented overhearing the talk of her husband and his friend on their favorite restaurants in Cairo, Beirut, and Damascus, the architecture of Aleppo and Alexandria, the destructive war in Syria, and the escalating political conditions in Egypt; in a nutshell, the dreams of yesterday that have turned into nightmares. The political talk about conflict zones runs against the restaurant and food as contact zones with a box of Syrian desserts on the table as a gastro-national metaphor of memory.

Tracing the journey of Syrian desserts from one place to another, al-Refai narrates how desserts can act as transnational tokens of friendship that connect people of different religions, races, ethnicities, cultures, and times. Brought by a friend from Damascus to Cairo, the box of desserts is taken by al-Refai's husband to Berlin for a Swiss friend who studied Arabic in Damascus thirty years ago. As Najwa al-Qatttan puts it, "identity itself appeared to rest on the palate" (721–2). Spotted by the Syrian waiter, the box of desserts brings nostalgic memories of the homeland. Detecting its psychological impact on the waiter who is moved to tears, al-Refai's husband insists on sharing the desserts with him. The visual scene is replete with auditory, gustatory, olfactory, kinesthetic, and tactile images. In a similar vein to the previous article, memory recalls gendered spaces and roles as intrinsic to identity formation. Writing the self, al-Refai documents,

> In the box there were desserts manufactured there, in the city of death and pistachios, the city of rose water, . . . the city of apricots, olives, missiles and exploding barrels. Each time I feel that the details of Damascus are being erased from my memory, my past life crystalizes in the shape of a piece of *baklava*; I take a bite and my mother emerges, elegant, holding the coffee tray to her friends on a sunny day. I smell the almond paste and I hear the laughter of the gathering there at home and sentences known to all who lived through such meetings: 'Have you heard of Om Hisham whose daughter married a good groom who's been living in France all his life?' I eat a piece of dessert with pine and I smell cigarettes coming out of my dad's small office. I overhear his conversation with one of his generation over Arabs, colonialism, Israel and the absurdity of the United Nations' declarations. ("From there, this is Damascus")

The box of desserts thus takes the reader on a journey through the lanes of memory into a gendered society where women and men in pre-war times used to occupy different spaces and engage with different topics. While women's main interests were marriage and domestic family affairs, men were occupied with more serious political matters. Food conjures the present war in Syria that is also interlaced with the colonial reality of Israel and the Palestinian condition signifying the interconnectedness of colonial and postcolonial times.

Back to the present, al-Refai takes the reader to the Syrian waiter who studies in Berlin and her husband's optimistic note of certainty that all will return to the homeland and start the process of rebuilding the nation. Cultural trauma is thus overpowered by a moment of solidarity and communion through food as a therapeutic medium. Bachelard's words are worth mentioning in this respect, "We comfort ourselves by reliving memories of protection . . . Memories of the outside world will never have the same tonality as those of home and, by recalling these memories, we add to our store of dreams . . ." (28). al-Refai's polyphonic narrative develops from the individual to the collective, manifesting an empowering collective memory. As she puts it,

> The Damascene land would never let us forget it. Sugar melts on my tongue as I approach our home there. I swallow the piece of dessert and share the box of desserts with a friend in Berlin; and he in turn gives half his share to a Syrian youth he meets at a restaurant. The youth adds the coffee they had to his check and my husband comes back with a new story about Syrian diaspora in Germany. ("From there, this is Damascus")

Food thus represents communal hunger for the land and nation. "The rite of eating and drinking together" and "the exchange of food" "constitute the confirmation of a bond" (Gennep 29) between the Syrians, a theme she re-iterates in "Siran, Yesterday and Today." al-Refai contemplates the ongoing "blood whirlpool" that culminated in the starvation of the besieged areas. The title she chooses acquires a historical dimension as the word "Siran," she elaborates, is used by the Syrians to identify that part that goes back to the Umayyad dynasty. Food recalls the pre-war identity, customs, traditions of civilians, and the present cultural trauma crystalized by Ghouta as a devas-tated conflict zone. The present excruciating scene of the humanitarian aids conjures up memories of Syria as the agricultural land of abundance that used to be rich with "fruits, citrus, almonds, walnut, wheat, olives, apricots and pistachios" (al-Refai, "Siran, Yesterday"). Nostalgia for the homeland is extolled through recollected scenes of Syrians spending their weekends gathering around food in Ghouta's orchards close to water channels.[2]

The rite of passage to Ghouta as a historical place is a gastro-national rite of identity formation that is countered by the reality of cultural erasure. Taking us through multilayered memory to pre-revolution times, al-Refai recalls the political corruption of authoritarian powers that transformed Ghouta's identity through the random encroachment of cement buildings. The recent air strikes waged by the regime on Islamists, and supported by Russia, have escalated the trauma of the civilians who are nostalgic for the bygone land of abundance once regarded as one of the wonders of the world. al-Refai adds, "Today, a friend of mine narrates how when she gave a child coming recently out of Ghouta a banana, the child looked at it and ate it with the skin. His mother blushed saying, 'He doesn't know fruits; he is three years old and we don't have fruits'" ("Siran, Yesterday"). Crystalizing cultural trauma and the splitting of Syrian identity due to the successive di-minishing of foodscapes, al-Refai draws an image of a contemporary Syrian Self entrapped between the past and the present:

> To be Syrian is to stretch your hand to a tree in summer and get an apple to eat after cleaning it with your hands and clothes. To be

Syrian is to receive a bowl of pure milk covered with a thick layer of cream from friends in Aleppo. To be Syrian is to stretch your hand to the apricot jam plate that has arrived from Ghouta and has been divided by the house lady between family and neighbors . . . To be Syrian today is to volunteer in gathering food, winter clothes or money for surgeries . . . To be Syrian today is to be stunned whenever you hear of human aids dropping on areas of people who have been willing to deprive themselves of the piece of bread they have to be offered to the guest. To be Syrian today is to live in a constant state of disbelief though you realize and acknowledge that the country you love is disappearing. ("Siran, Yesterday")

In other articles, Tamara al-Refai depicts women's resilience and the refugee kitchen as a performative/transformative ground. In his definition of resilience in war times, Brett T. Litz argues that, "Resilience most often refers to an outcome. . . . a person who often manages and reconciles a traumatic experience in the moment and over time is said to have navigated the impact successfully." The resilience, coping, and identity reconstruction of Syrian women in Jordanian refugee camps are examined by Karen Culcasi. As she puts it, "In this space . . . women socialize, laugh and have a little respite from their struggle, all while working on their embroidery" (464). In a similar vein, in her article "Recycling life," al-Refai delineates the resilient identity of female refugees through the polyphonic voices of women of multigenerational families where refugee camps substitute homes/kitchens that are cast in light of a land that is being reconstructed. Women are represented as weavers, preservers, and transmitters of cultural heritage.

In performing domestic chores, women struggle to recycle/re-inscribe Syrian identity and culture. The grandmother's cupboard, for instance, has an old tin biscuit box that is meticulously filled with organized pins, needles and colorful threads symbolizing the endeavor to pull together the fragmented threads of Syrian identity and the willful act of nation building. The same tin box emerges in the article "The brass key of return" to contain the key of forsaken homes recalling the Palestinian plight. Similarly, the old empty jars are used as spice jars; the leftover rice and chicken are recycled into a delicious *fattah* dish and chicken sandwiches; and the residues of soap are chopped and reused to perfume clothes in cupboards ("Recycling life").

Depicted as creative, energizing forces of life that breed lilacs out of the dead land, women defy displacement, poverty, and oppression through the kitchen as a fluid geographical space. As she puts it,

Everything other than the human being has multiple lives in Syria. The same thing is being reused in consecutive and different stages and is being re-circulated among different familial hands the way the human being plays a different role in his/her consecutive life stages. (al-Refai, "Recycling life")

Remembering collective Syrian identity that transcended sectarianism, al-Refai adds that recycling has never been associated in the Syrian mind with financial ability; it is only linked to the Syrians' ability to make use of everything, and "this in itself is an art we pride ourselves on possessing" ("Recycling life"). A great domestic housewife, she adds, is the frugal woman who possesses this art of recycling that "has been transformed into a tactic of survival for the Syrians" who make use of "a thing they may no longer have in the future due to . . . displacement, clinging to their dignity without manifesting their need for anything" ("Recycling life").

al-Refai consolidates "a sense of belonging," creating "communities" (Visser 109) of female agency from different Syrian refugees all over the globe. In Jordan refugee camps, al-Refai documents how an old Syrian woman cultivated different aromatic plants she acquired from a human rights organization that distributed food in tin margarine containers to be used for cooking. In Lebanon, another Syrian woman in a refugee camp recycled the old decaying tents that had been used for years into waterproof clothes for children. In Syrian homes, grandmothers dictate that things are never thrown away; things are not clutter as long as they are creatively recycled (al-Refai, "Recycling life").

The fluidity of female identity is detected in al-Refai's consecutive articles that develop with political escalations. Displaced, marginalized women gradually acquire visibility and centrality through culinary language as a medium that re-inscribes gender relations and foregrounds feminist geopolitics. The previously protected Syrian housewives become protective breadwinners, challenging "geopolitical power" and "paternalistic discourses of vulnerability" (Massaro and Williams 567) circulated by hegemonic imperial powers, Islamists, and authoritarian regimes. Using the kitchen as a political public space, women play the metaphorical role of cultural ambassadors negotiating identity. In "In the kitchen and politics," al-Refai documents the process of cooking that takes place in the modest fund-raised kitchen of her project "Zeit Zeitoon." The kitchen is delineated as a diplomatic, secular, contact/conflict zone where women disagree over recipes of different homes, ethnicities, and cities. As she narrates, "Kitchen talk for the Syrians is like talk on politics. We talk then disagree; we get anxious and cling to our views" ("In the kitchen and politics"). Female disagreement is cast in light of the Syrian crisis that is gradually resolved through tolerating differences, dissolving fissure, transcending boundaries, and practicing the politics of inclusion.

As a space of agency, kitchen generates hope and national solidarity. Mapping fragmented Syrian territories through the recipes of six women of different sects and ethnicities, al-Refai mingles them in a therapeutic potion. al-Refai narrates, "It seems that the 'Syrian kitchen' has the power either to trigger a whole crisis or to be the best program to call for tolerance, acceptance of and reconciliation with the other" ("In the kitchen and politics"). Kitchen and recipes as cultural bridges of communication and homogeneity expand temporally and spatially, horizontally and vertically to reconstruct an inclusive nation that embraces all cities, ethnicities and sects that have historically constituted the Syrian cuisine. The kitchen/homeland as a fluid space is remarkably signified by the intermingling of culinary and political languages:

> I agree on the basics: the pomegranate seeds that dance on minced parsley on top of the main course are inescapable; the pomegranate dressing on *fattoush* is non-negotiable. We will not negotiate the amount of garlic on chicken *fattah*. We will not sacrifice any piece of Nablus cheese, no matter how small it is, whether for the pie or the *knafeh* after extracting the salt. We will not deduce the quantities of the chili sauce used in *mjaddara*; and we will not substitute the fried bread with its oven toasted equivalent on *fattoush* (though lighter on the stomach). ("In the kitchen and politics")

The act of cooking transforms the kitchen from a place of being into a place of becoming through explicit negotiation of gender roles and spatial positioning as "in the intimate spaces of displacement women have taken on traditionally masculine practices . . ." (Culcasi 463).

The six women/cooks/diplomats/spokespersons are faced in their kitchen/homeland with red lines. al-Refai delineates a dramatic scene of negotiated boundaries:

> There are red lines in the kitchen like in political negotiations, a thing the six women arrived at after two rounds of shared work. As for possible concessions, the coastal woman insists on adding more lemon juice to the stuffed vine leaves and the Homsian woman agrees to somehow decrease the fat in the *kebab*. ("In the kitchen and politics")

al-Refai proceeds to document the demands and recommendations of every woman. The woman from Aleppo, for example, prides herself on her cultural specificity, yet hybridity, seeing Aleppo as "the kitchen queen" and "the Northern bride" whose cuisine has been enriched by the tips of the bygone Jewish and Armenian communities. The spices the Aleppo woman clings to are metaphorically depicted as "factions" the woman either utilizes or otherwise she "withdraws" from the negotiating act. Cooking is a multi-temporal/multilayered geopolitical act as the recipe the six women agree upon is metaphorically perceived as the Syrian map that is rooted in a long history of communal interconnectedness, multiculturalism, yet cultural specificity maintained.

The women's inclusive gastro-national discourse and their strategic positionality (Hall 2) contest the masculinist geopolitics of exclusion and hierarchy and reconstruct gender relations through envisioning female political leadership. Setting the strategy for the other women, the woman from the mountain area (Druze) quietly emphasizes the need for patience, rationality, and division of labor. "'Let's focus on priorities,' she says. What shall we do today and how shall we divide the work between us?" ("In the kitchen and politics").

In "No *fattah* in New York's kitchens," a more inclusive transnational perspective is acquired through the memory of a dinner gathering al-Refai was invited to in New York as a multicultural space. The invitation that comprised nine guests from different cultures, countries, religions, and ethnicities was preceded by the exchange of fifteen emails within two weeks between the hostess and guests. The successive emails are cast in light of a transcultural/political agreement on the meticulously selected food that "meets all the requirements" of "health" issues, "religious" affiliations, and cultural differences.

Memory of that gathering triggers other past memories of childhood and grants al-Refai a critical perspective on her home/homeland, signifying self-growth: "I remember the instructions we used to take when we were young from family elders; we accepted whatever they served us and never said that we did not like any kind of food . . . it was better to eat all what was served without debate" ("No *fattah* in New York's kitchens"). The "meaningful connection of this past to the current situation" (Neumann 336) grants al-Refai an understanding of collective identity formation in childhood and the oppressive patriarchal practices exercised on the Syrian self. The dinner gathering deconstructs the self/other binary rooted in nationalism; creates bridges; spreads warmth and empathy; and foregrounds coexistence and humanism as the constituents of home as an in-between space. al-Refai revisits the national cuisine, she—as a Syrian—prides herself on preserving, realizing that it actually cannot meet all the demands observed by the hostess. She narrates,

> I reconsider the list of names in the emails and see that most of them sound strange and mostly come from different ethnic and geographical origins . . . How admirable the freedom of opinion and expression is . . . How wonderful the feeling of respecting one's desires is; however, this should be intertwined with our belief that the other has similar desires that should also be respected or at least we should reconcile what we want with what others want. ("No *fattah* in New York's kitchens")

With the politics of inclusion extolled, the gastro-national discourse develops into a progressive transnational discourse depicting a world that knows no borders, though rootedness in one's culture is maintained. The kitchen thus becomes a political space that dreams not only of a better Syria, but of a better world. It is interesting to perceive the imagined home/homeland in light of Bachelard's words in *The Poetics of Space*,

> Sometimes the house of the future is better built; lighter and larger than all the houses of the past, so that the image of the dream house is opposed to that of the childhood home . . . This dream house may be merely . . . the embodiment of everything that is considered convenient, comfortable, healthy, sound, desirable, by other people. (81)

Utilizing the commemorative metaphorical language of food, al-Refai heals cultural trauma and revisits the meaning of home. Her culinary narratives and project "Zeit Zeitoun" represent "a project—at once a vision and a construction—that takes you 'beyond' yourself in order to return, in a spirit of revision and reconstruction to the political conditions of the present" (Bhabha 3). al-Refai's "art . . . renews the past, refiguring it as a contingent 'in-between' space . . . The 'past-present' becomes part of the necessity, not the nostalgia of living" (3). The selected articles develop from depicting cultural trauma as the product of the patriarchal struggle over geography and hegemony intrinsic to masculinist geopolitics to foregrounding a liberating discourse of feminist geopolitics. Though Syrian women preserve cultural heritage, they, nonetheless, negotiate identity and gender relations, shift ground, and interrogate the ongoing hegemonic practices exercised by Islamists, the nation-state and Western imperial powers. Using Scheherazade's counter hegemonic voice, al-Refai "decenters dominant geopolitical narratives," "challenges exclusions" (Massaro and Williams 569), exercises female agency, and anchored in hope, dreams of a more optimistic inclusive, transnational future.

Notes

1 For a brief history of the Syrian civil war see the BBC News report, "Syria: The story of the conflict." March 11, 2016. www.bbc.com/news/world-middle-east-26116868
2 Ghouta was exposed to chemical attacks launched by the regime and supported by Russians on Islamists, culminating in deaths of civilians. For a report on the conflict, see "Breaking Ghouta," www.publications.atlantic-council.org/breakingghouta

  In April 2016, a ceasefire was initiated during which the civilians embarked on their ritual journey to Ghouta. For a visual depiction of the ritual, see "Reviving the rituals of Siran Ghouta during ceasefire," www.youtube.com/watch?v=NGN6Eq83dWY.

Works Cited

Alexander, Jeffrey C. "Toward a Theory of Cultural Trauma." *Cultural Trauma and Collective Identity*, edited by Jeffrey C. Alexander et al., California UP, 2004, pp. 1–30.

al-Qattan. Najwa. "When Mothers Ate Their Children: Wartime Memory and the Language of Food in Syria and Lebanon." *International Journal of Middle East Studies*, vol. 46, no. 4, Special Issue: *World War I*, November 2014, pp. 719–36.

al-Refai, Tamara. "'An Thakerat Alraeha Walta'am," ("On the Memory of Scent and Food"). *Elshorouk*, 29 Oct. 2015.

———. "E'adat Tadweer Elhayah," ("Recycling Life"). *Elshorouk*, 7 Apr. 2016.

———. "'Fi Elmatbakh Waseyasa," ("In the Kitchen and Politics"). *Elshorouk*, 18 May 2016.

———. "Halab Madinat Alalf Qessa Wa Qessa," "Aleppo, the City of the 1001 Tales." *Elshorouk*, 17 Feb. 2016.

———. "Men Hunak, Hathihi Demashq," ("From There, This Is Damascus"). *Elshorouk*, 19 Nov. 2015.

———. "Siran Alams Walyawm" ("Siran, Yesterday and Today."). *Elshorouk*, 25 Feb. 2016.

al-Sadda, Hoda. "A 'Phantom Freedom in a Phantom Modernity'? Protestant Missionaries, Domestic Ideology and Narratives of Modernity in an Arab Context." *Rethinking History*, vol. 15, no. 2, June 2011, pp. 209–28.

Anderson, Benedict. *Imagined Communities*. Verso, 1982.

Bachelard, Gaston. *The Poetics of Space*. Translated by Maria Jolas. Penguin Books, 1964.

Barthes, Roland. "Toward a Psychosociology of Contemporary Food Consumption." *Food and Culture: A Reader*, edited by Carole Counihan and Penny Van Esterik, Routledge, 2013, pp. 23–30.

Bhabha, Homi. *The Location of Culture*. Routledge, 1994.

Culcasi, Karen. "'We Are Women and Men Now': Intimate Spaces and Coping Labor for Syrian Women Refugees in Jordan." TIBG, vol. 44, no. 3, Wiley & Sons, September 2019, pp. 463–78.

Desoucey, Michaela. "Gastronationalism: Food Traditions and Authenticity Politics in the European Union." *American Sociological Review*, vol. 75, no. 3, Jun. 2010, pp. 432–55.

Gennep, Arnold Van. *The Rites of Passage*. Routledge, 2004.

Hall, Stuart, and Paul Du Gay, editors. *Questions of Cultural Identity*. Sage Publications, 1996.

Litz, Brett. T. "Resilience in the Aftermath of War Trauma: A Critical Review and Commentary." *Interface Focus*, vol. 4, no. 5, Oct. 6, 2014, 20140008. doi: 10.1098/rsfs.2014.0008.

Massaro, Vanessa and Jill Williams. "Feminist Geopolitics." *Geography Compass*, 2 Aug. 2013, pp. 567–77.

Neumann, Brigit. "The Literary Representation of Memory." *Cultural Memory Studies: An International and Interdisciplinary Handbook*, edited by Astrid Erll, Ansgar Nünning. W. De G, 2008, pp. 333–44.

Visser, Irene. "Trauma and the Power in Postcolonial Literary Study." *Contemporary Approaches in Literary Trauma Theory*, edited by Michelle Balaev, Palgrave Macmillan, 2014, pp. 106–29.

Yuval-Davis, Nira. "Gender and Nation." *Ethnic and Racial Studies*, vol. 16, no. 4, 1993, pp. 621–32. doi: 10.1080/01419870.1993.9993800.

20 Revolutionizing Scheherazade

Deconstructing the Exotic and Oppressed Muslim Odalisque in Mohja Kahf's Poetry

Amany El-Sawy

As a Syrian American, Mohja Kahf contributes noticeably to Arab American visibility. Born in Syria (1967) and raised in America, Kahf attempts to bridge the gap between the West and the Middle East. She includes a diversity of voices and perspectives to break through the average reader's expectations that all Muslims are the same. In doing so, she consciously serves as a cultural intermediary between Muslims and Christians in America and attempts to deconstruct stereotypes about her culture and religion. Kahf uses Islam and veiling as a running theme throughout her work and mixes her life experiences into her poetry to speak about the intersections of feminism, Islamism, and American life from a personal perspective. This paper illustrates how Kahf opposes the Western, distorted symbol of the Muslim woman as an "odalisque" through the appropriation of the revolutionary Scheherazade. I deploy Kahf's *Western Representations of the Muslim Woman: from Termagant to Odalisque* (1999) to elucidate Kahf's presentation of Islamic Feminism as evident in her anthology *Emails from Scheherazad* (2003). Mohja Kahf, I argue, proposes a hybrid in-between subjectivity for Muslim American women that defies all hostility and hegemonic representations, and this is manifested through the portrayal of her revolutionary Scheherazade who writes "emails" and refuses to be marked as the "backward" Other. I consolidate Kahf's Muslim Feminist theory by illustrating how it agrees with the writings of other Muslim critics such as Fatima Mernissi and Sama Abdurraqib.

Mernissi marks out in *Scheherazade Goes West* the agency attributed to women symbolized by the Scheherazade figure, who has been silenced and reduced to an exposed odalisque in Western adaptations (50). The figure of Scheherazade changes her entire world and a brutal tyrant, Shahrayar, through dialogue and intellect: "The mysterious bond existing between pluralism and feminism in today's troubled Islamic world was eerily and vividly foreshadowed by the Scheherazade-Shahrayar tales" (Mernissi, *Scheherazade Goes West* 51). Mernissi's view is considered to be an act of rebellion against the harem hierarchy. Thus, Scheherazade goes beyond the sexual politics of gender war, carving out a newly possible, politically powerful subject position for Muslim women based on dialogue, equality, and mutual respect (Mernissi, *Scheherazade Goes West* 46).

Nevertheless, Suzanne Gauch notices that the empowered Scheherazade figure has been completely lost in Western adaptations. In a Western context, Scheherazade loses her prominent role as a narrator. By 1800, more than eighty editions of an Orientalist adaptation of Scheherazade as a slave to her master's pleasures and as a seductress were circulating from Russia and Europe to America (Gauch 27). The Westernized image of Scheherazade as an odalisque—a Turkish term for women slaves—contradicts her original role as victorious mediator in the tales. The European Orientalist culture was centered on visual codes and appropriations of Scheherazade based on Western fantasies of harems by famous painters such as Ingres, Matisse, or Picasso. These early Orientalist representations reduce Muslim women's bodies to sex objects. These images developed into the Hollywood and Disney versions of a meagerly dressed belly dancer in the twentieth century, which popularized the notion of a backward, monolithic, and unchanging Muslim world (Mernissi, *Scheherazade Goes West* 14). Such representations are in stark contrast to the dialogic nature of the original tales, displacing the authorial, self-defining act of storytelling by Muslim women for a visual objectified image.

Unlike what we see in such Western representations, Kahf's re-appropriation of Scheherazade helps her to weave the transnational, empowered voice with the torn subjectivity as "in-between" mediator in the legacy of *One Thousand and One Nights*. By doing so, Kahf has managed to survive a wave of hateful stereotyping surrounding American Muslim women. She embraces the revolutionary mediating role as a trans-culturally literate Muslim woman who deconstructs the exotic and oppressed representation of Arab Muslim women. Kahf successfully creates a fertile space for possible new subjectivities.

In her *Western Representations of the Muslim Woman: from Termagant to Odalisque,* Kahf traces the change in Western representation of Muslim women from Medieval and Renaissance times to the period of the early nineteenth century. Kahf confirms that the pre-Orientalist/colonialists' representations of Muslim women in European literature were different from the Orientalists' views. She argues that the Medieval and Renaissance representations do not construct the Muslim woman as veiled submissive oppressed victim. Kahf posits that:

> The image of the Muslim woman in Western culture has been a changing, evolving phenomenon . . . The Muslim woman occupies a much smaller and less central place in that narrative in medieval texts that she does in the texts of the nineteenth century. Her nature, too, is different. (Kahf, *Western Representations* 4–5)

Muslim women in Medieval literature, as Kahf explains, are described as a "termagant."[1] Her character is typically referred to as a high-ranking character, usually presented as "a queen or a noblewoman wielding power of harm over the hero" (Kahf, *Western Representations* 4). The character of the Arab Muslim woman in Renaissance texts, Kahf postulates in *Western Representations*, is constructed as independent and stubborn. The veil and the harem have always been associated with the status of Arab women and their seclusion, yet there is no reference of the veil and its submissive effect on Arab women in the literary texts of the Renaissance era. She argues that it was only with the advent of colonialism in the eighteenth century that the Arab Muslim female image first appears with the veil in Western representations, and the "harem" becomes the proper place of Muslim women in Western literary representation (Kahf, *Western Representations* 6). Since then, a great deal of the Western narrative "represents her as innately oppressed, veiled, secluded, and silenced. Nonetheless this characterization is entirely absent from the medieval representations" (Kahf, *Western Representations* 11). Thus, Kahf argues that the preamble theme of "harem" and its relation to the subjugation of the Middle Eastern Muslim female did not exist in the pre-colonial era.

Colonialism played a great role in the degradation and distortion of the image of Arab Muslim women. Laila Ahmed in *Women and Gender in Islam* confirms that "the issue of women only emerged as a centerpiece of the Western narrative of Islam . . . as Europeans established themselves as colonial powers in Muslim countries" (150). Kahf argues that the colonial activities in the Arab Muslim world in the eighteenth century were responsible for the emergence of literary narratives interested in representing Muslim Arab women as victims of their own societies and cultures. She asserts that:

> The 'rise' of the subjugated Muslim woman concurred with the build-up of British and French empires in the nineteenth century, which in subjugating whole Muslim societies, had a direct interest in viewing the Muslim woman as oppressed. (Kahf, *Western Representations* 6)

Thus, the augmentation of attention in the association of Islam with the oppression of women was clear in the eighteenth and nineteenth centuries. Relative to the growth of Western concern in studying the Islamic Arab world, an equally increasing interest in the study of the character of the Arab female emerged all at once. The emerging Western discourse in the eighteenth century explicitly associated Islam with the subjugation of the women.

Comparing the status of the Muslim women prior to the eighteenth and nineteenth centuries in Western narratives, Kahf says:

> Her figure simultaneously shrinks in subjectivity and exuberance. In the eighteenth century, the Muslim woman character turns into an

abject harem slave, the quintessential victim of absolute despotism debased to a dumb, animal existence. Then in the nineteenth century, this harem slave is rescued by the Romantic hero and recreated as the ideal of numinous femininity. (Kahf, *Western Representations* 8)

The study of Arab women and Islamic culture, therefore, became necessary new categories in modern literary studies. Paradoxically, such categorization has hardly represented the truth about Arab women's lives but rather largely confirmed the superiority of the Western culture over the oppressive Islamic system against women. In this sense, the inclusion of the victimized Arab women in modern Western literary studies became necessary to illustrate the importance of the colonial knowledge that constitutes the subjectivity of the colonized.

Contrary to Western feminist and colonialist beliefs, the veil does not suppress women; rather, the confines of a patriarchal society which reduces the condition of women are the reasons of women's repression as they limit their mobility. In "Under Western Eyes," Chandra Mohanty critiques representations of the veil as a "unilateral" institution of oppression, questioning the generalizations of the Western feminist perspective that condemns the act of veiling as a "control" over women or a "universal" symbol of "backwardness" (Mohanty 56). She condemns "Western feminism" and subsequent writings about third-world women for portraying the "average" third-world woman as leading an "essentially truncated life based on her feminine gender (read: sexually constrained) and her being 'third world' (read: ignorant, poor, uneducated, tradition-bound, domestic, family-oriented, victimized, etc.)" (Mohanty 56). That is, just as colonialist men use(d) a binary equating unveiled women with being educated and modern, and veiled women with being amateurish and backward, Western feminism has also universally reduced veiling discourse to a binary of oppressions and liberations within Muslim communities.

Kahf launches a cultural war against the hazards of the veil as she examines what veiling can achieve for women, not as a religious mandate or social pressure, but as a choice to express one's faith. Her representation of veiling restores to women the position of subject, wherein they are able to think, say, and act, rather than exist as mere objects victimized by a "vague villain." Samaa Abdurraqib claims that "Hijab Scenes" takes the course of identity negotiations as evidence for Kahf's poetic success in forcing readers to read differently, to read for and through bodies, and see how literature and reading practices shape people's perceptions of how bodies and subsequently how modes of dress are interpreted. Abdurraqib argues that wearing the veil is coded so clearly as a non-American practice that Muslim women's literary representations need to present to challenge stable and exclusionary notions of Americanness. She credits Kahf for having developed a new immigrant literary form "that includes veiling as a particular expression of Muslim

Americanness, rather than foreignness" (Abdurraqib 63). Kahf's success achieves a revolutionary intervention in US grand discourses by representing Muslim women's subjectivities not always reduced to the veil anymore.

Kahf's poetry aims to show the problems of the in-between people and to promote dialogue and understanding and helps to destabilize the ego-centric conviction of Anglo Americans as being the "self." Kahf addresses the multiplicity of her American readers through the shared ethnic experiences of racism and sexism. Nonetheless, she also stresses the universality of such experiences among people of any religion and background and thus transcends cultural differences. Abdurraqip states that the success of Kahf's poetry does not only offer the chance to negotiate the in-between state of Arab Americans with mainstream readers/discourses, but also artistically innovates 'ethnic' writing. Abdurraqib affirms that:

> In the end, Kahf is able to successfully challenge the traditional trajectory of Muslim immigrant writing. She does this by moving outside of both the stereotypical form and content of Muslim immigrant writing. (Abdurraqib 68)

Kahf confronts the homogenous norms of immigrant/ethnic literature, and by writing "emails" she refuses to be marked as the "backward" Other. Rather, she places her writing firmly in a present and American context and invites cross-cultural communication at a same level across all ethnicities within the America.

Kahf skillfully shatters the Western distorted symbol of the Muslim woman as an "odalisque." Since the eighteenth century, the term odalisque has also come to be associated with seduction. However, in direct opposition to these more scandalized Western fabrications of the women of the harem, the true circumstances of the odalik within the chambers of the Ottoman Empire "resembled a monastery for young [women] more than the bordello of European imagination" (Necipoğlu 180). Julia Kuehn highlights in "Exotic Harem Paintings" that Jerichau-Bauman's paintings were a mixture of "a woman's intimate knowledge of the harem, documentation, imagination" and attention to her European viewers' needs to see the East in an exotic light (Kuehn 46).

Nevertheless, in "Discovering Scheherazade," Ulrike Brisson claims that three German women who had access to the Middle Eastern harem challenged the traditional image of "the lascivious Oriental woman" (99). However, in an attempt to portray the little that they had seen as the whole story, they managed to confirm the Western ideal of the Eastern beauty while not fully comprehending the veiled Eastern woman in her harem. Evidence that the women artists lacked understanding of what they saw in their travels to the east is apparent in the way that all three artists perceived the veil. They found veiling to be a strange custom and despised it by describing the women as "ghost-like figures, they were enveloped . . . like corpses" (Brisson 102).

Kahf's ironic poetry depicts all kinds of reactions, positive and negative, veiled women have to deal with in their daily lives in America. In the "Hijab Scene" poems, she writes against the racism and objectification lodged at Muslim women whose oppression is always represented by the allegedly *menacing* veil. Through her first two "Hijab Scene" poems, Kahf condemns the view that the veil constitutes Otherness or restrictiveness, and ironically highlights that the appearance or clothing of other Americans may also be considered just as confining.

In "Hijab Scene #1," Kahf depicts the moment in which two different types of Americans come into contact and evaluate each other, "'You dress strange,' said a tenth-grade boy with bright blue hair to the new Muslim girl with the headscarf, his tongue-ring clicking on the 'tr' in 'strange'" (Kahf, *Emails* 41). There is dramatic irony in the poem wherein the boy with the blue hair and tongue rings is unconscious to his own unconventional appearance, which does not represent a mainstream American identity. Kahf satirizes the teenager's treatment of the Muslim girl who wears the veil.

Similarly, in "Hijab Scene #2," Kahf juxtaposes the image of Muslim identity with the image of American identity:

> You people have such restrictive dress for women,
>   she said, hobbling away in three-inch heels and panty hose
>   to finish out another pink-collar temp pool day. (Kahf, *Emails* 41)

The modern American woman views the Muslim woman's dress code as very "restrictive" and fails to see that she herself is being restricted by her high heels and outfit. By comparing the two cultural expressions, "Kahf illustrates how it is culture, rather than veiling, that keeps veiled Muslim women in liminal positions. Kahf illustrates that veiling is not incongruous with being American and with other American practices" (Abdurraqib 68). That is, being Muslim does not make any American less American and vice versa: being American does not make a Muslim any less Muslim.

In both poems, Kahf demonstrates that American identity is not extraordinary or monolithic in any way, so she ironically and rhetorically asks about the exclusion of Muslims from it. Both poems show the ways in which the representatives of non-Muslim American identity are inadequate in some way. While the American figures in both perceive the Muslim woman's veil as "strange" or "restrictive," the boy's tongue ring impairs his speech, while the heels and panty hose hinder the woman's ability to walk. Evidently, Kahf calls attention to how non-American Muslims are unaware of the notion that their appearance, habits, and lifestyles can seem just as constricting to others as the veil seems to them. She illustrates that a "hijab" is no different than other modes of dress, and it only serves as personal expression, rather than cultural markers of confinement.

Kahf opposes the false belief that the veiled Muslim women, that are visibly "un-American," cannot be part of the American society. Her poetry reveals that although these veiled women need to construct a narrative of their own and tell their own stories, Kahf's narrative can never be about contented assimilation. Therefore, Muslim women are compelled to construct a narrative of rebelliousness and resistance of hegemony and oppression. In Kahf's "Hijab Scene #3," she juxtaposes the image of the hegemonic mainstream Othering of the veiled Muslim woman with that of the Muslim woman defying invisibility and silencing. In the poem, the speaker makes a somber effort to become an active participant in American society. She volunteers to join the Parent-Teacher Association (PTA), but the school board refuses to acknowledge her presence. This scene is an example of the suffering and marginalization Muslim women experience in American society, and in educational institutions, in particular, but at the same time it reflects the power of the veiled Muslim woman, and her resistance of such oppression and refusal to be unacknowledged and made invisible.

American supremacy utilizes the veil as a powerful tool and sign to build unyielding barriers and misunderstandings between "us" and "them;" it employs the veil to make certain the continuity of fear and alienation of "the Other," and feelings of resentment and danger between the two opposing extremes. The veil as a visual marker that designates Muslims' difference from others put their allegiances into question regardless of their Americanness. Kahf proposes an example of a veiled Muslim woman whose Americanness is questioned in her poem "Hijab Scene #7" in which the speaker resists the American hegemonic stereotype imposed on her and refuses to be silenced. She says:

> No, I'm not bald under the scarf
> No, I'm not from that country
> Where women can't drive cars
> No, I would not like to defect
> I'm already American. (Kahf, *Emails* 39)

In this poem, Kahf challenges the image of Arab and Muslim women as silenced, humorless, and subservient individuals. She denies attitudes that attribute veiling to backwardness and employs violent imagery as an inversion of the injurious views. Moreover, Kahf counters American oppression with linguistic aggression. She uses a defensive and emphatic tone to condemn negative stereotypes that many non-Muslims possess about Muslims. The series of "Noes" that Kahf begins the poem with rejects the established beliefs that demonize Muslims and, in terms of identity, indicates that she is simultaneously Muslim and American, paving the way for a new hybrid identity that does not need to pit Muslims and Americans against one another.

Margot Badran in *Feminism in Islam* talks about the Western perception of Muslim womanhood that negates any agency to them to the effect that in popular discourses in US, feminism and Islam are perceived as "mutually exclusive positions" (Badran 1). Similarly, Mernissi highlights this paradox and claims that both Western and conservative Muslim perceptions of feminism are entirely mistaken. She states in *The Veil and the Male Elite*:

> We Muslim women can walk into the modern world with pride, knowing that the quest for dignity, democracy, and human rights, for full participation in the political and social affairs of our country, stems from no imported Western values, but is a true part of Muslim tradition. (Mernissi, *The Veil* viii)

In contrast to her negations, which reject stereotypes about Islam, Kahf marks the tonal shift in her poem with a series of affirmations and "Yeses," which speaks to the potential power that Muslim women can assert. She presents an alternative image in her counter-hegemonic narrative of an empowered Muslim woman who insists on being heard and has a voice of her own. She says:

> Yes, I speak English
> Yes, I carry explosives
> They're called words. (Kahf, *Emails* 39)

The Arab/Islamic feminist Eisa Ulen points out that many feminists, Western or Eastern, Muslim and non-Muslim, consider the veil as an oppressive tool, "urging complete unveiling as the key to unleashing an authentic liberation. For them scarves strangle any movement toward Muslim women's emancipation" (Ulen 46). Arab Islamic feminists have dealt extensively with such misconceptions and imperialist interpretations of this sign and struggled to create counter-narratives that highlight the genuine meanings of the veil within their cultural and religious context.

Kahf's poetry tries to shake the homogenized image of Muslim/Arab Americans and reflect the actual conditions of Muslim women's freedom and oppression through the portrayal of their heterogeneous identities. Kahf rejects the notion that reduces Muslim women to the veil, which has become the center of discussions in the East and the West. In both worlds the Muslim woman, the human being, and her suffering is forgotten and trivialized, but her hair and veil are foregrounded by patriarchal and hegemonic discourses.

In "My Body is Not Your Battleground," Kahf deconstructs the homogenized identity of a Muslim/Arab American woman through representing an empowered Muslim female speaker who asserts her identity and speaks out to be heard by the hegemonic discourse. In rejection of contemporary discussions of the Muslim veil, Kahf states that:

> My body is not your battleground
> My hair is neither sacred nor cheap,
> Neither the cause of your disarray. (Kahf, *Emails* 58)

Kahf refuses to listen to the oppressive voices that objectify Muslim women's bodies. These lines support Jasmin Zine's claim that in either case, forced veiling or unveiling, "Muslim women's bodies, whether in the Middle East or the West, continue to be "disciplined and regulated" (Zine 175). Kahf mocks those who believe liberation can be brought by shedding the veil and those who think wearing it will save them from their attackers. The speaker finds both parties irrational and neither one leading to true freedom nor development.

Moreover, Muslim women who wear the veil are denied agency and a voice of their own "to veil by their own volition, or to have their own cultural or political conscience" when they are constructed in this manner (Abdurraqib 59). Kahf discusses the issue of the Muslim woman's invisibility, especially if she takes on the Muslim veil that is a fetish and sign of oppression in the eyes of hegemonic discourses. She makes a reference to the rejection of the veiled Muslim woman who is made invisible within Western feminist circles. In Kahf's poem "Thawrah des Odalisques at the Matisse Retrospective," the speaker comments:

> No one wanted to know about us
> Statements were issued on our behalf . . .
> But wanted us up on their dais as tokens of diversity.
>   (Kahf, *Emails* 66)

"Thawrah" is the Arabic equivalent to "revolution." Kahf subverts the image of the Muslim odalisque by revolutionizing her. She postulates that veiled Muslim women are oppressed and silenced by those who cannot see beyond the veil, and the imperialist feminist agenda has no room for the concerns of Arab and Muslim women but urges them to be present in their feminist circles as "tokens of diversity." Abdurraqib emphasizes that:

> By overlooking the particularities of their veiling practices (or of their actual oppression) and reinforcing the boundaries between western women and the Other, veiling practices are linked to universal practices of oppression, sexual control, and nationality. (Abdurraqib 59)

Kahf realizes that the particularities of veiling have been and continue to be overlooked within hegemonic discourses and thus brings issues surrounding the veil and veiled Muslim women to the forefront in her work.

Nevertheless, part of Kahf's resistance to the prevailing hegemony is the appropriation of the Scheherazade figure as a modern muse and role model of a transnational, hybrid, and powerful Muslim woman. Kahf's Scheherazade is a modern figure who writes emails to her American audience; by doing so, she brings to light the Muslim feminist Scheherazadian root of the hybrid Arab American self. For example, in "Fayetteville as in Fate," Kahf places Arab immigrant paths in the myth of the "American way," highlighting the never fulfilled promise of rendering the America as a nation of "equal" immigrants. The poem bitterly traces the genocide of native people and multiple national settler colonials who all merge in "Fay'tteville's" environment. Nevertheless, Kahf sees this multiplicity and power imbalances as a call for agency, that despite the "fate" of all these people and all their differences living together, it is in their hands if they choose to communicate:

> but the open hand with the dirt in the creases
> makes a map both can read
> But who will coax them close enough to know this?
> Darlings, it is poetry
> Darling, I am a poet
> It is my fate
> like this, like this, to kiss
> the creases around the eyes and the eyes
> that they may recognize each other:
> *May their children e-mail one another and not bomb one*
>   *another*
> *May they download each other's mother's bread recipes*
> *May they sell yams and yogurts to each other at a*
>   *conscionable profit*
> *May they learn each other's tongue and put words into each*
>   *other's mouth Say Amen*
> *Say* آمين. (Kahf, *Emails* 6)

Although Scheherazade is not identified in this poem by name, the eloquent persona reveals her Scheherazadian subjectivity.

Moreover, in "Fayetteville as in Fate" Kahf stresses femininity as part of a Muslim women's identity but within a traditional Muslim perception of binary gender difference. For example, the Arab American female poet expresses her artistic gift in language, emotion and desire assembling kiss/love/write into an act of multiple and yet traditionally gendered forms of communication. Part of Kahf's strategy is then to cherish and relish Arab American femininity as part of her empowerment, which consistently contradicts the "Muslim woman as victim" trope that connotes femininity as inferior and by extension the orientalist value of Muslim/feminist/weak culture.

Kahf, through the mediating role of the transcultural Scheherazade, highlights the threatening reality and danger of the impermeable Arab/American divide. In "My Grandmother Washes Her Feet in the Sink of the Bathroom at Sears," she directly addresses the tensions and hazards inherent in the failed communication and cultural non-understanding on both sides. She communicates through the superficial misunderstanding between her grandmother, having to wash her feet for prayer during shopping, and petrified "Middle Western" ladies observing the scene— the irony being that in the end all these women cherish cleanliness and good manners above all, they just do not understand that about each other: "They fluster about and flutter their hands and I can see a clash of civilizations brewing in the Sears bathroom" (Kahf, *Emails* 26–8).

The contemplating Scheherazade embraces her position in the Middle East/West and keeps the door open for both Arab and mainstream Americans to walk through. The in-between status can be a position of power for American Muslim women if they speak both languages and understand both cultural codes. Kahf's Scheherazade gains her advantage as poet and storyteller via learning from other women: "it is from you I fashion poetry" (*Emails* 51). She constantly moves back and forth between cultures to undermine stereotypes on all sides, and she takes another part of her "power" from Islamic traditions of poetry and storytelling embodied by Scheherazade in the original tales.

Kahf opposes the restrictive Western representations of Muslim women. In her poem "So You Think You Know Scheherazad" (*Emails* 45), and addresses the distressing consequences for Western readers unawareness to surmise with "the demons under your bed / They were always there / She locks you in with them" (*Emails* 45) when encountering an empowered Scheherazade. She uncovers the Orientalist foundations of Western self-perception which distorts Muslim women's realties. In the end, she challenges both Muslim and Western readers to the power of the telling of a story:

> And suddenly you find yourself
> (. . .) landing in a field where you wrestle with Iblis
> whose face changes into Scheherazad-
> And suddenly you find yourself. (Kahf, *Emails* 45)

Nevertheless, Kahf's poems also concede the difficulties to find "one" self in a diasporic situation. The revolutionizing Scheherazade firmly rooted in an Eastern tradition and fluent in Western culture helps her to find herself in not just one woman, culture, or religion, but like a migrating bird through time and space she links herself to figures as varied as Eve after

Eden, Zainab, Malinche, the woman from the Oregon Trail, Harriet, Hagar, Nefertiti, Queen of Shaba, Zuleika, Mary, Dido, Cleopatra, Kadija, Aisha and many more (Kahf, *Emails* 85). Kahf's revolutionizing politics burst out of desperation against a threatening, homogeneous majority discourse about Muslim women. Kahf's Scheherazade rises from the ashes to take up her work as a cultural mediator who offers new perspectives to Muslim and other American women via her emails, but who replies?

To conclude, the post 9/11 decade has seen a surge in Arab American writing that squarely place Muslim cultures and identities within America and enjoy both critical and popular success, such as Mohja Kahf's poetry collection *Emails from Scheherazad*. This paper problematizes the Westernized view of the Muslim woman as a backward odalisque, yet veiled and modest and shows how Kahf exposes this orientalist dichotomy of veiling and seductiveness in her poetry. By giving these two contrasting views, Kahf revolutionizes the salient discourse—to put it in Edward Said's words—that the West had for centuries about the East as backward, silent, and feminine.

Thus, new spaces are created for Muslim womanhood that are neither flourished in Western Orientalist nor Muslim nationalist perspective: a hybrid in-between subjectivity for Muslim American women that defies all hostility and hegemonic representations. This is manifested through the portrayal of Kahf's revolutionary Scheherazade who writes "emails" and refuses to be marked as the "backward" Other.

Note

1 "Termagant" is an archaic English word associated with descriptions of Muslim women and means "overbearing, turbulent, brawling, quarrelsome woman; a virago, shrew, vixen." Oxford English Dictionary.

Works Cited

Abdurraqib, Samaa. "Hijab Scenes: Muslim Women, Migration, and Hijab in Immigrant Muslim Literature." *MELUS*, vol. 31, no. 4, Winter 2006, pp. 55–70.

Ahmed, Laila. *Women and Gender in Islam: Historical Roots of a Modern Debate*. New Haven, Yale UP, 1992.

Badran, Margot. *Feminism in Islam. Secular and Religious Convergences*. Richmond, One World Publications, 2009.

Brisson, Ulrike. "Discovering Scheherazade: Representations of Oriental Women in the Travel Writing of Nineteenth-Century German Women." *Women in German Yearbook: Feminist Studies in German Literature and Culture*, vol. 29, no. 1, 2013, pp. 97–117.

Gauch, Suzanne. *Liberating Shahrazad: Feminism, Postcolonialism, and Islam*. Minnesota UP, 2007.

Kahf, Mohja. *Emails from Scheherazad*. Gainesville, U of Florida P, 2003.

———. *Western Representations of the Muslim Woman. From Termagant to Odalisque*. Austin, U of Texas, 1999.

Kuehn, Julia. "Exotic Harem Paintings." *Frontiers: A Journal of Women Studies*, vol. 32, no. 2, 2011, pp. 31–63.

Mernissi, Fatima. *Scheherazade Goes West: Different Cultures, Different Harems*. New York, Simon and Schuster, 2001.

———. *The Veil and the Male Elite. A Feminist Interpretation of Women's Rights in Islam*. New York, Basic Books, 1992.

Mohanty, Chandra. "Under Western Eyes' Revisited: Feminist Solidarity through Anticapitalist Struggles." *Feminism without Borders: Decolonizing Theory, Practicing Solidarity*. Durham, Duke UP, 2003, pp. 17–42.

Necipoğlu, Gülru. *Architecture, Ceremonial, and Power: The Topkapi Palace in the Fifteenth and Sixteenth Centuries*. New York, Architectural History Foundation, 1991.

Said, Edward. *Orientalism*. New York, Random House, 1994.

Ulen, Eisa. "Tapping our Strength." *Shattering the Stereotypes: Muslim Women Speak Out*, edited by Fawzia Afzal-Khan, Massachusetts, Olive Branch P, 2005, pp. 42–50.

Zine, Jasmin. "Creating a Critical Faith-Centered Space for Antiracist Feminism: Reflections of a Muslim Scholar-Activist." *Journal of Feminist Studies in Religion*, vol. 20, 2004, pp. 167–87.

Index

Note: Page numbers followed by "n" denote endnotes.

For Product Safety Concerns and Information please contact our EU
representative GPSR@taylorandfrancis.com
Taylor & Francis Verlag GmbH, Kaufingerstraße 24, 80331 München, Germany

www.ingramcontent.com/pod-product-compliance
Lightning Source LLC
Chambersburg PA
CBHW071548110726
47908CB00007B/2041